Yui said some   ke
a curse. Her   t's
time to go."   nd
wrapped it about her waist.

"Go? Go where? We can't get out. The stairs
are blocked."

"We have to get to my father right away. He
needs to know what's happened." Yui wiped her
forehead with the back of her hand in a futile
attempt to clean away a heavy residue of dirt and
sweat. "Hold on!" She drew the energy bubble in
close and launched it from the platform. "We're
going for a ride."

Instantly, they shot upward.

Keiko's stomach plunged to her feet. The indigo
light was only a few feet from her face, but despite
its sizzle, she didn't notice any heat. She did hear
the roaring wind and the rumble of exploding
pavement as Yui rocketed high into the night sky.

In seconds, the whole city spread out beneath
her like a sea of stars. She should have been afraid,
but she was too overwhelmed by what she saw to
feel anything but wonder. For the first time since
her father's disappearance, she smiled broadly
and let out a delighted squeal as the ground spun
away beneath her.

KEITH YATSUHASHI

KOJIKI

ANGRY
ROBOT

ANGRY ROBOT
An imprint of Watkins Media Ltd

Lace Market House,
54-56 High Pavement,
Nottingham,
NG1 1HW
UK

www.angryrobotbooks.com
twitter.com/angryrobotbooks
A glimpse of the gods

First published in the US in different form in 2014
This revised Angry Robot edition published 2016

Cover by Thomas Walker
Set in Meridien and Montserrat by Epub Services

Distributed in the United States by Penguin Random House, Inc., New York.

ISBN 978 0 85766 615 4
Ebook ISBN 978 0 85766 616 1

Printed in the United States of America

9 8 7 6 5 4 3 2 1

For Kathleen

1
KEIKO

Tokyo, Japan

Keiko Yamada lifted her battered thirty-five millimeter camera and held her breath. The metal casing was cool against her feverish cheeks and smooth enough to slip precariously in her sweaty fingers. She knew she'd never take a clear shot like this, not with shaking hands and pounding heart. Fortunately, she wasn't here for the picture, not this one, and not the hundreds of others she could have taken but didn't. She was here for something else entirely.

She exhaled and peered through the viewfinder. *Maybe this time*, she told herself. *This time for sure*. Tokyo's glittering Ginza spread out before her like a sea of colored stars. The city was so foreign, so unlike her home in New York. Times Square certainly had its share of lights, but those were pale imitations of what now surrounded her. Here, twisted and interlocking neon tubes blazed like beacons, each pulse revealing a pastiche of corporate logos, Japanese characters, torii gates, and other unrecognizable images. It was a beautiful sight, just not the one she wanted.

Disappointed but still determined, she lowered the camera and scanned the street for yet another torii gate. Her late father had sent her to find one in particular, and for the first time since arriving in Japan, it felt close. She assumed he meant a torii like the spectacular floating one at Itsukushima Shrine in Hiroshima. Fifty-five feet tall and made of solid red-lacquered wood, the gate was as much a symbol of Japan as Mount Fuji. Keiko had seen it countless times on the internet, in pictures, and depicted on antiques in her father's store. Finding something that iconic, even in a city as large as Tokyo, should be easy.

Only it wasn't.

Torii gates were everywhere. Tall and lean, short and wide, they came in various shapes, sizes, colors, and designs. Some were made from wood, others from stone. All had the same basic shape: twin vertical pillars meeting a perpendicular crossbeam at the top. Keiko had pointed her camera at hundreds of torii without success. Instead of frustrating her, though, each failure – the current one included – hardened her resolve.

She tried to think back to the weeks leading up to her father's disappearance and apparent death, but her memories were a blur of tears and loneliness. Everything had seemed fine, right up until the day she came home to an empty house, a carefully placed note on the grand piano in the hall. Leaning forward, she recognized her father's firm hand, and read:

I leave a dream of me behind
To protect sun and spirit
For they are the light of my soul

Dazed, she lunged for the phone and called the police. "It's my father," she said when the 911 operator came on the line. "He's disappeared and... And... And he left a suicide note." The operator asked a question that took Keiko's numb head a minute to process. "Of course, I'm sure." Keiko may not have learned as much about her Japanese heritage as her parents hoped for, but she knew a *jisei* – a traditional Japanese death poem – when she read one. Keiko's father, Masato Yamada, was a dealer in Japan's finest antiques and art; Keiko had sorted and displayed enough jisei to recognize one when she read it. Her father's note was a jisei. No question.

Less than fifteen minutes later, a squad car pulled up to her house and parked on the street. Two officers climbed out. Keiko ushered the men inside, listened numbly to their basic questions, and somehow kept herself together when they said there was only so much they could do. Unless a disappearance involved children the police didn't officially consider it suspicious until after a set amount of time. Masato Yamada hadn't been gone nearly long enough for that.

Smiling sympathetically, the officers told her not to worry. Most of the time, the person turned up alive and well. They tipped their hats, handed her their cards, and went on their way. As soon as their car rolled down the street, Keiko snatched the poem from the piano. She crumpled the sheet and was about to hurl it at the wall when she noticed an envelope lying underneath. Heart pounding, she lifted the letter gingerly, turning the thick packet over in her hands. The back was blank, but on the front her father had written one simple word: *Keiko*.

Wide-eyed and trembling, Keiko tore at the paper, finding a Japanese passport bearing her name, an open one-way ticket from New York's JFK International Airport to Narita, a booking with something called Ancestral Travel, and – curiously – a short personal note that read: *Go to Japan in my place. Find the Gate. Your camera will show you the way.*

That was three weeks ago – three weeks of planning and packing before arriving in Tokyo, camera in hand, to search for one gate in a thousand. In a hundred thousand. Keiko didn't even know why. What was so important about a gate? Head shaking, she brought the camera back up to her eye, focused on yet another torii gate, this one in front of a makeshift shrine, and waited for… what? She had no idea, and that was part of the problem. A few seconds ticked by. The crowd swarmed in to block her view: commuters in business suits, a pretty woman with so many bags in her arms she could barely see, a teenager and his girlfriend, and a tall bald man who seemed to pause and glance in her direction before moving on. The look he shot her was strangely familiar, intimate even, enough for Keiko to keep her lens on him as he strode away.

His antiquated crimson robes were wildly out of place in the modern Ginza. They held her attention as much as his ageless face and the determined set of his shoulders. What was the odd white glow surrounding his body? A reflection? A trick of the light?

Keiko hoped so.

She considered going after him, but quickly stopped. Taking off after a stranger was never a good idea. Besides, she needed to get back to the tour group. She'd been gone a while – too long probably. If she didn't hurry back, they'd leave her behind.

Stowing her camera, she sprinted through the crowd. A large, brightly lit building loomed in front of her, and she skidded to a stop before a department store window. Inside, kimono-clad mannequins held cell phones and tablets. Outside, a hundred faces passed by her, all

Japanese. Her fellow Americans had moved on. They'd left her alone. Just like her father.

She cursed again, this time loudly. How could she have been so careless? Her first trip abroad and already lost. What would her father say? She didn't know what he expected her to do here, but this certainly wasn't it. She should have paid more attention to the time and not let that man pull her away. Not that she could do anything about it now, not unless she could roll back the minutes and choose a different path.

Frustrated, she checked her watch – another of her father's gifts. Swiss, gold bezel, mother-of-pearl face, automatic movement. It was an antique, but it looked and ran like new. She was only a few minutes late, but it was enough.

A feeling of hopelessness washed over her. Looking for a handful of people in a crowd this big was out of the question. She might as well search for a goldfish in the ocean. Her phone? A good option, or would be if she'd activated its international roaming before leaving Manhattan. Her only chance was to head for the tour's next stop and pray she reached it before they moved on again.

Reluctantly, she drew her map from her pocket. The Imperial Palace. It wasn't far, a cab ride away at most. If she hurried, she'd just about make it. Quickly stuffing the map into her jacket, she darted off. A clump of people swarmed over the wide intersection ahead, slowing her. She turned left, looked right. Craning her neck, she gasped as the crimson-robed man reappeared a few feet away. He glanced at her as he walked, almost, she thought, as if leading her.

Desperate, she locked onto him, following his wraithlike gait through a mob she swore parted for him. They broke around him, flowed back in, and when they opened again, the man had disappeared.

Keiko wheeled about, abruptly stopping when she spotted a small torii gate rising from the sidewalk. A pair of imperious dragon statues stared back at her from either side of what looked like an alley. Fiery, red-golden scales encased the one on the left while its twin wore stunning sapphire blue. Both were small, no larger than the bag slung over her shoulder, but for some reason she couldn't explain, they intimidated her. The camera she'd instinctively produced drooped in her hands.

She stood there as if frozen. Was this the gate? She wasn't sure, and she didn't know how to find out without further exploration. Indecision ripped through her. Charging ahead meant falling farther behind her tour. Could she risk it? Should she? A flash of crimson inside the alley drew her in. She inched a foot forward, and when a second flash came, this one appearing farther back, she sprang after it without thinking.

A few feet in, the cement walls on either side morphed into shimmering panels that reminded her of electrified fencing. They gave off minimal light, but the hairs on her arms lifted whenever she got too close. The air too had changed, no longer clean and fresh, it crackled as if dead – like a dried twig before a match.

Keiko cringed with each step. Coming here had been a mistake. If she turned around now, she could still make it to the Palace before the tour started. *Yes. That's it. Get back to the street. Go. Now!*

As she backed away, a burst of red and yellow light erupted in the distance, followed swiftly by the smell of ash and burning embers. Her pulse thudded. She needed to leave. Already, darkness filled the passage behind, where less than a minute ago lights from passing cars flickered along the walls. Had she turned around? She didn't think so, but she couldn't tell which way led to the street.

The light reminded her of Ginza, so she went that way, increasing her pace, trying not to think about the sharply rising temperature or the trickle of sweat running between her shoulders. *Not a fire*, she told herself. Any number of things could account for the heat – a restaurant maybe or a bathhouse. Her guide, Yui Akiko, had said something about public baths. She should have paid more attention. Not that it mattered. This looked like the only way out. It was either this or the darkness.

She moved into a quick trot, arms pumping, camera bag jostling, her nondescript flats clicking loudly against... what? It wasn't stone. Stone didn't pulse and thrum like it was alive. She tried not to look, concentrating instead on the opening that miraculously appeared ahead of her. At five hundred feet, it seemed like a godsend; at two hundred, a little less. At fifty, she began to worry. Waves of blistering heat slammed into her like a hammer, and before she knew where she was, her feet skidded to a stop at the edge of a sprawling courtyard. Water spilled from a globe-shaped basin in the middle of the cavernous space. Overhead, delicate trusses of brilliant silver ran from the top of one columned wall to the other, creating a transparent ceiling of spidery lace. Beyond the walls, random tongues of liquid fire belched into a red-tinted sky.

Halfway between the fountain and the entrance, perhaps a thousand feet away or more, a man materialized out of the rippling air. He was taller and more muscular than the man she followed through Ginza, with eyes that blazed like bonfires – wild and unpredictable one minute, pensive yet angry the next. A stark contrast, she thought, to the boyishly handsome face around them. He inclined his head, his tawny hair whipping in a nonexistent breeze.

As if summoned, two huge serpentine forms appeared – red fire on his left, blue ice on the right. They towered over him, their heads tilted as if listening. Unconcerned, he strode forward, placed his palms against the air, and pushed.

Keiko trembled violently, her gaze locked on the distorted space between them. Ripples spread outward from his hands like a spoon bouncing against gelatin, and the creatures… the less she thought about *them* the better. Again, the man pushed the barrier, and again it held. Rage mottled his handsome face. He motioned the fiery serpent forward.

Keiko's mind went numb. What the hell was this? She wanted to run, but couldn't get her feet to move. In her last few seconds of consciousness, the extraordinary image of a young Japanese man pulling back the hands of some great clock filled her thoughts. Sweat painted his face, his determined expression reminding her of her late father.

"Yui!" he shouted in an eerily familiar tone. "Come now, Yui! Come quickly!"

Yui Akiko staggered to a halt in the middle of a busy sidewalk. "Masato?" she whispered. Important people had a way of flashing through her head at odd times – Masato most of all. This time was different. It felt real. She shook her head at the impossibility. Masato was gone, had been for over a century.

An uncomfortable feeling of déjà vu washed over her. She looked back at her group and frowned. The roll! She needed to call the roll. Hadn't she done that already? A department store window spread down the street to her right, and she quickly shepherded the tour out of the pedestrian traffic, queued it up in front of the glass, and started to count.

"Keiko," she panted when she reached the end of the line. "Where's Keiko? Has anyone seen her?" Her normally breezy voice had slipped into the more comfortable tenor of command, clipped and decisive.

An older man in a tweed sport coat pushed his way forward with his obscenely young wife in tow. "I haven't seen her since we left that big intersection back there." He pointed down the street. "She said she wanted to take some pictures."

Yui struggled to keep her composure. "Tetsuo." She turned from the man and rounded on her assistant, a young, perpetually startled-looking student from Tokyo University. "Get the group moving again. We can't be late for the Palace." He started to protest, but Yui's steely glare silenced him. "We have a tight schedule to keep," she told him briskly, speaking in English for the tour's benefit. "I'm going back to look for Keiko. She can't be that far behind, a few blocks at most."

She snatched up her purse and pushed her way through the crowd. Keiko and her damn camera, she should have known. Every time she turned around, Keiko stopped and pointed the thing at whatever took her fancy – doors, bridges, and most especially torii gates. Yui needed to separate Keiko from that little metal box. And soon. It was probably the only way to keep her under control.

Yui snorted at the thought and hurried up to Ginza Crossing. Impatiently, she looked left, gauged the traffic, and was about to dart across the wide street when she glimpsed Keiko a block or so to her right.

Despite her Japanese features, Keiko was easy enough

to spot. Petite, she wore her short dark hair in a bob with layers that were all the rage in New York. The hair – like her expression – was uniquely whimsical. No Japanese could mimic that. Keiko might have Japanese features, but everything else about her was decidedly foreign, right down to the clothes she insisted on wearing to the Palace. Formality required a skirt and jacket. Isn't that what she'd said? The girl was odd, even for an American.

A cluster of pedestrians crossed in front of Yui, and she hurried forward, determined not to lose sight of Keiko now that she'd found her. Her luck held. Keiko stood a few yards away, examining the front of an ordinary granite building along Harumi-*dori*. The camera was out, of course, but strangely, she didn't use it.

Again, the crowd closed in, and this time, Yui zigzagged through it. She kept her eyes glued on Keiko, saw her move closer to the wall, pause, and then disappear completely.

No! Yui thought. *It can't be!* A thousand possibilities screamed through her head, and, as usual, she settled on the worst of them.

She ran a hand over her mouth and stopped in front of the building, hoping to find some sign of Keiko. As she drew closer, her dread increased. The wall remained solid and forbidding without seam or crease or opening. A flash of headlights illuminated something on the ground. Hands trembling, Yui looked down. There, where building met sidewalk, the top loop of a camera strap protruded from the bricks at her feet.

Yui stood motionless for several long seconds. Cars raced up and down Chuo-*dori* as they did every day. Pedestrians went about their business as if nothing strange had happened. They didn't know what Yui did, what Keiko's disappearance meant to them. To the whole world.

As if in a dream, Yui pulled a phone from her belt holster and dialed. Her heart pounded through the delay of a signal traveling thousands of miles across the globe. A man answered, and she released her breath. She gathered herself and spoke deliberately.

"It's Yui." She fought to keep her voice steady. "It's begun."

Keiko's eyes snapped open. How long had she been out? Minutes? Hours? Long enough for the tour to finish up at the Palace, probably. Long enough for that man to catch her. She dug her heels into the ground and bicycled until her back bumped against the wall, looking left, glancing right. A faint flickering at the far end drew her attention, and she turned her head toward it. Ginza? Was it possible? Dubious, she squinted at the light, measuring the distance.

Her camera lay on the ground a few feet away and, pulse racing, she lunged for it. The strap seemed caught on something, but it came free with a tug. The rest of her things had fallen and scattered, and as she hurried to gather them – a cache of film, two zoom lenses, a flash, her phone, wallet, and passport – a loud crack rocketed down the passage.

Keiko jumped. Tremors ran through her body; her legs felt weak. Eyes wide, she stared into the gloom, not wanting to see, unable to look away. A second ticked by, and then another. Shadows moved in the alley, advancing too quickly for her to recognize anything until it was right on top of her. Then – to her relief – Yui's lithe figure took shape, hurried over, and dropped to one knee.

The young guide's silky black hair had fallen partially out of the silver comb she used to keep it off her flawless face, but her blue suit and accenting red-and-white scarf remained as pristine as ever. Large chestnut-colored eyes studied Keiko, their golden flecks glinting in the darkness.

"You gave us quite a scare." Yui's expression softened. "Tokyo is the safest city in the world, but things *do* happen." Her voice was light and melodic, and her accented English added an exotic touch. This close, she looked no more than a year or so older than Keiko, her skin porcelain smooth, her lips as pink as cherry blossoms.

Beyond her, the shimmering walls had given way to gray cement, the strange ground once again pavement.

"You... You came back for me?" The rational voice in Keiko's head said it was Yui's job to look after her, but after weeks of tragedy, this small act seemed like a great kindness.

Yui smiled gently. "This city is large, confusing, and very crowded. It's easy to get lost here."

Keiko looked away and pushed her hair behind her ears. "I didn't exactly get lost. Not at first."

"That's how it always happens." Yui took Keiko's hand, patted it, and helped her to her feet. Despite Yui's calm exterior, the muscles just beneath her skin felt tight, tense. She tilted her head, a frown marring her otherwise smooth brow. "I'd be interested to know why you wandered off. Did you see something... something we can add to the tour, perhaps?" She said it lightly, but her expression was too intent for casual interest.

An uneasy feeling crawled up Keiko's back like a multi-legged insect. "No. At least... I don't think so."

"You don't think so?" Yui repeated, raising an eyebrow.

"I've been through a lot lately. I guess it finally caught up with me." The alley had returned to normal, and – now that Keiko had company – she thought she understood what had happened to her. "I sort of panicked when I realized I was alone. I didn't know what to do, so when this man showed up, I just followed him." She fanned her hands helplessly.

"A man. You followed a strange man in a city you don't know?"

Keiko shrugged. "I know it was stupid, but like I said, I was desperate. Besides, he looked like he belonged at the Palace. You know – tall, bald, dressed like a monk. I thought, maybe, he'd lead me there." She let out a long breath and lowered her head. "I followed him to an alley, but he disappeared before I got there. I think I passed out after that. Stress, you know? Jet lag, maybe. I dreamed the strangest things."

A look of alarm crossed Yui's face. "What things?" she whispered.

"You don't want to know." Keiko rolled her eyes. "Crazy stuff. Stereotypes. I was in a courtyard – or a temple surrounded by fire. A man was there too – big, maybe seven feet tall with burning eyes." She hesitated, licked her lips. "He... umm. He had these creatures with him. Dragons, I think. One red, one blue."

Yui flinched. She seized Keiko by the wrist and dragged her from the wall. "We have to go. *Now*!"

Even in heels, Yui ran amazingly fast. Ahead, an opening rushed up to meet them, another long rectangular slash in the dark. Outside, cars zipped up and down a wide street, briefly illuminating a steady stream of people. The familiar sounds of a bustling city filled Keiko's ears. A fresh sea breeze brushed against her face, and a strange tingling sensation coursed through her body, leaving her breathless.

She looked up to find Ginza once again sparkling around her. To her left, a row of red-lacquered torii gates leered at her from a side street, and though she knew they were harmless, she shivered at the sight of them.

2
SHIELDED

Once out of the alley, Keiko expected Yui to release her hand, but to her surprise, Yui increased both her grip and her pace. She squeezed through a gap in the crowd, swerved around a woman with a stroller, shouldered a young man with headphones out of the way, and darted forward as if determined to put as much distance as possible between the alley and their flight.

"Ginza Station is a few blocks away," she said as they passed a large building with rounded corners and a square clock tower on its roof. "The crowds are thicker there. We can't afford to get separated." Her gaze swept the streets ahead and – alarmingly – behind.

"Ginza Station? But that's the wrong way. Aren't we supposed to go to the Palace?"

"I know where I'm going, Keiko. You have to trust me."

They crossed another intersection, Yui speeding ahead, while Keiko ricocheted behind like an out-of-control trailer. A ubiquitous stairway opened before them, and Yui plunged into it with Keiko in tow. They reached the subway's wide, brightly lit concourse in seconds. The tiled floors, with their alternating shades of gray, were so like piano keys that Keiko half expected music to fill the air as she sped over them. Garishly windowed shops flashed by, here an electronics store, there a clothing boutique.

Yui's frantic pace continued until she reached a large bank of vending machines at the end of a crowded walkway. After buying a pair of tickets, she rushed down yet another flight of stairs, this one feeding onto the subway platform. Gleaming white walls met them at the bottom, the floor itself as clean as a hospital's.

Keiko had heard about Japan's pristine subway system, but she wasn't prepared for the reality. Awestruck, she wandered away from Yui and strolled about the station, taking in everything, including the elderly man with wispy white hair who swept the immaculate floors. Keiko wondered if he did it all day. From the looks of things, it was more than possible.

She left the man to his work and ambled down the platform, stopping when a slight breeze tickled her cheek. Instinctively, she turned and made her way back to Yui.

"What?" Yui asked. She was seated on a bench of pale wood by the stairs, her purse seemingly forgotten on the ground beside it.

"Isn't this our train?" Keiko tossed her head at the tracks.

Yui blinked. "Train? What train? We still have another ten minutes. There. Look." She pointed to an illuminated sign dangling from the ceiling.

"I don't care what it says – even if I could read it." Keiko sighed. Nobody ever listened to her. At eighteen, she was too young to be taken seriously and too old not to be. She shrugged. "Maybe we just got lucky. Maybe the sign's wrong. I don't know. The only thing I *do* know is that a train's on its way."

Yui shot her a skeptical look. This was a woman who thought she knew more than she did.

Keiko sighed again. She shifted her body toward the tunnel and waited for her hair to fan away from her head. "Here, see? A train pushes the air down the tunnel. You feel it before you hear it. Everybody knows that."

"This isn't right," Yui muttered. "Japanese trains run on schedule. That train would have to be a full ten minutes early, and that never happens... not ever." She stood slowly, woodenly.

"You're sure?" An irrational feeling of dread fluttered in Keiko's chest, some instinct both powerful and undeniably clear.

Yui nodded, her face grave. "*Yes*, Keiko. I'm sure."

Keiko moved away from the rails. The strengthening draft clawed at her, hot, dry, and stronger than it should have been.

"I've never felt that before." She clutched her throat.

Yui's head snapped toward the tunnel entrance. "What? You've never felt *what* before?"

"The heat. It's like an oven in here."

Face paling, Yui followed Keiko's gaze down the tracks. "Our train doesn't come from the left. It's a northbound train. They *only* approach from the right."

"What are you talking about?" Keiko started to say, when a throaty growl boomed out of the northern passage to silence her. Air rushed ahead of it in powerful blasts, each stronger than the last – blisteringly hot and accompanied by a hellacious glow that tinted the station's white walls with amber. "What was that?"

In a flash, Yui seized Keiko's jacket and forced her to the ground. "Stay down! You need to stay down! I didn't go through all the trouble of crossing the Boundary just to have you incinerated!"

Dropping to one knee, she dragged Keiko with her, her face lifting to meet the flickering glow. It churned faster now, coming down the tracks in a rush of sound and light. A wave of intense heat seared across the platform. Keiko's mouth went dry. She stared at Yui, but the question she wanted to ask died on her lips.

Yui wasn't paying attention to her. Instead, she stared into the light with an urgency that brought twisting knots to Keiko's stomach.

"Fiyorok," Yui hissed, scrambling back into a low crouch. "I was afraid of this." The first blast of air had loosed her hair, and it now whipped behind her, shining black silk hideously streaked with reflected flame. The image of the burning courtyard flashed through Keiko's head, the man's hands lifting, the creatures flanking him. Mesmerized, she started to stand. She had to know whether or not she'd imagined it. This felt connected, but she had to be sure.

She tried to worm her way around Yui for a better look, only to have Yui haul her back.

"*No*! I told you to stay down! No arguments! When I tell you to do something, you do it. Do you understand me?" A flash of golden light filled the chamber, and Yui shielded Keiko with her body. "Look away!" She raised her arms. "Protect your eyes!"

"What?" Keiko yelled.

A loud roar filled the chamber. She heard Yui's voice but couldn't make out what she'd said. Yui didn't seem to hear her either. She was about to repeat the question, when a great phalanx of fire erupted from the tunnel's mouth.

Dazed, she looked from one end of the subway to

the other, saw the horror, cursed her helplessness, her weakness. Passengers flared like torches. Paint peeled from stone, blackened, then ignited. Glass burst, metal melted.

Keiko tried to deny the reality, but acrid smoke and climbing temperature made it impossible. Her fist gripped the front of her shirt, the other lay rigid and trembling at her side. She imagined the touch of fire on skin, the sharp blistering pain, the sickening smell. Bravery failed her, reason failed her.

The firestorm consumed everything and everyone in the subway – everyone, she realized, but Yui, who knelt before her on the station's only remaining sliver of pavement. A lone figure kneeling amidst pulsating streaks of striated energy – indigo with faint traces of gold – that somehow held back the inferno. Her arms were thrust outward, crossed right over left at the wrists, her palms facing the fires, fingers splayed as though warding off a blow.

Keiko, a voice said in her head. An awareness followed it – a presence she recognized as Yui. *You need to do exactly as I say. I've raised a shield for protection, but I need to concentrate to maintain it. Stay down and keep out of my way. Do you understand?*

"Shield?" Keiko shouted. "What shield? What are you talking about? What's happening? And how are you talking to me like this? It's…it's…" She fished around for the right words and was just about to say "impossible" when a rumbling pulled her eyes to the smoking gash to her left. Fear froze her lips, and only a great effort convinced them to move. "We have to get out of here! We have to get out!"

Another growl echoed throughout the chamber, this one accompanied by an eerie staccato pounding. Keiko's pulse beat in time with the sound, the two growing louder in her ears. Light bloomed at the tunnel's mouth, alternating red and yellow, bringing still more heat.

Keiko glanced at the stairs. Too far. The thumping had already reached the tunnel entrance. Smoke stung her eyes, making it hard to see without blinking. A harsh scent filled her nose, and she recoiled, knowing the source.

She heard the northern passage collapse, the rhythmic pounding reaching it, growing louder. Slowly, as if invisible hands conspired against her, she looked back as the head of some terrible beast shot into the wrecked and burning station.

Glittering scales of red and gold sparkled through the smoke, vast armored plates that burned with an internal fire. A pair of huge spikes sprouted from the top of an enormous reptilian head, the long, snake-like body behind sporting a series of smaller, razor-sharp spears that began at the base of the creature's powerful shoulders and tapered toward its whip-like tail.

"I've seen you before," Keiko whispered, too enchanted to be afraid. "Back on the street, in front of the alley." She frowned. "But where is the other one. The blue one?" She crawled forward, but an invisible force slammed down in front of her.

Are you trying to get yourself killed? Again, Yui's voice sounded in her head. Fury burned her face.

Keiko tried to talk, but the huge creature silenced her. Its head swept the station, and when its gaze landed on Yui, its carnelian eyes blazed. "*AHK-KIIIIKKKOOO!*" it bellowed. Spittle dripped from its lips like liquid fire, torching whatever it hit.

Keiko recoiled, as much from the choking combination of smoke and flame as from Yui. Her heart thudded in her chest. She ran a hand through her hair.

"It knows you?" she panted. This wasn't happening. "I don't understand. What's going on, Yui? Yui, what's wrong?"

Yui's arms had fallen to her sides, and she staggered toward the twisted rails as if stunned. The creature towered over her, swaying from side to side like a giant cobra.

"Lower your shield!" it boomed.

The indigo light around Yui flickered like a guttering candle. Keiko's breath caught. That sphere was the only thing keeping them alive. If it went out...

Lunging forward, she grabbed Yui by the wrist and hauled her away from the platform's edge. Yui resisted, and Keiko tugged harder. She felt like she was dragging a wheelbarrow through mud. Sweat poured over her body, but at least the shield around them held firm. Yui was stronger than she looked. Feet planted, legs cramping, Keiko leaned back and pushed against the ground. The final surge was enough. Yui flew at her, and together they fell to the platform in a jumble of arms and legs, Yui on top, Keiko wheezing beneath.

The jolt reawakened Yui's mind. She gave Keiko a weak smile before climbing to her feet. "Thank you, Keiko." Straightening, she threw back her shoulders and spun to face the huge shape towering above her. "You shouldn't be here, Fiyorok! Go back to the Boundary. My father won't attack a guardian, but I will. If necessary."

The dragon brought its head down in a rush of orange fire. "Silly girl. You really think you can hurt me, don't you?" A great roar rolled from its throat, a laugh perhaps. "I admire your courage, but your ignorance is beneath contempt. You have so much to learn." Rearing onto its hind legs, Fiyorok inhaled sharply then thrust its body forward, jaws gaping. Smoke and flame issued from the creature's mouth, the two rotating into a single stream that slammed into Yui's shield and sent both Yui and Keiko careening into a far wall.

Up became down as they tumbled on, blood rushing in and out of Keiko's head like sand in a whirling hourglass. She tried to fix her eyes on a slab of broken concrete to keep from getting dizzy. That turned out to be a bad idea. She couldn't see where they were headed and was therefore unprepared for the impact. It jolted through her entire body, wrenching her gaze as they spun again, this time on an entirely different axis.

Yui righted the glowing orb before it hit anything else, and to Keiko's chagrin, headed back to the beast.

Amusement glinted in Fiyorok's eyes. "You are not worth the effort, little one. Go home to your father and enjoy what little time you have left."

The scarlet climbing Yui's neck made Keiko think of a thermometer dipped in scalding water.

"Don't listen to it! It's just trying to provoke you."

The dragon's gaze landed on her, and it laughed dismissively. "So, the Trickster's vaunted wisdom has finally failed him. How interesting. My master will be thrilled to hear it." Fiyorok turned its back and leaped for the tunnel. It smirked as it ran, as if daring Yui to follow.

For a moment, Yui seemed to consider it. Then, head shaking, she glared at Keiko. "What did you mean when you asked about the blue one?" Now that the monster had gone, the glowing orb around them became more pronounced.

"The other one?"

"No time for games. Did you see it? Do you know where it is?"

"They were statues – outside the alley. One was red,

the other was blue. I saw them again inside. With that man, the one with the fire." Keiko shivered. "They weren't statues then."

Yui said something in Japanese that sounded like a curse. Her eyes darted back to the tunnel. "It's time to go." She grabbed Keiko by the arm and wrapped it about her waist.

"Go? Go where? We can't get out. The stairs are blocked."

"We have to get to my father right away. He needs to know what's happened." Yui wiped her forehead with the back of her hand in a futile attempt to clean away a heavy residue of dirt and sweat. "Hold on!" She drew the energy bubble in close and launched it from the platform. "We're going for a ride."

Instantly, they shot upward.

Keiko's stomach plunged to her feet. The indigo light was only a few feet from her face, but despite its sizzle, she didn't notice any heat. She did hear the roaring wind and the rumble of exploding pavement as Yui rocketed high into the night sky.

In seconds, the whole city spread out beneath her like a sea of stars. She should have been afraid, but she was too overwhelmed by what she saw to feel anything but wonder. For the first time since her father's disappearance, she smiled broadly and let out a delighted squeal as the ground spun away beneath her.

3
FLIGHT

Keiko knotted her fingers together and tried to tighten her grip around Yui's waist. Her initial excitement had given way to an intense fear of falling. She didn't close her eyes, but she didn't look down either. Just thinking about the emptiness under her feet sent tremors crashing over her in waves. Her stomach flipped, climbed, then fell – first from their rapid ascent, and then again when the top of the Tokyo Tower flew by a hundred or so feet below. Another impossibility, one more thing for her mind to process.

Shinjuku's distinctive skyscrapers were a blur of concrete and glass, the twinkling lights of Shibuya sparkling like tiny diamonds. The sight drew her eyes, and against her better judgment she peered into the city. People still swarmed the sidewalks, as thick here as in Ginza, if not more so. They were too far away for her to see them as more than moving clumps separated here and there by headlights, neon, and garish buildings.

"You can let go now," Yui said, startling her. "The shield is large enough. I'm standing on it, and so are you. You have been since we left Ginza."

Keiko loosened her hold and tapped her right toe against the shimmering indigo light as if testing winter's first ice. She put more weight onto her foot then repeated the process with her left until she was sure enough to let go completely. "What *are* you, Yui?" she asked, stepping back gingerly. "The things you did today... I've never seen anything like it." Of course, she'd never seen a dragon either.

"You'll just think I'm making fun of you." Yui's body had gone rigid, and an odd defensiveness laced her tone.

Keiko raised her eyebrows. "Right," she drawled. "A dragon attacks us in the subway, and you're worried about me believing you. How does that make any kind of sense?"

Yui chuckled selfconsciously and some of the tension went out of her shoulders. "All right, but just remember you asked, OK?" Keiko nodded, and Yui let out a long, slow breath. "I'm the youngest of this world's elemental spirits," she said. "What the Japanese call *Kami*."

"Kami," Keiko repeated. "Like wood spirits or water sprites?" She knew a little about the Kami from her childhood; they were supposed to be spirits who embodied everything from wind to rivers to animals.

Yui gave Keiko a relieved smile. "Well that was easier than I expected. I really didn't think you'd believe me."

Keiko tapped a fingertip against the shield, tested her foot again, and looked over her shoulder at the smoldering sidewalks. "We *did* just leave a dragon behind, you know. How much more proof do I need? Which reminds me; you still haven't told me why that thing was so mad at you."

"It's a really long story, Keiko. Let's just say the dragon's master is very strong and very dangerous."

Keiko's eyes widened. "Dangerous enough to be

locked away!" She pictured the scene from the alley, seeing the handsome man and sensing something odd about him. Something off.

"You have no idea," Yui grunted. She shook her head. "My father didn't want Vissyus to know we were keeping an eye on him. I was just supposed to watch. I shouldn't have let his guardian see me. When my father learns about this…" She swallowed uneasily and glanced one last time at the chaos behind. Ginza was there, shining like a solar system in a larger galaxy.

Keiko followed Yui's gaze back into the city. A flash from somewhere closer drew her attention. It was nothing at first, a blip, a distraction, blazing a few blocks from where the glow of rescue vehicles winked red and white on the dark streets. Quickly, it became an inferno.

Flames roared upward in sheets of vivid fire, racing first north and then west before angling to Shinjuku in a pattern Keiko thought she knew. She'd seen it before – colored lines spreading out from a central point. Keiko's eyes widened as she remembered. She'd barely glanced at the walls of Ginza station; she was too busy careening behind Yui like a runaway trailer. Her subconscious caught the image, though, an image familiar to subway riders throughout the city. She saw it clearly, both in her head and laid out on the burning ground: the fires followed a subway line like a burning fuse, rocketing out of Ginza station and tailing Yui at high speed.

"*Yui!*"

Yui looked over her shoulder and muttered something under her breath. Her back was rigid, but her shoulders drooped. She reminded Keiko of a coach whose team was losing its lead. The fires closed, outrunning them. Already, they were plowing through Shinjuku like a white-hot saw. Keiko couldn't believe how fast they moved.

"What are we going to do?" Keiko's words came out like a squeak. She hung her head, cursing her fear. Yui needed more from her.

"Aokigahara," Yui said, as if coming to some decision. "That's where we'll go. My father put a Gate there. We should be able to lose Fiyorok in the magnetic storms." She pointed toward the vast forest beyond Mount Fuji. "It's farther than the Gate I wanted, but it's the only place I know that will confound Fiyorok's Searching."

"Gate? What Gate? Gate to where?" The dragon's roar tore through the skies and knowing what Yui was looking for became less important than reaching it. "How far?"

"Far enough," Yui said, her voice tight. She turned their shield southwest and accelerated.

The fires had reached Shibuya – close enough to feel their heat, close enough to hear the screaming. The famed crossing in front of the local subway station collapsed. Sooty clouds soared through the breach, a flaming mast following. Red-golden scales glittered at the base as Fiyorok rose from the ground in a sphere of incandescent fire. Windows shattered and neon tubes exploded.

Keiko was glad she couldn't see the carnage up close. People were dying there, probably many. Those who survived would carry their wounds with them for the rest of their lives – both physical and psychological. Her heart went out to them and their families, just as it had when the monster first appeared. She wished she could do something – anything – to help. But she was small, insignificant – a leaf in a hurricane.

Yui's almond eyes caught hers, the golden flecks burning like sunfire. She didn't speak, simply nodded. They shared a bond now, one of grief and helplessness.

It must have been worse for Yui. Gods – or whatever she was – were supposed to be omnipotent. What would a loss like this do to her? Already, creases formed around Yui's eyes and across her ash-streaked forehead. "You never told me what brought you to Japan," she said, sounding exhausted.

"You're asking me about that *now*?" Keiko was incredulous. This didn't seem like the time for small talk.

"I'm tired," Yui said – a grudging concession. "I need the distraction."

"What about telling me more about the Kami and why that dragon's chasing us?"

"That's a reminder, not a distraction. You need to tell me something that will take my mind off Fiyorok."

Keiko didn't think her ordinary life would help that much, and her recent history wasn't exactly cheery. Still, with a dragon pursing them, she'd do what she could. After bottling everything up for almost a month, talking might help her as much as it did Yui.

"It was my father's dying wish." Her voice was stronger than she'd expected. "He asked me to come, forced me actually."

"Forced you? How can a dead man force you?"

Keiko ignored Yui's lack of tact. Different cultures had different rules. "You didn't know him. When he wanted something, he made sure it happened. With me, he arranged everything, including travel and the tour."

Yui sniffed. "Fathers. They're all the same. You still could have ignored the request, though. You didn't have to step on that plane."

Fiyorok's bellow sounded closer. The light of its fires grew brighter. It was coming for them.

"Maybe not," Keiko said, trying to ignore their dwindling lead. "But if I stayed home, I'd never know why it was so important to him."

"He didn't tell you?" Yui's shield hurtled over Mount Fuji's graceful summit. Dragon fire tinted the snow the color of dried blood.

Keiko shook her head. "I don't know. Maybe he tried and I was just too preoccupied with my own stuff to notice." She chuckled miserably. "Funny thing is, now that he has my attention, the only thing he left for me to go on was a death poem."

"A jisei?" Yui perked up. Incredibly, Keiko's story was helping. "Those belong to the samurai. What did it say?"

Keiko didn't like thinking about the death poem. It made everything more real. She wouldn't see her father again, wouldn't hear his voice. It hurt.

"Something about leaving a piece of himself behind. To protect sun and spirit. Whatever that means."

Yui's face paled at the words. She looked shaken, as if Keiko had stabbed her in the heart. Obviously, this was more of a distraction than she wanted. Or needed. The shield surrounding them suddenly appeared less solid, and the golden bands within the indigo covering reminded Keiko of cracks in crystal. They blinked erratically as the whole shield flickered, held steady, then went dark.

Momentum carried them through the thin, winter-cold air. Keiko's terrified screams died in a wind that came from both nowhere and everywhere. Less than an hour before, she had thought she was safe. Her spirit had said otherwise. She should have listened to it.

Now, it tried to tell her something else. An ember stirred inside her, a survival instinct, a reflex. She reached out, but before she could touch it, Yui regained control of her shield and brought the glowing ball back to life.

"Are you all right, Keiko?"

Keiko gulped a mouthful of air and tried to steady her breathing. "Fine. You?"

"My concentration wavered. I'm all right now; it won't happen again."

"It's that poem, isn't it? It means something to you." Kami. Spirit. Jisei. Why hadn't Keiko made the connection? What had her father gotten her into? What did he know? Who was he?

"It's nothing." Yui said. "A coincidence. We can discuss this later. After we lose Fiyorok."

Keiko knew a dismissal when she heard one. She nodded silently. Better not to press. She prayed she hadn't upset Yui. The older girl was becoming important to her. She liked having someone else around, particularly someone close to her own age. A potential friend.

Her thoughts shifted to Fiyorok. She wanted to look, but didn't dare. Imagination put dragon breath on her neck, the smell of ash and soot filling her nose. She rubbed her arms as if to ward off a chill and kept her sights on the world ahead.

A neat semi-circle of lakes – five in all – lay outlined within the unblinking glow of hotel windows. Floating casinos dotted the shores, and a series of interconnecting highways, all filled with cars, linked the area to Japan's mega cities. Indigo light reflected on each of their surfaces, ghosting over the calm water like a phantom. A larger ball, a huge burning sphere of alternating yellow and orange, appeared close behind.

Chest tight, Keiko surveyed the area. How many people were down there? Thousands? Tens of thousands? They couldn't go there! Not with that demon on their heels. She had to stop Yui before they got too close, had to warn her off. But as she opened her mouth, Fiyorok's angry roar shattered the night.

Yui's head whipped around, her face grim. "Hold on, Keiko." She threw her shield into a steep dive. Keiko's stomach leaped into her throat. She thought she might well be sick. "Just a little farther."

A stream of fire cut through the air, barely missing them. It slammed into the earth below and spread outward. Flames threw back the darkness, light transforming what Keiko thought were rolling hills into thick, leafy treetops. Realization swept through her. Her heart soared. *The forest! That's what Yui meant. They would make it!*

The top of a medium-sized hill lay less than a mile west. Its eastern side fell away in a series of jagged cliffs and rocky promontories. Dense clusters of trees created an illusory canopy thick enough to hide the rugged bluffs below. Yui plunged through, the left becoming a blur of green, the right gray. Rotating her shield, she descended into the branches. Indigo light bathed magnificent fir trees on one side, a spectacular waterfall on the other.

Mist and spray wafted up from where the falls thundered into an unseen river, the world around them covered with a slick coating of ice-cold water. Yui continued down at a furious clip. She slowed before reaching the bottom, leveled out, and skimmed the surface of the wide river.

An ancient bridge spanned the emptiness several yards away. Built in traditional Japanese fashion, it sported torii gates at either end, while smaller matching posts supported the main span at regular intervals. Red lacquered paint stood out starkly against the deep green and gray that surrounded it, undimmed and unblemished by chip or scratch. It could have been built that very morning, though the way it melted into its environment spoke of an old, shared harmony between it, the gorge, and the falls.

Yui landed in the middle and extinguished her shield. A pair of carved dogs guarded the center, one for the front, one for the back. She placed a palm over the nearest and waited. Concentration lined her face, her body taut and ready.

"I thought you said it couldn't track us in here."

Yui shook her head in frustration. "Still so much to learn." Yui glared into the spray. "The magnetic storms will confuse Fiyorok's thoughts," she said to Keiko. "But the guardian already knows where we are."

Keiko looked from Yui to the darkened ravine. Apart from the thundering falls, the forest was unnaturally quiet. She held her breath, felt a rush of air hit her face, and recalled the subway as Fiyorok's shield drilled into the gorge. Its speed made it impossible to pull up, and the dragon hit the river like a falling star. Water boiled, steam climbing and spreading. Keiko heard the hiss of smothering fire working its way up the cliffs and into the forest. Yui's shield was still down, and she wore a satisfied smile. She stepped forward as if to attack.

Keiko moved to block her way. "I hope you're not thinking what I *think* you're thinking." The steam was still thick, but Keiko caught a flickering within the plumes.

"I can stop it!"

Light burst through the heavy clouds, alternating red, orange, and yellow as it worked its way down the river. A shimmer of indigo flashed around Yui's hand, the glow looking impossibly like a long spear.

"What about your father?" Keiko protested. The question brought a pang of jealousy. Yui still had her father. "You said you had to warn him. If anything happens to you, he'll never know. What's more important – fighting a fight you don't know you'll win or getting the help you said you need?" She tugged Yui's arm. "You've done it. You saved us. Sending the dragon into the river was brilliant. Now, let's go before it finds us."

Yui hesitated, seemingly weighing her options. After a moment, she lowered her guard. "You're right, Keiko; we should go." The glow around her hand faded, and she placed her palm over the stone dog's head.

A strange tingling rippled through Keiko's body as a hole opened in the air a few feet down the bridge. Peering through, Keiko thought she saw massive white walls climbing into the night sky.

Beside her, Yui brought her fist down on the small statue, shattering it. She then squared her shoulders and motioned Keiko forward.

"And we'll be safe there?" Keiko pointed at the portal. "It can't follow us?"

Yui shook her head. "I've destroyed the Keystone. The Gate will close as soon as we're inside. Neither Fiyorok nor its master will know where we've gone."

The hellish glow within the steam intensified, and Keiko heard the sound of something large moving back and forth through the water, as if searching.

"Hurry," Yui commanded, ushering Keiko into the opening. "This way."

4
RIPPLES

Aeryk Tai-Banshar, Kami of Air, lowered the phone with a remarkably steady hand. The perfect Florida day shining through the windows of his Miami office mocked him. The brilliant sun. The clear blue skies. Beautiful weather was supposed to make people feel good, lightening the mood and warming the heart. This morning did neither.

It's begun.

How could two simple words unsettle him so much? He'd waited for them for what felt like forever, dreading and dreaming about them. Now that they'd come, he wasn't ready. His thoughts spun in his head like leaves in a whirlwind. He couldn't think, couldn't pull the plans he made so long ago into focus. After an eternity, he still needed another few minutes to gather himself. Inhaling, he pushed his chair back, and – struggling to maintain an air of professionalism – walked to the woman seated in the plush visitor's chair.

One thing at a time.

"My apologies, Ms Montero," he said, reestablishing his disguise as enigmatic venture capitalist Eric A Aeronson. "I've just received some disturbing news. I'm afraid I'll need to reschedule."

"I'm so sorry, Mr Aeronson." Julia Montero looked genuinely concerned. "We can do this another time." She gathered her things and stood. Aeryk wouldn't have blamed her if she let her disappointment show. She didn't, and that impressed him.

"Thank you, but that won't be necessary." Tall as she was – five-eight or nine with long dark hair, a handsome face, and bright intelligent eyes – he still towered over her. He leaned against the desk to lessen the difference. "What you've discovered about hurricane tracking is very impressive. The National Hurricane Center tells me they've never seen anything like it. Based on their recommendation, I've decided to accept your proposal."

Julia gaped openly. EA Aeronson Ltd was the envy of the financial world, a conglomerate with a Midas touch. Its backing would make her research a reality.

"I don't know what to say. You won't regret this, I promise." She took his hand and shook it vigorously. "Thank you, Mr Aeronson. Thank you very much."

"You don't have to thank me. An early warning system with the accurate hurricane tracking software and satellite interface you've developed will go a long way to limit the loss of life. When more sites go online – " Aeryk fanned his hands – "who knows how many lives we'll save."

"I grew up in Florida, Mr Aeronson," Julia said, walking with Aeryk to the richly paneled oak door. "For as long as I can remember, I've worried about hurricanes. Every year it's the same: how many storms will we have? How strong will they be? I took my fear and tried to put it to use. It's as simple as that."

"It's been a pleasure," Aeryk said, grinning. "My attorneys will contact you this afternoon."

They shook hands one last time, and Aeryk watched her disappear into his outer office. Once she was gone, he closed the door, strode to the panoramic windows dominating the far side, and stared at a spot along the horizon, Yui's words ringing in his head. He pulled in another deep breath and drew himself up to his full height. Shoulders square, head back, he sent his thoughts past Biscayne Bay. He'd formed the words ages ago. Releasing them now lifted one great weight while bringing down another.

I'm coming, Seirin, he thought. *I'm finally going to get you out.*

Seirin, Kami of Water and Queen of the Oceans, didn't answer. Not that he expected her to. The Boundary held her still, would continue to hold her, if only for a little longer. The Gate to her prison was due east and a handful of miles from shore. How many times had he gone to it? More than he could remember. It was always in his thoughts, dominating his life – a life on hold, a life in purgatory. He couldn't think of anything else. His soul, his entire being, remained focused on a nearby speck of ocean.

Nearby? Maybe in miles, but the Gate itself might as well have been hidden among the stars. Proximity didn't matter; it never had. Time was all that counted: the moment the Weakening came, that delicate instant when he could break into the Boundary and free Seirin. Finally, if Yui was right, that time had come at last.

Yui. Aeryk tried to imagine how she was doing in Tokyo. If she was safe. He frowned angrily, wishing she'd told him more – about what she'd seen, what she faced. He probably should be more worried about her, but strangely, he wasn't. Her father, Takeshi, Great Lord of Spirit, had trained her well. Too well. Yui never offered more than she had to.

A family trait, Aeryk snorted. *And so like her father.* The last time Aeryk needed information, Takeshi was the one who withheld it. Now, his daughter did the same. Time moved on, but some things remained constant. He sighed, his mind working to unravel whatever puzzle Yui had left for him. A guardian sighting was always the first sign of a Weakening. Had there been others? If so, what?

Relaxing, he let his mind connect with the electricity flying through the air. He sorted all of it, discarding one piece after another until he found a news broadcast about fires in Tokyo, a subway collapse, and wild reports about an unknown creature.

An unknown creature. One. *Only one.* Fire made that Fiyorok. If this was the Great Weakening, then Akuan was out too. Out but not in Tokyo.

Aeryk's eyes flew open, his fingers rolling into tight fists. *No!* he thought. *No, no, no!* His trips to Seirin's prison came back to him in a rush. He wasn't the only one who wanted to see her. Long ago, Vissyus made her a promise. Insane and obsessive, he would have focused exclusively on the idea – made it the most important part of his existence.

Akuan was the promise's fulfillment. The guardian was coming, homing in on Aeryk's irresponsible use of power. Another city at risk, another population in harm's way. Heart sinking, he sent his gaze flying across the bay. Florida's beautiful weather already lured boaters out. He tried to count the number of ships, slips, and yachts cruising from one end of the bay to the other. How many people were on the water? A hundred? More? Each ship, from the smallest to the largest, carried anywhere from one to over twenty. The cargo ship steaming into port had a crew of at least forty. And then there was the city itself.

Aeryk grimaced. He had to get away; he had to go. If Akuan arrived and didn't find him, it would leave. Better for him to be away before that happened. Better for everyone. Sliding one foot behind his body, he started to back away from the window, when he spotted movement between Key Biscayne and Fisher Island. The calm water made the guardian's silhouette impossible to miss, but Aeryk didn't need the clarity to recognize Akuan's two hundred foot-long serpentine body. The dragon swam effortlessly but at high speed. Large white dots appeared behind it, growing and lengthening into large icebergs, a first for Miami's eighty-degree water. A wake formed at the top of Akuan's head, white foam curling above jade-green eyes, gathering force as it widened. Half a mile in front, the container ship's stern rocked up then down. The boat slowed to compensate for the rough seas, and in seconds, Akuan had caught it.

Aeryk almost felt the dragon's giant horns slice through the ship's keel. Sparks shot upward, some from the scrape of armor plate on metal, others from shorting wires. They showered the decks, igniting upended and leaking fuel canisters. Flood waters carried the fire through walls, under doors, and on into the engine room, where it fed a cauldron of heat, steam, and fuel. Powerless, Aeryk watched a series of explosions shake the superstructure. Huge chunks, blown from the deck, careened into the air only to fall like solid, deadly rain. Flames roared up to meet them, the sound deafening, even at a distance. Booms coupled with the hiss of vapor and the groan of dying metal, and, when the smoke cleared, the once-sturdy vessel was gone like a hole in the water.

Damn it, Akuan, Aeryk cried, summoning his power. *They're no threat to you! Leave them alone!* Raising his azure shield, he rushed ahead, the blazing orb solidifying around his body. His office window was nothing – as insubstantial as clouds. Breaking it would be easy, if conspicuous. People would see him. He wrestled with that. Did it matter? They'd already seen Akuan. Shield in place he lifted from the rugs, hating what he had to do, hating what was coming. His shield's outer rim sizzled a foot from the casements, half a foot, inches. He prayed no one was on the streets below.

Out in the bay, Akuan resurfaced and, chin lifted, swung its glowing green eyes toward him. A rabid leer broke over its snout. It had sensed him.

Swearing, Aeryk dropped the shield but couldn't stop his momentum. His palms slammed into the glass with a dull thud. The window shivered but thankfully held firm. He shook his head. That was careless – careless and stupid. He should have known better; he did know better. He couldn't even summon a fraction of his power without drawing Akuan like a beacon.

Freeing Seirin was significantly more complicated now.

Heart aching, he pounded his fists against the window. Screams sounded in his ears, loud and anguished. He barely recognized them as his own. This couldn't happen, not again. He had promised Seirin; he'd promised himself. The thought steadied him. He clung to it and drew his body to its full height. Willing his mind calm, he scanned the sea. The answer was out there. He just had to find it – and soon.

Akuan was already in the central bay. A boat swerved toward it, and then a jet ski. More craft closed, each eager for a look at the astonishing sight. But Akuan outpaced them. Only the fastest boat could keep up, only something like…

Aeryk whirled and reached for his phone. A tap of a button dialed his personal marina. "Russ?" he said, as soon as the dock master came on the line. "It's Eric Aeronson." The name he'd used for so long sounded funny in his ears.

Russ's energetic voice burst from the other end. "Good morning, Mr Aeronson. I've been expecting your call. I assume you already know what's happening." The man sounded thrilled. Aeryk wondered if he was the type to gawk at accidents on the highway.

"I can see it from my office." Aeryk struggled to keep his tone light. Akuan had disappeared beneath the surface, but the crystal clear Florida waters made the huge creature all too visible. "I imagine you're all busy down there."

"We're quiet, but that's to be expected. The other marinas, though… you should see them. People are falling all over each other to get their boats out. Everyone wants a look at the thing."

Obviously, word of the sunken freighter hadn't reached port. Aeryk knew he should warn as many docks as he could, tell them to keep people out of the water. He resisted the urge. The more boats, the easier for him to blend in until he was well away. He prayed Akuan would leave them alone. They weren't in its way – it wasn't after them.

Shame bubbled up within him. He fought it down and pressed the receiver to his ear. "Have the *Zephyr* fully fueled and ready to go within the hour. And tell David I'm just leaving my office. That should give him the time he needs."

He cut the connection, hurried to his executive elevator, and punched the button for the garage. Minutes later, he roared out of his building in a white

Lamborghini, heading south. The midmorning traffic was light, but hazardous considering his speed. He swerved around cars and squeezed into and through narrow gaps. The tires squealed loudly as they bit into pavement. Horns sounded all around him. Overhead, a news helicopter buzzed by like an angry wasp.

Aeryk scowled at it. He had one on the roof – why didn't he remember it? Akuan's appearance had rattled him. Badly. If he couldn't pull himself together…

The hum of the rotors gave way to a sinister hiss. Loud and chilling, it burst from the bay and rocketed upward. Aeryk recognized the sound; he didn't have to see it to know – Akuan's breath, a combination of ice and steam, different from Fiyorok's fire, but just as deadly.

He glanced in his mirror. A pillar of ice and foaming water burst from the bay. The strike tore through the air without melting, bisected the sky like a tilted horizon. Strong and powerful, it slammed into the chopper with enough force to push the fragile aircraft a mile back into the city. The helicopter shivered from the impact, held together defiantly, then came apart in clouds of inky smoke and flying metallic shards.

Aeryk tore his eyes from the carnage. His conscience told him to go back and help. He was the only one who could stop Akuan. But saving the city might mean condemning the world. Was he strong enough to just turn away? He imagined his sweat-soaked palms staining the leather steering wheel red. How much blood would cover his hands before this was finished?

As much as it takes, came the reply, *or other cities, other worlds, will suffer a similar fate.*

Stomach twisting, he pushed his foot down on the accelerator and sped toward the marina without looking back.

5
WINDSTORM

Aeryk brought the Lamborghini to a screeching halt at the end of the marina's long, flower-lined driveway. Smoke from its wounded tires clung to the hot pavement, the blue tendrils eerily reminiscent of Akuan, the pungent smell of Fiyorok. Akuan. Fiyorok. Both guardians free after so long. Knowing it would happen wasn't the same as living it. Not even close. His spirit felt heavy, chained. Reuniting with Seirin did little to dispel the sense of dread that shackled him.

He sat in the car, painfully aware of time's passage. The centuries had rushed past him, the waiting both eternal and fleeting. To his right, a pair of tall wooden doors blocked access to the docks. How easy it would be to let them stop him. To give in and turn away. Going through meant accepting what would come – the responsibility and the consequences. Could he live with that?

The voice of a reporter roused him. It came from his radio – young, terrified, female. She spoke about the helicopter, of the men and women inside, people she knew. They lost their lives to an unstoppable force, and she openly wondered how many more would follow.

Everyone's, Aeryk thought. *Once Vissyus returned.* He stared back at the white doors. A burst of air pushed them open. He vaulted from his car and sped between their blown hinges. Better to hurry. Less chance to change his mind.

Several yards in the distance, the marina's stucco boathouse dominated a quiet beach of manmade dunes, soft sand, and crystal clear water. Wide, contoured, and white, it looked like a large cumulus cloud had landed and anchored itself to the ground.

David Peterson, his young chief of the dock, waited just outside, a clipboard dangling loosely from his hand. He was perhaps a head shorter than Aeryk, with stylish, sunbleached hair and bright gray eyes.

He nodded as Aeryk approached. "Mr Aeronson."

"Good morning, David. Interesting day."

"To say the least." Apart from a slight tightening in David's voice and tension about his shoulders, the dock chief remained professional. "Are you sure about this?"

"No," Aeryk admitted. "I can't say that I am."

"At least let me call the Coast Guard. They can escort you out."

Aeryk raised a quizzical eyebrow. "A preemptive rescue? We both know the Coast Guard has better things to do."

David's cheeks colored, and he pretended to survey his clipboard.

"I know what I'm doing, David. It might not look like it, but I do." He placed a hand on David's shoulder. The company's official light-blue polo shirt rippled under his touch like a wind-blown flag. "You have a new wife. Shut down the marina and go home. You'll be safe there."

"What about you? You know what that thing did."

Aeryk stopped and stared into David's face. "I'll be

fine. Now, do as I say. Send everyone home and get out as fast as you can." He gave David's shoulder a reassuring squeeze and loped to the docks.

The *Zephyr* idled at the end of a lone jetty, the soft purr of its engine blending with the slosh of waves and the slap of fiberglass against bumpers. A fifty one-foot beast of a machine, the *Zephyr* outraced and outdistanced every other powerboat in South Florida. Its sleek hull and perfect aerodynamics hinted at speeds greater than the two hundred twenty miles per hour its engineers promised – speeds he never needed. Until today.

"Mr Aeronson?" David called from shore. "One more thing. I had a new sonar array installed on the boat. Silt builds up in the central bay, and trust me, you don't want to hit any shallows when going full out. With all that ice out there..." He left the sentence unfinished, looking as if he couldn't believe what he just said.

Aeryk nodded and climbed aboard. A tug on the ropes fore and aft set the boat free, and before long, he glided through the channel.

Out in the bay, icebergs bobbed in a direct line from deep water to shallow, some small, others as large as tankers. A few failed to reach the surface, and Aeryk thanked David for the boat's state-of-the-art electronics and the reminder to use them. Hitting an iceberg – even a small one – at high speed would tear the ship to pieces. He wished for a shield. Longed for it. Knowing he couldn't summon one only made it worse.

Frustrated, he slammed the throttle forward, careful to keep a close eye on the sonar. White dots lit the screen, though most remained several miles away. The largest and most stationary were probably ice, which made the rest boats. A lone object, huge, long, and fast, moved below.

Akuan.

Aeryk set his jaw and pressed on. A part of him desperately wanted to turn back and help the boaters. Leaving them was a death sentence, but attacking Akuan only postponed the inevitable. If he didn't rescue Seirin, the whole world would suffer. Better to hold his course, better for him, better for everyone. Almost.

Forcing the thought aside, he put his back to the bay. The Atlantic called him – seven miles distant. Six. Less. The way ahead looked clear both on the screen and off. Several curious anomalies bloomed in the lower corner, but they remained concentrated around Akuan. He glanced aft. Instruments couldn't show everything. Sure enough, a series of flashes erupted below the surface. Muffled booms sounded after them, muted by distance and water. The sonar's bleat became rapid, almost frantic.

A mile away, Akuan changed course. The dragon came about and drove for the nearest grouping of ships, diving so deep that its silhouette disappeared. Bubbles trailed behind it, the course straight, clear, and unchanging. Hunters became prey, and Aeryk had to force his hand steady on the wheel. He couldn't turn. He had to go on.

Aboard the foremost trawler, a big, barrel-chested man pointed at Akuan's wake and yelled something to the boat's pilot before picking up a large box and tossing it over the side. Seconds later, explosions sent seawater into the air.

Blast fishing. Those idiots! What were they thinking? No boat was safe now, not even his. Akuan would sink anything that moved. Already, the seas beneath the trawler had transformed. The gentle swells shuddered, and a slow, counterclockwise spin tugged at the ship's keel. Nearly imperceptible at first, it grew in speed and intensity.

The triumphant shouts coming from the decks turned to alarm. One fisherman in particular – thickset and sunburned – frantically twirled in his boat's flying bridge. He stared into the spiraling water with terrified eyes and drew a pistol from his waistband. Pointing it down, he fired off several rounds before Akuan's gaping jaws broke through the surface.

Nearly fifty feet long, they towered over the ship's cabin, one to port, one to starboard. Sea spray glittered on sapphire scales that snapped shut with lightning speed, pulverizing fiberglass and wood, shearing metal.

Akuan's tail surfaced sixty yards to port. One sweep splintered a handful of boats. Another pass capsized more. The remainder tried to run, only to find their hulls snared in a rapidly freezing bay. Ice covered a wide swathe of ocean, while below, Akuan's shadow could still be seen, this time heading for deep water.

Aeryk swore again and spun the wheel. The ice shouldn't spread far in such warm seas, but he plowed on regardless, catapulting over waves, soaring past deep troughs, guzzling fuel.

A rogue swell caught the *Zephyr*'s bow and shot it into the air. Aeryk's reflexes fired, and a shield flashed around him, bright and shining and unmistakable. He stared at it in disbelief. No! He didn't, he couldn't. A fraction of a second, that's all it took for his concentration to falter. He pounded his fist into the dash. Stupid, irresponsible, potentially catastrophic.

Across the bay, Akuan submerged and headed toward him at high speed.

The *Zephyr* was fast, but for all its horsepower, Akuan was faster. Aeryk considered abandoning the boat, but quickly discarded the idea. Shielded, he could outrun the guardian, but Akuan would sense his movements and track him. He couldn't allow that. Seirin was everything to him. He wouldn't let Akuan find her.

Desperate, out of options, he opened his thoughts. *Ventyre! Are you there?*

His guardian's response, though insufferable, came immediately. *My lord? Is that you? It's been so long. Are you still using the name the Sioux gave you, or have you chosen another one?*

Aeryk swerved away from a reef. Shallow water might slow Akuan, but it would freeze faster and hold ice longer. His only hope lay in the deep channels. *I need a localized squall in Biscayne Bay. Up by the big key. Do it now!*

Ventyre's mocking tone grew serious. *You haven't asked for direct intervention in over eight hundred years. What's happened?* Aeryk felt his guardian's Searching sweep the area. A sharp intake of breath followed moments later. *Akuan! I don't believe it. You should have called me sooner.*

The *Zephyr* zipped between a container ship and a tanker. *We all knew the Weakening was coming, Ventyre; we just didn't know when.*

Takeshi did, the guardian countered. *Why else is Yui in Tokyo? She wouldn't have been there if Takeshi hadn't ordered her to scout the city.*

Ventyre… Aeryk warned.

No, my lord. You've beaten yourself up about the Weakening ever since you first learned about it. I've held my tongue for long enough. The Weakening wasn't your fault. Takeshi is outside too. He could have stopped you from attacking the Boundary, but he chose not to. Did you ever ask him why?

Aeryk hadn't. Not in over a billion years. The guilt had been too much for him, so instead of confronting Takeshi, he simply avoided the topic whenever he and the Spirit Lord met to plan. *What's done is done.* He sighed and thought about the Weakening, and the more he thought, the more he knew Ventyre was wrong. He'd attacked the Boundary as hard and for as long as he could, hoping to find some way to free Seirin before the prison fully formed. He failed, of course, succeeding only in puncturing random spots across the Boundary's layered surfaces. Undamaged, the barrier might have held indefinitely. But now? Now Vissyus could break free if the damaged sections aligned into what Aeryk called the perfect Weakening. The odds against one were astronomical, which was why none had ever happened before.

Opening the engine, he sent the boat flying across the water. *Gates,* he thought. *Keystones. The Boundary. Why did Takeshi make everything so difficult?* Akuan quickly halved the distance between them and came up to surface depth. Its horns speared through the waves like splayed fingers. Rainbows danced within the cast-off brine, a violently foaming wake boiling behind it. Without a distraction, it would overtake him in minutes.

It's really not that complicated when you think about it, Ventyre piped. *You just have to think of the Boundary as a huge building. The Boundary itself represents the building's walls. The Gates are the doors to individual rooms – or worlds in this case – and the Keystones are both room numbers and unlocking mechanisms rolled into one. Getting the doors open is the only tricky part.*

As much as I love debating this with you, guardian, I'm running out of time. For now only Aeryk, Yui, and Takeshi knew how to open the Gates, and that advantage wouldn't last if Vissyus got a good look at them. Even insane, the Fire Spirit was far too strong and far too brilliant to let a simple door stop him, no matter how well reinforced or confusing. Takeshi might as well have shut the entrance with lace.

You're running out of time? Ventyre squawked. *I'm the one who has to hold Akuan off. It's been nice knowing you, my lord.*

The storms, Ventyre! Don't make me ask again.

As you wish. The guardian sniffed its offense but did as Aeryk asked. A warm gale blew in from southern waters, and Aeryk braced himself for the collision of low-level tropical air and the cooler atmosphere aloft. The skies darkened, thunder boomed in the distance, and the loud sizzle of rain on water raced inland.

Undeterred, Akuan swam on – course unchanged, speed unchanged.

They needed something more dramatic. He thought of the shark hunters and Akuan's reaction. *Bring the lightning,* Aeryk called. *As much as you can. Hit Akuan until it hurts. And make sure you key the strikes to the squall. It has to think you're in there. Nothing else will pull it away from me.*

I've never been suicidal, Ventyre said dryly. *Akuan will suspect a trap.*

Even if it does, it won't ignore a direct attack.

Ventyre grunted its assent. *And what will you do? You can't hide the Keystone forever, not if you want to activate it.*

Cyclones, Aeryk said. *I'll raise one around the Keystone then litter the ocean with a hundred more. We've prepared for this, Ventyre. I'll be fine.*

Provided Seirin doesn't kill you once you're inside. I'm sure she's furious with you.

Aeryk ignored the remark. He opened the throttle just as a series of lightning strikes rained down from above. Blindingly bright, they hammered the seas above Akuan. Electricity spiderwebbed over its horned crown like a glowing net.

Enraged, Akuan lifted its head from the water and fired a blast of ice into the clouds. Rain turned to snow, but the lightning continued, strong and relentless. Most originated in the squalls to its left. Akuan turned and sprang at them like a loosed arrow.

Coming your way, Aeryk told his guardian. *How long can you hold it?*

Hard to say. With all the storm activity up here, it might assume we're defending the Gate. If that's the case, you'll have more time. Once you start forming cyclones out to sea, though – that's when it will realize we've tricked it.

Which is why we'll need to form as many spouts as we can. Aeryk checked his instruments. *I'm just leaving the bay now. Given my current speed, I should be near the Gate in about twenty-five minutes. Keep it busy until then.*

I'll do my best, but I won't make any promises.

Aeryk grunted his understanding. He returned his attention to the ocean, occasionally checking the *Zephyr*'s GPS to make sure he was on course. The world beyond Key Biscayne was deceptively calm, and, except for a few white clouds, the eastern sky remained a clear and sparkling blue.

A large arrow-like shape cut through it, following him. It was roughly the same size as a passenger plane, though longer in the nose and tail. Electrical charges flickered across its big avian body, and Aeryk could have sworn he saw the glint of lavender eyes regarding him with a mixture of curiosity and worry.

I don't remember asking you to shadow me. Despite the words, he welcomed his guardian's presence.

I am not *shadowing you.* Aeryk thought he heard the disgusted ruffling of feathers. *I'm preparing the atmosphere.*

Of course.

Hundreds of waterspouts, the guardian squawked. *Difficult to form and maintain over so small a territory. You wouldn't want them to fail before you're inside the Gate, would you?* Ventyre emphasized each word as though speaking to a child.

Aeryk winced at the thought. *No, guardian. You're right. I wouldn't.*

I didn't think so. The wispy clouds thickened, and Ventyre slipped into them. *I can't believe you survived this long without me.* Its voice faded in Aeryk's head, and when it came back, a mischievous piping filled it. *You'd better hold on. Things are about to get a little rough down there.*

It began with a sharp spike in surface temperature. Sultry air swirled upward, and strong, convecting atmospheres pulled water into the sky. The first cyclone solidified several hundred yards to the *Zephyr*'s port side.

Aeryk sent the boat into a wide, sweeping turn to avoid it only to have another form in his path. He felt the current shift, noted how the engine protested. Waterspouts were everywhere, immense vortices that tugged at the boat from different directions. The Keystone was in the one off his starboard bow – calling him, leading him.

He came about and adjusted his heading to compensate for the increasingly rough seas. The hull shuddered as it turned. Waves battered the bow, pushing him back like a giant hand. He glared at the twisting water, felt time slipping away. Behind him, a row of undulating sapphire humps sliced through the ocean. Akuan's mane fanned out below the surface like beds of sea-green kelp in a riptide.

Aeryk's fingers tightened around the *Zephyr*'s throttle. He jammed it forward as far as it would go, and while the boat did its best against the rolling ocean, the hull wasn't built for this kind of punishment. It lurched over a ten foot-high wave, the propeller spinning in the empty air. The stern groaned ominously, and Aeryk knew the fight was over.

Releasing the wheel, he stepped back, aware of the *Zephyr*'s disintegrating aft section. The mid deck went next, then the seats. Unconcerned, he watched them fly into the sea and disappear. Waves lashed at him, the ocean reached for him, but his momentum carried him through the air. His air. His domain. It was where he belonged, where his power remained unequalled. Let Akuan try to follow him. It was strong, but he was stronger.

Instantly, he opened his thoughts. A globe of dazzling blue burst to life around him. How could he have been so long without it? Its return calmed him, helped him remember who he was, and what he could do. In that moment, Eric Aeronson ceased to exist. In his place, Aeryk Tai-Banshar, Kami of Air, Commander of the Winds, and King of the Heavens, soared toward the massive cyclone.

A soft glow pulsed deep within it. He smiled. Seirin was there, there beyond the Boundary. Waiting for him. His heart felt close to bursting. After an eternity apart, they would be together again.

6
CONFRONTATIONS

Aeryk turned his back on the sinking *Zephyr* and catapulted into a divided sky. Clear blue sparkled in the far distance, a world away from the black storms blanketing the Florida coast. Less than a mile from him, an immense cyclone tore through the ocean. He looped around the spout, first once, then again. Each pass brought him closer to the cascading water, closer to the Gate. Closer to Seirin.

Anticipation sent shivers through his body. The horror of the bay, of Akuan's reappearance and its implications, fell from his shoulders like shaken snow. Only the massive spout existed for him. Her Gate was there. Inside. Waiting for him.

Banking sharply, he plunged through the spinning water and into an enveloping darkness. Shadows swallowed everything, the gloom leeching into his soul, clawing at him, waking a suppressed past, an ancient wound. He saw the smoking remains of a great battle, felt his shame at arriving too late. The Boundary had claimed Seirin, and his power was useless against it. She wouldn't know what had happened to him, why he wasn't there to face Vissyus, why he didn't try to free her.

That memory haunted him. He thought about turning back, considered asking someone else to open her Gate. Takeshi could do it. This was his fault. Let him face her anger. But Takeshi wouldn't agree. He'd set the Keystones in random places. Seirin's was here in the Atlantic, while her actual palace once dominated an area of the South Pacific. Aeryk ran a hand through his dark hair. *Needle in a haystack.*

Are you all right, lord? Ventyre called into his thoughts. Despite the distance, his guardian sensed his discomfort and moved to help. Ventyre's power sizzled through the clouds. Lightning flashed, and his thoughts cleared. A presence lingered behind the unraveling night, a dissipating scent, a fading silhouette. *Lon-Shan's in here,* the guardian warned.

Aeryk's eyes shifted to the darkness. *Lon-Shan's Gate is over a thousand miles away, and even it wasn't, Lon-Shan can't interfere; he's behind the Boundary, Ventyre. He can't get out.*

You don't know that.

Of course I do. Takeshi said the Kami are locked away. They can't get out unless one of us opens their Gate from the outside.

With all due respect, my lord, the Weakening changed that. Perhaps describing the Boundary as a house was a mistake. It's more like a giant, multilayered sphere. Each layer rotates around the core for added security. When the Weakened parts align, the integrity of the specific cell – or world – at the core is compromised. Takeshi repaired what he could, but he could only do so much. To keep the imprisoned spirit from escaping, he added a specific protection. Strength is the indicator – lesser Kami can pass through a Weakened section of the Boundary like water through a screen. The Gates will catch anything stronger than a guardian. That's why guardians can escape during the Weakenings.

Aeryk flinched whenever Ventyre mentioned the Weakening. *I know all about that, guardian,* he snapped more harshly than he should have. *The Boundary keeps strong Kami trapped, Lon-Shan included. He shouldn't be here. I need to find out more before I open Seirin's gate. Vissyus might be using him to watch us.*

No, lord. You're not thinking. Lon-Shan isn't working for Vissyus; he's working for himself, He still blames you and Seirin for Vissyus's madness. As far as he's concerned, your power made you irresponsible. He thinks you have to face justice.

That doesn't explain why he's here. Or how for that matter.

It explains everything. Lon-Shan's weak, barely stronger than the strongest guardian. In some ways, he's less sane than Vissyus. Lon-Shan is cold and calculating; he planned for this, my lord. He set it in motion.

Aeryk cursed his shortsightedness. *How long have you known?*

About Lon-Shan? Ventyre asked. *Since Takeshi told us how the last battle ended; the rest came over time. I've watched many guardians reappear across the world. Some were strong, like Fiyorok and Akuan. Others less so. That's when I realized how Lon-Shan was closer to slipping back into the world than any other spirit.*

Aeryk's eyes widened in understanding. *Because he isn't that much stronger than the strongest guardian.* Why didn't he see it before? The Boundary didn't consider Lon-Shan a threat; it simply ignored him.

Aeryk made that mistake once, he wouldn't make it again. Dismissing Ventyre's rising protests, he threw his mind into the air. A single thought brought hot, dry winds from the west to sap the squalls. The darkness faltered, only to grow again when a new storm broke from the cyclone. Instead of shredding it, Aeryk let it grow. He summoned the thermal currents of the Atlantic jet and bound them to ferocious hurricane-force gales. Lances of air pinwheeled around his shield, gathering speed and momentum. He aimed them at the black clouds, but as he readied his strike, Ventyre's alarmed cries shattered his concentration.

Leave him, lord. Akuan's a much bigger threat. The ice dragon has already frozen a good part of the bay to cool the air. Your cyclones need tropical warmth to feed them and we've already lost a dozen or more to the cold. The next one could be yours. I understand you want Lon-Shan to pay, but you really need to think about this.

Aeryk hesitated. He wanted to hurt Lon-Shan. Severely. Unfortunately, that meant taking more time than he had. Just finding Lon-Shan's hiding place would be hard. He slowed his shield. Water broke around him like waves against rock, vaporizing at the touch and adding steam to the maelstrom. Still nothing. Best guess then. Turning, he spotted a clump of black clouds massed inside the spout's outermost layers – as dark as midnight and free from lightning. Not a Gate – the Weakening! Some of Lon-Shan's power rode the darkness through it.

That made him more dangerous than Aeryk expected. He could show up anywhere – just like he did before. Grimly, Aeryk recalibrated his air lances. Tropical, moisture-heavy air surrounded him. He seized it, blowing the warmest, densest portion into the upper atmosphere. Sickening green overwhelmed the once-black clouds, and an eerie glow radiated from their depths. Lightning arced from one to the next, the first flash shredding the clouds, the second shattering Lon-Shan's hold on the darkness. Daylight filtered through heavy cloud cover and pain-filled screams sounded over the thunder as

Lon-Shan retreated back into the Boundary.

Ventyre, Aeryk panted. He hadn't used this much power in a very long time, and it tired him more than it should have. *Where's Akuan?*

Too close now, less than five miles.

It'll be enough. Aeryk wiped sweat from his forehead. Inhaling, he let the air fill him. Heal him. *You've done what you can. Pull back to Hurricane Point. The remaining cyclones will fall apart as soon as I'm in the Gate. I don't want you anywhere near Akuan when that happens.*

Ventyre seemed to consider this. *As you say, lord. Just be careful. You don't know what you'll find inside.*

Of course, Aeryk said, brushing the comment aside.

He put his guardian out of his head and cut through the cyclone's remaining layers. This close to the center, they spun with crushing force – enough to carry an aircraft carrier or rip an oil rig from its moorings. Not enough to stop him, though. Not even close.

In seconds, he burst through. Clear skies greeted him, the ocean below calm and sparkling under the bright spring sun. He barely noticed. His attention remained riveted on the golden trident in the eye's center. As tall as a redwood, though slim and delicate, it stole Aeryk's breath and refused to give it back.

A thought would free the Keystone, one simple thought – so easy and yet so agonizingly difficult. Sending that command meant realizing a dream. Or maybe ending one. He shook his head and berated his weakness. Seirin might be hurt or angry, but she still loved him. She had to.

Aeryk rubbed his eyes and tried not to let his fear get the best of him. Instead, he focused his mind and sent the unlocking order into the trident.

Immediately, shimmering light surrounded the object.

A trio of emerald beams fired from the prongs, unfolding like a fan as they rocketed into the sky. Far below, a blue circle appeared within the glowing green rays. Rippling seas spread out beyond, endless but for the vast atoll rising above the waves, calling to him from the other side.

He rushed for the giant spout, passing through the Gate in a burst of azure light, moving so fast he almost forgot to destroy the Keystone. He did so with a bare breath of his power. In moments, devastating downdrafts dropped from above – incredibly powerful, impossibly strong. They smashed into the trident with the force of a great hammer.

The haft shattered, the prongs dissolving like salt in water. Akuan wouldn't know where he'd gone – not now. Not ever.

Satisfied, he turned away and headed for the atoll.

The dagger-like cliffs looked more formidable than he remembered. On Earth, they eased their way into the sky as if stroking the horizon. Not here. Here they reared up, tall and jagged, from a base of razor-sharp coral. Frowning, he slowed and headed for a gap in the limestone walls, only to stop when a sharp command erupted in his thoughts.

Stay where you are, lord, it called. *You do not have permission to approach.*

Aeryk's stomach twisted. Seirin's guardian knew him. They were friends. At least, they used to be. A quick Searching showed it beneath the waves, close to the atoll's foundations and coming up fast.

The great serpent burst through the surface in rainbow-filled showers. A head the size of a bus lifted through the spray, familiar aquamarine scales radiant in the sunlight. Wise eyes stared out over a blunt snout, and a long neck undulated to the tides' rhythms. The normally inert turquoise stripes running the length of its two hundred ten-foot body pulsed with living energy, and Aeryk couldn't decide if that meant the guardian planned to attack or defend.

We don't have time for this, Kirak, he said stiffly. Whatever game it played, it did so at Seirin's command. *Fiyorok appeared less than an hour ago in Tokyo. The Boundary opened a Gate near Ginza to warn us.*

Takeshi? Kirak asked.

Aeryk shook his head. *Yui told me. Takeshi's daughter has grown into a powerful young woman.* He let the news hang in the air before adding, *Akuan's free too. Vissyus's new guardian is right outside trying to find a way in.*

Alarm flickered behind the guardian's midnight blue eyes. After a moment, it bowed its head. *You may enter.* Aeryk nodded respectfully. He opened his mouth, but Kirak stopped him. *Hold your thanks, lord, until you see what awaits you.*

The words brought a sour taste to Aeryk's mouth. He nodded to Kirak, grateful for the warning, but hating it all the same. The words reminded him how foolish he'd been, how blind. As far as Seirin was concerned, his coming here wasn't about freeing her; it was about him and the hurt she suffered because of his broken promises. Ashamed, he lowered his head and turned away, unable to meet Kirak's eyes as he vaulted into the air and flew over the atoll's sheer cliffs.

Below, a narrow strip of grass separated lush tropical flowers from sun-splashed beaches that disappeared into a sheltered lagoon roughly a mile in diameter. In the distance, Seirin's palace sprawled over an archipelago of towers and flying spans. White walls tinted with pink coral gleamed under the sun.

A fifty-foot representation of the Earth perched precariously at the edge of the foremost island. Water rolled from each of the seven seas, joined a wide river, and, hitting the edge, tumbled over a seven hundred foot-high precipice.

The palace steps began near the river's source, some three hundred yards away. They climbed from a marble walkway, leveled out after a flight, then climbed two more before ending at a pair of gilded double doors. Inlaid with mother-of-pearl and carved to look like an underwater seascape, they remained closed as Aeryk came down on the top landing and let go of his shield. A pair of lionfish statues stood guard on either side, their poisonous spikes raised aggressively.

Aeryk ignored the statues and continued on to the doors. A blast of air pushed them open, and he strode into the elegant throne room beyond. Sunlight streamed in through tall windows, the floors tiled with clear crystal that provided a spectacular view of the lagoon below. Often, he had strolled across them with Seirin's hand in his. She'd point to one fish or another, then would quiz him on their names until he got them right. When they finished, they'd sit side by side before her coral throne, their feet dipping into the rectangular moat surrounding the high seat, her head on his shoulder.

He sighed regretfully and let the memory go. The throne was empty now, the protective water still but for a swarm of bubbles wafting up from the depths in a lazy line. Lost in thought, he watched them reach the surface and ripple away. More followed, too many for coincidence. A second stream mimicked the first, then a third, then more, one after the other, firing and forming and drawing what appeared to be a shimmering curtain around the throne.

Aeryk stared into it, his knees weak, his stomach tight yet lurching. Soft emerald light glowed on the other side, and the scent of tropical flowers filled his nose. The shimmering curtain quivered, the fizzing stopped, and the whole watery wall collapsed with a loud splash.

Behind it, the woman who haunted his dreams sat regally upon the throne, her beauty undimmed despite the eons. The golden hair he remembered framed her face like a halo, cascading in loose ringlets over slender shoulders. Only her emerald eyes were different. They blazed with elemental fire, a challenge issued, barium put to flame.

Aeryk drew himself up and tipped his head in a formal greeting that went unreturned. The face of Seirin Bal Cerannon, Queen of the Oceans, Mistress of the Waves, and Lady of Water – the woman who owned his heart since the beginning of time – was a storm of unbridled fury.

7
DARKNESS

Lon-Shan slumped into his throne and ran a hand over his eyes. He frowned at the red streaks coating his fingertips. He'd been careless. How many times did he tell himself to stay hidden? Drawing the others' attention was a mistake he couldn't afford. Aeryk was bad enough, but the Lord of Air wouldn't keep the knowledge to himself. Lon-Shan's thoughts shifted to Takeshi Ahk-kiko, the Lord of Spirit. No one knew how strong *he* was. Calling Takeshi enigmatic was like calling the sun warm. Vissyus was right to distrust him.

Takeshi was the first and the oldest of their kind. Some said he used his power to summon the other Kami out of the void, teaching them how to turn thought into matter and create physical bodies for their spirits. Lon-Shan remembered sensing that very call, leaving the darkness behind and waking to a new world. Figures surrounded him, beacons of power in human form: Takeshi and Teras to his left, Aeryk, Seirin, Roarke, and Botua to his right. Others came later, none as strong the first seven, himself included – if barely.

At first, Lon-Shan's fellow Kami were a close-knit

group with Takeshi their de facto father figure. But as the younger Kami grew in strength and knowledge, they became more independent. They started questioning Takeshi's wisdom, Aeryk and Seirin more than the others.

Only Vissyus was different; Vissyus treated everyone as an equal, and while he occasionally disagreed with Takeshi, he never openly rebelled. If he thought Takeshi was wrong, he'd try to prove it first.

Seirin never cared about proof, and Aeryk was too blinded by her to stand up for what he knew was right. But she blinded Vissyus too. Lon-Shan noticed the glances he cast at her when she wasn't looking. Lon-Shan remembered the longing and the sadness, and he hated Seirin even more for it.

Vissyus was Lon-Shan's only friend, the only one who visited Lon-Shan's compound, the only one who didn't dismiss or ignore the Shadow Lord. And now he was gone, gone because a woman asked him for a favor. Did Seirin even know how Vissyus felt about her? Lon-Shan doubted it. Disgusted, he crushed the handkerchief in his fist. Seirin would pay for this. Aeryk too. Even if it took an eternity. Even if the payment destroyed the world. Exhaling, he opened his mind to his guardian. Pain lanced through him. Again, he saw the lightning, this time in afterimages that seared his soul. Another few breaths steadied him, and he quickly formed words before the pain returned.

Streega, he called, somehow keeping the strain from his thoughts. *Summon my disciples. The Great Weakening is upon us. We have to prepare them for what's to come.*

As you say, lord, his guardian answered. *And what of Brother Norwoska? You said he was a special case.*

Lon-Shan mulled his options. *Send for him last, I*

want my followers to remember his entrance. Don't convey the message yourself. Have a disciple do it, one who needs... humbling.

Yes, lord.

Lon-Shan released the guardian, his body tensing through stabbing pains. Curse Aeryk and his lightning; curse them all for what they'd done. He smiled coldly. They'd taken him for granted one time too many.

Paitr Norwoska paced the deserted square like a caged animal, casting the occasional disgusted glance into a veiled sky. *A few minutes short of midday,* he guessed, *and a hell of time for a meeting.* His gaze swept over the city plaza, dark thoughts swirling inside his head. Six hundred years he'd served Lord Lon-Shan. *Six hundred years!* He'd been faithful, more faithful than any other disciple. What good had that done him? Not only was he the last to learn about the meeting, he had to hear about it from Martin Szwaskova. He and Martin were friends, more than friends. They were also rivals; they both knew it.

Lon-Shan brought Martin into the dark city a week or so after the Shadow Lord found Paitr, bleeding and left for dead inside his art studio in old Prague. When was that? 1785? The Czech renaissance was in full swing. Mozart was still alive, and an artistic and architectural revival swept through the capital. Quality paintings were in high demand, and, for someone like Paitr, who had no talent himself but still admired the craft, opening a gallery proved both satisfying and lucrative. At least until three men, off-duty soldiers by the look of them, broke into his gallery and stabbed him multiple times before looting the store.

As he lay dying, red blood oozing across the wooden

floors like spilled paint, Lon-Shan stepped from the shadows. "The strong always think they can terrorize the weak," he said, kneeling beside Paitr. "Poor Paitr. What if I said I could make them and everyone like them pay? All you would have to do is agree to join me. How does that sound to you?"

Paitr didn't ask where Lon-Shan came from or who he was; he simply swore himself to the stranger, figuring he had nothing to lose – his store was empty and his veins were quickly following. He was already dead. Only he wasn't. One minute he closed his eyes in pain, the next he was lying in a soft king-sized bed surrounded by servants. His service started a day later, his training as both warrior and general shortly thereafter.

Now, centuries later – after working his way through Lon-Shan's ranks, after years jockeying with Martin for position and favor – here he was, waiting for Martin to lead him to Lon-Shan's estates. The thought made Paitr nauseous. He swept an arm in disgust, and a granite slab in the middle of the square blew apart. He needed to deal with Martin, but he had to be careful. If he let his anger get the best of him, he could kill his friend before he found out what he needed. You couldn't get anything out of a dead man. Chewing his bottom lip, he looked across the square. A few columns stood haphazardly around the open space. Paitr squinted between them and just made out the hazy outline of a man at the far end.

Martin.

He'd know that fluid walk anywhere. It irritated him – the confidence, the grace. Martin strode through the city like he owned it. Paitr had to show him otherwise. Instead of waiting, he waltzed forward and met Martin in the middle of the park, below a statue of the winged victory.

"Right on time as usual." Martin grinned.

Paitr detected nothing suspicious in his friend's face, but rising to power here meant controlling emotion. He inclined his head and smiled in return. "I wouldn't have wanted to disappoint you, Martin. Not after you went through the trouble of sending that messenger for me to enjoy."

"Think nothing of it. You'd have done the same for me. Come on, we don't want to be late for the meeting. Lon-Shan awaits. It's the first time anyone's seen him in over one hundred and fifty years." Martin clapped a hand on Paitr's shoulder and lowered his voice to a conspiratorial whisper. "Something big is happening, Paitr, something momentous."

He slid his hand down until his arm rested around Paitr's shoulder and gestured at the sprawling mansion across the street: a building that – despite the daylight – lay hidden beneath an unearthly blot of blackness.

8
SIMMERING

Keiko backed away from the closing portal, a new fear bringing sweat to her skin. Everything about her surroundings – from the shimmering walls to the strange stones at her feet – reminded her of the gate in Ginza Prefecture. "Why are we back here?" she panted, spinning around, her eyes wide and wild. "We're not safe. We have to go."

"Keiko?" Yui asked, frowning. "What's the matter with you?" She looked as if Keiko had just proclaimed the grass purple.

"*We have to go*!" Keiko said again. "The dragons will find us; they can't be that far away."

A look of realization crossed Yui's face. She smiled softly and nodded her understanding. "I'm sorry, Keiko. I should have explained. The Boundary is like an infinite maze with many hidden and locked doors. Keystones and Gates are the only way in or out. Like a corridor, the Gates open into specific areas of the Boundary. This one is as far from Vissyus as possible, I can assure you. We've managed to keep its location from him because we don't allow strangers to enter. You are a very special case, but let me remind you: a secret only lasts until someone gives it away." Yui's eyes drifted meaningfully to Keiko's pack. "I don't want to take your camera, Keiko, but I will."

"Yeah, right." Keiko mumbled, unable to take her eyes from the spot where the Gate had closed. "Whatever you say." It wasn't as if she needed the camera anymore. Her father's note said it would show her the way, and it had. Come to think of it, she'd barely taken any pictures – not any real ones – since arriving in Japan; she'd been too preoccupied looking for that elusive gate. Still, she was attached to the little metal box and giving it up would be like losing the last piece she had of her father. She still remembered the first time he taught her to use it, telling her to focus her thoughts as she focused the lens. "The trick," he'd said, "is to know how something will look when frozen in time. Learn that, and everything else will fall into place."

"I mean it, Keiko," Yui warned, folding her hands together, the tips of her index fingers touching, steepled. Indigo light flared around them, and a hole opened in the wall before her. "This is important."

"I know. I know," Keiko replied. She'd given her word. Did Yui really think she'd risk Vissyus finding them? After what she'd seen in Tokyo? No way.

The new Gate led into a narrow corridor. The same shimmering walls stood on either side while overhead, gauzy light surrendered to blackness. The two girls continued on in silence, Yui leading by less than a step, Keiko keeping pace. Eventually, the passage opened into an enormous courtyard several miles wide and likely twice as long. Traditional Japanese gardens filled the space, while broad grassy lawns and neatly paved avenues separated them from one another. Stars sparkled in a moonless night, their light reflected in the many pools and fountains woven throughout the grounds.

In the distance, an impossibly massive yet graceful structure thrust from the earth, layer upon layer, into the higher reaches of the dark sky. If it hadn't been for the magnificent pagoda-like design, the building might have passed for a small, snow-covered mountain.

"The White Spirit Castle," Yui intoned. "Fortress of House Akiko. Shirasagijo Castle in Himeji City is a pretty good replica, though on a much smaller scale. Himeji was a scheduled stop on our tour. Sometime next week, I think."

"I'll take your word for it." The castle's size and grandeur overwhelmed Keiko. How could anyone build something so huge, and more importantly, why? Fortresses were supposed to protect people. The greater the threat the bigger the walls. And these walls were big. Bigger than any Keiko had ever seen.

Motioning Keiko in closer, Yui reformed her shield and zipped up to the gates. "My father disapproved of the shogun's arrogance," she said as they flew. "He didn't punish Go-Mizunoo right away, of course. Instead, he waited until the egotistical little man finished building the castle before stripping his authority and restoring the emperor to power. To be honest, I think he was just looking for a reason. Another Weakening had started, and he needed the people to believe in imperial divinity again. If the Boundary failed, we were counting on our monks to take care of the people while we dealt with Vissyus."

A dull ache grew behind Keiko's eyes. Her guidebook said Himeji's castle was almost seven hundred years old. *Seven hundred years*. And Yui had been there during its construction. To Keiko, Yui looked maybe twenty. Then again, she'd also talked about the Kami and how they ruled the Earth before man took his first steps. Keiko craned her neck and stared up the castle walls. The fortress had to be the biggest building of all time. What had she gotten herself into?

"Aeryk Tai-Banshar's palace at Hurricane Point is just as big," Yui said, following Keiko's gaze – and thoughts – up the donjon's central tower. "Taller too. Our shields come in handy," she added with a wry grin. "No lifts in either place."

Keiko rolled her eyes. "You don't have to remind me how much I need you, you know." She gestured at the castle, waving her arm up and down to emphasize its scale. "I'll be lost as soon as I step inside." She tilted her head, a sarcastic grin breaking over her face. "At least I still have a guide to show me around."

"That all depends," Yui sniffed, lowering the shield to the ground and extinguishing it. Being called a guide obviously irritated her. "I have no idea what my father has in mind for you." Eyes bright, she lifted her chin, her voice sounding inside Keiko's head. *Isn't that right, O Great Lord of Spirit? I trust you know what's happened.*

I do indeed, a masculine voice replied. *We were fortunate to have the last Yamanaka in Tokyo to warn us.*

Yui's body went rigid. Her head snapped up, and the muscles in her jaw tightened. She stared at Keiko, her expression at once incredulous and outraged. "Yamanaka," she hissed. "You didn't! You couldn't!"

Keiko's reaction was outwardly milder; inside, it was every bit as visceral. *The voice,* she thought. *How did it know?* The Yamanaka name was a secret.

A warm bath is waiting for you at the springs, the voice went on. *Refresh yourselves, but do not take too long. Vissyus has pulled his guardians back into the Boundary. He was close to learning what he wanted, and I'm afraid Akuan, at least, will soon leave again. I will see you both in my chambers shortly thereafter. Pay close attention to the time. I take it that won't be a problem for you, Yamanaka-san.*

Keiko shook her head as if compelled. Time... The idea tickled the edges of her thoughts. It was important somehow, something related to her father's business. Something he said was unique to both of them.

Good. I'll expect you soon then. The voice fled, the low rumble of opening doors replacing it. As if summoned, a pair of white-robed monks emerged from the castle and approached. Their eyes remained lowered as they stopped before Keiko and Yui and bowed deeply.

"This is Brother Seki," Yui said, gesturing to the stocky, square-faced monk on the left. "He's here to take you to the baths."

"What about you?" Keiko assumed Yui would accompany her.

"Brother Toda and I are off to my father's study. I have to brief him on tonight's events."

"But he said he already knew," Keiko protested.

Yui snorted. "He always says that. And for what it's worth, he could have been with us in the subway, and he'd still want a full report. That's just how he is." Turning, Yui strode toward the castle. "I will meet you as soon as I can."

"I could use a briefing too, you know," Keiko called after her. "I've earned one."

Yui paused without turning. "Soon," she said bluntly. "I promise. She disappeared around a far corner, leaving Keiko alone with Brother Seki.

"Might as well get this over with," Keiko sighed, motioning the monk to show her the way.

The walk through the castle was a blur of incredible

images. Keiko tried to fix them in her head, but gave up when they ran together. After what felt like hours, they came to yet another door. This one was of paneled oak and stood open to reveal a steaming pool. The monk excused himself with a bow and left her alone. The pool sat invitingly at the edge of a steep cliff. Without anything else to do, Keiko walked over, disrobed, and lowered herself into the bubbling cauldron with a long, satisfied sigh.

Outrageously hot and steamy, the volcanic water worked its way into her kinked and tired muscles. A string of bubbles wafted up from the stone seat. Keiko halfheartedly put her hand down to find the source, but apart from a few spots where the rocks were uneven she didn't find any gaps or holes. A heated bottom perhaps? The uncomfortable image of a lobster dropped into a boiling pot flitted through her head. She pushed it aside and tried to tell herself the springs were natural. Not an easy feat in a place like this. Peering about suspiciously, she crinkled her brow and inched toward a far corner. Several pools similar to hers lay scattered about the rocky cliffs, each separated from the other by tall walls that looked to Keiko like part of the original landscape. She planted her hands firmly onto the edge and pushed herself up for a better look.

"Leaving already?"

Keiko dropped into the water with a loud splash and spun around. Yui stood at the edge of the pool, staring at Keiko with an amused grin. She'd changed into a kimono dyed rich indigo and shot through with sunfire strands. Her hair was back and twisted into a bun to hold it in place.

"Yui?" Keiko sputtered, her hands desperately trying to cover her body. "What's the matter with you? I'm in the bath. I'd appreciate a little privacy."

"A private bath?" Yui mocked, her laugh reminding Keiko of tiny brass bells. "In Japan?" Yui's fingers reached for the obi that held her silk kimono together. In a flash, the garment dropped from her shoulders and fell into a neat puddle of multicolored fabric at her feet. She then eased into the pool and took a seat at the far end. "The baths feel good, don't they? Sometimes, I think they can cure just about anything." Closing her eyes, she leaned back and rested her head on the stone lip, unaware of Keiko's discomfort.

"Including modesty, apparently," Keiko muttered under her breath. Watching Yui undress so casually brought a slow burn to Keiko's cheeks. It wasn't enough that Yui was smart. Oh no, she was smart, courageous, magically powerful, and possessed an impossibly perfect figure. Keiko had taken good care of herself, but...

Life wasn't fair.

Scowling, she sank sulkily into the hot, mineral-tinged water and let the heat continue working on her tired body. Soon, her mood lifted, and she smiled contentedly. Yui was right: the bath *did* feel good. Good enough to soothe her wounded pride. Good enough to lessen the grief and loneliness she'd experienced since her father's death. They were there – they would always be there – but the holes they left in her life were healing.

"Yui?" she said, sitting up. "You still haven't told me what's going on."

Yui's eyes glittered mischievously. "Of course I haven't. I *am* Japanese, after all."

"No you're not! You might look Japanese, and you might speak Japanese, but if you're a Kami, then you can't *be* Japanese. Come to think of it, you don't really sound Japanese either."

Surprise shot across Yui's face. "You can tell?"

"Well, yeah. It was a little hard at first, but that was because of all the Americans in the tour. Once they were gone, I started to notice a difference."

Yui shook her head. "You really are your father's daughter," she said. "The truth is, the Kami communicate more with thoughts than voices. When we do speak, it's in a language unique to us. Your mind simply translates what we say."

"If you're trying to say I'm hearing what I want to hear, then why doesn't the word chocolate come up more often?"

Yui chuckled again. "Because you're not hearing what you want to hear; you're hearing what I say as you expect to hear it. To be honest, it's incredible your subconscious adds Japanese – or what you believe is Japanese – to my speech patterns. That's pretty remarkable."

Keiko wiped sweat from her cheeks, using the motion to whisk a stubborn tear from the corner of her eye without Yui noticing. "The only Japanese I know comes from the stray bits I picked up around the house or from a book I kept hidden under my bed. We were in America during a difficult time. I didn't want to be any more different than I had to."

"But you *are* different. More different than you realize. Different doesn't have to be bad, Keiko. Sometimes it just means 'special' or 'unique'."

"Maybe," Keiko said tiredly. "And I think you're right about not hearing what I want to hear, because what I really want to hear is what this is all about." As tired as she was, she drew back her shoulders and shot Yui a challenging stare. "We both know you're stalling. A lot of people died tonight; I'd like to know why."

Yui's expression was smoother than the pool's surface.

"I'd think it was obvious," she said. "My father wants to be the one who tells you."

"And you're OK with that? Your father knew who I was right away. He was expecting me. You've been with me for – what – two weeks, and you had no idea." Yui bristled at that, and, seeing the opening, Keiko decided to go all in. "Speaking of which," she continued, picking absently at a nail. "A *tour guide*? Seriously? What kind of father does *that* to his daughter." Yui blushed furiously and stared into the water. "Wait... You don't mean... Yui? Did *you* choose to be a guide?"

"It seemed like a good idea at the time," she mumbled without looking up. "I was supposed to watch the Gates in Tokyo. Japan used to belong to Vissyus, long ago, back before he broke the world apart. Most of our war took place on what is now Asia's east coast. It's why we have so many Gates here. Some are fake to confuse Vissyus, others are here so we can keep a better eye on the Kami behind them or so we can enter and leave the Boundary from different places – again to keep Vissyus guessing."

"And that's why the Gate to this fortress is here?"

Yui nodded. "Guarding Vissyus up close is better – and more dangerous – than from far away. He'll see this as our usurping his rightful home, but..." Yui fanned her hands. "What choice did we have?"

"And the guide part?"

"Since my father used random artifacts for the Keystones, a guide seemed like a natural choice." The hint of an embarrassed smile appeared on Yui's face. "I needed a disguise that let me go to multiple historic sites regularly. One that made sense."

"A disguise," Keiko said flatly. "You needed a disguise to visit historic sites in a city of over thirteen million people? Call me crazy, Yui, but I don't think anyone would have noticed one person's comings and goings given the numbers."

"Being a guide made access easier," Yui said, doing her best to defend herself. Her expression said she knew she'd lost the argument. "I didn't have to go through security or have to pay or…" Her voice trailed off when she noticed Keiko's raised eyebrow and crossed arms.

"We just flew from Ginza to Mount Fuji in a little energy ball, and you expect me to believe you couldn't get around those two roadblocks?" Keiko grinned triumphantly. "You didn't even think about it did you?" Yui blushed again, and Keiko shook her head in amusement. "Looks like we both have a lot to learn." She offered her hand. "Tell you what; I'll help you with the stuff you don't know about my world, and you do the same for me with yours. Deal?"

Yui stared at Keiko's hand like it was a viper. "I don't know, Keiko. What will my father think?"

"That you're smart enough to get advice when you need it," Keiko said seriously. "Look… Your father, my father – neither told us what we needed to know before asking us to do something for them. They've kept things from us. We'll keep this from them. Think of it as payback."

"*My* father has his reasons. The Kami of Air and the Kami of Water, Aeryk and Seirin, ignored him and look how that turned out."

"I would," Keiko grumbled. "If I actually *knew* how that turned out. Come on; you have to give me something. No harm no foul. Your father doesn't have to know."

"He's Lord of Spirit, Keiko. He'll know."

"Fine. How about the short version then? You know… the basics. Leave the details to him." Keiko crossed her arms and sank deeper into the bath. "I won't meet with the Great Lord of Spirit without knowing a little. I'll look like an idiot if I do. You can't do that to me; you can't do that to my father."

Yui stiffened. Her cheeks colored as if slapped. "That's not fair."

Keiko settled back, saying nothing. The air between them felt charged. Time seemed to grind to a halt. Finally, Yui shook her head in defeat. Instead of a direct answer, she pointed at a well-preserved tapestry on the nearby wall. "Do you recognize that image?" she asked.

Keiko snorted. "My father sold antiques; of course I know it."

"Explain it to me."

"It's a nineteenth century kabuki-stylized piece depicting Storm God Susanoo's slaying of the dragon Orochi. It's world famous. I assume it's the original."

"Yes, Keiko. And as false as every other Japanese myth. The Storm God never confronted the dragon for one thing, let alone defeat it. And he wasn't called Susanoo. That name and the god who wore it are fabrications my father created."

Keiko leaned forward. "Aeryk. That's your Kami of Air." Yui nodded slowly. Now they were getting somewhere. "But why?" Keiko pressed. "Why change anything?"

"To stay hidden while preserving some record of our past. We wanted Vissyus to think we were trapped in the Boundary instead of free and planning against him. He's insane, but he's not stupid – far from it. Vissyus was the smartest of all the Kami, brilliant in fact. He still is. He's also the most powerful." Yui's eyes drifted from the tapestry to the night sky. "Seirin, Aeryk, and Vissyus were best friends. It was only natural for Seirin and Aeryk to ask Vissyus for help. I was too young to remember Vissyus before his madness, but my father said he was the best of us. *A beacon in the night*, my father called him. Vissyus looked at the universe and saw wonder – so much so that he wanted to unlock every one of its secrets." She smiled sadly. "He promised to help Seirin and Aeryk, said he knew how to test the blending of elemental Kami. Days later, the volcano holding his palace home erupted. That's when they found out."

"What?" Keiko said breathlessly. She was leaning even farther over, her chin barely above the water. "What did they find?"

"Each Kami has a guardian protector, a lesser elemental spirit to act as a counselor and aide. The guardians take the shape of huge beast-like animals: a thunderbird for Aeryk, a sea serpent for Seirin, a dragon for Vissyus, and so on. When they found Vissyus... he had two: Fiyorok, the guardian we all knew, and Akuan, a guardian of ice."

"Do you think he chose an ice spirit intentionally? If I was experimenting, that's what I'd do: go all in just to make sure."

Yui started to answer, paused as if thinking, then continued. "I'll leave that for my father. I've told you the basics, most of them anyway."

"What about the Boundary? Where did that come from?"

"Ah yes," Yui said. "The Boundary. Thank you for reminding me. My father brought the Boundary to trap Vissyus, as I said before. Infinite worlds lie beyond it, each one accessible through a specific Keystone like the one we passed through to get here. Or the one you somehow opened into Vissyus's prison."

Keiko winced. "That was an accident. I didn't know what I was doing."

"Perhaps. But just remember: your father sent you here to find a gate. Funny how it happened to be the most important gate on Earth. I don't believe that's a coincidence, and neither should you. The Boundary's been weakening for some time. Likely, it was calling out to us; we just didn't hear it."

Keiko sat back and rubbed her temples. "But why me? I'm nobody. I had no idea what I was doing. If I did, I never would've left home."

Yui picked up a bar of soap and rubbed it into a deep, foamy lather. "And yet here you are, arriving just in time to give us the warning we probably would have missed. Apparently, your father knew you better than you know yourself, even if he didn't prepare you for the coming war."

Again, images of her father filled Keiko's head. She saw him leafing through an old Japanese manuscript, recalled his proud expressions when she used her camera, then remembered how he rarely looked at the pictures once they had them developed.

"I can't believe your father knew mine," she muttered, pushing the memories aside. "I can't believe any of this."

"We both knew your father," Yui said. "He was a fixture here for a very long time."

Keiko's heart thumped in her chest. Maybe she wasn't alone after all. Hope built within her, but she tamped it down. Believing meant opening herself to more pain, to being alone again. She wasn't ready for that.

"It just doesn't seem possible," she said, as much to herself as to Yui.

"No less possible than dragons in Tokyo? Or an ancient fortress as large as a mountain and yet invisible to all around it?" Yui sighed, and her eyes took on a faraway look. "You don't look much like the Masato I remember.

But you *do* remind me of him. He possessed incredible abilities. No one was a match for him, not even the instructors. He defeated them so handily that Father sent him to train with me. I had a distinct advantage because of who and what I am, but he learned quickly; he came very close to beating me more than once."

"You spent that much time with him?" Jealousy prickled Keiko's skin.

She'd been the center of her father's life, even when her mother was alive. As much as she wanted Yui's friendship, she didn't like the thought of her father sharing so much with another woman, certainly not one so young and beautiful.

"He was the closest thing I've ever had to a friend. Masato didn't care who my father was, and he wasn't afraid of him."

Keiko lowered her head to hide her discomfort. Yui's face gave nothing away, but secret longing laced her tone. Within, Keiko sensed the breath of denied possibility and withheld dreams.

"Masato was the most respected disciple Father ever had, and he left as the most powerful. Everyone here knew who he was and how important he would become to the imperial throne." Yui propped her head against the stone lip and gazed into the stars, melancholy painting her smooth features. "The Yamanaka family is the oldest in all of Japan, older even than the imperial line. The *Kojiki* says Emperor Jimmu was a direct descendent of the Sun Goddess Amaterasu, but his ties to us were more tenuous than those of the Yamanakas."

"Kojiki?" Keiko interrupted, finally finding something else to focus on. "What's that?"

Yui smiled whimsically. "Ostensibly Japan's great creation myth."

"Isn't calling a myth ostensible a bit redundant?"

Yui's grin widened. "I suppose it is, but the Japanese accept the myth as reality. Ask anyone if they believe in the emperor's divinity, and more often than not they'll say yes. MacArthur forced Hirohito to renounce the claim, but it didn't make any difference."

"And the *ostensible* part?"

"The Kojiki that Japan knows is complete fiction, something my father created to confuse Vissyus. As I said before, if we released a true record of our history, Vissyus would know we survived."

Keiko snickered. "God's diary!" She spread her hands expansively. "Imagine the implications."

Yui closed her eyes, her lips compressing into the telltale line of someone fighting down laughter. "In the fake Kojiki, Japan's power rests in the hands of the divine emperor."

"And the truth?"

Yui let out a long breath "The truth." She licked her lips as if deciding how much more to say. "Since my father founded Japan, the Yamanakas have always been the power behind the throne – at least when they weren't inside the Boundary training." Keiko opened her mouth, but Yui held up a hand. "Father never considered making the Yamanakas emperor, if that's what you're thinking. He didn't want his disciples to govern directly. Too much power in the hands of a single person, no matter how stable or moral, is never a good idea. Vissyus's fall was all the proof we needed."

"If my father was so important," Keiko asked, "then why didn't he stay in Japan? Why all the secrecy? What happened to him?"

"Several years into Masato's service, rebel daimyos sent their samurai into the palace. Masato died defending the emperor, or so the reports claim."

Daimyos. Samurai. Japan hadn't had those for over a hundred years. Keiko's father couldn't have been that old. Could he? Again, faint images swirled in her head. A newspaper with a picture of Babe Ruth on the cover, a woman in a yellow dress holding a matching parasol as she climbed into a horse-drawn carriage, San Francisco in ruins, her father's home, untouched and yet open to anyone who needed shelter.

"If Masato Yamanaka died in Tokyo," Keiko said, trying to shake the pictures from her head. "Then how...?"

"My father *didn't* tell me." Yui looked away. Though her face remained still, Keiko heard the bitterness. Yui felt betrayed. "I should have known. The story never sat well with me. Masato could defeat any man or group of men. It wouldn't matter who they were or how big an army they brought with them. The Masato I knew would have obliterated them."

"I don't see what any of this has to do with–"

"With you?" Though she'd regained her composure, Yui's eyes blazed like sunlight through heavy clouds. "Masato sent you to us, his jisei makes that clear enough."

"But *why*? What did he expect me to do?" Keiko's spirit reawakened. After weeks of wandering aimlessly through life, worried about her future, having a goal – even if she didn't know what it was – set her soul on fire.

Yui shook her head. "I don't know. But I think it's time we find out."

9
MEMORIES

"My father was a dealer in fine antiques," Keiko said again, drying her hair and wrapping a towel around herself. She moved purposefully, hoping the delay would douse some of Yui's anger. "I never thought he might be the oldest thing in the store."

Yui – clearly impatient – wound an identical towel about her own body. Keiko noted how the fabric clung to Yui in ways it never would on her. She let out an exasperated sigh.

"Sorry?" Yui threw a second towel over her head and quickly blotted her hair. "Did you say something?"

"Me?" Keiko said, sourly. "No, of course not." She did her best to hide her feelings, knowing her expression had gotten away from her. Fortunately, with the towel still over her head, Yui had missed it. "It's just that... since I got here, I've been having these memories – things I can't explain. Some of them happened a long time ago."

Yui paused and turned to regard Keiko. The towel she had used on her hair now draped around her shoulders, silken black hair spilling over it to frame her flawless features. The golden flecks in her eyes blazed, reminding Keiko of sunlight.

"Masato's power could account for that, or it might be yours. Your father is dead, yes? You're sure? You know for certain."

Keiko shuffled her feet uncomfortably. "Well when you put it that way…" She heaved a sigh. "I don't really know what happened to him. I came home one day and he was gone."

"And that's when you found his jisei. Did you notice anything else?"

"Nothing other than this weird feeling of emptiness. I don't know how to explain it really." She licked her lips, not wanting to talk about it. "I just knew he wasn't there anymore. I could tell. I… Yui, wait!" But Yui had already gathered her kimono, settled herself back into it, and headed for the door. "Yui? What's wrong?"

Keiko snatched a plain white robe hanging from a wooden peg on the wall and followed the other girl into a wide hallway that led away from the hot springs at the rear of the castle and continued into the central donjon. Corridors randomly opened up on one side or the other, each heading off to some distant part of this massive fortress. The ancient tapestries lining the walls sported traditional Japanese renderings of rugged, tree-lined mountain landscapes, while overhead, large globes set into ornately carved fixtures of jade and brass glowed softly at regular intervals. Not so long ago, Keiko would have marveled at the sight, openly gaping at the shining orbs and wondering what powered them.

"I thought you accepted everything too easily," Yui said as Keiko caught up to her. "A dragon, flying, things that would have any normal person questioning their sanity."

"I question my sanity every day, Yui. That's what sane people do. It's called coping."

"You know what I mean," Yui snapped, her cheeks flushed. "Your family possesses a part of our spirit, Keiko. Either you've reacted calmly because your subconscious recognizes our history through it–"

"Or–"

"Or Masato left a piece of himself inside you."

Keiko's eyes widened. "Is that possible?"

"Bodies die, but souls live on. Most go unnoticed, but Masato is different. He was with us for a very long time. His soul is stronger. He'll have some control over how he manifests. Masato can't create a vessel for himself, so he'll hijack the next best thing."

Keiko felt as if her still damp skin had frozen. "What are you saying, Yui?" Mixed emotions erupted in her head. She'd come to Tokyo to find out what happened to her father. Learning he might somehow exist within her was both comforting and disturbing.

Yui muttered something that sounded like a curse. "Fathers. Yours, mine. They use us like puppets." She stared at Keiko. "I'll need to look into your thoughts to know for sure. Will you let me?"

"What do we do if you find something?"

"Let's just see if I'm right first. We'll deal with the rest later. OK?"

Nodding woodenly, Keiko followed Yui to the near wall. "Do I need to close my eyes or something?"

Yui chuckled and shook her head. A moment later, Keiko felt Yui's presence slip into her mind. She inhaled bravely. The image of a nosy guest snooping through medicine cabinets flashed into her consciousness, eliciting another wry laugh from Yui.

"I think I found something," Yui said. "It's one particular memory." She frowned. "It's almost as if he left it there on purpose – like he wanted us to find it."

"You won't know until you open it," Keiko said reluctantly.

Yui grunted something that sounded like agreement.

Abruptly, Keiko felt as if her head had been sucked through a straw. Her world inverted and folded, and, when it stopped, she found herself standing in the dining room of their California house. A calendar tacked to a door showed the year, 1942, and as usual her father had neatly crossed off the days until Sunday, February 22nd. A plump, aproned woman with light hair and a freckly face was clearing the table when the doorbell rang. Wiping her hands, the housekeeper went to the door and opened it.

Two big men in long raincoats and wide-brimmed hats stood on the threshold. "FBI," the one in front proclaimed. He flashed a badge and shoved his way inside. "You need to come with us – your family too." He thrust a letter forward and waved it importantly. "It's all in here." Snapping his fingers, he sent the second man into the house.

Masato stepped into the hall, tall, lean, and imposing. In his dark suit and bright red tie, he looked younger than Keiko remembered, less careworn. His eyes found the maid, and he dismissed her with a gesture. "You don't want to do this," he warned, glaring at the agents. His tone, while neutral, had an edge to it. Keiko knew the signs. Keiko's father didn't anger easily, but when he did, people stayed out of his way. This time, his rage was beyond anything Keiko remembered. Masato's eyes smoldered with fury, and some unseen power rippled beneath his skin like a coiling snake. Keiko shrank away from the vision. The man was her father, and yet he seemed like a stranger.

The agents didn't sense the danger; they simply reacted

to Masato's resistance. The first man moved to block the door, while the other put his hand into his coat and drew a revolver. The bright sheen of its barrel dimmed as he lifted the weapon, and by the time it was even with Masato's eyes, it looked hopelessly corroded.

Stunned, the agent turned the gun over in his hand and stared at it in disbelief. Something about the movement bothered Keiko. It looked labored, unnatural. She was about to examine the man's hand more closely when his screams pulled her eyes back. Whatever had happened to the gun was working its way up the man's arm. Worn patches appeared all over his sleeve, his torso shrank into his suit, his head shriveled and wrinkled, and his once-muscular legs gave out beneath him. By the time he hit the floor, he looked like a mummy in a fashionable, albeit threadbare, suit.

The surviving agent backed away from his fallen colleague. "*What the hell*?" Wide-eyed, he waved his hands at Masato, who now moved toward him. "Stay away from me! Don't come any closer!"

Ignoring the threat, Masato strode over to the man and lifted his fist. The letter lay crinkled within, blue light swirling around it. The man stared transfixed in terror, unable to look away. Not even the burning paper distracted him. He screamed.

"Miss Ryan!" Masato said over the man's wailing. "I'm going to Miami for a few days. I'll be back as soon as I can. Until then, let no one into the house. Do you understand? *No one*." His head came about and his eyes held her. A strange periwinkle light glowed around his irises. "This won't take long, a few days at most."

"Yes, lord," the maid bowed, unfazed. "Give Lord Aeryk my regards."

"I will," he assured her. "He was right to recommend

you to me." Nodding his goodbye, he half dragged, half shoved the remaining man out the door while lugging the dead agent behind him.

Keiko's memories flashed forward to the next century. She was a young girl, maybe six or seven, rushing straight to her parents' San Francisco antique shop after school instead of going home. Thick fog clung to the city for most of the day, but as she made her way down the street, the wind kicked up behind her to clear a path to her father's building. Oddly, the rest of the city remained blanketed. Keiko giggled, imagining the mist had parted for her alone.

When she reached the shop, she pushed the door open and skipped inside. A strong gust blew it back just as she tried to close it. Frowning, she placed both hands on the frame when she noticed a man at the threshold. He was tall with an athletic frame, a handsome face, and piercingly blue eyes whose color shifted from one moment to the next. Instead of a suit, he wore a pale blue shirt over a pair of tailored pants.

"Can I help you?" Keiko asked when he walked in.

"That won't be necessary." Her father emerged from the back room with a carefully wrapped package tucked under one arm. "I have been expecting him." He bowed to the man, who returned the gesture with a smile. "Keiko, your mother is in the back unpacking a new shipment. Please go help her."

Keiko wiped her hands on a cloth hanging from a hook near the register and headed toward the store's loading dock. Just past the door, she stopped and, doing her best to stay hidden, peeked through a gap in the curtains.

"Mr Yamanaka," the man said. "It is good to see you again. I'm sorry to keep moving you around like this, but it's the only way to keep you hidden."

"It's fine, Lord Aeryk. A man who doesn't age stands out. I understand the need to relocate every ten years or so."

Aeryk nodded sympathetically. "But this time is different."

Keiko held her breath. A man who doesn't age? What was that supposed to mean. Intrigued, she leaned forward intently.

"I'm afraid so," Masato said with a frown. "I have Keiko to think of now; I don't like the idea of uprooting her while she's still in school."

"And your wife agrees," Aeryk said, pulling up a seventeenth-century Japanese chair of black lacquered wood with a severe torii-styled back.

"She lived in the White Spirit Castle long enough to understand what this life is like and why it's necessary."

Aeryk placed his large hand on Masato's shoulder. "I'm sorry, Masato. I've never approved of arranged marriages. I didn't think Takeshi did either. If I'd known, I would have spoken to him."

"My wife is from the greatest family in Japan. Her bloodline goes back to Jimmu, Japan's first emperor."

"That's not what I meant, and you know it. Either way, I'm sorry."

"Thank you, lord." Masato bowed again, lower this time. "Both for the sentiment, and for helping me here. America is so different from Japan."

"The least I can do," Aeryk shrugged. "You lived through some very difficult times here. I just wanted to help you any way I could."

"I am in your debt." Masato lifted the package he brought with him from the back and placed it on the counter. "Please accept this gift on behalf of my family.

I found it on a recent trip to China and thought you should have it."

Touched, Aeryk examined the finely wrapped object. He pulled the loose end of a lilac ribbon, and the paper fell away to reveal a sea serpent carved from rare aquamarine marble streaked with turquoise. The creature's eyes were blue diamonds, its fangs mother-of-pearl. Keiko thought it was the most exquisite piece she'd ever seen. Her hopes for a closer look were quickly dashed, however, when the man placed it into a well-padded box.

"Thank you, Mr Yamanaka," he said thickly. "This means more to me than I can say."

Masato beamed at him. "Excellent. Two gifts exchanged, family for family. May both survive the storms ahead."

"Storms I can handle, my friend. It's fire that worries me." He turned to go, then paused. "A word of advice: try to fit in as much as possible. Leave Japan's language and its culture behind. Especially for Keiko. Make her as American as you can. I'm sure you know how to do that."

Masato nodded and then bowed as the man headed for the door. An azure light flared around the retreating figure, and everything went dark.

Again, Keiko felt the odd, uncomfortable, straw-like inversion and found herself back in the hall with Yui storming back and forth in front of her.

"They knew!" Yui cried. "They both knew, and neither one bothered to tell me."

Keiko took a step forward and placed a hand on Yui's arm. "They didn't tell me either," she said steering Yui into the corridor. "Come on. I need answers too."

They continued on silently for a while. By the time

they reached the apartments, Keiko was so turned around she knew she'd never be able to find her way back to the baths on her own.

"Your rooms." Yui swept her arm toward a staid door of lacquered oak. "Change quickly. I'll be back for you in a few minutes, and then we can see my father."

"I'll be ready," Keiko promised.

Yui gave Keiko a curt nod before striding back down the hall. When she finally disappeared, Keiko opened the door and hastened into the large sitting room on the other side.

Sparsely decorated, it contained only a low, rectangular table with a vase filled with fresh lilies at its center and a row of pillows neatly arranged along the walls. The faint click of her door latching behind surprised her, and she made a mental note to ask Yui why an old traditional Japanese palace like this was built with doors instead of the more common sliding panels she'd seen throughout the tour.

She headed to the far side of the room, where a second door opened into a small bedchamber. Inside, she found the clothes she'd worn that day – all neatly cleaned and pressed – atop a simple wooden dresser. Another pile sat next to them, similarly folded, containing a set of fine white silk pants, matching top, and short kimono complete with sash.

Never one to give in to ostentatious displays, she did manage a guilty twinge as she drew them on. She slid her feet into the pair of comfortable yet sturdy slippers left beside the clothes and a set of hiking boots and raced from the room just as Yui turned a far corner.

The other girl strode toward her with a languid feline grace, every movement a perfect combination of poise, power, and agility. She wore robes similar to Keiko's, though instead of plain white, hers were streaked with a deep, almost purplish blue and tied with a sash embroidered with sunbursts. She'd pulled her hair away from her face and pinned it in place with a pair of black lacquered sticks that shone dully under the soft light.

Keiko fell in behind without a word and they padded along to the end of the corridor, where a large, ornately carved door swung back on its hinges. Beyond, a broad staircase disappeared into the darkness, one side climbing up, the other down. Yui lifted a hand, and the now familiar indigo light flashed around it. The lamps along the walls, once hidden by the gloom, blazed to life.

As her eyes adjusted, Keiko saw they now stood on a meager landing. The floor was fully carpeted with a thick, crimson rug accented along the edges with white-and-gold bands. Halfway up the wall, a sturdy railing of carved oak twisted its way beside the steps to provide support for those who needed it.

Instinctively placing a foot on the stairs leading up, Keiko slowed when she noticed Yui heading in the opposite direction. The young spirit stopped, her quizzically raised eyebrow halting Keiko before she took another step.

"I take it we're not going up." Embarrassment heated Keiko's face. She simply assumed they'd meet Yui's father at the top of the tower.

Yui shook her head and folded her arms into the sleeves of her kimono. "This is a fortress, Keiko, not a hotel. The main hall needs to be the most secure room in the castle, easily defensible, and easy to escape when retreat is the only option left to us."

She looked away and proceeded down the steps, while Keiko fought to close the distance.

"Right," Keiko said, half to herself, half to Yui.

She drew herself up to her full height, painfully aware how much taller Yui was. After several flights, the stairs opened into a cavernous antechamber lined on either side by huge white-lacquered pillars that looked like arms reaching to heaven. Ahead, a pair of immense ironbound doors, the first sliding shoji-like panels she'd seen since entering, remained closed.

Power resonated strongly from the chamber beyond, enough for her to feel through the thick metal and wood between them. A similar, though slightly weaker, force slammed into her from the side, and she turned, pulse quickening, to see Yui staring back at her through a nimbus of vibrant indigo.

Knees wobbly, Keiko reached for one of the wooden columns to steady herself.

Do not be afraid, my child, a gentle voice said into her mind, the same one that had spoken to her at the gates. *I've looked forward to meeting you for a very long time. The soul of Japan rejoices at your return, Yamanaka-san. Welcome to your ancestral home.*

Home. The word rolled through Keiko's body like church bells. Three weeks ago, she wondered if she'd ever have a home again. She lowered her head and thanked her father, wherever he was, for bringing her here.

10
TEMPEST

"Aeryk," Seirin proclaimed in her breathy, musical voice. "After all this time. Imagine my surprise when Kirak told me you'd come." She brushed a strand of golden hair from her forehead, careful not to disturb the waves cascading over her shoulders in sunfire ringlets. Stunning emerald eyes glowed behind hooded lids, Seirin's full lips drawing into a dangerous grin. She kept her chin lifted imperiously, as if daring him to challenge her moral authority, which, truth be told, wasn't that solid, all things considered.

Not that Aeryk could tell her that without pushing her further away. Instead, he let her anger roll from his shoulders as he strode to the wide pool and stared up at her, taking in her turquoise gown, with its studded pearl accents and a delicate belt of finely woven platinum strands cinched about her waist. He'd given her both, and now she used them against him. He opened his mouth to speak, but she raised her hand to cut him off.

"Don't! Just don't! I don't want to hear your excuses. I don't want anything from you."

Aeryk stopped at the edge of the moat. The water

between them could have been miles across, as real a divider as the years and the Boundary. "I know you don't," he said when he found his voice. "And I don't expect you to. You've suffered. I understand that."

Seirin's glare intensified. Her long lashes fluttered in front of pale green pupils, as clear as the rains, as limpid as tears. "Don't patronize me, Aeryk!" She slammed her fists onto the arms of her throne. Ripples spread out beneath it. "You don't know what it was like! You don't know anything!"

"No," Aeryk admitted. "No, I don't. All I know is what I saw and what Takeshi showed me after the fact." He spread his hands in supplication. "I have no idea what you went through. But I want to. Show it to me, Seirin. Show me what really happened during the battle. Please."

Seirin sat back in her chair. "You want to know," she said, her voice a low and menacing whisper. "All right, Aeryk. Since you asked so politely." Flicking absently with a finger, Seirin increased the room's humidity. Images played across mist and cloud, pulling him closer. Air and water fused into one atmosphere, and before he understood what was happening, Seirin seized his mind and dragged him into her memory.

Seirin crouched behind a huge sheltering boulder at the top of a high mountain range and waited for Roarke's signal. At this height, the howling wind came from everywhere, cutting through her green tunic and pants like a thousand icy needles. Whenever she found a spot that offered some protection, the frigid gale sliced in from a different direction. She shifted once, and then again, this time not from the cold but from nervous tension. A part of her worried Roarke would change his mind about the attack at the last minute and turn away, leaving them to deal with Vissyus without him.

The Earth Kami was soft spoken for such a big man, but he had a gentle heart and was more sensitive than anyone would think after setting eyes on his massive figure. Though he said little, Vissyus's madness wounded him deeply. He and the Fire Lord spent a good deal of time together, each comparing the other's power, Roarke bringing the raw materials, Vissyus heating and forging them. Always withdrawn, Roarke seemed more so recently, and Seirin had her doubts about his commitment to this battle, doubts that began when Roarke argued against shields.

Seirin understood Vissyus would sense a shield's power and thereby give them away. Still, understanding didn't make her feel better or less exposed. And why was Roarke in charge anyway? How had that happened? She didn't remember agreeing to it, which meant – as far as she was concerned – she didn't need to follow his orders. Seirin Bal Cerannon was strong, independent, and peerless. No one commanded her. No one ever had.

Which, she admitted ruefully, was exactly how she had ended up here, preparing for a fight no one wanted. Once again, she'd been selfish. So in love that her judgment – never great to begin with – had clouded. Damn the prohibition against having a child and damn the law. She and Aeryk were two of the world's most powerful Kami; they could do as they liked.

Only they couldn't. Takeshi saw to that. He said blending elemental power into one body was potentially deadly. Whenever she conceived, whenever one of the Kami conceived, Takeshi blocked a spirit from entering the new body. Without a soul, the husk died almost as soon as it started growing. Yui was the exception; ostensibly a concession from Takeshi to see if having children was safe. Seirin believed Yui's birth had more to do with Teras's desires than Seirin's nagging.

Undeterred, Seirin convinced Aeryk to look for alternatives, conducting secret experiments at Aeryk's fortress, she teaching him how to wield her water, he giving her his air. Clandestine meetings led to more experimentation, and before long they were sure they could safely fuse air and water into a living body – even one as small and vulnerable as a baby's. All they needed was a way to test the idea before bringing their proof to Takeshi, and Seirin knew exactly where to go for that.

Vissyus hated Takeshi's interference as much if not more than Seirin did. Intrusive, he called it, an affront to both science and nature. Seirin's request to prove Vissyus right was enough to secure his support. With a hug and a shy kiss on her cheek, he promised to prove, beyond all doubt, how right her instincts were.

Tragically, what seemed like a good idea at the time had turned into a colossal mistake. Less than four months since asking Vissyus for help, Seirin found herself here, inching toward a gap in the protective stone wall while a now insane Vissyus sent his power rampaging unchecked across the globe. Wind howled past her, blowing her hair around her head like golden pennants. Brushing the strands from her eyes, she swallowed uncomfortably and peered out of her shelter.

Vissyus's island home, a massive yet broken volcano, reared from the ocean like a gigantic tower. Despite the damage, no other mountain stood as tall, no peak covered as much ground. The caldera alone towered forty thousand feet above the seas, measuring a staggering six hundred square miles. Once, Seirin thought the solitary peak was a perfect melding of earth, air, and sea; today, it looked more like a lonely prison. She'd never get her answers now. Turning away with a leaden heart, she moved to a second opening in the rock, her mind reaching out to Roarke.

The Earth Spirit stood behind a similar barricade less than two miles down the range. Even at a distance, his massive seven-foot frame was easy enough for her power-enhanced sight to spot. Roarke wore his traditional rust-hued robe over skin as dark as rich soil. His hammer remained looped in his iron belt, but his posture spoke of readiness. His silver eyes caught hers, and he nodded. *Are you ready?* he asked.

Lon-Shan, Lord of Spirit, interrupted before she could answer. *I still say we should talk to him. We don't really know what's happened. What if it's temporary? How can you condemn him without knowing that first?*

Roarke shook his head. *We can't take that chance. Vissyus is strong enough to destroy the world; he was halfway there two weeks ago. We were lucky he stopped before he went too far.*

Seirin closed her eyes and sighed. Vissyus had done so much for her. Shouldn't she do something for him? *Lon-Shan is right, Roarke. Vissyus is our friend. We have to try. We owe him that much.*

Roarke's hesitation lasted less than a second. He'd made up his mind, and nothing they said would dissuade him. *It's too risky. Vissyus is strong and fast, and in his current state he could strike without warning. I'm sorry, Seirin. We don't have that luxury. If Aeryk were here, you know he'd agree with me.*

But Aeryk is not here, Lon-Shan countered. *You say we don't have time to waste on a friend; the same goes for Aeryk. He knew the timetable, and for whatever reason, he ignored his promise – to Seirin, to you, and to the hundred or so Kami he asked to stand with us. We need to make a decision, and we need to make one now.*

A decision on something Seirin believed settled. Anxiously, she lifted her gaze to the skies, formed a

Searching, and cast her thoughts into the air's moisture.

Aeryk. Where are you?

The wind whipped in answer, but Aeryk's power was strangely absent. Aeryk Tai-Banshar, Kami of Air, no longer commanded the gusts swirling around her. She cast a Searching into his palace at Hurricane Point. Empty. Worry gnawed at her, desperation filling her widening Search. Her mind swept over the large continent, heading northeast from Aeryk's fortress and up to a range of jagged mountains. Nothing. Worry became panic and by the time her Searching reached a dark ravine, her hands were shaking. Aeryk was her future and she his. She couldn't lose him. Not now, not after everything they'd sacrificed. She pushed ahead, forgetting Vissyus and Roarke and their building conflict, when Lon-Shan's voice filled her head, pulling her back.

Seirin! We need your vote. His tone had an edge she hadn't heard before. A sharpness. Had she wandered that far?

She steadied herself for what she was about to say. Roarke wouldn't like it, but he'd understand. Eventually. *I'm sorry,* she said. *But I agree with Lon-Shan. If there's even the slightest chance, we should try.*

This is a mistake. Roarke flung his arm at the volcano. His robes billowed around him, and ash dusted his dark skin. *We won't have another chance. Fail, and we die.*

Seirin lifted her chin. *I've made up my mind. I'm going to talk to him; he'll listen to me.* She ignited her shield and pushed from the high peak in a blaze of emerald light.

You're not going anywhere near Vissyus, Roarke rumbled. *I promised Aeryk I'd keep you safe. If that means burying you inside the mountain, I'll do it.* He dropped to one knee and placed his palm on the ground. Silver light rippled outward in concentric rings before fading. In seconds, stone columns shot from the ground to ring her in.

Seirin arched an eyebrow. Look out for her? She was stronger than either Aeryk or Roarke, and while she understood this was Aeryk's attempt at chivalry, he seemed to need looking after more than she did. She glared at the Earth Spirit and advanced. Emerald light met silver. Sparks exploded from the impact, and cracks appeared in the stone pillars.

Buried deep beneath the mountains, Lon-Shan made a throat-clearing sound with his thoughts. *I'll go. I'm better equipped for this than either of you. I can hide in the shadows until I'm out on the plain. Vissyus won't know I'm there until I want him to.*

Seirin didn't like it. No one should go in her place. Even so, Lon-Shan's argument had merit. Nodding, she released her power. *There's an underground river not far from you. A tributary flows from the mountains and travels through a deep gorge on its way south. This early in the morning, the eastern cliffs keep the riverbed in shadow. You should have enough cover until you're in place.*

And then what? There's no shade on that plain – no power well for me to use. If that's where you want me to go, you'll need to rectify that.

I can't build a shelter without Vissyus knowing, Roarke grumbled. His reservation was easy enough to read, but if sending Lon-Shan meant keeping his promise to Aeryk, he'd do it. *A grove runs along the mountains not far from your location. Botua's there. I'll have her move a section onto the plains for you. That should give you the protection you need.*

Thank you, Roarke. That should do. Please send my thanks to Botua as well.

With that, Lon-Shan slipped into Seirin's river and headed for the plain and his meeting with Vissyus, Lord of Fire.

Seirin watched him disappear as she paced anxiously about her mountain sanctuary, occasionally peering through the slim cracks between the stone, and surveyed the land below. A stiff land breeze had taken the worst of the volcano's soot, smoke, and ash out to sea, though here and there patches of gray dust swirled over the vibrant green of forest and grassland. Where an expanse of open fields had been, a small knot of trees and underbrush sat just beyond the eastern lip of a gorge, their shade reaching to the western side.

She smiled grimly and sent a Searching into the deep shadows below. Lon-Shan was there, exactly as promised. He acknowledged her, and then went silent as he waited for Vissyus. Lifting her hand, Seirin redirected her thoughts from the Shadow Spirit to Roarke. *Lon-Shan's in place. We can begin whenever you're ready. Just remember, we're trying to get Vissyus's attention, not provoke him.*

Don't worry. I know what I'm doing. Roarke's thoughts rolled from Seirin, dove into the ground, and spread out. Forty thousand feet below and twenty miles to the east, light tremors rattled the shoreline. Roarke quickly deepened them into long sustained quakes. The Earth groaned. Great tracts of land broke apart, soil and ocean pouring into widening fissures. Water met magma, and the two rocketed to the surface as pressurized steam.

Seirin's gaze shifted to Vissyus's volcano. She had expected movement, a response, something. But the mountain remained quiet. *You're too far away. The quakes have to reach the island.*

I can't do that without threatening him. Agitation thrummed through Roarke's words. *This can't look like an attack.*

But this *was* an attack. Or the beginning of one. Changing the name didn't change the reality. They'd come for Vissyus, and the only reason they didn't want to threaten him was because he was too strong for them. For all of them together.

Seirin closed her eyes. *Would a storm be enough?* The words came reluctantly, as if dragged from her chest. Everyone loved Vissyus, and though he returned the feeling in equal measure, he held a special place in his heart for Aeryk and Seirin. The three of them were as close as any friends could be. Staring at his ruined home and trying to reconcile the devastation with Vissyus's gentle and generous nature brought Seirin to tears.

A big one might. If you target the caldera's interior, he'll know you're here. Roarke didn't say her presence was enough to pull him out, and she was thankful for it.

"I'm not sure I can do this," she breathed. Aeryk was right; she shouldn't have involved Vissyus. She'd been so sure he'd know what to do, so confident in his incredible intelligence. She buried her face in her hands. How was she supposed to live with herself?

By saving him and bringing him back. Seirin hadn't expected an answer, least of all from Lon-Shan. *The longer he stays in there, the longer Roarke has to change his mind.*

Seirin lowered her head. She breathed in steam, drew in sea spray and smoke-choked moisture. Lon-Shan was right. Hesitation brought doubt and second-guessing, and they were well beyond that.

Swallowing reluctance, she threw her mind into the air's moisture. Her thoughts touched the rising steam and chilled it. Low-level warmth mixed with sudden cold and spiraled upward in strong cyclonic winds. Overhead, white clouds gathered, darkening as they expanded into severe lightning-filled storms. Thunder boomed, and lightning stroked the waves below. These, Seirin fueled with undersea currents, stealing power from the quakes and building them into breakers hundreds of feet tall.

The first line rolled toward a west-facing beach. Their surge would swamp the land and drown everything for miles. Seirin set her jaw and hurled one wave after another toward shore.

A familiar voice rose above the roaring seas. "Teacher?" Vissyus called. "Is that you? Why are you making Heaven cry? Is it sad?"

Seirin's heart faltered. Her waves collapsed, and her storms broke apart. She put a hand to her chest to slow the pounding inside. *Yes, Vissyus,* she thought. *We are all sad.*

He laughed then, a fresh and innocent sound against the ruin. "Don't worry. I have something here that will make you happy. Let me show you."

Seirin's heart thudded wildly. Show her? Show her what? Foreboding settled on her shoulders, as real and as heavy as the mountain beneath her feet. She waited for a moment. And then another. Before the next, the volcano exploded. Vissyus's sunfire shield emerged from the broken crown and climbed into the sky with the slow majesty of a newly risen star. Incandescent flames bathed its surface, sparks racing throughout like miniature solar storms.

Vissyus floated inside, head back, arms outstretched. He gestured to his left and then to his right, and two smaller orbs flew up from below, one blazing red, the other arctic blue. Ice flew from the latter in an array of spears, the former adding to its master's inferno with streams of carnelian fire. Together, they crested the fallen volcano, moved over the ocean, and headed for the coast.

Their approach withered the earth. The seas boiled below them, and sandy beaches turned to glass. Away from shore, grasslands ignited like millions of slender torches. Wherever Vissyus's thoughts went, destruction followed. Joyously, he atomized one random target after another. Guarded mountains fell, and the pools Seirin protected vaporized. To his right, Fiyorok, a dragon guardian with shining red-golden scales, lashed the land with fire, while several thousand yards to the left a second dragon coated the ground with ice.

Sapphire scales covered the unfamiliar dragon's two hundred foot-long body. A billowing mane the color of foaming seas ran from just behind its brows, through a row of horns shaped like an inverted crown, and down its back to the tail. Outwardly, it was magnificent, but the inside, where its spirit should have burned brightly, was empty.

Vissyus pointed at the blue shield. "Look what I've made for you. Its name is Akuan, a guardian of ice. A part of it is you; a part of it is me." He stabbed a finger at the ground. "Go, Akuan. Show them what you can do."

Akuan. The name clung to the air like windblown snow. Seirin paled and backed away. Water Kami were her responsibility. Why hadn't she known about this? Because she'd been at Aeryk's palace, too busy luxuriating in their newfound love to even care. A stark line now separated that blissful past from this desperate present.

Her gaze followed the guardians' flight. Fiyorok landed in a field of burning grass, Akuan on a suddenly frozen lake. Vissyus dropped behind the dragons and lowered his enormous shield. Laughing heartily, he strode up a low hill and stopped to survey his surroundings. Childlike innocence filled his face, and his large muscular body trembled with giddy excitement. His red shirt was soiled, and ash covered his black pants. The long gray cape fluttering behind him looked more like a tattered flag or shredding smoke than the once regal cloak Seirin remembered. His whimsical expression said he either didn't know or didn't care about his appearance, only that he'd had a very good time reaching his current state.

He approached the small cluster of trees Botua had moved onto the plain and frowned. Leaning forward, he cupped a hand to his mouth. "Teacher? Are you in there?" His half-whispered, half-sing-song tone prickled Seirin's skin. He held his head at an angle as if listening. When no answer came, he pursed his lips and tried again. "Teacher? You can come out. I found you. It's my turn." Another silence followed, and Vissyus's frown deepened. Power swirled around him. He lifted his arms and thrust his hands forward. "No more hiding. My turn now."

White light flared around his opened palms. Sparks flashed and died quickly. Too quickly. In seconds, they came again, though this time the light had moved from his hands to the trees. A sizzling followed, and then a sharp boom. The accompanying light was blindingly bright and equally abrupt. Seirin blinked, and when her sight cleared, ashy stumps stood in place of the once-proud trees. A black sphere hovering over the charred ground was the only untouched space within the charred glade.

Light-damaged and without the protective shadows of the trees, Lon-Shan's shield unraveled. The Dark Spirit stared up at the much taller Vissyus, his face hard, his eyes glinting before the fires.

Confusion and disappointment played across Vissyus's features. He shook his head, his tawny hair spraying out like a corona. "Only you? I don't understand. Where are the others? Where is Teacher? I know she's here; those were her storms." He lifted his chin and spun in a circle.

"Teacher! Come out, Teacher. You have to see what I made for you!"

Lon-Shan said something in reply. Seirin couldn't hear what, but Vissyus's reaction was swift and chilling. He wheeled, his red-and-yellow tinted eyes flaring. Power radiated from his body – strong, unstoppable, and seemingly limitless. He clapped his hands together and motioned Akuan forward. The dragon obeyed, bounding down the hill in a blur of blue and green. Frost marked its passing. Grass curled and browned. Brittle leaves snapped. Rough ground became icy sheets.

The color drained from Lon-Shan's cheeks. He backed away, but his feet landed on smooth ice, and he went down. He tried to stand, but his feet slid out from under him. Again he tried, and again he fell. Panicking, he grasped for his shield. Black motes swirled around him, only to have the flames sear them away. His face was pale, and sweat matted his hair.

Two hundred feet away, Akuan prowled forward. A cold triumphant light burned in its eyes. Jaws agape, it thrust its head forward and spewed ice-laden fog into the air.

Instinctively, Seirin reached for her shield. *Lon-Shan!* she called. *Are you all right? Lon-Shan? Answer me!* Energy pulsed around her in bright emerald wisps.

On the plains, Vissyus stopped and cocked his head. He looked first east and then west. His gaze followed the land's contours and surveyed wood, field, and mountain.

A terrified voice broke the silence. *He knows where we are!*

More followed, some distinct, others unintelligible whimpers.

What's happened to him?
He's burning everything!
Has anyone heard from Lon-Shan?

And then, *Where's Aeryk? We can't defeat Vissyus without Lord Tai-Banshar.*

Seirin bit her lip. Aeryk. Where *was* he? What if something had happened to him? Trying not to think about Aeryk was as hard as ignoring the battle below. Both fought for her attention, the former beyond her control, the latter seemingly so. Together, the two immobilized her. Her body seized. She couldn't process what her eyes saw.

Vissyus continued to walk across a wide plain, his burning eyes glued to the mountains. Closer to her, a dark winged shape rocketed through the dense fog with Lon-Shan cradled in its claws.

My lord is injured, the guardian said, banking sharply to the west.

How bad is it, Streega? Concern laced Roarke's tone. *Lon-Shan is too important to lose.*

Streega shook its horned head. *I'll do what I can, but until I know the extent of his injuries, I can't make any promises.*

Seirin watched the large bat-like guardian retreat. *Let them go, Roarke. Lon-Shan was only here to cover us.* He was lucky to be alive. Akuan held too much of Vissyus's power. More than any guardian should.

He was also a scout. He can touch Vissyus's shadow and anticipate his movements. Losing that puts us at a disadvantage.

Aeryk's absence put them at a greater disadvantage, but Seirin didn't want to say that to Roarke. Instead, she widened her Searching to compensate for Lon-Shan's loss and found Akuan at the bottom of a low rise, craning its neck as if listening. On the plains, Fiyorok did the same. A ball of icy blue energy burst to life around Akuan, red and orange surrounding Fiyorok. Both shot upward and disappeared into the clouds.

Their abrupt departure made Seirin uneasy. They wouldn't leave on their own, which meant Vissyus sent them away. But why? To make himself look vulnerable? Would he do that? Could he? She needed to warn Roarke about this before he ordered another attack.

But Roarke had already started. His thoughts drilled deep into the earth. Spikes broke free and flew toward the valley. More followed, splinters carved from mountains, slivers hundreds of feet long – spears of iron, stone, and other hard metals.

Vissyus responded with a wide grin. He'd issued a challenge, and Roarke replied. Together they would play, power against power, skill against skill. For a second, Vissyus didn't move. Then, seemingly too late, he brought his sunfire shield to life around his body. The massive orb pulsed once, and then again, each flash leaping farther away before solidifying into a blazing shield. One or two of Roarke's missiles sliced through, only to disintegrate into a fine powdery spray; the rest melted or burned to ash on contact. Sparks fell in orange showers, but before they hit the ground, Vissyus seized them and drew them close to his shield. Faster they swirled, gaining speed and blending with fire.

With nothing more than a graceful unfurling of his fingers, he hurled fire at the towering cliffs. The mountains had called to him, and his power echoed back. A mimicked response, a child's game, power sent, power returned. Large swathes of mountain disappeared, reduced to smoke and liquid slag. Many lesser Kami, afraid for their lives, abandoned their positions and fled in terror. Those who could still command valiantly tried to rally, an impossible task with Vissyus atomizing heavily fortified escarpments with ease. The chaos left Roarke alone and unsupported in the middle of their rapidly disintegrating line.

As Vissyus's attacks closed, a small, willowy figure exploded from a densely wooded forest and raced forward. Delicate flowers peppered hair the color of fresh ivy. She wore a saffron shirt over loose olive-green pants, muted shades that kept her hidden until she reached a fortified glen. Redwoods – tall, strong, and resistant to most fires – ringed it.

Seirin's breath caught. *Botua? Botua, no! Don't! Stop!*

You know I can't. Worry tightened Botua's normally breezy tone. *My forests are more vulnerable to fire than anything else on the planet. They clean the air, Seirin. What would happen to Aeryk without them? What happens to the world?* Igniting her yellow shield, she crouched and pressed her palms into the earth. A soft golden glow swirled around her hands, identical to her shield's hue. Overhead, a loud whistling filled the air, a shriek that became a hiss and then a roar. Clouds split, and Fiyorok dropped through the void they left behind.

Seirin glanced up, and her hopes died. No! Not like this. *I can't just leave you there. Fiyorok is coming!*

Botua closed her eyes in resignation. *I'm not giving you a choice.* Her palms stayed on the ground despite the threat from above. The yellow light cut through grass, racing toward Vissyus, pacing Fiyorok to see which reached its target first. *My guardian is our only chance. Vissyus attacked Lon-Shan, but he left Streega alone. He knows the law, Seirin. He won't hurt a guardian. Kloran will tell him we want to talk. I just need to get his attention first.*

Fiyorok landed at the edge of the forest and stalked ahead. Nearby trees smoldered, but the dragon held its fire. Miles away, Botua's guardian burst through the ground beneath Vissyus. Vines wound about his legs, their yard-long thorns plunging into his legs to hold him.

Seirin's knees weakened. *What are you doing? You can't hurt him like that. He won't understand. Stop it, Botua! You don't want to anger him.*

Botua's face hardened, but she didn't answer. Seirin tried again, and this time Botua threw a shield around her thoughts to keep Seirin out. Desperate, anxious, and afraid, Seirin forced her gaze back to Vissyus, expecting a retaliatory strike.

Instead, the Fire Spirit grew still. The vines stirred something inside him: a glimmer, a memory. The longer he stared at them, the more his confusion lifted. Recognition flashed in his eyes, a welcoming smile forming on his lips. He bent to stroke the dark green leaves. His touch sent an orange light rippling through them. Sparks danced then caught, and before long the once-lush fronds lay withered and burning at his feet.

Vissyus stared, confusion contorting his face. "Kloran? Kloran, what's wrong? Wake up. You have to wake up." Anguish twisted his mouth. His eyes reddened, and his shoulders drooped. Stooping, he gathered what he could of the shriveled plant and pressed the leaves to his chest. "I'm sorry. I didn't mean it. It was an accident." Tears rolled down his hardening cheeks, his hands clenching angrily. Rising like a great, smoky plume, he cast a furious gaze into the wood. "*Botua!*" he cried, lifting a trembling fist. "Look what you made me do! This is your fault. I have to punish you."

Seirin reeled. Dazed, she staggered away from the cliff until her back hit cool stone. She fought for breath, but her lungs conspired against her. *Kloran's dead. Botua's guardian is...* Her eyes flew wide. Botua! She'd forgotten about Botua. Hurting a guardian hurts its Kami. At best, the Forest Spirit was stunned, at worst...

Frantically, Seirin gathered her shattered thoughts

and sent them cascading into the steep ravine to her left. *Kirak,* she called, summoning her guardian. *I need you. We're going after Botua.*

A deep blue glow appeared in the darkness, growing rapidly as her serpent guardian roared up to meet her. Its huge head appeared first, the blunt snout, the wise eyes. Turquoise scales shot through with aquamarine stripes shimmered like sunlit water along its long body.

Seirin waited for Kirak to clear the gorge before vaulting over the cliffs. The guardian followed without speaking, drawing moisture from the lakes and rivers and feeding the liquid to her as they fell.

Water spiraled toward Seirin in wispy streams. She touched them, changing their temperature with a thought – ice above, steam below. The two collided, and black clouds formed in the saturated air. Below, Fiyorok moved deeper into the woods. Fire ate large swathes on Fiyorok's right and left, with more falling directly ahead. Seirin couldn't see Botua through the smoke and thick tangle of leaves and branches, but she knew where Botua's thoughts came from, and that section of the wood remained undamaged. Hope warred with fear in her heart. What would she find when she reached it? What would she see?

Fighting worry, she ripped her storms open and let the deluge flood the forest. The rains would slow Fiyorok's fire, but only for so long. As if sensing her need, Kirak dropped down beside her, and together they closed. Four thousand feet. Three. Less.

And then, with the trees in sight, Akuan burst through the clouds above and fell on her like storm-driven hail. Its arctic blue battle shield shone vibrantly against the blackened sky, its bared teeth white and glistening. Kirak pulled up, rolled, and put itself between them. The two guardians collided in a blur of shield and scales, their bodies twisting and turning, each one fending off the other's attacks.

Seirin wheeled about. *Kirak!* She redirected her thoughts into the water below and formed whatever moisture she seized into turgid cannons.

No, mistress! Save Botua. Go to her. Go now!

Seirin hesitated. Her thoughts rolled back to Kloran's death. A violent severing of the Guardian Bond incapacitated both guardian and spirit. If anything happened to Kirak... Fear racked her body. What should she do? Helping Kirak would cost valuable time.

And Fiyorok was closing.

Her mind made up, she banked away from the grappling guardians and raced into the forest. What hope she had died the farther she went. Fiyorok had moved faster and farther than her floodwaters. Little remained of the tall trees securing this part of the glade, and two wide tracts of scorched earth and soot-dusted ground led into and out of the area. Wherever she looked, she saw smoldering ruins. Her hands covered her mouth and nose. Grimly she pressed on, certain of what lay ahead.

She found Botua in a bed of blistered sunflowers. Most of the olive skin was burned beyond recognition, but the face – Botua's face – was peaceful and remarkably untouched. Quietly, somberly, Seirin landed beside her. She stood there motionless for what felt like forever. Eventually, her knees buckled, hitting the ground with a dull thud. Botua's hand lay exposed next to her body, and Seirin grasped for it. A tear rolled from her cheek and onto their intertwined fingers where it held for a moment before succumbing to the heat.

11
ABSOLUTION

Aeryk's thoughts left the past and slammed back into his body. His knees weakened and collapsed and only reflex brought his hand down on the floor before he tumbled into the moat. Sweat coated his face and streaked his clothes. He peered up through damp hair and caught Seirin's eye. Emerald light shimmered through the beaded water on his eyelashes, more glinting off his damp cheeks and nose. Across the water, some of the hurt and anger melted from Seirin's face as she reached into the liquid dampening his skin. Her touch was light, tentative even, as if she feared his rejection as much as he feared hers.

Memory and emotion passed between them, as much from one as to the other. He held his breath as she processed what she felt from him, his pain, isolation, and helplessness. The more she probed, the more the air between them thawed. She wanted to forgive him; he sensed her searching for a reason. Could he give her the one she needed before he told her everything?

He stood and started to speak, but she stopped him with a sad shake of her head. "I can't believe you didn't know. All this time... I was so sure you left me there on purpose."

"I would never do that to you. We promised to make things right, Seirin. And we promised to do it together."

He stretched an arm to her, but she pulled away.

"Why didn't you come sooner?" A hint of pain was still visible on her face, a touch of distrust in her stunning emerald eyes. "You knew where I was, and you obviously knew how to reach me. Why did you make me wait? How could you let me believe what I did? About you and me... about us?"

"I tried," he blurted. "I tried so hard I almost set Vissyus free right after we caught him."

Seirin cocked her head. "We?" she asked, suspicion casting more shadows over her face. "You weren't alone?"

"No," Aeryk admitted. "I was at first, then Takeshi reappeared with a barrier he called the Boundary. I don't know how, but he pulled the whole battlefield and every surviving Kami inside."

Seirin's expression tightened. "Takeshi," she repeated, her tone flat. "I should have known. Vissyus never trusted him. He said Takeshi knew we'd out grow him someday, that all those rules and laws he made us follow were just a way to control us."

"I thought so too, but there was more to it than that. A lot more." Aeryk inched forward until his toes hung precariously over the moat. "Takeshi was trying to protect us, Seirin; he left to build the Boundary because he knew something was wrong – with us, with Vissyus, with everything. He was right too. We came so close to destroying an entire planet. Without the Boundary, we would have." Aeryk lowered his head and looked away. "I almost did it by myself. I didn't know what the

Boundary was at first, so I attacked. I hurt it – bad enough to damage random layers and create the Weakening." Sighing he caught her eye again. "We're all responsible for this, and it's up to us to make things right."

"How many?" Seirin said in a barely audible whisper.

"Just the strongest, those of us who ruled all the rest: you, me, Takeshi, and Roarke."

Seirin's lips thinned, a concerned look spreading over her face. "What about Lon-Shan? He was injured. He's all right isn't he?" Aeryk hesitated, adding to her agitation. "Aeryk? What's wrong?"

"Lon-Shan blames us for what happened to Vissyus. He thinks we need to pay." Aeryk let out a long, slow breath. "Lon-Shan wasn't trying to fight Vissyus; he was trying to save him. That's why he went onto the plains. He thought, wrongly, that Vissyus would see him as a friend – his only friend – and stand down. When that didn't work, he intentionally provoked Vissyus into attacking you… starting by having Botua move her trees to shade him."

"No! It's not true. I don't believe it! I won't. Lon-Shan's a friend."

Aeryk shook his head. "Lon-Shan always thought we looked down on him, and in a way he was right. Vissyus was the only one who really treated him like an equal. The rest of us barely gave him the time of day, and when we did, we patronized him. Don't think he couldn't tell the difference, Seirin. Denying it simply proves my point." Sighing, he ran a hand over his chin. His mouth felt dry, bitter – as if he'd eaten dried bark. "Lon-Shan killed Botua; he tried to kill me too. Before the battle, he sent an army into the mountains to stop me. That's why I was late, Seirin. Not because I didn't want to be there, and not because I'd forgotten. I was late because Lon-

Shan ambushed me."

Blood drained from Seirin's cheeks, leaving them wan and pale. "My fault," she panted. "Stupid. Selfish." Anguished, she flicked her wrist and sent boiled-up seawater from below in a rush of white foam. Brine lashed Aeryk's body, liquid whips slapping the side of his face. He caught her radiant eyes behind the storming water. Hope glimmered within, a flickering similar to a fire's tinder, waiting for him, testing him, needing him to save her from herself.

Instinctively, he hurled his thoughts into the air and blasted the moisture away. His memories suffused the gales, and a host of images cascaded around her. She nodded to him, a barely perceptible tilting of her head. He would show her what happened so they could grieve together and move on.

Seirin noticed the wind first. It blew against her face and teased her hair: strong, insistent, and steady. Aeryk's azure shield soared through the air beside her like a miniature Earth.

Aeryk.

Emotional knots twisted inside her. She'd been so angry, so hurt for so long. Inhaling, she opened her thoughts and let him guide her through his memories. She felt as if she was with him, experiencing what he had, each sensation unexpectedly real and vibrant. Curious, she fell in behind his shield. What would he show her? What was strong enough to keep him away?

The storms ahead thinned. Mountains, so like dragons' teeth, appeared on either side, casting the world around her into shadow. With a start, she realized where she was.

Hurricane Point towered over a wide peninsula fifteen

hundred miles southwest, while Vissyus's island fortress sat in the middle of a huge gulf thirty-five hundred miles or so in the northeast. She remembered mapping this route with Aeryk in the days before the battle. They'd flown practice runs together to determine both distance and time. Pulse quickening, she followed him into a deep gorge.

Black marble lined the walls, adding to the darkness. Only a small sliver of blue sky remained visible overhead, enough to illuminate a strip near the top of the canyon, but no more. Something about the gloom troubled her, made her wary. She felt as if she was being watched. Her skin prickled, and the hair on her arms and neck stood.

Aeryk moved as if he sensed it as well, his flight slow and cautious. He fired a Searching into the walls and, finding nothing, he asked his guardian if it felt it too.

I didn't notice anything out of the ordinary, Ventyre said into his mind. Its voice always reminded Seirin of a finely played pipe. *Shall I double back and scout the way for you?*

Aeryk shook his head emphatically. *We can't afford the delay. The staging will take time. I'd rather do it myself than leave it to the others. They're not ready for this.*

Aren't you the seasoned warrior? Ventyre mocked. *And just how many battles have you been in? Let me think… Was it a hundred? Fifty? Ten? Two? The numbers go up a little if you include the arguments you've had with Lady Seirin, but since you lost those, perhaps they shouldn't count.*

Seirin smirked nastily at Aeryk's burning cheeks.

You know what I mean, he grumbled. *They have no idea what we're up against.*

And you do?

Aeryk sighed. *No. Not exactly. I haven't seen Vissyus since the madness, but that doesn't mean I've forgotten how strong he is. If his psyche is as damaged as it feels, we'll have a very hard day ahead of us.*

Then you'd better pick up the pace. The sooner we arrive, the better.

Whatever you say, guardian. Aeryk chuckled, then grew serious. *I don't like the feel of this place. I'll be glad to be clear of it.*

A familiar voice hissed at him from the shadows. "But the master wants you to stay. He ordered us to keep you here. Lord Lon-Shan commands, and we obey. Stay with us, Lord of Air. Stay with us while our lord helps Vissyus escape."

Seirin gasped. Streega? Impossible! Streega had been on the plains. She'd seen it. She spoke to it.

A cold breath grasped for her from the darkness, and whispered voices came at her from every direction. "Lord Vissyus will escape. He will deal with the traitors and then he and our lord will rule this world in peace."

"The master promised us."

"The Lords of Fire and Shadow will rule over all."

"Nothing can stop them. We are their army. Our lord created us to do his bidding. All hail Lord Lon-Shan! All hail the Kami of Shadow!"

Seirin pushed a hand against her lurching stomach. It wasn't real. It couldn't be! Shame burned in her heart. Aeryk. How could she face him? All those years, her accusations… She'd been wrong… about everything. A cold wind buffeted her body. Aeryk was right: Roarke defied Lon-Shan, and the Shadow Spirit made him pay.

Dropping next to Aeryk's shield, she circled him protectively. Lon-Shan took Botua – she wouldn't let him have Aeryk too. Reason said she couldn't do anything to help a memory, but the gesture comforted her nonetheless, especially when the first creature appeared to her left.

Darkness hid all but its grasping hands. These Aeryk severed with a shearing wind. Ghastly slurping and smacking sounds replaced an incomplete scream. Seirin heard the beat of wings all around them. Her head whipped left and right. She caught a hint of movement before a horde of bat-like shapes erupted from the shadowed mountainsides. If not for their size – and numbers – Seirin could have easily mistaken them for the much larger Streega.

My lord? Ventyre called back, clearly alarmed. *I heard screaming. What's happening?*

I don't know… an attack of some kind… they claim to serve Lon-Shan. Aeryk drew hurricane force winds into the chasm, ripping the wings from some of his attackers while hurling others into the walls like dolls. The survivors regrouped and charged again. *You have to tell the others about this. Lon-Shan's betrayed us. He might even be working for Vissyus. Get to Seirin. You have to help her.*

What about you?

I can take care of myself. These aren't guardians; the laws against attacking them don't apply. And as long as I know Seirin's all right, I'll be fine. You have to protect her, Ventyre. I don't know what I'd do without her.

Seirin felt as if she'd fallen into one of her whirlpools. The world spun. Up became down, right became wrong. Why didn't they know about this? How long had Lon-Shan plotted against them? If she'd suspected, if she'd had a hint, she'd never have listened to him. Botua might still be alive. How much blood was on her hands? She wanted to scream, but no sounds came from her tightening chest.

As if sensing her distress, Aeryk's vision sharpened; the sounds increased. She smiled thinly. He knew. He knew and he was trying to distract her. Warmth spread throughout her body. His heart was still hers. Fighting down guilt, she set her sights on the unfolding battle.

Aeryk continued his relentless attacks. She saw the worry on his face, felt the tension in his body. He fought, but not for his safety; he fought for her. A fine tingling prickled her skin like the light touch of a feather. She'd been so wrong. Her heart soared. Kami died, and heaven help her, she barely felt it.

Ventyre? Aeryk called, agitated. Only then did Seirin realize the guardian hadn't responded to him. *Ventyre. Did you hear me?*

Ventyre's voice, when it finally came back, was murderous. *Yes, lord. I hear you. Unfortunately, the situation has changed... Streega is here. I think it intends to stop me.*

Aeryk's eyes turned from sky blue to slate. *Lon-Shan?* he asked, angry now.

There is no sign of him.

Which means he's either at the battlefield or gone into hiding. Aeryk cursed under his breath. *I don't care what you have to do to get past Streega. You have your assignment, and that guardian is in your way. Deal with it.*

Ventyre's response was a mix of surprise and sympathy. *I'll do what I can.*

Aeryk lifted his face to the orange-tinted sky. Shockwaves from some faraway cataclysm sent tremors through rock and air, befouling winds as the morning's tranquility shattered. "Vissyus," he said sadly.

Head shaking, he returned his attention to the surrounding nightmare. Tornados flew horizontally from his fingers, thin funnels that sucked in everything in their path. They shredded wings and peeled flesh as they spun through the ravine, the spray from the creature's wounds painting the rocks with blood.

He dumped the whole crumpled mess to the cavern

floor and summoned devastating macrobursts to clear the rest of the area. The downdrafts smashed what was still aloft to the ground like a hammer. With nothing left to slow him, he threw himself forward in a blur of stunning blue light.

His passing scarred the landscape, towering peaks reduced to amorphous pillars of limestone and basalt. Their onceproud outlines now reminded Seirin of rotting fangs. In the distance, a new ocean sparkled beneath the sun, and beyond that a wall of shimmering white energy climbed from the depths of the ocean to infinity.

Ventyre! Aeryk directed his thoughts at the streak of lavender light in front of the wall. The guardian banked away and hovered over the waves.

My apologies, lord. I tracked Streega to this spot, but when I arrived, I found myself facing… that. Seirin saw the guardian gesture at the energy band with its sleek avian head.

And even though you didn't know what it was, you decided to approach it?

I cast a Searching first, Ventyre quipped. *Was just in the middle of it, in fact, when you interrupted me.*

And Streega?

Inside, at least from what I can tell. Something caused it to break off and race back here. If I had to guess, I'd say Lon-Shan called it in to protect him. Ventyre snorted. *Some protection. Got itself trapped along with its master.*

Aeryk waved a hand dismissively. *We can't worry about Lon-Shan now. Look!*

As if drawn, a ring of clouds formed halfway up the energy wall, rotating from west to east and picking up speed.

It's shrinking, said Ventyre. *I don't understand.*

Aeryk shook his head, inched forward, and then froze, his body trembling. Like a clearing sky, a portion of the barrier rolled back to reveal a scene of unbelievable beauty. An endless parade of worlds appeared before him, each connected to the other by pathways of soft white light. Some were little more than crystal globes within which perched what looked like miniature landscapes – here a forest, there a stone mesa.

Seirin barely had time to inspect them before the wall's gossamer lining returned, but what she'd seen was enough. Roarke's fortress was in one of those orbs, a pristine ocean in another. She knew what that meant, and if she did, then Aeryk certainly had as well.

Already, she saw his shield move forward again, this time flying up at an angle. He fired a short series of microbursts into the thing's outer layers, obviously hoping a strafing run would perforate it. His second strike – a huge rotating updraft – should have peeled it back like a piece of fruit. As he wheeled around, though, a column of intense light shot down from above to blind him.

Seirin held her breath as he landed at the edge of what was once a verdant plain, a tall, armor-clad man standing between him and the dying battle.

Supple plates the color of a dawn sky cascaded in waves from wide epaulets to give his upper body the illusion of constant movement. The hilt of a sword peeked over his left shoulder, a companion secured about a belt at his waist. Aeryk didn't seem to recognize him at first, but she did – the armor wasn't familiar, but the face… she knew it all too well.

Takeshi? How? Why?

"I don't know where you've been or where you came from," Aeryk snarled, his right hand raised, open palm thrust forward menacingly. "But I want you out of my way! Now!" Air swirled, the power of a hurricane spinning ominously around his wrist.

Takeshi Akiko remained relaxed despite the threat. He rested one gauntleted hand on the pommel of his belted sword but made no move to step aside. The sound of crumbling mountains swept in from the west, while from the east came the sickening crack of the Earth's crust breaking apart.

"I told you to get out of my way! Seirin's in there." Aeryk stabbed a finger at the dwindling orb behind Takeshi, his face stricken enough to touch Seirin's heart. "I have to get her out – I have to save her."

"Your lady is fine, as are the others. Those who could still be saved."

Aeryk's expression softened at the news, though his shield, a translucent globe of azure blue, remained in place.

"And Vissyus?" he asked.

Seirin winced, waiting for the accusation that – thankfully – never came.

"Alive as well, if imprisoned." Takeshi's face remained neutral. "A better fate than he deserved under the circumstances, but the best I could do."

"What do you mean? Does this have something to do with that… that…?" Aeryk fired a blast of weaponized air toward the strange glowing ball.

"Boundary," Takeshi said, inclining his head at the orb. "It is called the Boundary. It will protect us while we do what must be done." He smiled at Aeryk's puzzled expression. Seirin's blood grew hot. Takeshi was toying with him. "I came here to ask for your help, Lord of Air, as you have already guessed."

Aeryk's eyes widened. "Why should I help you? I don't owe you anything. If you hadn't left when you did, none of this would have happened. You picked a fine time to reappear. Why did you wait until the battle was already lost? We could have used your help. Seirin, the others... how many are dead or captured because you've been away?"

"You know what Vissyus can do," Takeshi replied. Seirin noted the angry gleam in his brown eyes, the only hint of emotion on his otherwise smooth face. "No civilization, no world, is safe so long as he lives. We must finish him, and neither one of us can do it without the other."

"Look around you. What can we do against this?" Aeryk swept an arm around his body. Concentrated gales followed the motion, slicing through burning rock and strata.

"Now that we know what we face, we can better prepare. We will use the time we have to rebuild the world our war destroyed. But we will do it from the shadows. Vissyus can't know we're free."

"Why not just leave him there and be done with it? The world's suffered enough. We wanted to banish him, and now – apparently thanks to you – it's done. Our first task should be to free the other Kami."

A good question. Seirin held her breath as she waited for the answer.

Takeshi's expression, though sympathetic, was firm. "The Boundary wasn't meant to last forever, my friend. At least not around Vissyus." Seirin suspected he'd rehearsed these words many times. "We can't unlock it piecemeal without damaging it. If there was another way, I would take it, I assure you, but Vissyus's power limits what we can do. His shield makes him invincible, whether trapped or not. The Boundary can hold him, but it is not a permanent solution."

"You seem to be very familiar with this *Boundary*."

Aeryk's voice was a low and menacing whisper. "I've never seen it before. How do you know so much about it?"

Takeshi shook his helmeted head. "I will say more after you've agreed to my terms. You are not the only one to make sacrifices, Lord Tai-Banshar. My wife is in hiding, my own daughter trained as a warrior from birth."

"Seirin's in there," Aeryk said, as if that explained everything. "I won't help until you free her. I'll do it myself if I have to."

The words sent a warm rush through Seirin. He'd put her ahead of everything else. How had she doubted him?

"Foolishness!" Takeshi stepped aside and waved a hand.

A fiery sphere appeared within the Boundary. Even from a distance, Seirin felt Vissyus's consciousness lashing out in waves of infinite flame. Insanity turned what should have been rage to joy, the anticipation of breaking and destroying driving him to the peak of ecstasy.

"You've done enough already. Your little exercise weakened the Boundary, shortened its lifespan. I will not risk any more harm. The Boundary remains closed until we are ready. I did what was necessary, now I ask you to do the same."

The Weakening! Seirin thought. Aeryk created the Weakening just as he'd said. She stared into his azure eyes to see if he knew what he'd done, only to watch them pale to a frigid Arctic blue.

"I'm not leaving without her."

They argued for some time – said something about Gaiyern, Takeshi's guardian, and the Boundary – but Seirin was no longer listening. She'd heard what she needed to hear, seen what she needed to see.

An eternity of wondering was over now, her questions answered, her torment obliterated in a few short minutes. It was as if Aeryk had taken a torch to the layers of ice around her heart. He hadn't abandoned her – he did everything he could to free her, risking death, confronting Takeshi. That was love at its purest. For the first time in recent memory, her spirit lifted from the ground, and she no longer felt so hurt or helpless.

Before she realized what she was doing, she was on her feet, launching herself forward. She passed through Aeryk's flickering memories without seeing them. Only the startled man in the middle of the hall mattered to her, his earnest, hopeful face, piercing blue eyes, and boundless faith. She threw herself into his arms, sobbing joyously as she wrapped hers around him.

He didn't say anything, didn't let go. He just held her and waited until she was ready. She smiled and sighed into his chest, safe and whole again after what felt like forever.

Aeryk could have held her throughout eternity, neither speaking, nor moving. He'd forgotten how much she completed him, forgotten in a way only her presence could soothe. He wished they could savor the moment a while longer. Telling her what was to come seemed unfair, cruel even. She wouldn't want him to withhold it, though. They'd suffered enough misunderstandings.

She must have sensed the change in him – a slight tightening in his arms, an elongated breath – because she craned her neck and stared into his face.

"I shouldn't have doubted you." She never took her eyes from his. "I didn't at first, but then…" Her voice trailed off, and she looked into the distance. "So many died. I don't know, maybe I thought you could have saved them. It was easier to blame you than face the reality."

Aeryk stroked her cheek. "You didn't lose faith, Seirin. You wouldn't have let me see you if you had."

She blushed but refused to look away. Taking his hand in hers, she lowered it from her face. "Vissyus's Boundary is failing, isn't it? That's why you're here. Takeshi made you promise to stay away until the last possible moment." Aeryk tried to answer, but she put a finger to his lips to silence him. "I hope you've used your time wisely. We'll need every advantage we can get." Again he tried to speak, and again she silenced him. "Before you tell me, there's still one thing I'd like to know."

"What is it?"

Her glorious eyes hardened. "Lon-Shan. Tell me where I can find him."

12
AFFINITY

Vissyus swam through a clear blue sea, the Teacher's presence drawing him like a magnet. He shook his head, the motion strangely languid. He didn't remember leaving his volcanic fortress or crossing half the world to reach this spot.

Swimming felt natural, though. He swayed in time with the sea, matching its rhythm with undulating strokes. Had he always loved the oceans this much? He didn't think so. They doused all but his fiercest fires. Why was he here then? He tried to think, but his thoughts were a jumble of emotion and fractured memory. This meant something to him, he knew that much. Something about a guardian.

Oddly, his mind conjured the image of a man encased in a shimmering prison. He sat on a gigantic throne, his body slumped, his head down as if sleeping. A magnificent red-golden dragon watched over him. It looked concerned and oddly jealous.

Vissyus watched the creature drop its muzzle and nudge the man, just as something bumped his own shoulder. The hit came again and one last time. He frowned then shook off the sensation.

Whatever drew him here was gone now, faded away like that strange upside down whirlpool. An odd sense of loss filled him. He'd been close. So close. But to what? Sighing, he turned his long body and headed back, only to pause and lift his head.

A faint tickling called to him, this time coming from a high mountain nearly six thousand miles east. Two vast inland seas cradled it on either side, a perfect spot, it seemed, for him to search.

Grinning widely, he plunged beneath the waves and set off. He would find it this time, for certain. Nothing and no one could stop him. They never had, and they never would.

13
TREACHERY

Paitr fought a suspicious frown as he followed Martin across the empty square. What did Martin know that he didn't? The thought made him uncomfortable. He'd have to coax it from the other man. Carefully.

"Have any details of the meeting leaked out?" he asked – a safe question. It implied neither knowledge nor ignorance.

Martin shook his head, quickening his pace. "Nothing specific. And not for lack of trying. With so many disciples milling about, you'd expect some leaks. Lord Lon-Shan's kept everything to himself, it seems."

"How many?" Paitr asked.

"How many what?"

"Disciples, Martin. How many nobles?"

Lon-Shan's disciples had become notoriously provincial over the years. The centuries spent jockeying for favor made them paranoid. Only a direct order from Lon-Shan could lure them out. Paitr drummed his fingers nervously against a thigh. Why hadn't he been told?

Martin shrugged. "All of them."

Paitr nearly stumbled. "*What*? You're sure?"

"Fairly sure, yes. I didn't have a list to check, but I saw enough of them." Martin put a hand on Paitr's shoulder and leaned his head close. "Some of the fools are using the creatures our lord gave us to pull their carriages."

Paitr's jaw dropped. "Are they insane? Arrogance is one thing, but this… This is exactly what we're fighting to stop." He shook his head. Their lord would not be pleased.

Lon-Shan had spawned the beasts from his guardian, and while they lacked Streega's intelligence, they retained much of its ferocity. Their lord ordered his disciples to turn the brood into an army. That took commitment, determination, and patience, something Paitr's compatriots obviously lacked. But an army for what? Martin believed their forces would sweep across the world and usher in a new order. Paitr wasn't so sure. Conquering armies showed discipline and at least some semblance of humanity. Lon-Shan's showed neither. His forces were little more than a huge pack, and packs didn't conquer or rule; they destroyed. He was missing something, something important. Something he needed to know before the fighting started. Thunder rumbled in the distance, and he glanced into the brewing storm. "That's funny." He scowled. "I don't remember hearing anything about rain. Do you, Martin?"

The other man shrugged. "Who can say what our lord has planned. A downpour would go a long way to obscure daylight outside the palace grounds."

Paitr wasn't convinced, peering constantly over his shoulder as he walked. "You might be right. Still, I'd rather be inside when it breaks." More thunder boomed, closer and louder this time. "Come on. We'd better hurry. It wouldn't do for us to present ourselves to Lord Lon-Shan drenched to the skin."

They trotted over another street, cut across the central boulevard, and headed toward the unnaturally dark mass surrounding Lon-Shan's private compound. Paitr glared surreptitiously at Martin. Doubt gnawed at him. He should have kept a closer eye on the man. Martin was more than a rival now; he was a threat. The time had come for Martin to have an accident.

Paitr mulled the possibilities as they reached the darkness surrounding Lon-Shan's estates. Its huge shadow spread out before him, at once sucking and reflecting what was left. He walked into it then headed for the high walls – gated and studded with black pearl and onyx – ringing the looming buildings beyond.

A single pillar stood to the left of the gate, blacker than everything else around it. It was taller too, over one hundred fifty feet, possibly more.

"Odd," Paitr mumbled. "I don't remember that tower."

"No," Martin agreed. "It wasn't there the last time I was in the palace."

Paitr wondered when that was. He hadn't been inside for over fifty years – not since the last Weakening. His gaze scanned the tower, and he stiffened.

"What?" Martin said.

Paitr grimaced. The fool didn't even have enough sense to lower his voice. He lifted a hand and hissed for silence. "I thought I saw something. Up there – near the top of the tower. A large door, maybe two."

"I don't see anything." Martin sounded incredulous, but when he saw Paitr shield himself, he did the same.

"There." Paitr pointed to a spot well over their heads. "Did you see that?" The tower shivered. Realization slammed into him. Horrified, he shrank back. How could he have been so stupid?

Instantly, he released his shield and dropped to one

knee. With any luck, Martin would remain shielded. The insult would cost him his life. His eyes shifted to Martin, but then froze as a great, bat-like wing peeled away from the tower. A second followed, exposing a leathery body with wide shoulders and powerful arms ending in talons. Midnight eyes peered down at them over a short, snarling muzzle.

"How dare you!" Lon-Shan's guardian boomed. "Disciples are not allowed a shield within the gates."

"Forgive us, Lord Streega!" Paitr cried. "We didn't know."

"Every disciple knows! It is the law."

Cold sweat trickled down Paitr's neck, his heart stopped for a moment, and he waited for a blow that didn't come. The seconds stretched on, but he didn't look up. He didn't dare. He should be dead, unless the guardian had something worse in store for him. The thought made him shudder.

"I should have killed you, Brother Norwoska," Streega said. "But your devotion to Lord Lon-Shan has earned his favor. He will overlook this incident."

Paitr put a hand on his chest. He could breathe again.

"Training our army was a difficult task. Many tried, but you are the only one who succeeded. Tonight, our lord rewards you. He will name you first disciple."

Paitr's eyes widened. His body came alive as if jolted. He wanted to laugh, to cheer. "Thank you, Lord Streega." He lowered his head in respect. "I am honored."

"Your gratitude means nothing to me," Streega said, abruptly shifting its attention to Martin. "As for *you*... Lord Lon-Shan is most disappointed in what you've become."

Martin squirmed under Streega's black gaze.

"I hope you enjoyed your last assignment. Delivering

messages to a liege is an important part of an aide's duties."

Martin tensed, but he made no sound.

"Every leader needs a lieutenant. Brother Norwoska is no different. You are to serve him until he's had enough of you. If he is not satisfied with you... then you are mine."

Martin swallowed noisily. "It will be as you say, lord."

Streega's head came down in a rush of wind. It faced Martin, studied him from a few inches away, close enough for Paitr to smell blood on its breath. Poor Martin – he must have forgotten to guard his thoughts.

"You can't keep secrets from me, slave!" Streega growled, grinding Martin's body against the street with its mind. "You will do as you are told. If something unexpected happens to the master's chosen one, you will suffer. Have I made myself clear?"

Martin managed a wooden nod. "Yes, Lord Streega."

Streega continued to stare. After a moment, it pulled back and released its hold. "Lord Lon-Shan is waiting for you. You are free to go."

The pressure that kept Paitr at Streega's feet ended as abruptly as it had come. He stood stiffly and stared at the guardian, hoping for more assurances. Having a would-be assassin as an aide did not make for an ideal situation. When the fighting began, he'd order Martin to carry commands to the front. A necessary assignment, if a dangerous one. Accidents happened in battle. It couldn't be helped.

He bowed to Streega, spun on his heels, and hurried toward a set of heavy doors at the front of the palace. They swung back as he approached, revealing a grand foyer just beyond the threshold. At the far end, a pair of staircases branched out toward the east and the west wings.

Paitr took the stairs to the right, climbing effortlessly. Despite his brush with death, his heart was light. He'd pleased Lon-Shan. The reward his lord promised was within his reach.

Outside, the storm finally broke. The slap of large drops against stone added an eerie rhythm to the click of his boots. He reached the top and followed the corridor to the east wing and the library. Martin struggled to keep up, falling behind and shouting for him to wait.

"Hurry up, Martin," he called, poking his head over the stair rail. "How would it look if I arrived without my servant? I won't have you dishonor me now."

He'd wasted energy worrying about Martin. The man would pay for that. Sweat and hard labor were just the beginning. He smiled at the thought and turned to the windows. This was the most ferocious storm he'd ever seen. Windless, with drops the size of his fist, it had started only a few minutes earlier, and the courtyard below was practically flooded.

Martin staggered up the last few steps and lurched to a stop beside him.

"I don't like it," Paitr said. "Something about the rain feels... unnatural."

Martin snorted but quickly remembered his new station and muttered an apology. Ignoring him, Paitr reached for the library's heavy wooden door. He twisted its gilded handle and pushed his way inside.

Book-lined shelves framed a small path into a large room, rows of sycophantic disciples milling about a big fireplace at the far end. He glimpsed the black flames and smiled. Even the candles along the walls swallowed the light, dark where they should have glowed, like a negative of the natural world.

"Let him through," a voice within the crowd ordered.

Reluctantly, Lon-Shan's disciples parted in a swish of fine silks.

Paitr sneered at them – at their pristine swords and bejeweled clothing. They flaunted treasure as if it could earn what their weakness could not. How would they feel when the night was over? He grinned wickedly, deciding who to keep and who to discard.

The farther he went, the more hostile the mob became. Zealous stares bled with envy. The space between his shoulders prickled as if expecting a knife. His shield was down, but as he'd already learned from Streega, raising it this close to Lon-Shan could be fatal. Fortunately, hurting him in Lon-Shan's presence was probably just as fatal. What happened beyond the estate's walls was another matter. Not that he worried, though. Life here meant being overly cautious.

Eventually, he left the throng behind and came to Lon-Shan. The Lord of the Darkness, Weaver of Shadow, and King of the Night studied him from a high-backed chair of onyx and black diamond. His silvery hair framed a cruel, almost lupine face. He wore a belt of black opals over midnight clothes. The short but lethal daggers hanging about it in battered sheaths spoke of continuous use, as did the strong, weathered hands resting on the pommel of his great staff.

Sweat dappled Paitr's forehead. His last audience with Lon-Shan had been a long time ago. He'd forgotten how he felt in his lord's presence, the aura of power; those dark, almost malevolent eyes.

"Paitr Norwoska," Lon-Shan said in the gravelly voice Paitr remembered. "Come here." An invisible force seized the front of Paitr's shirt, dragged him forward, and threw him to the carpet in front of the throne. "Our long wait is almost over. The world outside beckons. Revenge awaits, my disciples. It is ours for the taking. No longer will the privileged ignore the work you do for them! The time has come to take what you've earned from those who claim it by birthright. Today, the oppressed and disregarded will overthrow our old masters. We will establish a new order, one of true equality and mutual respect."

Cheers erupted throughout the room, momentarily muffling the pounding rain. Paitr sensed an undercurrent of worry below the surface. Some of the disciples realized how poorly they'd prepared. He needed to uncover them before the campaign began – desperate men were dangerous men. He'd put them on the front lines.

Lon-Shan's thoughts blanketed the room, forcing mouths shut, silencing lips. His black eyes fell on Paitr. "Paitr Norwoska. You will lead our pilgrimage. You are my hand, Lon-Shan's first disciple!" Lon-Shan lowered his staff onto Paitr's shoulder. "Rise, Lord Paitr. Rise and face your soldiers."

Paitr wasn't sure if he stood by himself, or if his lord set him on his feet. As he steadied himself, his eyes locked with Lon-Shan's, and in the span of those few short seconds, his triumph crumbled. Outwardly, the Dark Spirit looked the same as he remembered, but something – a light in his eyes – reflected a hidden pain. Paitr's pulse quickened at the sight. How was that even possible? He was mistaken. He had to be.

A full goblet, that's what he needed. Quench his thirst, give him time to think, steady his nerves. The force of Lon-Shan's presence made it impossible to concentrate.

He eased his way back into the crowd, wiping a hand across his forehead. Dry. He'd been sweating. What happened to the sweat? In a daze, he searched for a glass with at least a few drops of wine at the bottom. He found one on a tray at the very end of the library, lifted it, and swirled it around in his hands. The blood-red liquid spun around the inner rim.

The idiot disciples hadn't seen what he had. The strange light in Lon-Shan's eyes – eyes that never glittered, never glinted, eyes that never showed anything but blackness – nagged at him.

Lightning flashed, closer now and followed half a second later by booming thunder. The rain beat down harder than ever, pounding against the windows as though trying to turn the estate's thick walls into rivers of slime. He raised the cup to his lips, empty. Odd. He didn't remember drinking. Another flash.

Something moved outside, briefly visible between the strikes.

The unmistakable figure of a woman appeared and then vanished, her beautiful face turned toward him, savage iron-green eyes glowing in the dark with a promise of violence.

Paitr gasped at the sight and dropped his empty wine glass in astonishment. He staggered backward, his mouth working soundlessly. Lon-Shan turned his dark eyes toward his favored disciple, searching, questioning.

"A woman, my lord!" Paitr shouted, half turning, his arm stiff, his finger pointing. "Outside… a woman in the courtyard."

Flash! Boom!

Lon-Shan's face registered both shock and fear. "It can't be," he muttered, as if seeing something for the first time. "It was all there, why didn't I see it – the storms, the dehydrated air, the punishing rains. Seirin! I know you're out there. Come inside, let me offer a proper welcome."

Silence followed his words. The rains pounded louder.

Another sound accompanied it, a roaring Paitr couldn't quite place. Just in time, he realized what it was, lunged for the windows, and raised a shield in front of them as a wall of water smashed into the Palace.

Lon-Shan thrust his body forward and squawked at the indolent disciples like an angry crow. "Fools! Get on your feet, you cowards! We're under attack!"

14
SPIRIT

The doors to the White Spirit's main hall rolled open to reveal a room of tatami mats and ancient Japanese art. Keiko nudged a foot forward and stopped, intimidated. "I don't think I can go in there."

Yui smiled encouragingly. "Why not? Walk through. What could be easier than that?"

"But. There's a god in there."

"Really?" Yui blinked mockingly, peered about the room, and then pressed her lips to Keiko's ear. "There's one out here too."

Keiko glared at her. "Oh, sure," she sniffed. "It's easy for you. He's your father. I've never met anyone even remotely like him."

"What about Vissyus? You stood up to him. Once you've faced the worst, nothing else should frighten you."

"I didn't exactly stand."

Yui smiled gently. "You know what I mean." She nodded at the doors. "Go on. You will feel better once you're inside."

Keiko doubted it. "Right," she said, half to herself, half to Yui.

Yui laughed easily and motioned Keiko forward, pointing to the stunning assortment of art and sculpture on the far wall. Vases and figurines decorated the various recessed shelves in what Keiko believed was age order – one shelf per era, one style per emperor.

"There you see?" Yui beamed. "I'm sure Masato's collections looked much the same."

Keiko managed a weak nod and slipped into the room beyond. The tightly woven tatami mats had a luxurious feel, and she curled her slippered toes into them as she walked. Amazingly, the tension that had built within her body lessened with each step. Once inside, she lifted her chin and gazed about.

Red-and-yellow silks covered a raised platform in the middle of the chamber. Her eyes found the circular crest emblazoned on the front – a radiant sun rising over the shoulder of Mount Fuji. Without knowing precisely why, she bowed to it. Straightening, she made her way to the very back of the chamber, where a suit of traditional Japanese armor sat in an elevated alcove.

Its supple beauty radiated a force equal to that of the dais in front of it. Instead of a traditional breastplate, tiny overlapping pieces cast in some crimson metal covered the cuirass like dragon scales, rippling as they descended, wavelike, from outward flaring shoulder guards. A matching helmet perched atop the neckpiece, a golden sickle adorning the forehead.

"Your father loved that armor," a rich, cheerful voice said from behind.

Startled, Keiko spun, lost her footing, and would have fallen had the speaker not reached out a hand to steady her.

He stood less than a foot away, tall and lean and wearing a silken kimono dyed as if to match the armor.

His strong Japanese features – high cheekbones and sharp Asian eyes – while kind, reflected both wisdom and power. Keiko swore she'd seen him before. When she tried to recall exactly where, though, her mind grew foggy.

"He stole it from me once," the man said. "I caught him at the gates, 'on his way to Tokyo to stop the emperor from opening Japan to the rest of the world'." He released Keiko's arm and smiled at her. "Your father was the most impulsive disciple I've ever had."

Impulsive? Her father? That wasn't how she remembered him. Unable to speak, Keiko chewed on a lip before offering what she hoped was a disarming smile.

"It was rude of me not to be here when you arrived. I was in my study, attending to something." He gestured to the sliding shoji behind him. "I am Takeshi Akiko, Lord of the White Spirit. Please accept my apologies. I hope my absence has not offended you."

Keiko shook her head. "No." The word sounded shrill in her ears. Mortified, she cleared her throat. "No, of course not. You just startled me, that's all." She fixed Yui with an angry stare. "You could have warned me, you know."

Takeshi laughed and ran a hand over his bald head. "There – you see?" he said proudly. "She may not look much like Masato, but there's no denying the temperament."

Yui gave him a loud, unladylike snort. "It's unseemly of you to gloat, Father, especially when you knew who she was."

"Gloating is every father's right and privilege, Yui-chan. You should know that by now."

Keiko stifled a giggle and let Takeshi lead her to the low table across the room. Soft silken pillows surrounded it on all sides – one for each of them – while an elegant if modern tea service perched at the table's head.

"Please," Takeshi said, motioning for them to sit. "We have much to discuss, and we might as well be comfortable." Yui joined Keiko at the table, and Takeshi waited for them to arrange themselves before lowering himself to the mats. "I hope you will excuse the informality. We do not have time for a proper tea ceremony."

He lifted the tiny kettle and poured a measure – first for Keiko, and then Yui, and then, finally, for himself. Finishing, he returned the teapot to its original spot.

"I am sure you have many questions for me," he said, sitting back. "Given the circumstances, however, I think it's best for you to tell me what happened in Ginza, what you saw, and perhaps even more importantly, what you felt."

The slow heating of her face reminded Keiko of the teapot in front of her. What she felt? She'd been scared out of her wits. Not exactly a proud moment, and certainly not one she wanted to share.

"I've never felt anything like it," she said, choosing her words carefully. Truth was truth, but if she could save a little face, she'd do it. "I wanted to run as far away as I could."

Takeshi lifted a peremptory finger. "But you didn't run, Yamanaka-san, did you? Not then and not when Fiyorok appeared. Any number of Kami would have, you know. I think you underestimate yourself."

"You seem very well informed," Keiko said, tartly. "Why don't you ask your daughter? She knows more about this than I do."

Face unreadable, Yui raised her cup and sipped, ignoring both her father and Keiko.

"You were the one who managed to sneak through the Boundary," Takeshi reminded her. "You found a way in, where Yui did not."

Pride bubbled up from somewhere deep inside Keiko. A sense of loss came with it. She did what her father asked her to do – rather quickly, looking back on it. But where did that leave her? What was she supposed to do now? She stared at Takeshi, half afraid to ask the obvious question. Unfortunately, staying quiet wouldn't give her any answers. She had to ask. Now. Or not at all.

"Why me? Why did it have to be me?"

"Why indeed?" A mischievous smile split Takeshi's lips. "Yui and I are very close to these events; too close, perhaps. Sometimes, a fresh perspective can see what a complacent one cannot."

"The subway," Yui said miserably. She set her cup down and lowered her eyes. "I never noticed the breeze before, and I didn't believe you when you told me."

"Yes," Takeshi nodded. "Listen to Yui, Keiko. I'm sure you would consider her to be a highly intelligent and observant young woman."

"It's hard to say." Keiko's words came out slowly. "We don't know each other that well."

Takeshi slapped his hands on his knees. "Then you'll just have to accept her father's word. Yui is extremely perceptive."

Yui blushed at the compliment and another jealous wave washed over Keiko. She missed making her father proud; she missed everything about him.

"If someone as quick and attentive as Yui can miss something so obvious, then perhaps – when it comes to the Boundary and the Weakening – I might miss something for much the same reason."

Keiko found that hard to believe. Everything about

the room spoke of meticulous care, and Yui's hints and comments about her father were completely in line with what she saw. Even the tea ceremony, something Takeshi said was informal, was perfection, something Keiko's own father never reached. More likely, he needed information only she could give, information Masato Yamanaka left in her head. She sighed nervously. "All right, Mr Takeshi. How do we start?"

"I need to review your memories. It's the only way. Will you allow it?"

Keiko shifted. "I'm not sure my memories are all there. They've been muddied since I stepped into the Boundary. Yui thinks my father tampered with them. Coming here seems to be bringing them back, but…" She fanned her hands helplessly.

Takeshi snorted. "I should have expected this. Your father possessed a unique talent, one that made hiding him – and you – easier." He lowered his cup to the table and stared into her face. Keiko felt his mind brush hers, vast, powerful, and wise. "My Searching can wait, I think. First, you need to learn about your family and how they fit into all of this."

Beside her, Yui tensed. This was important to her too. Her feelings for Masato Yamanaka were obvious.

"Your father served me during Emperor Meiji's reign. From 1872 until the Meiji Restoration in 1888. He presided over the most radical change in Japan's long history, and when he finished his task, I needed to remove him from power so the Japanese people could rule themselves, modernize, and prepare for this century's final Weakening. Unfortunately, the Emperor was against it. Masato was both his advisor and his friend. Much like the guardians are to us."

1872. Yui mentioned daimyos and samurai. Their time

ended with Emperor Meiji. Her father was a part of that? More than a part, if Takeshi was telling the truth. Keiko closed her eyes and rubbed them. Their Masato was so different from the one she knew – younger, certainly, but also fierce and impossibly strong. Strong enough to alter her memories, strong enough to live for more than a century.

"Yui said a group of daimyos killed him." Keiko's voice was small and sad. "But that's not what happened, is it?"

"No, Yamanaka-san. The emperor knew I called Masato back to the White Spirit, so he took the entire Yamanaka family hostage and refused to let them go. Meiji thought he could force Masato to choose between me, his emperor, and his family. He was wrong."

The room around Keiko went cold. She liked Takeshi. What if he did something horrible? Could she accept it? She had to. It was the only way to learn what happened.

"What did you do?" she asked.

"I sent a band of renegade daimyos into the palace to stage a coup." Takeshi said it as easily as if discussing his day. "Masato held them off while the Imperial Guard spirited the emperor and his family to safety. The fighting was short-lived, however, and the daimyos retreated, though not before setting fire to the palace. According to the Guard, Masato and all his family perished in the blaze." His tone changed then, and a knowing glint sparkled in his chestnut-colored eyes. "No one suspected him of setting the fire himself, or of leaving Japan for America."

"How could they," Yui said, half standing. "Masato was under Aeryk's protection. The Lord of Air made sure no one saw him leave – not an easy feat when a giant thunderbird carried him from Kyoto to San Francisco, in the middle of the night."

Takeshi's eyes drilled into Yui. So much power, all of it fixed on her. She withered a little but didn't back down. "I am trying to save the world." His voice was hard. "Masato understood that. He accepted his role without question. A continued Yamanaka presence in Japan meant civil war. I need a unified Japan when Vissyus returns. It's the only way to protect its people. No one could know what happened, not if the young government was to survive."

"You could have told *me*!" Yui's eyes burned like sunfire, her voice low and sizzling.

Takeshi's face hardened to match his voice. Granite looked softer by comparison. "Our samurai would have known! Your grief, more than any other, *had* to be genuine. Anything less and suspicions would grow. Many believed Masato would become your guardian. They knew it was impossible, but that didn't stop them from hoping. No human spirit has joined those ranks – none was strong enough, not even Masato. Our samurai weren't dissuaded, though. They all thought he was invincible. Your reaction confirmed that he was not."

Yui's cheeks turned scarlet. She looked ready to leap across the table. "You and Aeryk meet regularly at this castle; I've attended a lot of those meetings myself. I can't believe neither one of you told me he was still alive. Worse, you arranged a wedding for him. How could you do that to us?"

"Masato was no longer a part of the castle," Takeshi said patiently. "He asked me to give him a normal life, one that would match his increasingly mortal body."

Keiko groaned aloud. She massaged her temples to ease the ache blooming behind her eyes. "Can we just start at the beginning? Or at least as close to it as I need to know?"

Takeshi dipped his head in sympathy. "All right then," he said, sitting back and folding his arms. "The beginning it is."

15
ANSWERS

Takeshi's thoughts caressed Keiko's consciousness like a warm towel against cold skin. *Keiko?* he said into her head. *I need to see into your dormant mind and open the part where you store your experiences, the whole of your life. Can you take me there?*

I don't understand, Keiko thought, drifting peacefully in what felt like sleep. *How am I supposed to learn something I don't know from my own memories?*

You will see, Takeshi promised. *The memories, Keiko. If you please.*

Keiko nodded woodenly. *Yes, this way.* A pair of hands – her hands – appeared. Without thinking how they came to be there, she grasped the elegantly cast doorknobs in front of them and threw open a set of glass doors. She smiled over her shoulder and motioned Takeshi's voice to follow.

"Here." She spun around and pointed at one of the tall bookcases along the walls and stepped back, her slippered feet swishing on a tiled floor the color of rich cinnamon.

The room itself was a wide square, apparently ceiling-less, with high white marble walls. Her mind waking, she looked about in wonder, not so much at the graceful chair rails and baroque friezes, but at the seemingly infinite books. If these were her memories, the room should have been smaller, the shelves fewer. This wasn't right. Labels clearly delineated each row, and the years stretched back to the first part of the twentieth century.

Takeshi followed a step behind, tall, confident, and shining with power. He made his way to the big oaken table in the center of the room, drew back one of the matching wooden chairs and gestured for her to sit. Keiko ignored the seat and remained where she was, her mind reeling.

"I'll only be a minute," Takeshi told her. He disappeared between the shelves and returned with a pair of thin books. Sitting, he pushed one toward her and gestured for her to open it. "The truth lies in there." he said, pointing. "You need to open it. This is your mind, Yamanaka-san. I can't do it for you."

Keiko doubted that. More likely, he wanted her to face the contents on her own. Her sub-conscious didn't recognize the books, which meant they were new or deeply buried, neither of which made her want to open them. Palms sweaty, she placed a trembling hand on the closer of the two and threw its cover back.

Instantly, soft blue light climbed from the pages, lifting and swirling like a miniature shield before drifting to the floor. There, the blue glow expanded rapidly, and when it went out, the unmistakable – if young – figure of Masato Yamanaka, her father, dressed in the familiar robes and sash of the White Spirit, stood in its place. His head was shaved, like the monks in the castle, and his dark, piercing eyes had a startled, embarrassed cast to them.

Torn between joy and anger, Keiko didn't know whether to hug or hit him. "Pop? Oh no. No, no, no." She stepped forward. "This isn't happening."

"I assure you it is," Takeshi said from behind.

Masato's eyes widened, and he dropped to one knee. "My lord! I can explain. Keiko has the spark just as you suspected. I nurtured it as best I could but..." His gaze drifted miserably to the floor. "I didn't know what else to do. This isn't the sort of burden a father wants for his children."

"Sometimes we don't have a choice, Masato-san. You should have told me, though. It would have saved us a great deal of trouble."

Keiko had the distinct impression Takeshi knew already – which made her the last to find out. Ignoring him, she stormed past the table and chairs. The room shrank, whole swathes of tile tumbling away, the remainders resealing until Keiko stood toe to toe with her father.

"You should have told *me*!" Tears formed behind her eyes, but she refused to let them fall. "How could you? Your own daughter. You let me think you were gone." A few minutes earlier, she heard Yui say much the same thing. The anger, the pain – she understood them now.

"I am gone." Masato's tone was apologetic yet firm. "This isn't what you think."

"I'm afraid it's exactly what she thinks," Takeshi interrupted. "You were centuries older than any normal man when you left my castle. Away from my power, your body aged very slowly. A body dies, but a soul that's served me as you have endures. You understood that."

Ignoring Takeshi, Keiko strode up to her father and jabbed a finger into his chest. "You lied to me. About everything." She spun away, and the room she built in her head buckled, splitting down the middle, the floors and walls elongating, the distance between them increasing. Arms crossed, she tossed her head and refused to look him in the eye.

He inhaled, and his voice softened. "You are all that's left of the life I was supposed to have." He turned back to Takeshi and bowed formally. "I apologize, my lord, as much for keeping this from you as for Keiko's outburst."

"Daughters," Takeshi shrugged. "They are a constant challenge – so unpredictable. I have one myself, you know."

Masato straightened. He glanced at Keiko and cleared his throat. "No matter how much they grow, you never stop worrying about them."

"I've learned it's rude to talk about someone like she's not there," Keiko said, turning to face them. "Mother taught me that."

Takeshi laughed and pointed at her. "There, you see? Predictably unpredictable."

Keiko uncrossed her arms and threw them into the air. "I hope you're pleased with yourself." She paced angrily about the room. "Both of you."

"After what we did to Vissyus?" Takeshi said. "We don't have the right. I see nothing wrong with celebrating our victories, however. The large and the small."

He turned to Masato and nodded. Behind him, a thin book – no more than a sheaf of folded paper – wafted from the shelves. It drifted easily through the air, unfolding as it fell to the tiled floors between them. Pale light bloomed between its pages, as soft as the whispered voice that accompanied it.

Go to Japan in my place, it said. *Find the Gate. Your camera will show you the way*.

Masato's face reddened. "You found my jisei in her memories."

"I didn't need to. I knew the moment Keiko arrived in Japan. The Boundary was already looking for a messenger to warn us of the Weakening." He chuckled lightly. "It knew not to call Yui, and for that we should be thankful. I am wise enough to stay away from Vissyus, but Yui? She'd see an opening into his prison as an opportunity. Yui would want to attack him."

"Like the subway," Keiko breathed. She stopped pacing and shivered at the memory. The room around her darkened, and a deep roaring shook the walls. "The dragon, Fiyorok – I had to convince her to let it go. If I wasn't there, I'm sure she would have followed it."

"She absolutely would have," Takeshi said. "The same is true for the Boundary. Your presence kept Yui from reaching Vissyus. She'd never leave you alone, and she wouldn't take you with her. Your father forced her to choose between attacking Vissyus and saving you, knowing the Boundary would close as soon as you left it. He saved us, Keiko. This world, you, and Yui most of all."

Masato lowered his eyes and lapsed into elegant silence.

"What if Yui's right?" Keiko said. She rounded on Takeshi, fists raised. "Vissyus can't leave his prison. He's cornered. Finish him. If Yui's not strong enough, then what about you? You could do it before he breaks out."

"If only we had that luxury." Takeshi drew a deep breath. "No Kami goes near Vissyus's section of the Boundary, not Yui, not me, not anyone. You were the first to see him since the Boundary formed. Where your instincts told you to run, ours would have urged us to fight."

"And that's the only reason you kept him isolated?"

"Certainly not. Vissyus is dangerous and unpredictable. If we approached him and he felt us, if something went wrong..." He shook his head. "Against such power, a direct attack is as useless as it is foolhardy. We can't fight him. We never could, not even here. He's more powerful than any of us. That's why I created the Boundary – to hold him until we found a way to defeat him."

"Destroy the Boundary, then. He won't feel that coming. He'd never get a shield up in time." A part of Keiko's mind screamed at her. She was talking like them. The bookshelves along the walls morphed. They looked alarmingly like prison bars.

"I'm afraid I can't do that," Takeshi said. "The Boundary and the universe are interconnected now. Neither can survive without the other."

Keiko frowned, took a step toward him, then stopped. The air grew cold, ice slicked the tiles at her feet. "Mr Takeshi? What did you do?"

A tired smile cracked Takeshi's lips. "I discovered a way to weave a spirit into the fabric of time and space. When I finished, my guardian, Gaiyern, Spirit of Life, became the Boundary."

"Your guardian." Keiko remembered the rush of energy she felt when Yui led her out of the alley in Tokyo. She'd felt it again when they entered the passage on their way to the castle. Alive, she thought. It's alive. That's why he won't destroy it. "What then?" She leaned forward intently. Takeshi had taken their best option away from them. She should have known it wouldn't be easy. "How do we beat him?"

Eyes filled with boundless wisdom stared back at her. She found little comfort in them.

"My power begins and ends at the Boundary," Takeshi said. "Inside his prison, Vissyus's will is supreme. We could blast the universe to pieces around him, and he'd still survive. Outside, we have a chance. For this to work, we must free Vissyus and neutralize his shield."

Keiko stiffened. "You'll kill millions of people!" She gestured as if at the outside world.

Memories of fire overwhelmed her senses. She felt its heat, smelled the acrid smoke. Distant screams echoed beyond the walls. Somehow, she knew she'd only seen a fraction of what Vissyus could do. Her heart pounded harder, her throat so tight she could barely speak.

"You can't let him do it, Pop. Tell him." She looked at her father for help, but Masato was lost in his own personal misery.

"How long have you known?" he said without looking up.

Keiko's brow climbed. He was talking about this *now*?

"I am Lord of Spirit, Yamanaka-san," Takeshi said gently. "You cannot hide from me."

"So my role is over, then." Masato looked stricken, defeated. "You won't bring me back."

Bring him back? Takeshi could do that? Hope fluttered in Keiko's chest. Having her father returned to her was a dream come true.

"The time's not right," Takeshi said, at once confirming and dashing her hopes. "A Kami must summon you, and I won't allow that while Vissyus threatens us. Yui's the only one without a guardian, and love clouds her judgment – just as it did Seirin's all those years ago."

Masato's jisei rushed through Keiko's head. He wanted her to watch over Yui until she summoned him to be her guardian. That wouldn't happen now, not according to Takeshi. Masato Yamanaka wasn't coming back.

"I can do it," Keiko said, stepping forward. "*All* of it."

She stared into her father's face, proud and unafraid. An idea took root deep in her heart, and to her surprise, it refused to wither. Yui listened to her, took her advice.

Why not become her guardian? Takeshi said it was impossible for a human spirit, but she didn't believe it – not after the way he looked at her in his study.

Masato's face darkened. "No! You're not ready for this."

"Who else is there? Yui listens to me!"

"She listens to me too," Masato snapped.

"That was a long time ago. Keiko is Yui's best chance, maybe her only one. Yui knows how to fight; she needs someone to tell her how not to. Would you deny her that?"

"No," Masato admitted. "No, of course not."

Takeshi clapped a hand on Masato's shoulder. "Don't worry, Yamanaka-san. Your time will come. Until then, I release you from all of your oaths – all of them, Yamanaka-san – except the one you swore to me. Remember *that* the next time the White Spirit summons you."

A look of wonder crossed Masato's face. "Thank you, Ahk-Kiko-sama." He bowed, and then – once upright again – walked over to Keiko and wrapped his arms around her.

"Do you plan on telling me what that was about?" Keiko said into his chest. His embrace – so familiar, so comforting – brought fresh tears. She'd missed it so much.

Instead of answering, he leaned in closer and dropped his voice to a whisper. "I know what you're planning, Keiko-chan, and I'll do whatever I can to help you. Just remember, a guardian's greatest strength is its wisdom, not its power. Yours may Awaken in time, and it may not. Try not to worry about it. Concentrate on keeping Yui from harm instead. The rest will take care of itself." He pulled back and touched a finger to her forehead as his body shimmered. "I'll be here until you no longer need me."

"I'll remember," Keiko promised, scrubbing her tears away.

Keiko hugged herself as Masato's body dissolved. Once he was gone, Takeshi held his hand out to her. She took it and let him lead her from the room, only to stumble into him as he came to an abrupt stop. "What is it?" she whispered, suddenly alert.

"We are no longer in your mind, Yamanaka-san," Takeshi said. "Something is happening. The Boundary speaks. Be silent and listen."

Keiko yelped as the marble floor tumbled away to leave her hovering several thousand feet above a range of rounded, alpine mountains. "Where are we?"

"Our bodies are still in the White Spirit," Takeshi said. "But our minds float above the Carpathian Mountains." He waved an alarmingly spectral hand over the forested landscape.

Romania. "But why?" Keiko wrapped her arms around her body to suppress a shiver. Her father's embrace seemed like a distant memory. "What are we doing here?"

Takeshi's face was grim. "A friend needs us. The Boundary brought us here to help."

Keiko shook her head wildly. "We can't help anyone like this! We're… we're like ghosts."

"We are not ghosts, as you will soon see." Takeshi's voice had lost all of its wry humor and now boomed like thunder. "Your father showed you what a disembodied spirit can do, and I am much stronger than he."

A flash of movement caught Keiko's eye, and she slid her gaze reluctantly toward it. She reached for Takeshi with her free hand only to remember they didn't have physical form. An immense wake cut across the surface of a distant sea, waves fluming ahead of some huge object before easing. Foreboding filled her soul. Whatever was out there had submerged, but Keiko still felt it drawing closer.

"Akuan," Takeshi said. "It is Akuan."

16
FIDELITY

Kirak's gaze bored into Lon-Shan's compound. How long had Seirin been down there? Minutes? Hours? She'd breached shield and wall easily enough, but Kirak expected as much. Lon-Shan felt safe here, and he'd kept his defenses down. That would change. Already, his power filled the dark shield overhead, hardening the outer layers. Kirak worried about the barrier catching Seirin, but she punched through just as the shield solidified, a streak of green against the blackened sky.

Kirak stifled a relieved sigh. "Did he see you?" the serpent asked as she slowed to a halt a few feet away.

"Oh, yes, my guardian. He saw me. I made sure he did." Seirin's deep, musical voice was throaty and wild, her expression a study in cold fury. The sunfire tresses framing her face made her look like an avenging angel, though instead of billowing robes, she wore an open-necked blouse of hunter green over matching leggings held in place with a slender platinum belt.

"You're going to die, Lon-Shan." She stared grimly at the thunderheads. "Those who trusted you will have justice."

They'd left the Boundary the day following Aeryk's arrival. After a tearful goodbye, Seirin led Kirak from the Air Lord, across a wide, untamed ocean, and into what Aeryk called the Carpathian Mountains. Lon-Shan's Gate lay hidden somewhere inside, on a peak, Aeryk said, where its Keystone caught and used sunlight to secure the Dark Spirit's Boundary.

Seirin found the stone at the end of a highland trail half hidden in the tangled undergrowth – a spherical orb of polished gold nestled within a stone basin. A quick thought opened the marker; a quicker one closed it again once they were inside.

"I am not convinced I agree with this course of action, mistress." Kirak flew up to Seirin. "Forgive me for repeating myself, but alerting the Shadow Lord of our presence seems most rash."

"We've been over this," Seirin said impatiently. "Lon-Shan won't come out. He doesn't like confrontation." Her mouth twisted. "That's what his generals are for."

"You're not serious!" Lord Aeryk hinted at Lon-Shan's depravity, but Kirak hadn't expected anything like this.

"It buys him the time he needs to run."

Kirak swung its head back to the walled mansion and exhaled sadly. An odd rippling near the foundations drew its attention, and it eased a Searching toward the disturbance. Lon-Shan's shield appeared in its mind – a large black dome, devoid of reflection, and, apart from the distortion, perfectly smooth. As Kirak watched, a rectangular gash opened in the obsidian wall. Garishly clad men poured out, swarming the square, dark spheres forming around their bodies.

The weakest quickly lost control and exploded. Shields winked out, and blood rained from the sky. One flamboyantly dressed man underestimated the diameter needed to encase his whole body and subsequently severed his head from his neck. Those who survived cackled at those who didn't.

Repulsed, Kirak turned back to Seirin. "How will you keep them away from us?" It noted how the mob quivered and shifted, the whole lost without an obvious target. "They don't look like much of a threat, but under the circumstances, we don't need the distraction."

Seirin smiled gravely and lifted a hand over her head. Water poured from the clouds, pooling midway between them, stretching and thinning until Kirak found itself staring at a translucent replica of its mistress. Refracted light filled the form with color, yellow hair flowing over hunter green clothing.

"A perfect little copy," she said after a careful examination. "A false Seirin for a false friend."

As though working a puppet, she sent the decoy toward the outskirts of the city. Once there, it turned and lifted its hands. Jagged bolts flew from them, sizzling light that careened off walls and statues before falling harmlessly into the middle of the gathering battalion.

"There she is!" a squat, pinched-featured man shouted.

The mob's attention shifted, and a ringing chorus erupted throughout the city. As one, Lon-Shan's followers lifted from the ground in a mass of shield, cloth, and chaos. Two men collided and fell back to the stones. The rest gathered into a messy formation that sprang off after Seirin's double.

"That should keep them busy." Seirin slipped into the thunderheads. "Let's go."

Kirak followed her into the clouds and widened its Searching. Thus far, nothing stirred in the city – not now, and not after Seirin unleashed her storms. The

Shadow Lord's followers weren't likely to withstand the huge, spherical rain; their feeble shields weren't strong enough. Nor would they find much shelter if they were fortunate enough to land. The deluge turned puddles to lakes that quickly overflowed and fed slime-filled streets. Lavish estates became sunken ruins, buildings collapsed, and every now and again, a bloated body surfaced only to wash away with the rest of the refuse.

Lon-Shan's pulled his shield closer to the compound, Seirin called. *Streega must be out already.*

Kirak blasted a Searching over a wide area, but apart from the swiftly running water, little moved beneath the powerful rains. The men that vacated the shield were gone, the square submerged. In the southeast, a huge bat-like shape soared over the city, wings spread despite the black globe surrounding it.

I have the guardian, Kirak reported. *Near the corner of the estates and climbing.*

That's closer than I expected, Seirin muttered. *And in the way. I'll need to adjust my approach. Can you keep Streega away until I'm inside?*

It will be down long before you reach the shield. Kirak lowered its head and set an intercept course.

Just be careful. Streega escaped the last battle. A guardian that can survive Fiyorok's fires is one we need to watch. She paused. *We should weaken our Bond for this; we don't want to end up like Botua.*

Kirak ground its jaws together, expecting the request but disapproving all the same. Seirin had worked feverishly, almost obsessively, since their imprisonment to perfect a way to insulate their shared minds from the guardian. Botua's death still haunted her; she saw what could happen to a spirit when its guardian died.

Kirak? Seirin called. *Are you there? Did you hear*

me? Streega plowed through the air beneath them, accelerating. Coming in fast. It had cleared the tallest buildings and wrapped its wings around its body like a grotesque obsidian cannonball.

Yes, mistress. I heard you. They'd practiced this over and over again, but the sensation, while not uncomfortable, always left Kirak feeling empty. Weakened. This time was no different. A hole opened in Kirak's spirit as soon as their shared Bond dissipated, a gash, a wound that wouldn't heal until Seirin refashioned the link. Kirak turned and tried to put her out of its mind.

Streega made that easier. Lon-Shan's guardian cut through the clouds ahead and closed on Seirin. Before it reached her, Kirak ignited the bioluminescent stripes along its body and focused on the huge bat shape. A thought mixed the turquoise light of Kirak's body with the blue of its shield. Rain carried both in a display of refracted brilliance. Power thrummed through Kirak's scales, building like a blocked river. The first glowing beam fired from its left side, another flying from its right. Together they cut through the gloom in dazzling streaks that pounded against Streega's shield. Ragged holes opened along the outer coating, and before Streega could repair the damage, Kirak fired again. The second strike breached the black sphere. The third cut across hide. Smoke coiled from a wound at the nape of Streega's neck. More sprouted from the tight muscles along its back.

What remained of Streega's shield crumbled before the assault. One great wing came loose with a sickening snap. It bent at an odd angle, giving it the look of a defeated flag. A final barrage shredded the other wing before tearing it free. Endless red drops oozed from the tattered membrane to mingle with the rain as Streega fell into the flooded streets below.

Streega's down, mistress. Kirak reported. *You have a clear path to Lon-Shan.*

You wounded it? Seirin asked dubiously. *I haven't noticed any change in Lon-Shan's shield. Something's not right, Kirak. You need to be careful.*

Does he know what we've done with our Bond? It didn't seem possible and yet… Quickly, Kirak sent a Searching across the city. Jagged, toothlike tops fought to keep upright through drenching rains. Several collapsed when a rogue wave washed over them. Others simply surrendered to the current. Only Lon-Shan's mansion, some fifty or so miles toward the city center, remained untouched. Exactly as Seirin reported, the Shadow Lord's black-coated shield protected him from the worst of the flooding.

I don't think so. Streega's probably faking the injuries to lure you in. Her voice faded. *It can't reach me in time, so it'll try to kill you and hope that disables me.*

Kirak grunted, closed the connection, and refocused its attention on the floodwaters. Eddies swirled about the ruins, the strongest of which centered at the confluence of several broad streets. Smaller, less severe backflows appeared on the downstream side of ruined towers or above undercut objects. None gave Streega's position away. Kirak ground its jaws, fighting to remember where the guardian went down. Was it near the wide central square or closer to the giant statue of Lon-Shan that stood – headless – beside what looked like the top of a long suspension bridge? Both lay beneath several hundred feet of running water, water that could have carried Streega anywhere.

The square looked promising, except for its lack of cover. Streega couldn't hide there. A main thoroughfare seemed more likely, and the one cutting through the heart of the city was an ideal place for an ambush. Any one of its connecting streets could become traps, canyons with one entrance and one exit.

Kirak nodded and dropped at a steep angle, hitting the surface with a great, booming splash. Turgid water and clouds of stirred silt dropped visibility to a few murky feet, and Kirak switched to a Searching for both reconnaissance and navigation. The image of a ruined statue flashed by, a granite storefront, faceless buildings, lifeless bodies all flowing toward a gap downstream. The current was strong enough to carry Kirak into the intersection, and the guardian tilted the long fins of its upper torso to complete the turn. As it rounded the corner, it exhaled a stream of bubbles. There, a dozen or so figures floated above the pavement, spears piercing each chest, the hafts fastened to the iron chains anchoring them to the pavement. Some looked like the soldiers that followed Seirin's decoy into the clouds. The rest appeared to be servants. An odd shadowy haze swirled around them, one Kirak recognized as an explosive trigger.

Cursing, Kirak pulled its thoughts back and lunged for the safety of a side street. Mines! The men were mines. Turning men into killers was bad enough, but this? Distance. Cover. Kirak needed both. Veering left, it swam for the closest crossing street and braced itself. The detonation came as it rounded a sheltering corner, sound and pressure assaulting its ears, blast waves throwing its body into a tall clock tower.

Stunned, dizzy, and disoriented, Kirak momentarily lost control of its shield. The guardian couldn't focus, not visually and not with a Searching. Rubble assaulted its shield from multiple directions, a few pieces lancing through like white-hot pokers. Desperately, Kirak fought to repair its shield before another wave came. The first attempt brought a soft blue glow that sputtered and went out. The second failed just as quickly, and as it threw its thoughts into a third, Streega leaped from a smashed turret high overhead and slammed onto its back.

A blow landed below Kirak's skull, the next glanced to the right. Each rhythmic plunge tore through Kirak's skin, each brought agony. What little concentration Kirak had left died. It couldn't think, couldn't bring its power to bear. Without light, without a shield, it was worse than helpless. Kirak needed something unrelated to guardian power. But what? Its Searching landed on a network of crisscrossing bridges spanning the street ahead. Would they do? Maybe – given enough force.

"Give up, Kirak," Streega hissed, obviously noting Kirak's increasing speed. "Your mistress is finished. Lord Lon-Shan won't let her to survive – not after what she did to Vissyus."

"Vissyus?" Kirak gaped. "This is about Vissyus?"

"Of course it is. Seirin knew Vissyus would do anything for her. She manipulated him into helping her and it cost him his mind."

"You're crazy. She didn't manipulate anyone. Vissyus wanted to prove his theories as much as he wanted to help her."

Streega's mouth came down beside Kirak's head. "Is that what Seirin tells herself? We all know she used his feelings for her to get what she wanted?"

"Seirin and Vissyus are friends, nothing more. She's with Aeryk; Vissyus was the one who brought them together, in case you've forgotten." The bridges were closer now. If Kirak could just keep Streega distracted a little longer… "I think your lord's the one with the problem; Vissyus's madness left Lon-Shan heartbroken, and he's looking for someone to blame. He can't see the incident for what it was: an accident."

Enraged, Streega reared up and, bellowing in anger, plunged its muzzle into Kirak's aquamarine scales. Black spots threatened Kirak's vision, pain throbbing in five distinct spots along its back, two by the tail, two in the torso and one in the shoulder – hands, feet, and teeth. The water felt viscous, more tar than oil, the bridges unreachable.

Weak, but determined, Seirin's guardian thrust its tail, halving the distance to the bridges first once and then again. A slender arc flew by, too delicate for Kirak to use. Just to the west, a service road cut over what was once a low river. Thick support beams buttressed heavy stonework, strong and secure and meant to hold a great weight. Kirak dove for them. This deep, water pressure intensified with every foot.

Kirak compensated, but Streega, unshielded and not used to the depths, began to flag. Encouraged, Kirak tapped the last of its energy and raced for the bridge. Its head grazed the roof, and before it could prepare itself, a violent, nearly paralytic pain erupted across its back. Nausea brought bile up from its stomach, and it fought to remain conscious.

The lurching world didn't help, nor did the failing light. Shieldless and severely injured, Kirak's resistance faltered. Lon-Shan appeared in its head, his face a mask of rage and fear and hatred. His dark power seized Kirak's spirit, poisoning it with thoughts of defeat, of Seirin's death, and the severing of her Guardian Bond.

Kirak sensed the physical strike forming behind the psychological one. Instead of the dark missiles it expected, though, dull light filtered down from above, dispersing Lon-Shan's power. Kirak looked up. The bridge soared behind, the darkness receding.

Quickly, Kirak doubled back, this time over the bridge, and fired a Searching to reacquire Streega. The mined intersection was farther upstream than Kirak expected, ten to twenty blocks distant. Streega floated somewhere between it and the bridge.

Gashes riddled its black skin, and its freely flowing blood stained the water. Only the steady stream of bubbles escaping its mouth and nose said it still lived.

Seirin's warning sounded in Kirak's head, the need for care, the possibility of deception. Only this didn't look like a trap. A Searching would say for sure, and Kirak floated one into Streega. It crossed the distance, breached the tattered shield. Life beat within the wounded guardian, but a great emptiness sat where the Bond should have been.

"Lon-Shan," Kirak murmured. "What have you done?"

Images of Streega's grotesque mines flashed through its head. *No! Lon-Shan, you didn't, you couldn't.*

But Lon-Shan had been on the plains with Botua; he knew what losing a guardian meant to a Kami. He'd seen it up close, possibly even orchestrated it. Now, faced with his own guardian's death, he broke the Bond before it hurt him.

Immediately, Kirak whirled about and drove hard for the surface. Fifty feet below, the water around Streega quivered. A slow spin formed and quickly intensified into a gravitational vortex. It swallowed everything within reach, crushing matter near its base and sucking the remains into a lightless core.

Climbing away was more difficult than Kirak imagined. The big serpent gained ground grudgingly, one inch, and then another, clawing its way upward, willing its muscles to move.

The water above warmed. Shafts of light pierced the floods, and Kirak knew it was close to the surface. Nothing else moved away from the whirlpool, nothing else fought its way to the skies and freedom. Alone, Kirak ascended, a creature of the sea yearning for Heaven. Shield alight, it crested the waves. Safe – safe for now and away from the imploding whirlpool.

Kirak sighed sadly. Streega deserved better than this.

A muffled explosion tore through the city shortly thereafter. Water muted it, but it still seemed to batter Kirak's senses. Exhaling heavily, Kirak stole one last look at the epicenter and made a respectful bow.

"Farewell, Streega."

17
RETRIBUTION

Seirin raced through thick clouds and blinding downpours. Cold fury drove her on, the emotion strong enough to effect the Boundary's temperature. Sleet mixed with the rain, the pellets growing, hardening. Several hit the city with the force of falling meteors. Towers crumbled and large craters appeared in the ground only to have the floods swallow them.

Seirin swore at her lack of control and quickly fed warmth back into the clouds. Kirak was below – in the water – and she didn't want her guardian to fight through ice or worry the liquid might freeze solid. She had her own conflict ahead; she couldn't afford the distraction. The sooner she brought Lon-Shan to justice, the sooner this ended. For all of them.

Lon-Shan's sprawling complex was less than ten miles away. Ten miles from justice, minutes from death. This close, the estates looked like a gigantic octopus whose dark arms grasped greedily into the city streets. The middle bulged above the rest, covering several blocks like an ugly welt. Aeryk had warned her about it, though he offered few details. Finally, she understood why. No one adequately described a nightmare. It wasn't possible.

Thinking of Aeryk brought a warm blush to her cheeks, and for a second he seemed to be with her. His breath brought the thermal currents that fueled her storms, his arms the gales embracing her. Maybe, if she inhaled deeply enough, she could draw his presence into her body. Their time apart had been so long, their reunion too short. She wanted him with her, but she knew he was safer outside. Lon-Shan had wormed his way into Aeryk's spirit once already. They couldn't risk it happening again. Fortunately, her emotional walls were stronger than his. Not that she'd ever say so, but her power was more damaging. More deadly.

Lon-Shan's devastated city proved what she could do. Only the lord remained, and that was temporary. Soon, he'd join the soldiers whose souls he twisted. Their fate was as much his fault as Botua's had been. He would pay. This would stop. Here! Now! She summoned a new line of storms into the city. Lightning seethed through them, their surfaces roiling like typhoon-tossed seas. The flashes would weaken Lon-Shan's shadows, and the rain, withheld and straining within the boiling clouds, would eat away at his shield like acid.

The Shadow Spirit's defenses quivered under the onslaught, and Seirin quickly fashioned her shield into a long, thin pike. Angling down, she pierced the darkness with the ease of a needle through fabric. Inside, several buildings spread out before her, wide rectangular slabs clustered into a geometric compound of ebon marble.

The library dominated the east wing, and she landed in the same open square as before. She smiled at the tall, severe walls, three of stone, the fourth fronting a window of leaded glass that spanned the entire length. Without a shield to protect them, they were easily breached. She gazed at the stone gargoyles perched menacingly on buttresses and laughed coldly. What good were they? What use? Not even Streega could stop her; the guardian hadn't even slowed her.

A faint flickering pulled her eyes down. She remembered how Lon-Shan inverted light and shadow, recalling the black fire and the dark lamps she'd seen earlier. He'd never waste so much energy on an empty room, not with a battle raging within his walls. He was still there, right where she left him.

She frowned at that. Why did he stay? Was it arrogance or fear? He had to know it was over. Maybe he didn't understand what she'd planned. Maybe it didn't occur to him. In the end, she realized she didn't care; she simply seized the water about her feet, morphed it into an array of deadly projectiles, and hurled them at the library's wall. She followed a heartbeat behind, careful not to outpace them. It wasn't easy. Fury boiled her blood; she'd never been so angry. Her rage should have frightened her. Even at his most destructive, Vissyus retained a childlike innocence. He neither hunted nor purposefully killed. Not like she did now.

Ten feet from the ground, she extended her arms. At twenty, she called her power. A nimbus of gray tinged with green bloomed around wrists aimed at the window. The light raced to her hands, and she let it fly, twisting and thickening her power with a thought. By the time the whole slammed into the palace, her attack became a living maelstrom.

Windows cracked and shattered. Huge glass shards, some several feet from tip to tip, flew into the library beyond, where they came to a quivering halt. Two of Lon-Shan's soldiers disappeared beneath the falling gargoyles, their blood oozing into the enormous hearth, dousing the fire within. The violence seemed to die with the flames, but, as she'd hoped, the ensuing calm portended its return as eloquently as a hurricane's eye.

She waited for the sounds of shifting weight and rustling fabric to reach her ears before starting her attack. She thought she heard Lon-Shan's heart – a frenzied tattoo within the pounding rain – and realized she'd waited long enough. Fear wouldn't paralyze him forever.

Vaulting over the ruined sill, she charged the library. A gleaming trident burst to life in her hands, hot and sizzling against her palms and growing brighter as she landed before Lon-Shan's throne.

"Hello, Lon-Shan," she grinned. "I can't tell you how good it is to see you again. When Streega pulled you out of the valley, I feared the worst. Imagine my surprise when I heard you still lived. Not many stand against Vissyus and survive. How fortunate for you."

Across the room, Lon-Shan stared at her from his throne, his face a mask of shock, rage, and fear. "I don't know what Aeryk told you, but you were there. You know what happened."

"I know what I saw, but I didn't know what it meant."

His thoughts tested her mind, Searched for a way in. It was his way. He'd try to fill her with doubt, even amplify her despair. Her smile grew. He'd find neither.

Desperately, his eyes flicked to the library doors. "Seirin," he pleaded. "Let me explain. It was Vissyus. He killed them. You watched him do it."

"Only after you provoked him!" She pointed her trident at his chest. It flared satisfactorily. "You sent Botua between Vissyus and the mountains. You knew she'd be on her own. She's dead because of you!"

Lon-Shan's lips thinned. "She's dead because of *you*,"

he snarled, his demeanor changing from fear to disgust. "If you hadn't been so selfish, none of this would have happened. Vissyus would still be sane, Botua would still be alive, and the world would still be whole."

"Blaming me isn't a very smart strategy, Lon-Shan, and it's not going to help you. You have to pay for what you've done."

"Why? Because you say so? Who's going to make you pay for what you did to Vissyus? Who'll make you pay for what you've done to me? You came here – to my home – and intentionally leveled my cities and murdered my men. They didn't have a chance against you. Did you even see their faces, Seirin? Would you remember what they looked like? Do you care? You and the others are so self-absorbed you don't see anything you don't want to. Do you realize this is the most you've ever spoken to me? Ever?" His face grew hard, bitterness tightening his features. "Vissyus was the only one who spent any time with me... And you ruined him!" Enraged, Lon-Shan raised his ebon shield and exploded from the throne. A stream of black tracers appeared in front of him – long, thin, and deadly.

She deflected the attack with quick arching sweeps of her trident. The sickening sound of unraveling matter filled her ears, and she was thankful for the noise. Lon-Shan's words cut her more than any attack ever had. She had to get them out of her head. Why wouldn't they go? Her rising anger and her need to silence him only validated what he had to say. She could have let him go, could have turned around and left him alone with his darkness. But she didn't. Her blood was so hot; she couldn't think, couldn't do anything but concentrate on the barrage pushing her back from the heavy double doors, countering him here with lances of water, there with liquid daggers.

"Attacking Aeryk was a serious mistake," she snarled, using anger to hide her guilt. "If you stayed hidden, we might have forgotten you. It would have been easy. You're not that memorable." She stepped lightly from one foot to the other, ready to strike.

Lon-Shan ignored the insult. "You're not a killer, Seirin. You couldn't kill Vissyus, and you can't kill me."

Seirin grinned maliciously. "A woman's prerogative. I've had a very long time to think things over."

Botua's charred body floated out of some locked section of her mind. Her will hardened. She'd learned the cost of hesitation. Things were different now. Lon-Shan *would* face justice. She lifted her eyes to his, saw the fear, anticipated the attack.

Black daggers came at her heart, but instead of trying to deflect them, she dropped her trident and reached into the floodwaters. At her command, the temperature plummeted, ice replaced water, and a frozen curtain rocketed up to the ceiling to shelter her.

Lon-Shan's rounds collided with the barrier and imploded. Hundreds of tiny gravity wells formed along the ice, small whirlpools that dragged matter into shrinking cores. They pulled her defenses into their dark, cyclonic centers and turned her wall into a writhing sea of liquid and gas.

Seirin held her ground, her body coiled and ready. She slipped her mind into the splintering ice and seized the water molecules within it.

Oblivious, Lon-Shan continued to reform his vortices. He inverted matter, weaponized it. A look of triumph contorted his face, but as he tried to fire at her, his expression crumbled. Fear gripped him, from his worried eyes to his trembling body.

Beyond his hands, the attack he'd so carefully crafted vibrated to a halt. Seirin savored the moment.

"Water seeps into everything," she said. "Even your darkness. If you were stronger, maybe you could take it back. As it is, though…"

Slowly, the dark spheres moved, not at her, but back toward him.

"Seirin, no! You can't…"

"Tell that to Botua." Seirin's voice hissed from her lips like escaping steam. "At least I will be quick. The others would take their revenge one piece at a time." She stared into his eyes for a long moment. "I am sorry, Lon-Shan, but you brought this on yourself."

With a thought, she forced Lon-Shan's water-laced missiles into his shield. Swirling darkness met solid obsidian. The latter welcomed the former, as if reclaiming a part of itself. Lon-Shan recoiled. The color drained from his face; sweat poured over it. Seirin's thoughts touched the liquid. Quickly, she morphed it into sharp needles and let them hover inches from his skin. She held them there, emphasizing his helplessness before driving them in.

Lon-Shan screamed; his body thrashed wildly. A lone thought rushed past her, and before she could counter it, he pulled back his darkness. Night gave way to instantaneous day, clear and incredibly bright. It lasted only a second before the darkness rushed back in. Not long, but long enough to blind her.

Unable to see, Seirin turned to her Searchings. They blanketed the room and found a barrage of black spears heading toward her. Too little, too late. Her power condensed the surrounding air. Water formed in huge pools that hovered over the ruined carpet.

The clustered projectiles sliced through, but not

before she unleashed the liquid's crushing pressure. Muffled explosions broke an uneasy silence, then faded away. Blinking, she brought tears to cleanse her eyes, and the library came back into focus. Wind and rain blew in through smashed windows, tattered paper and bits of fabric swirling into the air. Apart from the wreckage, the room stood empty.

Lon-Shan had vanished.

Coward. Where are your shadows now? The thought made her pause. Lon-Shan hated confrontation of any kind. This could be a trap. Better not take any chances.

She reached out with her thoughts. *Kirak! I need a report.*

I am here, mistress, not far from the palace. Kirak's comforting presence warmed her senses, and she opened her mind to it. *Lon-Shan? Have you finished him?*

The words triggered the guilt she'd so far suppressed. She tried to smother it. *Did Streega survive?* She knew what the answer would be, but she had to make sure.

Anger rolled through the slivered Bond. *Lon-Shan sacrificed his guardian before its defeat could hobble him.*

He did what? Seirin's stomach knotted. She didn't want to hear the rest, but she knew she needed to. Holding her breath, she waited for Kirak to continue.

The master killed the servant to save himself. This is worse than anything we imagined, my lady.

Seirin tried to speak, but she couldn't gather the words. This was all her fault. She'd started it. Lon-Shan was right, not that that excused him. Lifting her shield into the air, she hovered over the floor. Her power churned the floodwaters beneath into dangerous swells.

This is the end, Kirak, she said. *If anything happens to me, it will be up to you to tell the others.*

Kirak tried to protest, but she cut it off. *Nonnegotiable.*

I have to settle things here before we meet Vissyus. Without waiting for an answer, she reformed her trident and, gripping it tightly, rocketed through the ruined doors and into the hallway.

A line of blood coated the sodden carpet, but the trail abruptly ended halfway down the hall. *Healed himself.* She raced on, tracking him through the east wing, down two flights of stairs, and into a seemingly endless corridor. As she rounded a corner, her Searching detected another volley closing fast from the far end of the hall.

He needed to do better than that. Nothing short of a dark, spatial vortex could stop her now. She smiled coldly. And he'd try it too – at least she hoped he would. All she needed now were the floodwaters. Her thoughts reached into the library and drew them out. At her command, a wall of water rushed into the hall. Spray dappled her shield, then large drops, and finally a deafening wave.

Arms outstretched, she banked to the left in a wide, rolling arc and let it overtake her. Her fingertips grazed walls, ceiling, and floor. Water followed the movement, and she spun faster. Gravity would drag it into a swirling, pressurized funnel. She nodded grimly. Let Lon-Shan deal with that.

By the time the lances reached her, she'd turned the hall into a muzzle. Water streamed past her like liquid cannon fire that swamped Lon-Shan's missiles and instantly crushed them. The door ahead offered even less resistance, the wood splintering into a thousand pieces, and took a good chunk of wall away as well.

Seirin followed the water into the space beyond. A quick Searching revealed interlocking iron girders and a ceiling made from a single glass panel that, while beautiful, seemed wildly out of place. Lon-Shan had opened a large portion of his palace to the sky, something she was at a loss to explain. He hated the stars and the moon alike. Why wouldn't he blot them out? She shrugged. It didn't matter. The skylight provided an easier escape than she anticipated.

Apart from the roof, everything else was suffocatingly devoid of light, perverted in much the same way the library had been. Tiles of smoky marble lined the floors, the walls paneled with mahogany or some other dark wood. No plants, no flowers, nothing sustained by sun existed here. She glimpsed a subtle glint on the iron latticework above her, but even that seemed dull, almost dead. A raspy wheeze came from somewhere within the tangle of girders.

Calmly, she Searched the darkness.

Lon-Shan stood on one of the many beams overhead, silhouetted against the rain clouds. Even from this distance, she could make out the tired slump of his shoulders, the heavy rise and fall of his chest. His face was a ruined mass of dried blood and torn flesh that accentuated the burning hatred in his eyes. He'd try to finish this quickly. It was his only chance. He needed to throw everything he had into one massive strike and pray it defeated her before she could counter.

She hoped he didn't realize his mistake too soon.

Hurling her thoughts into the water, she manipulated it at its most basic, molecular level. The procedure was simple, really, too simple for what it would do. She shook her head as she worked, mourning the loss of Vissyus. He'd suggested this in exchange for her teachings. Bitterly, she realized just how high a price she'd paid. When she finished, she reinforced her shield and lowered herself into a cauldron of newly formed heavy water.

"That's not going to help you, Seirin!" Lon-Shan

shouted. "You can't hide from me here." His voice rasped like the scrape of sandpaper across rough wood. "I know what your guardian reported to you. But that overgrown snake failed to tell you how I withdrew Streega's strength before I killed it. Guardian blood magnifies my power. You're not the only one with tricks. I'm going to stop you now. For Vissyus."

Beneath the surface, Seirin kept Lon-Shan firmly in her sights. Water distorted her view, but she adjusted. The ripples above smoothed enough to see him building darkness in his hands like a sliver of stolen space. A sickle moon appeared through shredding clouds to frame his head with horns.

Her heart beat once, and then again. She saw his gaze sweep across the water, felt his Searching cut through its depths. When it reached her, she opened her mind to it, showed herself, and vaulted into the air. She sped through iron girders, threaded her way through a forest of cold metal as a black energy sphere hurtled toward and then past her. Overhead, Lon-Shan screamed in outrage.

Seirin's escape took Lon-Shan by surprise. He expected the same ferocious assault she used to drive him from the library. She'd beaten him. They both knew it. Why then, did she stop pressing and pull back? It wasn't like her. What had she done? Impulsively, he glanced back to the floodwaters. He tried to reform his shield, but a series of earth-shattering concussions broke his concentration.

The water… She'd done something to the water.

He could still see his dark matter reacting with it, changing and expanding into a roiling mass of nucleic energy, a furnace as bright and as hot as the sun. It moved inexorably toward him. Despite the heat, fear lashed his body like a cold, arctic wind.

He grasped at the girders to keep from falling, but his hand disappeared in flame. Pain raced through his body, the acrid smell of burning flesh amplifying it. His dreams burst with each blister, his future as torched as his peeling skin. An outraged howl escaped his lungs.

Eons of planning destroyed in an instant. He'd come so close. How had it gone so wrong so fast? Despair washed over him, more pronounced for its finality – the last emotion he'd ever know. No. Not the last. As if born from the flames, a wild fury raged through his body. Vissyus could perform this trick with a hundred times more force. The idea brought another emotion. A cruel smile split his scalded lips. He laughed, hoping with his dying breath that his friend would kill the remaining Kami and finally bring peace to the world.

18
ICE

Vissyus woke to a world of dark, brackish water. Cold seeped into him, and he quickly formed a shield to push back the chill. Blue light, the color of winter ice, glowed around him, illuminating an undersea world. The shade was pretty and familiar, and the shade matched the huge, icy chunks forming around him.

He watched them rise to the surface before putting his head down and plowing ahead. A nagging thought tickled the back of his mind. Did this happen before, or had he dreamed it? He recalled a warm sea and raging storms. The ice was different, the water colder, murkier. Only the insistent pull on his thoughts remained the same. He tried to think, but the harder he concentrated, the more fragmented his thoughts became. Visions of towering cyclones gave way to shimmering walls, a volcanic island, and a regal dragon of red and gold. They looked familiar, but as he tried to place them, a second consciousness roared out of the darkness.

It swam alongside him, steering his body, assuming control as his mind wandered. He drifted, feeling free. His thoughts stretched further than he remembered, no longer bumping against that curious wall. A wild fire ignited somewhere far to the east in a forest of huge trees. To the south, a small volcano rumbled to life. The seas around an icy continent warmed, massive chunks melting, breaking free.

He turned his attention west and followed an invisible trail toward the shore. It called to him, filled his senses. This time, he knew what it was. He closed his eyes and let the feeling wash over him, dimly aware of the darkness closing around him, dragging him back as if through a portal.

"Teacher," he breathed, the name exploding around his head in a wash of icy bubbles. "I have found you."

Keiko's body may have been safe and warm in the White Spirit Castle, but her mind registered a sharp change in temperature. In Tokyo, intense heat preceded Fiyorok's arrival. Here, it was the cold. The other dragon was coming. She was sure of it. Frantic, she studied the Black Sea, fighting to accept what she saw. A layer of ice had formed several miles out and now raced toward land. Keiko had never seen anything like it. The seas didn't freeze that fast – not in the coldest winter, and certainly not in the middle of spring.

"Vissyus's guardians grow stronger." Takeshi floated in the air beside her. His words were grim, but he seemed more thoughtful than worried.

Keiko didn't share the sentiment. The thought terrified her. She remembered what Fiyorok did to Tokyo. This, though different, resonated with the same sense of violence.

Ice crystals appeared in the air above a coastal village. They swirled ominously beneath the May sun as if mocking it. Below, a dark shape, so like Fiyorok, swam within the frozen sea, heading for shore. A large crowd had gathered along the docks. Many pointed excitedly into the bay, while others wandered in from the streets, their heads tilted skyward, bewildered expressions on their faces.

Keiko's heart went out to them. They had no idea what was coming.

Akuan was clearly visible beneath the ice. The people watching from shore began to back away as it rushed toward them. Those behind pushed forward, crushing the ones stuck between. Angry shouts erupted from the mob, anguished cries and terrified wails adding to the chaos. Pressure built from either end, the whole disorganized mass corralled into a small spit of land between the abutting beaches as Akuan exploded through the ice and roared into town.

As Keiko looked down, the world lurched around her. Blue sky became stone buildings and streets slick from melting snow. She gazed about to reorient herself. This was the second time in a short span in which her surroundings changed abruptly. The last was fairly benign. She'd been too far away to notice the details. Here, though, in the middle of the village, the horror was all too vivid.

People streamed past – men, women, and children – mindlessly fleeing. Panic made them selfish. Few stopped to help friend or neighbor. A woman with a wailing infant in her arms stumbled, lost her balance and fell. Keiko tried to grab her, but she passed through Keiko's arms and hit the ground with a loud thud.

The crowd behind didn't slow. Keiko turned to face it, waving her arms and shouting for the people to stop. As they closed, an icy blast shot through the street sweeping forward and freezing whatever it touched.

"No," Keiko pleaded. She covered her eyes, and when she looked again, she gazed into a sea of icy statues. "No. Oh, God no!"

Takeshi moved closer. "What do you think I should do, Yamanaka-san?"

"I don't know!" she cried, spinning to face him. "Something. Anything!"

"We have no form. Our options are limited."

"I don't care." Keiko replied. His composure rankled her. "You can't just let them die."

"And what of the law? No Kami can attack a guardian – the Law of Binding Trust forbids it. We cannot and will not attack them, not even in self-defense. I make every Kami agree to that before I allow them to summon a guardian spirit. The agreement becomes part of the binding. They cannot break it."

Keiko balled her hands into fists. "How are you supposed to stop the dragons if you can't fight them?"

Akuan had reached the town square, an open plaza with a tall fountain in the middle. Its claws ripped up the cobbles, its tail smashing the fountain from its base. Water sprayed in every direction and then froze into what looked like a blooming flower.

"A decision, Yamanaka-san. We're running out of time."

Keiko blinked at him. Why was he asking her? She tried to focus. Saving people should be easy. What did the law matter when lives were at stake?

"Lure it away," she said finally. "Out of the city. Somewhere without as many people."

Takeshi nodded. He looked pleased. "Excellent choice!" Reaching down, he grabbed a fistful of snow and tossed it into the air. The flakes swirled around them, spinning faster and faster. A white glow burned in the center, coloring swiftly to vibrant emerald. Takeshi lifted a hand, and the green orb rocketed into the skies.

"Akuan is here for Seirin," he said, as if that explained everything. "Come, Yamanaka-san. We still have to keep the dragon from reaching her." His spectral form lifted from the ground and headed after the glowing ball.

Keiko followed closely, wondering how her mind knew what to do. She glanced back at the town with a heavy heart. Akuan had rampaged through the village's narrow streets. Blood splattered toppled buildings and torn pavement, it flowed into gutters, pooled at the sides of the road or sizzled within burning debris.

A four hundred-foot cathedral stood at the end of the trail, Akuan's claws gripping the tall spire, the guardian's body coiling, its head tilted like a hound on the hunt. When its gaze locked onto the glowing green globe, a triumphant bellow burst from its throat.

Takeshi had slowed long enough for Keiko to catch up, while ahead the mysterious ball raced eastward toward a range of alpine mountains. Akuan vaulted into the air after Takeshi's decoy, sapphire scales sparkling regally in the bright morning sun.

"Why aren't we leading it back out to sea?" Keiko asked.

Takeshi shook his head. "Akuan follows Seirin's trail. She flew in from the west and stopped before she reached the Black Sea." He pointed at a distant peak. "The Gateway she used to re-enter the Boundary is there."

"But that means we're leading it right to a Gate! Yui said we weren't supposed to do that; she said we couldn't let Vissyus learn how to use a Keystone."

An enigmatic smile slid across Takeshi's face. "I didn't say anything about opening the Gate," he said. White light flickered around his body, and the world lurched again. This time, they rematerialized over a mountain summit. "My guardian protects the Boundary. And while the law prevents me from attacking Akuan, Gaiyern faces no such restrictions."

"Guardian? I don't see a... You don't mean *that*!" Shading her eyes with a hand, she stabbed her finger at the mountaintop, where a spherical orb of polished gold lay within a stone basin. She had so much to learn and so little time.

Takeshi's face somehow managed to look both serene and affronted. "Already you know enough to recognize a guardian? You are a quicker student than your father was."

Keiko shrank a little into herself and looked away. Again with the mouth. Grimacing, she turned back to study the gleaming stone, when it abruptly cracked open. A shining pillar lanced upward. Keiko thought she saw a figure standing within it – enormous and as clear as glass. Lights swirled beneath its translucent skin, more than she could count. Somehow, they reminded her of a starry sky, a vast, infinite space teeming with galaxies.

Akuan pulled out of a steep dive and circled warily. A bubble of arctic blue pulsed around its body before steadying.

"Akuan's shield," Takeshi said. "The Boundary blunts most of it, but don't let that fool you. Vissyus is still strong enough to protect his guardians with or without the barrier. A direct strike will only stun it, as you're about to see."

Keiko managed a wooden nod. She couldn't speak. The sight of two spectacular guardians had stilled her tongue. She'd never be like them. She was nothing in comparison.

The glow around Takeshi's guardian faded enough for Keiko to see the figure raise a hand. Blinding light burst from its palm as Akuan came about, catching the dragon just between the horned crown and the mane. The impact knocked Akuan into a tight downward spiral. Another light, this one from the Keystone, rushed out to hit the dragon just as its great body smashed into the ground.

Dirt flew hundreds of feet into the air, the earth shook, and avalanches rolled down the mountains. Keiko ducked her head as the debris raced toward her. When she looked up again, an odd shimmering covered the dragon's body, building in intensity before dissipating. When the light finally vanished, Akuan was nowhere to be seen.

"As I thought," Takeshi whispered. "He didn't alter the Binding." He smiled broadly. "Good. I have found his weakness."

Keiko frowned at him. "Where did it go? What did you do to it?"

"Me?" The question seemed to surprise him. "I assure you Akuan's removal had nothing to do with me. Vissyus felt Akuan's wounding and retrieved the guardian before it suffered any permanent damage."

"Felt the wounding? You mean you hurt him?" Keiko's heart leaped, only to have Takeshi douse her hopes.

"I'm afraid not. But it proves he left the Bonding unchanged." He looked to the west and nodded as if to someone she couldn't see. "We need to get back. A word of warning, though: say nothing about Masato's reappearance to Yui, not even if she asks you directly. Understood?"

Swallowing hard, Keiko bobbed her head. She didn't

have to ask why. She knew, and she didn't disagree.

"Good," he grunted, dropping his head crisply. "You did well, Yamanaka-san. You made the correct choice and saved hundreds of lives. Your father was right – power is more than strength. It's the ability to save or destroy."

Keiko blushed. Takeshi heard what Masato said to her. He had to know what she wanted to do, and he didn't dissuade her. The thought sent her spirit soaring.

"We need to return to the White Spirit." He held out a hand for her. "We wouldn't want our tea to get cold."

19
PHOTOS

The world around Keiko blurred again, and she was vaguely aware of her mind tumbling from one end of the globe to the other. Finally, blinking and dazed, she found herself right back where she started – seated comfortably in Takeshi's chambers with Yui on one side, the monk on the other, and a steaming pot of green tea on the low table between them.

Yui reached for the kettle and expertly refilled their tiny cups. "Did you find what you were looking for, Father?" Her tone, though light, betrayed her curiosity. "You were gone longer than I expected."

"Questions eventually lead to answers, Yui-chan," Takeshi said blandly. "Sometimes, however, the answers are also questions."

Yui fixed Takeshi with a flat, irritated look before returning the pot to its place on the table. "If you will excuse me, Father." She stood and made a halfhearted bow. "I will prepare more tea. This is likely to be a long night."

Takeshi stared thoughtfully at the ceiling as Yui's footsteps retreated to the side panel.

"You'll have to tell her eventually." Keiko waited until Yui closed the shoji behind her before speaking.

"Perhaps. Though I rather think it will become irrelevant. She's not the only one who's suffered, and the sooner she realizes that, the better. Roarke Zar Ranok sacrificed his heart, Aeryk and Seirin their innocence." He closed his eyes as if savoring something long since gone. "Vissyus lost more than any of us. The Great Lord of Fire lost everything that made him who he was."

Yui returned through the shoji with a lacquered tray filled with cookies, sweet-cakes, and a fresh pot of the same green tea that now swirled, stone cold, in the cup at Keiko's wrist. She set the tray on one corner of the table and proceeded to arrange the platters precisely, beginning with the cakes, which – to Keiko's great disappointment – she placed in front of Takeshi.

Keiko's frown deepened as Yui lowered the cookies next to the cakes. Her stomach growled loudly at the sight of them. Politely ignoring the rumbling, Takeshi removed two of the sweet-cakes and a handful of cookies before passing the plates to Keiko. Yui was already seated by the time Keiko filled her small dish to overflowing, the eyebrows on her face climbing to match Keiko's growing pile.

"Are you going after Akuan?" Keiko mumbled, her mouth so full that the words came out in a muffled mess.

Yui rounded on her father. "Akuan? You saw Akuan?"

"The ice dragon was searching for Seirin near Lon-Shan's Gate," Takeshi admitted.

"I can't believe you didn't tell me! This changes everything. We don't have time to sit here and talk. We need to finish our preparations and–"

"It changes nothing!" Takeshi slammed his hands onto the table. Teacups rattled, the hot liquid rippling precariously close to the edges. "We made our plans for a reason. You need to control yourself, Yui!"

The room fell deathly quiet. Takeshi's gaze swept over the two women, holding them, daring them to speak. Dark red splotches colored Yui's cheeks. She lowered her head and kept it down throughout the silence.

Beside her, Keiko cleared her throat and reached for the tray in front of her once more. "I don't know about you, but I'm starving. I haven't eaten a thing since lunch." She selected a moist cake and transferred it to her already full plate. A second followed, then another. Before long, cookies and cakes flew across the table in a blur of golden brown and sugary white. When the tray was empty, Keiko lifted a large wafer, bit into it, and waved the remaining piece airily. "This is *so* good," she said between bites. "I love pastries. I just can't help myself. It's like an instinct, you know? A compulsion." She glared at Takeshi. Her voice, though breezy, had a steel edge to it. "Some people don't think before they talk, others keep secrets. Me? I lose my mind for a good piece of cake."

Takeshi folded his arms over his chest and chuckled. "You have a unique friend here, Yui. I hope you appreciate her."

Yui's head remained lowered, but Keiko caught the hint of a smile.

"As for secrets – I think Keiko's waited long enough to learn about hers."

Keiko swallowed and dropped her hands to her lap. Blood roared in her ears. She inhaled to calm her pounding heart and nodded. Yui remained as she was.

Across the table, Takeshi smiled kindly. "Every spirit has a power," he continued. "Can you guess what forces your father controlled?"

Keiko was about to shake her head, when a rush of images flashed through it – the mummified agent in her father's house, different decades, her father speaking to her as she looked through a viewfinder, telling her to focus her thoughts.

It was so simple.

"Pictures," she said after a pause. "Captured moments. He could do something with time."

Takeshi beamed at her. "Yes, Yamanaka-san. He had the ability to manipulate how a person passes through time."

Keiko exhaled forcefully. "So that's how he did it." She stared – wide-eyed – at Takeshi. "That's what the camera was for; he used it as a training tool to help me focus my mind." Her hands trembled as something new occurred to her. "You want me to do that, don't you? Take us back to the beginning so you can show me what started all this."

Takeshi knitted his fingers together and leaned forward. "Though we could test your theory now, I don't think you are ready. For this, I will maintain control." Takeshi cupped his hands around the kettle and collected the steam wafting from the spout. "We begin with Seirin. Tragedy fills her spirit. She remembers anything connected to her power." He let the small cloud hover above his palms before casting it into the room, where it expanded. "Her memories call us through her element. Breathe it in, let her steam fill you. You will see what she saw, experience it as she lived it when the world was young."

Keiko's mind drifted, and she felt control slipping away as she merged with another consciousness.

"A word of warning," Takeshi said, his voice fading. "After Seirin, we'll move on to Vissyus's trace memories.

Prepare yourself, his are strong and powerful. I will anchor your thoughts to mine to keep his madness from sweeping you away. We finish with Seirin's reaction to what she's done. Only then will you understand who is responsible for what."

Keiko swallowed nervously. This was why she was here; backing out meant letting her father down. She couldn't do that, not to him and not to herself.

EARTH
THE DISTANT PAST

20
INNOCENCE

Seirin Bal Cerannon, Queen of the Oceans, looped her arm through Aeryk's and stretched up to kiss his cheek. His skin was warm to the touch, and it dimpled into a smile just before she pulled away. She loved the feel of his body against her, his white shirt as soft as the clouds around the tower. At any other time, she would have pressed into him, wrapped his arms around her like a blanket. But she was too anxious, too preoccupied with what they'd come here to do.

Hurricane Point was the ideal location for this test, soaring the edge of a great peninsula, touching land and sea and sky. Aeryk claimed he could see the whole world from the top of the Observatory, and maybe he could.

Seirin wasn't looking at the world, though. The horizon called to her, so far away, so elusive. She tried to ignore it, but the distance pulled at her – insistent, mocking even. Out there, ocean and sky merged into a single line, a line that never really existed. Until today. Today, she'd take that illusion and make it real. Nothing would stop her. Not now, not after waiting for so long.

Teras's recent pregnancy had awakened an insatiable hunger in her, a primal need unlike anything she'd ever known. A child! Teras had a child. It was a miracle. The answer to an eternity of questions. Could the woman survive a collision of powers within her own body? The blending of elemental forces was dangerous, the ramifications unknown. Would a child survive it?

Takeshi promised to let her know as soon as he ruled out danger, but Yui's birth had come and gone, and Takeshi still found reasons to delay. Let Yui mature, let her power manifest. Years passed, and Takeshi's excuses continued. Seirin was tired of waiting.

Aeryk shifted nervously beside her. "Are you sure this is safe?" he asked, not for the first time. "No one's ever done this before."

Seirin's contented sigh became irritated. They'd been over this a hundred times. He questioned, she answered. Her heart told her having a child together was safe, but he wanted guarantees.

"I asked Vissyus a few days ago." Incredibly, she managed to keep her tone light. "He assured me it was."

Aeryk frowned, his face uncertain. "We should have asked Takeshi. He'd know better than anyone."

"He refused to tell us," Seirin replied, unsuccessfully keeping the heat from her voice. How many times had she asked him? How many times had she walked away disappointed? "We have to do this for ourselves. It's the only way we'll know." She worked her lips into a full pout. "Unless you don't really want to."

"Of course I do." Aeryk's response was satisfyingly quick. "It's just that... This is his prohibition, Seirin."

Seirin twined her fingers around his. "I know you value Takeshi's opinion. I do too. But Vissyus doesn't think it's dangerous, and I believe him. He'd never let anything happen to us." She gave him a shy smile. "He convinced you to share your feelings with me. As far as I'm concerned, that makes him the smartest man in the world." Releasing his hand, she squared her shoulders and headed for the large, open windows. "Right. Let's do this."

Halfway across the floor, she hit a wall of solid air and stopped.

"I trust Vissyus too," Aeryk said, walking up to her. "But that doesn't mean I'll let you go first."

His words gave rise to conflicting emotions, the ice of anger, the heat of elation. He was worried about her. A warm rush coursed through her body. She wouldn't take that from him – his kindness, his need to protect her. Finding him, loving him, was the best thing that had ever happened to her. What had she done to deserve him?

"All right, Aeryk. But you have to stop if anything feels wrong. Promise me."

He brushed a kiss over her lips, his mouth lingering, the words *I promise* lilting through the space between them. His barrier opened. Warm, tropical air rushed through to fill the void. He strode into the breeze and made his way to the east-facing arch. A blue nimbus erupted around his body, his sky-blue eyes becoming slate gray.

Seirin's heart pounded wildly in her chest as he drew his power. She held her breath.

At first, nothing happened. But then, as she reached out with her mind, she felt Aeryk's spirit slip into the Earth's waters. He used the power in ways she never thought possible. One minute, he manipulated the tide, the next its temperature. Rip currents formed far below the surface, riding against the tides to whip the turquoise waters into violent, white foam. A vast vortex swirled upon the seas below, but only for the moment it took Aeryk to heave it into the sky.

Seirin gasped as he took control. She watched in stunned satisfaction as the whirlpool bulged, inverted, and twisted into a turbulent column. Sea spray lashed the castle's alabaster foundations; rainbows sparkled before it. And then it ended.

Aeryk lowered the cyclone back into the ocean. Seirin felt his power leave the water, felt it leave her body. Loss flitted through her, overridden by jealousy, and finally impatience. She hungered to know him the way he now knew her, to see the world through his spirit. Why would Takeshi forbid this? What harm could it do? She found it hard to believe he never tried with Teras. Yui's birth validated their emotional commitment. Then again, what if they *had* tried… and failed? What if Aeryk was right and Takeshi knew something she didn't?

No. Vissyus would have warned her. Where Takeshi relied on instinct, Vissyus took a far more theoretical approach. His faith rested in the physical, not the metaphysical. He analyzed and dissected – if he'd found a flaw he would have said so.

Reassured, she hurried to Aeryk, spun him by the arm, and searched his face. "Aeryk? Are you all right? Did it work?"

Aeryk placed a finger under her chin and lifted. "Beyond our wildest dreams." He beamed at her, his blue eyes shining like a summer sky.

She pulled away, determined not to let his piercing gaze distract her. "I have to know," she breathed. "I want to *feel* it." She gestured to a point just beyond the beaches where the waterspout had only recently collapsed. "I let you understand me, and now it's your turn." She stroked his cheek. "*Please*."

He flashed an encouraging smile, placed his hands on her shoulders, and turned her to the huge, arched window. "Do you want me to tell you anything about it?"

She shook her head. "No." She shrugged out of his grip. "I don't want to know. I want the experience to be pure." She flared her shield and cast one last look at him before launching herself into Hurricane Point's sultry air.

Excitement sent her pulse racing. Instead of working the atmosphere from the safety of the Observatory as she'd planned, she climbed to the top of the tower's domed roof and landed, not at the edge, but in the middle, the peak, from which she could gaze into the horizon. From here, she'd see everything as she felt it.

A gentle breeze – light and southeasterly – streamed over the warm bay, where it picked up moisture as it made its way to the Point.

She slid her thoughts into it. The bound elements served as a conduit to their gaseous states – a wall she always noted but never tried to breach. Until now. Thrusting her spirit forward, she broke through. Her mind touched the vastness of Heaven, and its enormity stunned her. Not even her waters reached so much of the world. Deserts diminished her, earth drank her in, used and then discarded her. But the air... the air was different. Where water cleansed and purified, air consumed and dissipated. She needed to know how and why and what it meant for Aeryk to wield this power.

Feet planted, body taut, she pulled her thoughts out of the comfortable air-born water and hurled them into the atmosphere. As with Aeryk, nothing happened right away. Then, she felt a slight change in the temperatures aloft and below. Pressure dropped, the air cyclonic and rising.

Thunderheads formed swiftly, tall and dark and anvil-topped. They surged over Hurricane Point, where they fed off the warm, tidal waters. Dark shadows blanketed both land and sea in an eerie dusk-like light. Lightning strobed from cloud to cloud, the wind moaning fiercely.

She let the storm slam into her body. Her senses quivered with each electrical strike, her heart thumping in time with the thunder. Overhead, funnel clouds broke from the main storm to touch down along the beaches in a flurry of sand and water.

Seirin drove them out to sea before calling a fresh land breeze to dry the air. Smiling triumphantly, she launched herself from the tower. Laughter, like the tinkling of a waterfall, replaced the rain's staccato thrumming, her shield more vibrant than the sun. She flew over the waves in a wide arc that eventually brought her back to the Observatory. Her feet barely touched before Aeryk embraced her. His strong arms lifted her from the diamond floors, and together, they spun about the room as if dancing.

They continued to practice long into the night. The following day, they rose early and began again. By midday, they were exhausted. They broke from their work and wandered to the pristine beach below the fortress.

"Do you still want to tell Takeshi?" Seirin lay beside Aeryk on a blanket of soft, white sand, gazing into his face while he studied the sky.

"He'll find out sooner or later. Better to tell him than have him discover it on his own." His brow puckered. "The problem is finding the right time. Yui keeps him so busy."

"Isn't she beautiful?" Seirin placed her head against him and traced a finger across his chest. "She'll be taller now. We haven't seen them for a long time."

Aeryk chuckled. "All right, Seirin." He ran a hand through her hair. "You win. I'll contact Takeshi and ask if we can visit in the next few days."

A shadow fell over them. Seirin looked up to see Takeshi Ahk-Kiko, Lord of Spirit, standing on a low rise a few feet away. She inhaled sharply. *Did he know? Is that why he'd come?*

"Teras would like that," Takeshi said, his crimson robes rustling in the light breeze as he walked. They always reminded Seirin of blood.

"Takeshi." Aeryk smiled. "This is unexpected. What brings you to Hurricane Point?"

Takeshi folded his hands into his sleeves. "Vissyus. The three of you are very close. I thought you might answer a question for me."

Seirin sat up quickly, sand flying. "What's he done?"

Takeshi must have suspected something. But since he didn't confront them, he couldn't know exactly what. Bringing Vissyus into it troubled her, though. He'd put the pieces together soon enough.

"Done?" Takeshi raised a questioning eyebrow. "He hasn't done anything. It's what he might do that troubles me."

Seirin masked a guilty flinch as best she could. "What do you mean?"

"Elemental powers shape our view of the world – you with water, Aeryk with sky. Vissyus's ideas come from the transformative power of heat and fire. He believes we'll eventually need to remake ourselves in order to survive. Yui represents a validation of his thinking, an evolutionary step in our physical and spiritual growth."

Seirin relaxed. This wasn't about them, at least not yet. She needed to keep it that way. Takeshi's concern for Yui would do. Mollify that, and he'd probably leave happy.

"If it's a validation of his thinking," she said, "then there's no need to worry. He'll simply run his tests and come to us with the results."

"His whole theory is flawed." Seirin caught a hint of frustration in Takeshi's normally calm voice. "Evolution is generational. Forcing it is dangerous. Vissyus doesn't understand that. He never will."

The certainty in Takeshi's tone chilled her. "Have you been looking into the future again? Did you know he could do that, Aeryk?" Aeryk gestured helplessly, and she frowned at him before turning back to Takeshi. "I'm sure Vissyus didn't mean any harm. Still, I'll let him know how you feel."

This only seemed to agitate the Spirit Lord. "You will see him soon?"

"In a few days. We made arrangements to visit his fortress."

"You need to be careful with him, Seirin. His brilliance has made him arrogant. Don't let him drag you into something he can't control."

"Nonsense." Seirin managed a bright tone. Inside, her stomach twisted. How much *did* he know? They'd been so careful. "There's nothing to worry about. It's just a misunderstanding, that's all."

"I hope you're right, Seirin, because if you're not…"

Seirin patted the sand beside her. "You're just tired. Come. Sit with us. When was the last time you had any rest?"

Takeshi made no move to join them. "Not since Yui was born, which brings me to the other reason I wanted to see you." The air went cold. Aeryk's hand found hers. Saying nothing, he simply squeezed. "I have a task ahead of me, a sabbatical of sorts."

"A sabbatical?" Seirin barely suppressed her incredulity. "Does that mean you're leaving? Takeshi... you have a new family."

"Yui and Teras will accompany me. I may be gone for a very long time."

Seirin's heart fluttered. "Will we be able to reach you?"

The previous day was merely a prelude of the future she craved, one abruptly and indefinitely postponed. She believed Takeshi would let them have children once they brought their findings to him. If he left...

"I am afraid we will be completely secluded."

"*What*?" The pressure on her hand increased, but she yanked it away and stood to face Takeshi. "I don't understand. How can you do this to us? You gave your word."

Takeshi's eyes flashed, the only visible emotion on his otherwise smooth face. "As did you, though apparently you have reconsidered."

"What's so important?" Seirin challenged, ignoring the accusation. "What's making you go?" Dangerous swells built behind her. Waves thundered against the shore.

"A tear falls into a pool, and its ripples carry us into a storm." Takeshi's voice remained as calm as a meadow despite the roaring ocean.

"No more riddles, Takeshi! Why are you leaving?"

"Change comes. It is my responsibility to master it. Other than that, I cannot say. The future hides behind a veil, but I see enough to know it brings chaos." His shield shimmered to life, soft and white. "Forgive me, Seirin." His body began to dissolve. "I must attend to this."

"*Takeshi*!" She threw her thoughts into the moisture

around him, freezing him into a crystal statue that
shivered and then shattered, its emptiness matching
her hollow heart. She'd failed to hold him. Spinning,
she brought up her shield and burst from the ground.
Takeshi forced her hand. She had only one place left to
go.

"Seirin!" Aeryk shouted, racing over to her. "What are
you doing?"

"I'm going to see Vissyus." They'd come so far, only
to have their accomplishments brought to a shuddering
halt. She needed more, wanted more, even if it meant
turning her back on the law. "Takeshi won't help us,
Vissyus will."

Aeryk skidded to a stop, mouth agape. "No! Seirin,
you can't. You heard Takeshi. He warned against this."

"I am no longer interested in what Takeshi says or
does. I'm going... with or without you."

21
DESCENT

Seirin hurtled over Earth's lone continent in an emotional daze. Anger churned her stomach, soured it. She couldn't think, couldn't breathe. Everything she wanted, every dream she ever had, seemed shattered beyond repair. How could Takeshi do this to her?

She flew faster.

Vissyus would know what to do. He was strong and brilliant and confident in his abilities. Takeshi and Aeryk were careful; Vissyus was not. No other spirit could do what he did. None dared.

A range of towering mountains reared up ahead of her, and she sent her shield into a dizzying climb. She cleared the peaks and quickly found herself shooting over a lush basin of rivers, meadows, and grass. Up ahead, the ocean sparkled under the midday sun.

Vissyus's volcanic home dominated a cluster of islands less than fifty miles off shore. Its massive yet elegant cone climbed high into the heavens, the crater at its summit a staggering forty thousand feet above the seas.

Seirin's spirits lifted at the sight. She crossed into the volcano and headed for the immense fortress floating in the center of the six hundred-square-mile caldera – sleek, black, and imposing. Its mountain-tall towers looked like hardened magma, the roofs and gates like solid smoke. Polished lava tiled the courtyard, so like marble yet not, while strands of silver spun over the open space like a spiderweb.

Vissyus waited for her on top of the foremost wall. Rising thermal currents whipped his tawny hair, the dazzling, fire-laced eyes beneath searching her face. Sometimes, he seemed more like some wild, untamed force than a physical being. His choice of a charcoal-colored coat – tapered at the waist, flared at the leg – completed the picture, and the long cape fluttering behind him like smoke gave his tall, muscular body the look of a volcano come to life.

He smiled, and the illusion melted. The warmth in his boyishly handsome face reminded her of a hearth in midwinter. He would know what to do. She was sure of it. She glanced over her shoulder to make sure Aeryk still followed, nodded to him, and started down.

Landing, she hurried over to Vissyus and hugged him tightly. "I'm so glad you're here."

His hearty laugh brushed her cheek like a summer breeze. "Where else would I be? You were here just over a week ago. I told you I planned to test a new theory. Don't you remember?"

"Of course I do." That wasn't exactly true, nor was it patently false. She'd been… preoccupied. "You're always conducting experiments. How am I supposed to keep them all straight?"

"Maybe because this one has to do with you." He lowered her to the ground. "Why are you here, Seirin?" Somehow, he always knew when something troubled her. "What's happened?"

She tried to look away, but his earnest gaze held her. "Takeshi. He came to see us this morning." She gestured at Aeryk, who had just touched down a few feet away, his face grim. He nodded back, urging her to continue. "Aeryk and I had made a discovery of our own."

Yellow fire danced in Vissyus's eyes. "You did it then? It worked?"

"Yes, it worked," Seirin snapped. Recalling their success frustrated her. They were so close. "It worked exactly as you said it would."

"And Takeshi stopped you?" Anger and sympathy played across Vissyus's face. His big hands bunched into fists. "He had no right."

"I'm not sure he'd see it that way." She turned and walked to the stone railing. The shimmering orange beyond mystified her, liquid without water, closer to Roarke than to her. No matter how often she reached for it, it always eluded her touch.

"Elemental forces are connected," Vissyus protested. "I proved that when I built these islands."

"Roarke might disagree," Seirin said. The Earth Lord hid his irritation well, but Seirin knew he saw Vissyus's bold hijacking of earth as blasphemy. "Spirit is set apart, you know that. It's probably why Takeshi doesn't understand."

"I'll make him understand. I can prove it again if I have to – with something else."

"I'm afraid you won't get the chance." Tears built behind her eyes. She fought them down, stopping all but one from rolling down her cheeks. "He's gone, Vissyus. Said he had something important to do. Teras and Yui… they've gone with him."

"Gone? What do you mean?" Vissyus demanded. "Gone where?"

"We don't know," Aeryk said. "He wouldn't tell us."

Vissyus ran a hand through his hair. "This is all my fault. I should have been more discreet. I asked too many questions about Yui, and he became uncomfortable."

"We should have told him what we planned to do," Aeryk muttered.

Seirin glared at him. She thought they'd settled this. "We *tried*. We approached him any number of times, remember? What else were we supposed to do?"

"He asked for patience."

"Why are you defending him? He tricked us into saying more than we should have. He just wants to keep Yui away from us. I told you we should have come here first." She crossed her arms and turned her back on him. "I thought this was important to you."

"You know it is. But…"

Vissyus cleared his throat. "What if there's another way?"

Seirin's breathing quickened. A glimmer, like morning sun on closed lids, warmed her spirit. She spun to face him. "You've learned something? I *knew* you could do it!" She beamed at him.

"I haven't done anything yet," Vissyus cautioned. "The theory hasn't changed, but I think I know how to test it. You've already taken the first step."

"Thanks to you." Somehow, Seirin managed to hide her impatience.

Vissyus blushed slightly at the compliment, though his face remained serious. "The rest is more difficult. And more dangerous. There's a difference between using your power to command various elemental forces and pulling them into your body."

Aeryk frowned. "I don't see…"

"You will. Once I show you, you'll understand."

"I think we need to know more about this." Aeryk's eyes had taken on the steel blue-gray Seirin associated with worry. "Vissyus, if it's dangerous..."

"Discovery is always dangerous." Vissyus clapped a hand on Aeryk's shoulder. "It's why we run tests."

"What do you want us to do?" Seirin said, moving between the two men.

"I need you to show me what you've learned. Since Seirin will bear the brunt of this, we should begin with water."

Aeryk stepped forward protectively, but Seirin held up a hand. "It's all right, Aeryk. I'll show him. My teaching was easy enough for you to follow, I'm sure Vissyus can keep up with me."

Vissyus made a florid bow. "As you wish... *Teacher*."

Somewhere far beneath them, the Earth groaned. A lone volcano in the northwest erupted in anger.

Seirin barely noticed. She placed a hand on Vissyus's wrist and pointed into the caldera with the other. "Pressure and temperature are the easiest places to start, especially for you. You can use your element as a gateway into another, but you have to remember to let go before the transfer. If you don't..."

"You're manipulating the foreign element and not controlling it," Vissyus finished. He swept his arm over his volcano. "That's how I shaped these islands, not with earth, but with heat."

"You didn't have to make it look like a dragon, though," Aeryk chuckled. "Roarke will never forgive you."

Vissyus shrugged and fanned his hands. "Maybe if I'd made it look like Botua?"

Adolescent grins broke out on both men's faces, only to fade when they saw Seirin's disapproving stare.

She sniffed airily then turned serious, describing what they'd done. She spoke softly yet firmly before motioning to the fountain behind them.

"We'll use your fountain," she said. "It's close and small enough for you to sense each particle. After you've mastered that, we can…"

Vissyus swiveled his head over his shoulder and made a calling gesture with his hand. Power shimmered around his unshielded body, fiery red and incandescent white burning in his eyes. A thick column of water appeared over the volcano's south-facing wall, peaked hundreds of feet above the topmost turret, and, as though hitting some invisible shield, ricocheted back toward the lava bed.

"I live on a chain of islands," Vissyus grinned. "Water is never very far away."

Seirin staggered back. That wasn't the point, and he knew it. Somehow, he took control of the coastal seas without her sensing it. She shuddered at the implication, at once proud, jealous, and frightened.

Beside her, Vissyus seethed with power. An aura of dazzling yellows, reds, and oranges sizzled around his body. He summoned geysers from the surrounding ocean. Up they climbed, soaring above the caldera before arching into the fluming lava, where they instantly boiled away. Their steam wafted upward and took shape. A white bulb appeared from nothing and bloomed into a breathtaking flower.

"Water lilies," Seirin breathed. "So beautiful."

But how had he done it? She turned to him, and an ominous chill settled over her. A storm raged inside his burning eyes. Emerald light ringed his golden pupils, then, as she peered deeper, the color shifted to sky blue.

"What are you doing? Vissyus, wait." She glanced

helplessly at Aeryk, who stormed forward. He started to speak but abruptly stopped and turned his head.

There, coming in from the western sea, a blast of tightly focused air blew across the caldera, then climbed. The steam-borne lilies still wafted over the lava, but instead of blasting through them, the wind carved at their edges until a majestic white crane emerged, wings unfurled and neck stretched toward the horizon.

Seirin noticed Aeryk's stunned expression. He hadn't felt it – Vissyus commanded Aeryk's element without his knowing. Foreboding cut across her heart like a sudden squall. She took an involuntary step back. Maybe this was a mistake. Vissyus stood a few feet away. She could stop him – she just had to ask.

Her thoughts flashed back to Teras and Yui. Despite the danger, despite her fears, Teras had never looked so happy. Seirin had to have that. She wondered what her child would look like. Boy or girl? Golden locks or rich brown? A lifetime growing, learning, teaching, and nurturing – together. With Aeryk.

All thought of stopping Vissyus evaporated.

She shot a meaningful glance at Aeryk, imploring him to stay back. Like her, he'd moved to intervene. Worry creased his forehead, his body tense, rigid. Thankfully, he obeyed her unspoken command. His wooden nod said her reprieve was temporary. She exhaled. It would be enough – please, let it be enough.

Eventually, the glow of power around Vissyus winked out. He whirled to meet them, a look of delighted wonder on his face. "I was right!" he said triumphantly. He looked first at Seirin, and then at Aeryk. "I just need to test one more thing."

Seirin stiffened. She wanted to shriek and lash out and sweep Aeryk away so they could forget about tests and trial and danger. Why couldn't they just do what love demanded? Her heart told her she was right. What harm could it do? The image of Vissyus's eyes came back to her. She thrust it away. This had to happen. Today! Now!

She slid her hand into Aeryk's and gripped it. "How long?"

"A few days at most," Vissyus's tone made it sound like an apology. He gazed at the hand Aeryk held with a strange, almost melancholy expression. "Evolution isn't always successful. Rejection is a very real possibility. We need to be sure. One last test, Seirin. I promise. And then we'll know."

"Just be careful," she said. "And please hurry."

"Yes," Vissyus replied, his voice thick. "Of course."

22
MADNESS

Vissyus drummed his fingers on the arm of his throne. The black stone was hot to the touch, the seat's temperature kept just below its melting point, soft enough to mold to his body, firm enough to comfort it. At least that's what it normally did. Today was different. Today, Seirin's anguish wreathed his spirit like smoke.

He remembered the feel of her lips against his ear, the brush of her breath, the words, "I'm so glad you're here," caressing his soul.

No! He couldn't think like that. She was with Aeryk. He accepted that a long time ago. They were right for each other. Instinctively, he knew that. Knowing didn't ease the pain, though. It was there. Always.

Sighing heavily, he pushed the thought from his head, stood, and headed to the long flight of stairs before the throne. Seirin needed him. Needed him in a way Aeryk couldn't equal. The thought lifted his spirits. He quickened his pace and hurried down the steps, determined to complete this last test faster than he promised. She would remember this forever – the day Vissyus made her dreams come true.

Fiyorok waited for him in the large amphitheater several yards from the base of the stairs, volcanic light shimmering over its red-golden scales, its eyes a stunning mix of yellow and orange. The dragon lifted its large reptilian head as he approached and nodded a greeting.

"Thank you for coming, my friend," Vissyus said, dropping his chin in reply.

"I am a guardian," Fiyorok shrugged. "You summoned, and I obeyed."

"That doesn't mean I can't be grateful. Are you ready?"

Fiyorok nodded again. "I understand both the theory and the risks, though I'm not sure I agree with the method. Without a comparable test subject, the results could be flawed, possibly tainted."

"Which is why I'll channel everything through the Bond. I'll feel the discrepancies, Fiyorok, and adjust for them."

Fiyorok considered this. "You'll need a perfectly controlled environment, something better than what we usually use." It flipped its head at the ring of five-foot tall stones surrounding its body.

"Something like this?" Vissyus threw his thoughts into the nearest post. Light flared high into the chamber. The stones to the guardian's left and right ignited, and a solid wall of fire spread from one to the next. "An external shield," he said, answering Fiyorok's unasked question. "Identical to the one around the fortress, only smaller."

Instead of impressing the dragon, however, the declaration seemed to agitate it. "How much power does it take to hold two shields? What if you need to protect yourself? You might not have enough energy."

Vissyus waved a hand. "You worry too much."

"The nature of a guardian, I'm afraid, especially one

with a lord as reckless as you."

"You think everyone's reckless." Vissyus laughed.

"Why wouldn't I? You try to make the impossible possible. If the others understood how dangerous your experiments really are, I doubt they'd come within a thousand miles of you."

"Seirin knows," he said, a little too defensively. "And she still asked me to help her."

"She's desperate, my lord. Takeshi didn't give her the answer she wanted. She had nowhere else to go."

"Takeshi made promises he didn't keep. He tricked her into believing them and then left. He left, Fiyorok!" Vissyus ignited the air, shadows scattering, embers ablaze. "I won't do that to her."

"No Kami has ever called a second guardian. The strain is too great. You'll never control it."

He'd heard enough. Nothing Fiyorok said could change his mind. Seirin would thank him. She'd love him, if only for a moment.

"I am your lord," he said bluntly. "I will do this! Prepare yourself!"

Fiyorok's yellow eyes deepened to orange. Though it nodded, its expression was openly skeptical.

"Good." Vissyus exhaled to clear the tension in his chest and cast his mind into his guardian. Threads of yellow flame guided him to the body's energy sources, past muscle and bone and tissue and into the very spark of life. Carefully, he mapped what he saw, copied everything – committed it all to memory. His consciousness seized the incandescent filaments and pulled them out of Fiyorok. They wavered in the air beside the guardian like a candle at the end of its wick, at once bright and fragile.

Vissyus looked at it in wonder. *Was this how it felt to*

create life? Was this why Seirin wanted it so badly? The nascent light flickered in front of him, as if beckoning. He reached for it, poured his will into it, and then stood back to watch it grow.

A long body identical to Fiyorok's formed behind a veil of shimmering yellow fire. Blue streaks slashed across its surface. Green followed, and then boiling white. The familiar red-golden scales became sapphire blue, and the dagger-like spikes running from shoulder to tail dissolved into a mane of sea-foam green.

Vissyus approached his work… his *masterpiece*. The muscles in his legs felt heavy. He took another step, but a wave of dizziness stopped him. Ignoring the sensation, he moved forward to inspect what he'd done. The shape surprised him. He didn't expect such a drastic change. But the more he thought about it, the more he understood – function matched form, though how anything anticipated the guardian to come, he did not know.

"An incredible achievement, my lord." Despite the words, Fiyorok sounded strangely subdued. "Are you all right? You look tired."

Vissyus massaged his neck where a dull ache gnawed at the back of his head. He pushed the pain aside. "I'm fine," he lied.

The dragon's eyes shone through the shield, probing. "This is a delicate procedure. I suggest you rest before continuing. We can't afford a mistake."

"I said I was fine," Vissyus snapped. "I'll rest when we're finished."

He shouldn't have spoken like that, but the pain had become more insistent. It meant something. What, though? Why couldn't he think? He could ask Takeshi. The old monk had an answer for everything – when he decided to share, that is. Seirin learned that the hard way.

Vissyus frowned. Hadn't Seirin said something about Takeshi? If he could just remember...

"My lord," a voice said, anxious, insistent.

Vissyus lifted his head. The fires were so beautiful.

"*My lord*," Fiyorok called again. "The body won't survive in this heat, a few more minutes at most."

Vissyus blinked and shook his head. "Yes. Yes, of course."

He stood back and hurled his thoughts into the heavens, searching, calling. Time slowed. A minute crawled by, and then the next. Only the slow, steady pounding in his head marked its passing. Finally, after what felt like ages, a dim light tickled the air around the inert body. The glow wavered for a moment and then burst outward to form a shield of cool, arctic blue.

The dragon's chest heaved. Its heavy lids rolled back to reveal jade-green eyes. "I am Akuan. Spirit of Water and Ice. Where is my mistress?"

Vissyus approached the shielded stones. "Welcome, Akuan. Lady Seirin is not here. I have summoned you to serve in a different capacity."

Confusion flitted across Akuan's face. "I don't understand. The Law of Binding Trust..."

"...should not concern you. I am Vissyus, Spirit of Fire."

"I know who you are," Akuan answered.

A fading voice in Vissyus's head asked if he still knew himself. What was happening to him?

"Takeshi's law clearly states..."

"A Kami makes its own laws!" The pain came from everywhere now, piercing Vissyus's spirit from the inside as if looking for escape. "If I decide to take a second guardian, who will stop me?"

"I don't know what this is about, lord," Akuan shrank back. "But you need to stop. Whatever you've done has affected you. You are clearly not yourself."

"I will NOT stop!" Vissyus thundered. Such insolence. If the guardian didn't do as it was told, he would punish it. "I made a promise. Vissyus keeps his promises! I called you, and now I will Bind you."

He didn't expect resistance. The Summoning gave him the control he needed. Answering Akuan's questions had been a measure of courtesy. That time was over now. His thoughts surged forward, first to Fiyorok and then on to Akuan. The air crackled with power – ropes of fire, wires of ice, opposing helices wrapping around each other, red and blue light twisting together, merging, blazing, and after one final burst, winking out.

Vissyus Searched the Bond. Had he done it? He checked the buffers. They seemed undamaged, and yet, as he walked over to Akuan, his every movement felt labored, as though he waded through quicksand. Fatigue, he guessed. Completing the Binding required more energy than he expected. He peered into the fiery ring. Fiyorok stood at Akuan's side, head down, mind at rest, tired, but outwardly fine. Akuan remained alert, respect shining in its pale blue eyes.

"I don't understand," it said. "How is this possible?"

"The world changes, Akuan. Tradition, law, and even fear keep us from changing with it. We stand in place while creation remakes itself in order to survive. A hundred years ago, the Lady of Light gave birth to our first child, a girl who would presumably show beyond a shadow of a doubt how to take love and give it life."

"I don't see the relevance. Binding two guardians is–"

"Not just two guardians," Vissyus interrupted. "Two

fundamentally *different* Kami."

Akuan's face contorted in horror. "You're using me to simulate that child's conception – two elemental forces fused into one spirit." It shook its head vigorously, revolted. "This is beyond dangerous. Can't you see what it's doing to you?"

"Doing to me?" Vissyus frowned, puzzling over the words. Finding nothing in them, he shrugged. The movement brought a fresh throb. "It isn't doing anything to me."

"You're holding and channeling both powers," Fiyorok grunted, rousing itself. "They're at war in your mind. I warned you not to leave yourself unprotected."

"That can't be," Akuan protested. "I'm not affected."

"You're at the end of the chain," Fiyorok explained. "Our lord is first, then me, then you. He holds the most power, which means he's under the most stress. We need to call for help. I'm too weak. You'll have to do it for me. Use your natural link to Lady Seirin. Hurry, Akuan! Before it's too late."

"No!" Vissyus shouted. "You will *not* worry Seirin with this. I forbid it." He had *not* failed. Vissyus never failed. Apparently, he needed to remind them.

Energy roared along the Bond. He'd almost grown accustomed to the accompanying pain, so intense now it bordered on pleasure. At his command, Fiyorok went completely silent. Akuan's attempt to reach Seirin ended, though not before the troublesome guardian called out to her.

"You do not have permission to speak with Seirin." He wagged a finger. "I won't let you ruin our surprise before it's ready." He forced the dragons to nod, then grinned. "I'm so glad we agree. I need to confirm my success. A simple Delving should do it. Hold still now."

As he focused his power, a small voice at the back of his head railed against him. It came like the shadow of something once important, a part of him now lost. He grimaced. First the incessant pounding and now voices. He'd accede to neither.

The Delving swept through Fiyorok, into Akuan, and then, oddly, into another pathway. Frustrated, though curious, he followed, not knowing where it led, hoping for the confirmations he sought. He felt the world's forges churn in the depths, felt its waters boiling and freezing and falling from the sky into boundless catch basins. The two forces were connected and yet locked in eternal conflict.

Fiyorok was right. He'd made a horrible mistake. In his dreams, he and Seirin were together. This experiment shattered that illusion. Their elements weren't compatible. Joining them was dangerous, potentially deadly. It was just a dream, but it meant the world to him. He loved her – Heaven help him, he loved her more than anything.

Lowering his head in defeat, he pictured her in his mind. Her dazzling smile, her flawless face. He grasped at the image and held it tight, knowing it was the last thing he'd remember.

The tears on his cheeks helped, their salt so like her oceans. He felt them driving toward him, immense and unstoppable; the thought of her powered them forward. On they rolled, and when they reached his fires, instead of the drowning he expected, they ignited waves of explosive energy. His world came to a stop. Time stood still, and then, within that eternal moment, Vissyus felt his mind shatter.

Rage, innocence, and intelligence splintered into divergent personalities. One mourned for Seirin, while a second stared incomprehensibly at his failure. The most dominant, the one tied to his fires, watched the violent dissolution of matter with wonder.

23
REGRET

Seirin woke from a troubled dream. Immediately, she threw off her sheets and paced about her room, hugging herself. Some unknown water spirit had tried to contact her. It felt important, urgent even. She had to find it.

Unfortunately, what should have been a simple Searching turned up nothing. She frowned. Maybe if she'd been home, where her power was strongest, instead of here at Hurricane Point. No, location shouldn't make a difference. She could learn what she wanted here, and she would learn quickly.

Grabbing her robe from a nearby chair, she raced for the door. The Observatory would be her first stop, the perfect place from which to survey the world. If she could find the source of the message then…

Her hand had just touched the handle when a series of deafening explosions rocked the fortress. Casements rattled, and the floors shook. She struggled to stay on her feet, gripping the door to keep from falling. Her body went numb. Something terrible had happened.

Immediately, she launched herself at the windows. Pure green light exploded around her, glass burst and fell away like showers of stars. The Observatory tower loomed ahead, while in the distance a hellish glow painted the sky. She climbed. The seconds it took to reach the top seemed agonizingly long.

Her bare feet slapped against the diamond floor, and she let out a relieved sigh. Aeryk stood in front of the far windows, gazing northeast, his body rigid.

"Aeryk? Aeryk, are you all right?"

His answer cut across her like an arctic wind. "Vissyus. I think… Seirin, something's wrong with him."

She stiffened. "That's ridiculous. Nothing's *wrong* with him."

Aeryk lifted his arm and pointed east. "Volcanoes are erupting. Hundreds of them… all over the world."

"Impossible. Where's the smoke – the ash?" It wasn't true. It couldn't be.

"He cleansed them." Aeryk turned. His eyes were red, and the look he gave her held self-loathing. "You know what that means."

The air in the Observatory grew cold. She backed away. "No. I don't believe it. I *won't*!"

A puff of air wrapped itself around her and gently carried her toward him. "See for yourself."

Reluctantly, she forced her gaze into the world. The eruptions had quieted, and while Roarke and Botua had already started to repair the damage, she still saw the scars – mountains broken, forests burned, here and there new lands forming in the oceans.

"I sent Ventyre out to check on him after the first few eruptions. That was hours ago."

"And?"

"He never came out."

Seirin's legs felt weak, her throat constricted.

"When Vissyus didn't answer, Ventyre cast a Searching

into the volcano. He has a second guardian – a water spirit."

"Why would he…?"

Aeryk tightened his embrace. "His mind is gone, Seirin."

Seirin's eyes widened. The dream! The spirit called to her, tried to warn her. As if unlocked, she saw it again, this time more clearly – fire and ice, rage and innocence, twisted together and yet shattered into a hundred pieces. She couldn't stand. This was her fault. All of it.

"What have we done?" she whispered.

WHITE SPIRIT CASTLE
THE PRESENT

24
IMPETUS

The steam dissipated, but Seirin's memories lingered. Keiko put a hand on the side of her head. She had the distinct impression she'd seen something else, something unrelated to Seirin. The heat had triggered a hidden memory, and the boiling vapor only enhanced the feeling. No matter how hard she tried to remember, though, the thought eluded her.

Shrugging it off, she looked through the fog and found, to her surprise, the Boundary's shimmering walls in place of Takeshi's study. Below, the image of a smoldering planet greeted her: the Earth, her planet, her home.

The history Takeshi conjured stayed with her, filling her soul with sorrow. To the last, Seirin tried to right her wrongs. She led an army of Kami past a great plain ringed with mountains. Vissyus was there, beyond an eastern sea, waiting for her. He emerged from his volcanic stronghold – shield enshrouded – like a rising sun. Guardians rushed his dragons, only to die by the hundreds, immobilizing master and mistress alike.

Fiyorok incinerated a beautiful spirit with lush green hair and yellow eyes as Seirin raced to save her.

Mountains rumbled and fell, the great continent split into seven smaller landmasses, and the seas rushed in to force the shards apart. In the distance, a wall of rippling energy dropped from Heaven to surround the battlefield. It spun faster, separating the Kami apart, isolating them.

Seirin's mind went dark, and Keiko woke to find herself here, inside the Boundary with Takeshi and Yui. She was glad to have them nearby. An odd sensation haunted her, the unsettling feeling of a hidden watcher. Neither Takeshi nor Yui seemed concerned, and that comforted her. She shook off her unease – mostly – and stared down at the broken planet.

"So that's what started this," she whispered.

Takeshi drifted over, and she leveled an accusatory look at him. Anger churned within her. Was the emotion hers, or did the feeling come from somewhere else? She wasn't sure. For some reason, the sight of Takeshi, calm and serene after everything he showed her, brought an uncharacteristic rage.

"Why did Seirin need permission to have a child?" she demanded. Seirin craved a family and Vissyus, his love for her unfulfilled, hoped to win a piece of her heart by making her dreams come true.

"The more power one has," Takeshi began, "the greater his influence over the lives of others. We do the best we can to teach personal responsibility, but sometimes we dream too hard and want too much."

Keiko tried to hide her irritation. What kind of answer was that? "*You* had a child." She crossed her arms. Her face felt hot, flushed.

Takeshi nodded. "I couldn't let the others take the risk. We didn't know what would happen when the parents' powers merged."

"But Yui's all right – more or less. She proved it's safe."

"Yui only answered part of the question, I'm afraid – enough for Aeryk and Seirin to draw the wrong conclusions." Takeshi must have sensed Keiko's confusion because he continued before she could interrupt. "Air and water. The two are eternally connected. Regrettably, I had no way to know how important that was until Yui was old enough for her power to manifest. She is of light and spirit – again, both are compatible."

"And when Vissyus ran his test, he combined water with fire instead of air," Keiko said, understanding what Takeshi was trying to tell her. "That's why it didn't work!"

"Which is why Vissyus created buffers. He thought he could blunt the conflict – or at least hold it in check."

Keiko recalled Fiyorok mentioning buffers. The guardian didn't think they'd work either. Odd. That memory was foggy, and recollection faded as fast as it had come.

"Balance and harmony are created when opposing forces counterbalance one another. No matter how strong Vissyus is – and he is exceptionally strong – he simply couldn't stop the inevitable war between them."

Keiko frowned. "He had to know how dangerous it was."

"I believe he did." A distant, almost wistful look haunted Takeshi's eyes. "Yui can explain this better. She's always been more of a romantic than I."

Yui flickered into view next to her father, her dark glare appearing before the rest of her. "Haven't you ever been in love, Keiko?"

"None of your business," Keiko blushed. "I don't see how my personal life is relevant."

"It's absolutely relevant. People in love do things they wouldn't ordinarily do; the simple becomes complicated. Aeryk and Seirin Bound their identities together – mind, body, and soul, forsaking their independence, searching for common ground, sharing... everything."

Keiko's eyebrows slid to the top of her head. "You really *are* a romantic."

"Unfortunately," Yui continued, plowing over the interruption, "neither realized how much Vissyus loved Seirin or what he would do to make her happy. Vicarious love is the hardest of all."

"That doesn't excuse him, Yui." Keiko tried to keep her voice as gentle as she could.

Yui's eyes burned with anger and sadness. Condemning Vissyus meant condemning herself. Something like that could tear a person apart.

"No one is trying to excuse him, Yamanaka-san," Takeshi said. "We're simply presenting the history. Our goal isn't to absolve Vissyus, it's to stop him."

"Stop him," Keiko repeated. "Not save him." Her spirit felt heavy. After seeing Vissyus for herself – the old Vissyus – she wished it could be otherwise. He wasn't the villain she wanted him to be.

"I have no other choice." Takeshi said, bowing his head in defeat. "His spirit is broken. He's become a powerful and unpredictable force. We can't let him do as he pleases. He'd kill everyone."

"You sound like you're talking about a rabid animal."

"Worse, Yamanaka-san – much worse. An animal's first reaction is to protect itself. Everything else is secondary. Instinct takes over where reason and thinking fail. Not so with Vissyus. A sliver of his mind survives – enough for him to remember fragments of what he was and what he can do." He paused, as if thinking. "Have you ever watched a child build sand castles?"

Keiko nodded.

"What usually happens?"

She shrugged. "The child knocks it down before it's

finished. Or right after."

"Children enjoy the unmaking more than the making." He looked at her intently. "Unless they're angry. That's when the unmaking turns violent. Imagine *that* in a Kami." A shadow flitted over Takeshi's face. "Vissyus will burn this world to a cinder. Unless we stop him."

Keiko tried to swallow a sense of foreboding. The enormous space closed in around her. An uncomfortable tickle surfaced in the deepest part of her head. It moved to her fingertips, so like the connection she felt to her camera and yet profoundly different – more... powerful.

Takeshi hadn't taken his eyes from her. "His guardians are still bound to him. His strength and power are still intact, even if his mind isn't. Without a moral compass to hold him back..." Takeshi fanned his hands.

Keiko had stopped listening. A slight hiccup in her surroundings – a lurch like a needle skip on an old phonograph – drew her attention. Odd the others didn't feel it, especially Takeshi. They *were* inside his Boundary, after all. If the Boundary and his guardian were one and the same, he had to know when something was wrong. Didn't he? She searched the space.

Yui had just called Takeshi over, and the two dove into some private conversation an arm's length away, Yui making small gestures while her father listened. Several feet below, the air rippled and then calmed. A figure slowly took shape, barely visible at first, but solidifying. Keiko's heart faltered. She recognized that boyish face, that tawny hair. A chill swept through her as eyes like burning fire landed on her. She wanted to scream, but an external will immobilized her.

Vissyus.

Horrified, Keiko watched him raise a finger to his lips, an impish smile making him look like a lost cherub. Limitless power reached for her, a net of woven insanity – threads of innocence, filaments of madness, the whole coated with quicksilver. It passed over her, sliding away toward the two figures in huddled conversation. She felt it land on Takeshi, heard Vissyus's exhalation. An astonishing transformation came over him. All trace of his playful demeanor evaporated, and a very different person peered out from those fiery eyes, this one wild and hurt and angry.

"Mr Takeshi!" Keiko cried, tugging at Takeshi's sleeve.

Takeshi brushed her aside. "In a minute, Yamanaka-san. Yui and I have something to discuss."

Vissyus's expression immediately became warm, almost paternal. So many changes, so fast.

"Yui?" he exclaimed. "Can it be?" His eyes flicked back to Keiko. "And already Bonded." He pressed his palms together in a gesture that reminded Keiko of prayer, touched them to his lips, and whispered hungrily through them. "I sense the stars in you." He giggled happily. "Star child. I was right! I knew it!"

Takeshi whirled, an arm raised protectively in front of his daughter. Shock registered in his eyes, his body tense and ready.

Vissyus looked equally stunned. Then, as recognition played across his face, an almost primal fury erupted throughout his body. Steam issued from his mouth, black smoke curling from the corners of his eyes. Keiko had never seen anything like it. She shrank back, fear tightening her throat.

"*You*!" Vissyus roared. He stood and drew himself up to his full height. A whip of fire flew from his hand like lightning, its scarlet flames dancing in the darkness. Fast and deadly, the thongs looped around Takeshi's neck before he could raise his shield. "*Trickster*! *Betrayer*! You promised to help her!"

He tugged on the whip, and Takeshi staggered forward. The smell of burning flesh filled the air.

"She suffers because of you. All this time." He lowered his head, and his voice became sad. "I tried to find her. I never stopped trying. Lon-Shan showed me how to move through the Boundary. Not intentionally. Like you, he never knew I was watching. I have learned more than you can believe, more than enough to make you... uncomfortable."

Takeshi's paling face brought a cruel satisfied grin.

"Did you really think the Boundary would fool me? Its pathways are interconnected and easy to navigate. I knew you'd come here. All I had to do was wait for the Weakening. You should have checked the internal walls." His lips pulled back into a rabid snarl, the red-golden eyes above glowing manically. "Foolish man. Time to pay!"

Keiko had never felt so helpless. She needed to do something, anything. She moved forward. Vissyus glanced at her and she froze, but not before she threw her thoughts at Yui.

What are you waiting for? she urged. *You have to help him!*

Yui's shield sprang to life, and a lance of pure light flashed between her fingers – indigo hafted and tipped with yellow-white. Keiko followed its arc as Yui swept it up and then down, severing Vissyus's whip with one quick slice. Yui brought up her other hand, and a stream of blinding, sunlike rays flew from her opened palm.

It slammed into a disc of living fire – a fragment of Vissyus's shield – its size insulting, its message chilling. Vissyus had blocked her as easily as a blade of grass. Unless Yui had something else up her sleeve, this fight was over before it started. Keiko hoped Yui knew when to cut her losses. But, to her dismay, Yui charged.

Power exploded around Vissyus in a blaze of red and orange fire. Takeshi raised his shield in an arc to surround Yui and Keiko as well as himself. Yui somersaulted through its narrowing gap, dropped to a crouch to avoid the fires, and then prowled ahead to continue the fight.

Vissyus's eyes flashed like heated coals. "Trickster. If my noose is too good for you, perhaps I can find something more *poetic*."

He still held his whip in his right hand, but as Keiko watched he snuffed it out. In its place, small, nucleic spheres formed over his opened palms. They hovered there like miniature suns, spinning in tight, fast circles.

For one long minute, nothing happened. Each spirit measured the other, waiting for his opponent to move first. Takeshi's gaze remained locked on Vissyus, but when he moved, it was toward Yui.

Yui shrugged away and stalked forward.

"*No*!" Takeshi shouted. "He's too strong! Fall back. Yui! Fall back!"

"He's right in front of us, Father! We can finish this!" A reformed javelin sizzled in Yui's hand, her eyes bright, determined.

Vissyus smiled at her, unafraid.

"I said *fall back*!" Takeshi said, more firmly this time. He threw his shield at Yui's. "We have to run. We have to run if we want to survive."

White light surrounded indigo. Takeshi slashed a hand at the Boundary's shimmering wall, and Yui's shield hurtled toward it. A second slash lifted Keiko by the back of her robe and hurled her in.

Reality twisted sickeningly. The disturbing image of flushed refuse filled Keiko's head, and she was grateful when the brilliance ripped open, spilling her hard onto the tatami mats of Takeshi's chambers. Unshielded, Yui tumbled past a moment or two later and rolled to a halt by the far wall. An angry welt decorated her forehead, which she fingered gingerly.

Keiko hurried over. "Are you all right?" Her voice sounded ragged in her ears.

"I'm fine," Yui said with a weak smile. "Thank you, Keiko. You have saved me."

"Again," Keiko grinned.

Yui nodded. "Again. But more importantly…"

The air behind them shimmered, and Takeshi stepped into the room. He touched his knuckles together and muttered under his breath. Pure white light lanced from his fingers. Keiko turned her head and covered her eyes to avoid temporary blindness. When the glow died away, the opening had disappeared.

Yui glanced at him. After Vissyus's attack, she wore her affection openly.

Takeshi stood alone on the other side of the room, sweating heavily, his chest heaving. He seemed to sense their eyes on him, strode over, and helped them both to their feet. A long, sinister burn ran around his neck. Yui stretched a hand to examine the wound, but he pushed her away.

"We don't have time for that now! Gather your things. You leave for Nepal within the hour. I opened the Boundary in a way Vissyus can't, but he still could have seen something to help him understand its construction. Our time is now significantly shorter."

"But we just got here!" Keiko bit down a growing emptiness. She didn't know if she could make the castle her home, but she'd like the chance to try.

Yui whirled to face her father. "What makes you think I'm taking her with me?"

"A Kami should have a protector," Takeshi said.

Keiko's pride burned at the words. She knew he trusted her to watch Yui, and while he hadn't used the word *guardian*, he inferred it. "We're in this together, Yui. We have been since Tokyo. You know that."

Yui looked helplessly at her father. "She hasn't Awakened yet, and even if she had, she doesn't know a thing about controlling her power."

"And you don't know how to use yours in a real fight. Training isn't the same as combat, I assure you. Even I take my guardian into battle, and I've been in more than enough; this will be your first. Going alone when you don't have to is both reckless and foolhardy."

Yui crossed her arms. "She's a liability."

"She's a Yamanaka. And more than capable." Takeshi walked gingerly to the elevated platform in the middle of the room and placed a hand on the cloth representation of Mount Fuji. "We need to release Roarke, Spirit of Earth, and I cannot leave. Japan is a nation born from all the forces now at war. The seas surround it. Wind protects it. A restless Earth shakes beneath it, threatening its volcanoes." His hand curled into a fist. "I won't abandon it now."

"I can do this, Yui," Keiko said, stepping forward. "It's what my father wanted."

Yui hesitated, and Keiko saw the conflict raging through her. She thought she understood. As Takeshi Akiko's daughter, Yui couldn't have many friends: protocol wouldn't allow it. No wonder her feelings for Masato developed the way they did. They'd spent a good deal of time together, much of it alone. He was gone now, and no one else could fill that role for her, certainly no one within the castle's hierarchy. Until Keiko.

Yui reached a decision. She exhaled, and some of the tension left her body. "All right," she said. "You can come."

25
SURVIVOR

Paitr Norwoska huddled in his shield, afraid to move and afraid to remain where he was. Rubble covered him, blocked his view. He didn't know whether he should bless the ruin for keeping the truth from him or curse it for leaving him alone with his pitiful fear. At least he was still alive, a small miracle as far as he was concerned, especially when his lord probably wasn't. He wondered how long he would last without his god. Lon-Shan's power created this place; what would happen without him? A bitter laugh burned Paitr's throat. All those years of service, all of it wasted. He sighed. If only his lord had granted the immortality he promised.

Pushing himself to his feet, he made a wide sweeping motion with his arm. Dark tendrils leeched into the fallen rocks like cancerous cells, filling every seam and fissure. A simple outward thrust blew the debris into the decimated landscape beyond. He stared at the devastation for a moment before flying to the top of a twisted girder for a better look.

The once-impressive city now reminded him of a muddy river delta. Water sluiced through the streets, the newly emergent sun coloring the brown liquid to bronze. He shaded his eyes from the glare and tried to locate some sign of life. Apart from the floods and the breeze-stirred refuse, he found nothing but stillness.

How did this happen? he wondered. Who *was* that woman? Where did she come from? Paitr had never seen anything like her – beautiful, majestic, and deadly. She commanded the rains the way Lon-Shan commanded the night. His fellow lords couldn't stop her; Lord Streega couldn't stop her. Lord Lon-Shan himself hadn't even slowed her.

The thought was enough to stop his heart cold. He stayed there for a long time, half dazed, half rudderless, reliving his life's choices. His eyes traced a glowing orb in the skies. It tugged at his mind, and he frowned – focusing on it, probing, looking closer.

A man hovered inside, tall and imperious. Red-golden eyes moved over the ground as if searching. They touched a ring of mountains, flared angrily, and moved on, though not before melting half the range. The red dragon floating next to the man opened its jaws and raked the flooded city, leaving it steaming like a boiling pot.

"You cannot hide from me, Trickster!" the man bellowed. "There is nowhere left to go!" He laughed then, a wild, roaring sound that hurt Paitr's ears. "I know the Teacher was here. This place reeks of her magnificent power. What have you done with her?"

Paitr watched the man approach, neither slowing nor pausing. His fires flared once against the darkness before he disappeared into the striated wall. Less than a heartbeat later, a second figure materialized a mile or so to the east. Unlike the first, this one remained spectral.

"He's moving easily through the Boundary," it said,

turning to the shimmering wall above. "How long can you keep him inside?"

The Boundary flashed in reply. "I can hold until you are ready."

Paitr staggered. *Alive? That thing's alive. But that's impossible.*

"Seirin's completed her task," the ghost continued. "Aeryk will make sure she's in Tokyo to meet the others."

The figure turned its head, and for a moment, Paitr thought it stared at him, maybe even smiled. He blinked and shook his head. When he looked back, the specter was gone.

Exhaling thoughtfully, Paitr lowered himself onto a slab of upturned marble.

To meet the others, he thought. *So. This is a war, a personal one.* Finally, something he could understand, something he could use. A child learns the ways of the world from his parents, and he'd learned his lessons particularly well. Strike from the shadows, bring the unexpected. He laughed. What did he care if these gods blew the world to pieces? He was dead anyway. Already, he felt Lon-Shan's power leeching from his blood. Vengeance was what he wanted. Vengeance against the powerful, just as Lord Lon-Shan promised. For the first time since his lord's death, he knew what he had to do. Standing, he took one last look at his master's humbled palace and flew into the air.

Below, an angry line – etched into earth and building alike – marked the end of the blast radius: everything beyond remained untouched. The stark division between normality and chaos stayed with Paitr as he approached the broad plain on the outskirts of the city. His sprawling, fortified compound lay a few miles ahead, jutting out of the distant flatlands like a mesa.

Thick walls surrounded it, and lookout towers sprang up at each of its four corners.

Paitr banked toward a squat building in the center of the grounds, feeling no guilt at becoming one of the elites he thought he despised. People needed leaders, and he was all they had left. A short balding man waited for him before a pair of imposing doors. "Have you summoned the staff to the main hall?" Paitr asked as he touched down onto the hard cobblestone driveway.

"Everything is exactly as you wanted, my lord. I collected them as soon as you commanded it. You will find every person working within these walls lined up and ready for inspection."

"Very good, Josef. I will be with them shortly."

"It will be as you say, my lord." Josef bowed and made his way back through the entrance.

Paitr barely noticed him go. His eyes were on the mountains – what little remained of them.

Tokyo. That's where she was headed – one of the most densely populated cities on Earth. His troops would like that. They'd like it very much. Spinning, he strode through the double arched doors.

Ten minutes later, he was back outside, his shield reformed and thickened to carry the servants he'd stuffed into a ball of black energy. Josef was there as well, dutifully seeing his lord off with assurances that all would be in order when he returned.

Paitr wasn't listening. He had more important matters to attend to at the moment, and he feared time was already running short.

Without waiting for the obsequious little man to finish, he pushed from the ground and set a course that would take him deep into the mountains. Icy winds brushed against his shield, tiny droplets of crystallized water sizzling and vaporizing as he pressed on. His blood boiled, and the closer he drew to the caves, the faster it surged through him.

The entrance appeared in a gap between two snow-covered ridges and again when he peeked around the shoulder of a mountain. Dropping down, he cut through a high ravine. An immense gate of stone crisscrossed with iron bands and sealed firmly waited for him on the other side. It rumbled open as he approached, revealing a darkened burrow and a single, black passage.

Inside, he made his way through the network of tunnels until finally – several miles below ground – he broke into a large cavern. Thousands of glittering eyes turned toward him in anticipation, silent, hungry, and ready. Lord Lon-Shan's secret army gazed at him in anticipation.

A thin smile split Paitr's face. Slowing, he brought his dark sphere to a halt halfway between the floor and the ceiling, lifted his arm, and whipped it as if throwing. A big, black ball broke from his shield and sailed effortlessly over the horde, arching higher until it burst to reveal a young woman in pleated skirts. Terror paled her pretty face. Her eyes were wide and wild, her shrieks growing more frantic.

Paitr gave her another minute before her mind disintegrated.

The swarming mass below followed her flight. A few of the beasts refused to look away from him, however. Did they recognize him, or were they too hungry to care? They needed a reminder. A thought yanked the woman upward just as a clawed hand reached for her ankle. The creature howled angrily and tried again.

Paitr lowered her, only to jerk her back up. The sweet smell of her fear filled the air. "I decide when and what you receive!" he shouted.

Lon-Shan once said the beasts were like Streega, and if that was true, maybe he could bind them. He didn't have his god's power, of course, but he had food. If that wasn't enough, they'd kill him. He wasn't afraid, though. Without Lon-Shan, he was dead already.

Enraged, he dropped the girl into the horde, pulled a second ball from his shield – this one holding a chambermaid – and let it fly. A stable boy came next, and then a groundskeeper. He threw again and again, and when he'd run out of servants, he blasted the far wall to pieces. Below, a sea of dark eyes watched him, the sounds of feasting paused.

Paitr nodded knowingly. Food – that's what they responded to. Outside, he could give them all the food they wanted. The woman who destroyed his dreams wouldn't know what hit her.

26
FAITH

Aeryk turned his back to the sealed Gate off Florida's coast and flew east with a heavy heart. His time with Seirin had been too short, more blissful dream than reality. She was gone now, racing off into danger because of Lon-Shan. He wanted to go with her but understood why he couldn't.

Accelerating, he blasted over the ocean and climbed toward an immense cumulus cloud southeast of Miami. A tunnel into the vast mist opened with a thought, and he dove through its billowing walls. White lumps gave way to the great hollow cone where his ancient fortress sprang out of layered altostratus clouds, building turret upon turret over soaring balustrades. He needed neither Gate nor Keystone to enter his ancient fortress; he hadn't been at the great battle, and the Boundary never claimed him. Instead of leaving his castle on the wide peninsula where he built it, he uprooted the foundations and sent the whole into the skies above Seirin's Gate. If he couldn't be with her, then being close would have to do.

Climbing past the palace's base, he reached a broad

plateau halfway up where the granite ramparts leveled off. Ornate buildings perched atop the landing, tall and lean, with rounded and rolling parapets to match the look of the cloud surrounding it.

Once, when Seirin came to stay with him, she said Hurricane Point's elegance reminded her of a glistening cake. He smiled, relishing the inference.

The largest structure – a tower of pure white marble – lanced into the sky from the heart of the main citadel. He aimed for the great blue dome at the top, landed on the western side, and hurried to the open windows.

"I don't like this," he muttered. "I can't believe I let her talk me into it."

A light rumble, like the sound of distant thunder, rolled up from behind, startling him. Aeryk cursed himself for not sensing the thunderbird's arrival. He noted neither its approach nor its landing. He turned his head, and detected a touch of amusement in its sharp, lavender eyes.

"You find something funny, guardian?" he said.

"No, my lord. Nothing at all." The guardian's slender, triangular head tilted to one side, tufted jowls fanning outward from the base of its golden beak. "I see you're trying to win a settled argument." It preened a wing the size of a small airliner's, trying not to look smug. "So much time has passed, and yet so little has changed. Tell me, lord, have you ever won a debate when she was still in the room, or do your victories come after she's gone?"

"You need to watch what you say."

Ventyre shrugged. "I'm only speaking the truth. We both know she's better equipped to deal with Lon-Shan than you are. Lon-Shan knows how to manipulate you."

Aeryk scowled. "One of these days, you'll stumble over that glib tongue of yours." He clasped his hands behind his back and walked toward the window.

"Vigils never solved anything," Ventyre pressed. "Either do something or find a distraction."

Aeryk ignored the comment and paced the Observatory's diamond floors, head down, stomach churning. Seconds stretched into minutes; time passed, though how much, he couldn't say. Hands clenched, he glanced out the eastern window for what seemed like the thousandth time. Where was she?

Ventyre, now perched at the ledge, swept the skies for some sign of movement. Time crawled. One second. Two. Finally, the guardian's trumpeting voice broke the silence. "I see her, my lord! She's dropped her Masking and is making her way across the Atlantic. Judging by her speed, she should be here soon." The large bird whipped its long neck away from the edge of the Observatory and stared back at him, relief softening its avian face. "She is uninjured!"

Aeryk drew in a breath to steady his racing heart. He turned on his heels and stalked – one labored step at a time – to stand beside his guardian, anxiously scanning the skies, first by sight and then with a Searching.

He found her cutting through a tropical storm two hundred miles south of Bermuda. The rains mirrored her tears, the winds her agonized cries. Grief tore at her heart, guilt making it worse. Ventyre didn't think she was hurt, but he knew differently. Frustrated, he slammed his fist against an arcing support beam. Lon-Shan was another lost spirit, another death on their hands. How much was enough?

Ventyre's concerned thoughts tickled his mind, but he refused to answer. Instead, he leaped from the tower and threw his shield at the gates. That's where he should have been, not up in the Observatory, not pining for her like a jilted lover. She needed him, now more than ever. He wouldn't disappoint her. Not this time.

His feet touched down at the far end of the castle's large rectangular courtyard, and he skidded past an exquisitely sculpted fountain. Ahead, a slender white bridge ran from castle to cloud. Seirin's emerald shield landed at the far end, held for a moment, then burst open like a soap bubble.

In seconds, he was bounding toward her. His arms opened then closed about her like a vice. Safe, she buried her face in his chest and seized his shirt with her hands. Drawing him closer.

She lifted her face to his, her tears nearly breaking him. "What have we done, Aeryk?"

"We didn't know." Aeryk shook his head. "Lon-Shan, Vissyus… we didn't know."

Seirin swayed against him, and he moved his hand to her elbow.

"I think I need to get you inside. We can talk more later." Without letting go, he led her into the main hall. A ramp to the right spiraled into one of the grand turrets along the outer wall. He half expected her to slip free when they reached the tower, but she simply pressed into him as they climbed to their chambers, opened the elegant white door, and stepped into a large room. Turquoise tiles, covered here and there with white area rugs, ran from one wall to the other. The furniture, most of which was carved from multi-hued coral, always reminded Aeryk of great reefs peeking out of a tranquil sea.

Seirin excused herself and walked into an adjoining chamber. When Aeryk heard the soft fizz of a fountain-shower, he settled into a large, shell-shaped ottoman to wait. She re-entered a short while later in a soft gossamer dress of cerulean blue. Touches of pink-blended white accented a top that fell away diagonally to bare her right shoulder. Short, it barely reached to mid-thigh, and as soon as he saw her dressed for bed, he let out a relieved sigh.

"Afraid I was heading out again?" she chided. "The thought did occur to me, but when I saw this," she plucked at the front of the dress, likely exposing more than she intended, "I realized how tired I was. It was nice of you to remember it."

"It gets warm in the tropics," Aeryk shrugged. She'd deal with her emotions when she was ready. Pushing now would be a mistake. "And the humidity makes it feel worse than it is. A good host plans for his guests' needs."

"*Really*?" She laughed, her voice light if tired. "Too bad we don't know anyone who can – I don't know – summon a breeze? Cool the air perhaps?" He opened his mouth to speak, but she touched a silencing finger to his lips. "Well, then, *host*, since we can't do anything about the weather…" She draped her arms about his neck and kissed him deeply.

"I should have trusted you," she said when she pulled away. "I lost hope, I'm sorry."

Unable to meet her gaze, he lowered his eyes. "I made a promise, and on the most important day of your life, I failed you."

Seirin brushed his hair with her fingers and searched his face. "You didn't fail me. I didn't understand it at the time, but I do now." She kissed him again and then wormed her way under his arm, adjusting her position to make herself more comfortable. Golden hair spilled over her forehead. Her chin drooped drowsily to touch her chest. She lifted her hand to cover a yawn.

Aeryk swept the strands away and sat motionless on the corner of the chair for several long moments, luxuriating in her presence.

Finally, when her breathing deepened and her body relaxed, he carried her across the room and lowered her gently onto the soft, quilted bed. He brushed a kiss across her lips, backed out of the room, and made his way back to the Observatory.

The cavernous space was empty, its diamond floors reflecting the orange glow of the setting sun. Aeryk crossed the room and stopped at the eastern-facing windows. A velvety darkness crawled across the sky, newly emergent stars twinkling within it.

Another day gone, one day closer to Vissyus's return. Moments became increasingly important. The new day would come, and when it did, at least he'd have Seirin at his side. Her happiness was all that mattered to him. He watched the sun drop below the horizon, swearing he would defend her to the very end.

27
PUPPETS

Vissyus's mind swept over a forbidding landscape of rock and ice. The urge to turn the whole canyon into a heap of molten slag bubbled within him. He hated the cold, tolerating it only for Akuan's sake. Akuan. Fury boiled Vissyus's blood when he thought of his guardian's wounding. The Trickster would pay for that. No one attacked his child without punishment.

"The Keystone is close," he said to Fiyorok. The guardian's awareness flickered beside his – sometimes merging, sometimes separate. "I can feel it."

Fiyorok's thoughts burned, and Vissyus felt a rush of heat in his chest – or was it Fiyorok's? He couldn't tell. "You wish me to attack?"

Vissyus shook his head, the motion quick yet energy consuming, as if he moved a large object. "The Trickster sent emissaries to other Gates. He'll do the same here."

"What if he sends the girl?"

The girl? Vissyus hadn't considered the possibility. What would the Teacher think if Fiyorok hurt the girl? He licked his lips with a long tongue. Fire dripped down a golden chin. He thought he felt it.

"I can't be with Teacher unless I'm free," he said. "I need to know how to open my Gate, Fiyorok. Everything else is secondary."

Fiyorok's answer became a blur of distorted sound. Vissyus felt his mind pull back, his eyes falling on a sleeping Akuan. Fires plumed beyond shining black walls. He was back and yet not. A part of him returned to watch over Akuan while another part remained with Fiyorok. Waiting for… *her*.

He smiled, hoping Fiyorok was right. The Trickster wounded his child, and now he would return the favor.

Keiko sat at a wooden table, a tray of smoked meat and bread before her. The rest of the inn looked like something from a renaissance fayre, though with a decidedly eastern flavor. Tables identical to hers filled a cramped dining room, with benches for seating instead of chairs. The serviceable bar hugging the far wall appeared to be made from the same wood as the tables, benches, floor, and just about everything else, though the dim guttering candles made it hard to tell for sure. At least the air was warmer than she expected, but then the village was on the fringe of the Himalayas, not in them.

This early, the place was deserted. Even the innkeeper, a happy-faced little man of about fifty, had disappeared, presumably to prepare the day's menu. Not that Keiko minded. As much as she liked him, she didn't want him around when Yui returned. The young Kami was unpredictable. Keiko had no idea what she'd bring back with her.

Her eyes drifted to the inn's door for what seemed like the hundredth time. She was about to go back to her meager meal when the hinges creaked and Yui stepped over the threshold, a wizened man in a fur-lined coat following a step behind. Something about the man held Keiko's attention. His gait was wooden, mechanical even, and though he navigated the dining room's clutter easily, his eyes never moved. It wasn't natural, not even for a blind man.

Yui reached Keiko's table before he did and lifted her hand. The man stopped.

"This Sherpa returned from a climb two weeks ago." Yui nodded to the figure behind her. He was taller than Keiko, but not by much, with strong, weathered hands and dark eyes that reflected... nothing.

"What did you do to him?" The man's vacant expression and slack, bearded jaw unnerved Keiko. Combined with the jerky way he moved, he might as well have been a marionette, another piece of wood for the inn.

"What?" Yui said, blinking. "I don't–"

"I'll ask you one more time..."

"I'm controlling his soul." Yui shrugged. "Someone tampered with his memories. This is the only way to reach them without him remembering."

"Controlling his soul?" Keiko spat. "Do you even listen to yourself? You can't just go around messing with people like this. Well, you can – apparently – but you shouldn't. It's wrong."

"We need information before we approach Roarke's Gate," Yui said primly. "This is the only way to get it. If Roarke's guardian is out there, it won't wait for us to identify ourselves, not with Fiyorok and Akuan on the loose."

"That doesn't give you the right to hijack a man's soul." Keiko thumped her fist on the table. "Look at him." The Sherpa continued to stare ahead, neither moving nor speaking. He gave Keiko the creeps.

Anger flickered behind Yui's eyes. "His memories are important. I can't reach them any other way."

"You're treating us like puppets. We're better than that, and so are you."

"Lord Roarke is doing what he can to protect himself. What do you suppose would happen if he found this man wandering around near his Gate? Do you think he'd just let him go without interrogating him?" She leaned forward. "You wouldn't want *that* to happen, I promise you."

Keiko shivered but refused to back down. "It still isn't right."

"None of this is right. That's why we're here – to make sure it doesn't get any worse. Roarke has an important part to play. He proved it before; he can do it again."

Roarke had rebuilt what Vissyus destroyed. Keiko remembered hearing Aeryk tell Seirin as much when Takeshi sent her into the water Kami's memories. She folded her arms and slumped back into her seat. Her gaze shifted to the Sherpa. He might as well have been a mannequin. She flicked her thumb at him.

"Let's get this over with," she sighed. "His legs will be killing him by tomorrow."

Yui grinned. "He climbs mountains, Keiko. I'm sure he'll be fine. Shall I have him report in English so you can understand him?"

"Does he *speak* English?"

"Nepali and some Mandarin."

"Then how…?" Keiko waved her hand in surrender. "Yes, Yui. English is fine."

Yui flipped her wrist, and the man awakened. "Two weeks ago, a group of Chinese hired me to lead them up Kanchenjunga," he said, his voice thin and reedy. "I refused at first. It is a sacred mountain. Few go there, and fewer return. They offered a great deal of money. I am not a wealthy man, and my family is large. So, I accepted.

"We began our climb just over a week ago. Half of my team abandoned me at the foothills after a strong tremor. Kanchenjunga is a quiet mountain; quakes do not happen there. My men said we angered the Mountain God. I did not believe and continued on. That night, as we made camp, a fierce squall blew through the range. I left my tent to secure our gear when I saw it."

The wooden bench beneath Keiko creaked as she leaned forward. "What? What did you see?"

"A stone giant covered with snow and moving through the storm." The Sherpa stared straight ahead as he spoke, reminding Keiko of a ventriloquist's dummy. She threw a harsh glare at Yui. "It ran from a shimmering light, but it wasn't fast enough. The light overtook the figure then winked out. When our eyes adjusted to the darkness, we found nothing but the snow. The giant had vanished."

"Malog. Guardian of stone." Yui glanced at the Sherpa and waved her hand dismissively. The man promptly turned and strode from the room with a wooden gait.

Keiko lifted her chin after the man. "That will wear off, won't it?"

"In a few minutes. I had to erase this meeting from his mind. If I can pull hidden memories from him, Vissyus can as well. We can't take any chances." Yui turned her face to the door. "Once his thoughts are clear, his consciousness will return."

Keiko disapproved but kept her comments to herself. She'd said her piece and didn't need to belabor the point. Gathering her small pack from beneath the table, she followed Yui into the street. Once outside, her spirits lifted. She liked the village's simplicity – dirt roads, wooden homes, shingled roofs, rich green pastures filled with livestock. It felt more grounded than the cities. Even the people, scraping to make a living, seemed more alive than their urban counterparts. Here, they made their schedules around the planet's natural rhythms. They didn't dwell over missed buses or canceled meetings. They just... *lived*.

Yui guided her down the village's only street, retracing their steps out of town. They had landed behind a steep hill to minimize the risk of detection and would leave the same way.

"I take it you got what you came for," Keiko said as they walked. She inhaled, drawing in the rustic scent of tilled earth and woodsmoke.

"I did. I needed information about Roarke's guardian before we approached the mountain."

"That it's out, you mean?"

Yui shook her head. "On the contrary. I wanted make sure it was back inside."

A herd of goats scampered across their path, ending with a little girl brandishing a stick above her head like a sword.

"Do you want me to ask why that's important, or do you just plan on telling me?" Keiko watched the girl with amusement. The smoky smell grew stronger.

"If Malog sensed another power in the valley, it might attack before we identified ourselves. We can't afford that."

"No. I don't suppose we can. How long will it take us to get to the Gateway?"

"Not long." Yui smiled wickedly. "Of course, it would go faster if you learned how to form a shield and fly for yourself."

"Until I slammed into the side of the mountain," Keiko

grumbled. "Digging me out would take you a while."

Yui raised an eyebrow. "And what would that teach you?"

"That you'd leave me behind," Keiko said softly. "Just like everyone else." She bit her lip and looked away. "I'm sorry. I shouldn't have said that."

More people hurried across the street, this time moving in the opposite direction. Yui threaded her way through the crowd and stopped in front of Keiko. "It's all right," she said firmly. "I forgot what you've been through. I know how it feels to be left behind. My mother, Masato." Smoke cut through the air between them, the wind catching Yui's silken hair, swirling embers glowing against it like stars. "I won't do that to you. I promise."

"What if this power I'm supposed to have never comes? Your father says it will, but I don't feel *anything*."

The confidence Keiko felt in Takeshi's castle seemed like a distant memory. All that talk about her family and its abilities. A part of her thought the power would materialize as soon as they were on their way. It hadn't. Maybe she was wrong about this. Maybe she should have stayed behind. She shook her head.

"I'm letting you down, Yui. You were right. I'm a liability."

Yui's expression softened. "I was mistaken." She smiled warmly. "It's nice having someone to talk to. That may not seem like much to you, but it means a great deal to me."

"But I want to help. It's why my father sent me. So far I haven't done anything but watch."

"Like in the subway?" Yui said. "Or in the White Spirit? Your observations saved our lives, Keiko. Keiko?"

But Keiko had stopped listening. Several young men carrying buckets came at them from the left, shouting and gesturing as they ran. She tensed. Something was wrong.

"What is it?" Yui asked.

"The whole town's in an uproar. Don't you feel it?"

Yui blinked and then cursed. "This way."

They dashed down a narrow side alley, past rows of simple homes and into a small farm. Thick clouds issued from a medium-sized barn, an angry glow visible behind its open doors. To Keiko's surprise, a crowd of villagers surrounded the same Sherpa Yui questioned at the inn, obviously consoling him.

Yui signaled for Keiko to wait and approached the group. When she returned, her face was ashen.

"Yui? What's wrong?"

Anguish played across Yui's face. She covered her eyes with a hand and drew in a deep breath. "This is his home." She nodded at the Sherpa. "He went straight to the barn after leaving the inn. One of his sons was changing the oil in a tractor when he arrived. His mind must not have settled... He... he tried to light a cigarette, but his hands didn't work right. He dropped the match into the oil. This is my fault." She lowered her head. "You tried to warn me, but I didn't listen."

"I didn't know this would happen." Keiko placed her hand on Yui's arm. "And neither did you."

"I was arrogant. You were right about using people." She looked back at the burning barn. A large beam gave way with a groan. It fell in a shower of orange sparks. "I know better now."

The townspeople contained the fire in the dying barn, but that wouldn't matter to Yui.

"Is there anything we can do?" Keiko asked.

"I've already seen to it. I paid the villagers to rebuild the barn." She inhaled. "And the man's son is very sick –

leukemia. I made sure I healed him before I left."

Keiko stepped close to Yui. "You can do that?"

"We have the power to heal ourselves." Yui's voice was quiet. "I tethered my mind and body to his until I removed the sickness. We're not supposed to do it, but the Sherpa was my responsibility, and I failed him."

Guiding Yui away, Keiko headed back to the main road and out of the village. "You know," she said, hoping to change the subject, "that power could come in useful up there." She pointed to the distant, snow-covered mountains, swept a hand over her silk kimono, and frowned. "We're not exactly dressed for a climb."

Yui shook herself back to life with each step, and by the time they reached the sheltering hill, Keiko thought she'd put the incident behind her. Hopefully, not too far, though. Yui needed to remember it.

"A Kami doesn't worry about the elements," Yui said. "You'll be fine."

"I'm *not* a Kami," Keiko sniffed.

"A guardian then."

Keiko's feet faltered. "A guardian?"

"Yes, Keiko." A knowing smile curved Yui's lips. "It's what you wanted, isn't it?"

Keiko wished she could stop her cheeks from flaming. "How did you know?"

Yui continued to walk along the dusty path, and Keiko hurried to catch up. They rounded a curve in the road and continued on until the hill obscured the small village.

"I am the Lady of Spirit. You can't hide something like that from me. Protector? Honestly, Keiko."

"I never said that. Your father did. And according to him, a human can't be a guardian. He said it's impossible."

"And yet you persevere. Why is that?"

Because it's all I have, she wanted to say. Instead, she kept her mouth shut and quickened her pace, hoping Yui wouldn't press her. Thinking about being alone brought her grief back. She faced an uncertain future; if she couldn't be a guardian, what would she do?

When they neared the spot where Yui's shield burned a light ring in the grass, Yui stopped and leaned in close to Keiko. "I can help you. I command spirit, too. I can turn you into a guardian, if that's what you want."

As much as Keiko longed to accept, she pulled away. A surge of unexpected anger rolled through her body like a river of molten rock.

"Just because you say I'm a guardian doesn't make it true, you know. You can't wave your hand and make things all right. No one can." She clamped her mouth shut as soon as the words left her lips, but the damage was done.

Pink streaked Yui's cheeks, and when she spoke, her tone was frosty. "Forgive me, I won't mention it again." She headed for the charred ground without waiting for Keiko.

"I'm sorry," Keiko said. "I appreciate the offer. I really do. I just don't think you can decree something like this. I need to earn it. On my own. It won't mean anything if I don't."

Yui nodded slowly. "No; it's OK. I know what it's like to live with someone else's expectations."

"I'll bet you do." Keiko grinned. "I guess that means we both have something to prove." She looked up at the mountains. Though distant, they loomed over her – tall, cold, and forbidding. "We better not die trying."

28
AVALANCHE

An hour later, Keiko found herself back in her familiar spot behind Yui, soaring over an inhospitable range of glacial summits, precipitous slopes, and ice-walled ravines. The crystal-clear skies offered a perfect view of the range, and Keiko admired the sight for as long as she could. When they were within a few thousand feet of the highest peaks, Yui began a gradual descent.

"*This is incredible!*" Keiko beamed. She cast a disgruntled look at Yui. "Can't you slow down a little. It's not every day you get the chance to see something like this, and certainly not *like* this." She gestured toward the immense, snow-covered mountains below, the image surprisingly undistorted despite Yui's indigo-tinted shield.

"Unless you've learned how to slow your time stream, we can't afford the delay."

"You know I haven't," Keiko said sharply. "Too bad, too. Look around, Yui. Appreciate the world you're trying to save."

"I know, Keiko. It's beautiful. I understand that. Unfortunately, it's also a distraction. I need you to think about your power. Focus on your thoughts, then train yourself to push them beyond your body."

Keiko nodded. Yui was only trying to help, but the constant reminders bordered on nagging. Absently, she wondered if Yui nagged Masato too. She doubted it.

Yui studied Keiko for a moment, then – apparently satisfied – threw their shield into a dizzyingly steep spiral. Keiko's stomach lurched to her throat, making it impossible to say anything until they leveled out. Ahead, the rough outline of a massive, glacier-formed mountain burst from the earth in a series of peaks and summits. At nearly thirty thousand feet, it dominated the landscape, sprawling over a wider area than Everest's taller, yet leaner, footprint in the northwest.

Yui banked toward it. "Kanchenjunga. We'll find the Keystone in a hidden valley halfway up."

She flew toward a razor-thin gap where one of the mountain's five peaks split away from the foundations. A wide gash cut through the formidable clumps of up-thrust earth to separate one section from the rest. On its west-facing slopes – well concealed by a large overhang – another smaller fissure lay between the foothills and the steep rise to the summit. The gash was so well hidden that had it not been for the slow plume of fog rising lazily into the sky, Keiko would have missed it.

"Are you sure you're in the right place?" she asked dubiously. "I can't see a thing."

"I'm sure. I may not be able to see it, but I *can* sense it." Yui zipped toward the fog-shrouded section of the mountain and into a narrow ravine. Mist reduced visibility to a few feet.

"Can you sense the walls too?" Keiko grumbled. "I'd hate to slam into one when we're going this fast, shield or no shield." The fog was thicker here and curiously warm. Even within the shield, she'd felt the change in temperature almost immediately. She didn't like it. "There isn't a volcano in the area, is there? Or hot springs?"

"No, there are not. We wouldn't allow such a blatant display of Vissyus's power so close to Roarke's Gateway. He's been through enough. Apart from the pair of Buddhas we set to watch the valley, we've kept this entire area as pristine as possible."

"But what about the mist? This is the only spot on the mountain that has any. Don't you think that's a little odd?"

"Perhaps, but Roarke and his guardian wield considerable power here. Either one can touch the Earth's core. Releasing that much heat could account for the fog?"

"Maybe," Keiko conceded. "I think we'd better keep our eyes open, though. Something doesn't feel right."

They shot through a nearly invisible cleft between twin rock outcroppings and into a narrow valley that dropped a thousand feet or more before leveling out. Blue sky occasionally showed through the water vapor in slivers of light, the gorge's sheer walls framing them.

Yui grew increasingly tense the farther they flew, and something about her words made Keiko uneasy.

"Roarke is a friend, isn't he?" Keiko prodded. "You don't think he'd attack us, do you?"

"Vissyus doesn't give opponents second chances, and Roarke will strike if he doesn't recognize the intruder." Keiko started to speak again, but Yui interrupted. "Roarke knows what this Weakening means. He can't afford to lower his guard if the dragons are loose. But, in answer to your question: yes, Keiko, Roarke is a friend. Still, the sooner he knows who we are, the better."

Yui had a habit of revealing things like a veil dancer, one tantalizing piece at a time. Keiko crossed her arms and cocked her head. "Is there anything else I need to know?"

"Just keep your eyes and ears open. And watch for anything that seems out of place."

"You mean like two young women flying through the air in a glowing purple ball?"

"You know what I mean. We have a way to go yet, and until we pass between the Buddhas, we are vulnerable."

Keiko's lips curved downward to form a disgruntled frown. "I'm not sure I like the sound of that."

"You will like it a great deal less if we find ourselves trapped between here and the ravine. An avalanche at this time of year is a real possibility... and there are other dangers to watch out for as well."

"Whatever you say," Keiko added, pointing. "I still think there's something strange about that fog. It gives me the creeps."

Yui grunted. "I heard you the first time. The source must be somewhere up ahead. It's probably just Roarke testing the Weakening."

Scratching her head, Keiko peered uneasily into the gloom, her imagination conjuring all sorts of hidden dangers. "Can't you do something to see what's out there?" Yui didn't seem to take the warning seriously. Keiko thought she put too much faith in Roarke's ability to keep threats away. Something told her they needed to be more careful.

"A Searching you mean?" Yui shook her head. "It's too risky, especially since I don't know for certain if Malog went back into the Boundary. We need to be very careful how we approach the Earth Lord. Announcing our presence first is best for all of us."

"But how can you find the Keystone without a Searching?"

Yui raised an eyebrow. "I sense the Boundary because it's a manifestation of Gaiyern, my father's guardian. I still need you to help me scan our surroundings, however. We don't have the luxury of a Searching, and we wouldn't want to stumble over anything in this fog, even if it turned out to be a friend. Do you think you can do that for me?"

Keiko responded with a deep breath and perfunctory "yes." Yui was more careful than she suspected. She relaxed a little, her eyes drifting to the ground below, disconcertingly visible between her feet.

She leaned out for a better look and spied the vague outline of statues in the distance – two of them flanking a ragged hole in the mountain. Unlike the Buddhas she'd seen in Japan, these two stood with their feet planted firmly apart, their arms crossed over the familiar paunch. Rolling fog spewed from the opening between, and while it was thinner than she expected, it still made her uncomfortable. Yui said they would be safe once inside. Looking down, she wasn't so sure.

She assumed Yui would drop below the clouds and head for an area where the vapors were thinner, but to her surprise, instead of skirting the clouds, Yui headed right for them, the top of their shield coming within inches of a rough-hewn archway leading into what looked like a tunnel.

"Yui?" Keiko croaked.

"It's all right. I'm just using the fog to hide our approach. It's a much safer alternative than a Masking. At this range, the sudden surge would give us away too soon."

Keiko frowned. "A Masking?" She had so much to learn.

"A Masking is a way to hide," Yui explained. "Once it's in place, we become invisible. Even our thoughts are shielded. Unfortunately, forming it leaves traces. Anyone who knew what to look for would know we've arrived. By traveling within the fog, we avoid that little complication."

"What good is all this power if you can't even use it when you need to?" Keiko asked. When did hiding mean giving yourself away? It was ridiculous.

"You wouldn't feel that way if the roles were reversed," Yui replied blandly. "It isn't about limitation, but what my father calls balance and counterbalance."

"I don't–"

"New techniques require new defenses. That's why no one holds an advantage for long. Power has its limits. Strategy and cunning are more important than strength and skill, Keiko. They always have been."

Keiko didn't see Yui as much of a planner. The thought made the walls feel stiflingly close.

They continued the rest of the way, busily scanning the fog for signs of movement. With the world around them lost behind a curtain of white, it was a challenge for Keiko, but she persevered nonetheless, determined to uphold Yui's trust in her.

A subtle brightening overhead indicated an end to the passageway, and Keiko breathed a sigh of relief as the dense bank dissipated. With more room, the fog wafted in several different directions, though the light air currents continued to push the bulk of it into the dank tunnel behind, where it then thickened.

Once free of the mist, a breathtaking valley spread out before them. Smooth and almost perfectly vertical cliffs climbed toward one of Kanchenjunga's many peaks. To the right, a floor of tumbled stone sprang perpendicularly from the edge of one wall, crossing in front of them until it ended at the razor's edge of a bottomless chasm. Arcing bridges of ice randomly bisected the open space, all that was left of once-solid rock, eroded and whittled by time and element.

Yui swept the entire length before circling back and landing in front of a pile of large boulders. The air was a peculiar mixture of warm humidity and clammy chill.

"Watch your footing," she warned when Keiko's feet touched down with a squishy plunk. "The floor is slick with condensation, and there are a couple of puddles as well."

None of the debris slowed her as much as it did Keiko, who picked her way around the puddles and random stone formations so cautiously that Yui had already reached the cliff by the time she'd caught up.

Yui studied what appeared to be an ancient pictogram, crudely carved to look like a large man hefting the Earth onto his burly shoulders.

"I take it this is what we came for," Keiko panted. Yui barely acknowledged her. Keiko shivered and rubbed her arms vigorously. "Well. Let's get this over with. The sooner we're out of here, the better. I don't know why, but I feel like we're being watched."

Yui's hand stopped inches short of the Keystone. "What did you say?"

"I said it feels like someone's watching." She shivered again. "I don't know where it's coming from, but it doesn't feel friendly."

Yui whirled about and cursed. "How could I have been so careless?"

Without explanation, she shoved Keiko behind a mound of broken rock and padded away from the Keystone. "I felt it too, but when no attack came, I thought I was mistaken. I should have realized it would be here." Yui stalked this way and that like a panther, her shield flaring against her body. "Why didn't I see it? The condensation, the melting ice, the fog." Turning, she looked at Keiko with furious eyes. "Be ready. We have company."

Keiko's heart sank. She'd been afraid of that.

A series of detonations rocked Kanchenjunga, booming and echoing throughout the valley. Keiko expected them to come from the mountain's roots – like an earthquake. Instead, they erupted from one of the stone bridges spanning the abyss.

She saw a flash of red out of the corner of her eye, a slender ribbon of rock hanging suspended in space. It toppled into the depths with a loud groan, and as it fell she glimpsed glittering golden scales within the debris. A pair of fiery eyes locked onto them before disappearing over the edge.

Keiko's knees buckled, but she managed to stay on her feet. "Fiyorok," she breathed.

Frantically, she searched for Yui, leaning out from a heap of boulders with her hands over her head. The other woman stood a few yards in front of the stones, purple-and-gold light shimmering around her.

"Yui! Don't do anything stupid!"

A wall of fire belched up from the pit to swallow her warning. She shouted again, and again the heat snatched the words away. Smoke mushroomed up from the depths, whipping across the valley as it climbed and partially hiding Yui from sight. If not for the shield, Keiko would have lost her completely. She relaxed a bit only to tense again when a new glow appeared high above her head.

At first, she thought the light came from a single

source, but as it advanced, it halved into twin globes. She couldn't see much of the shape she knew followed the eyes, but instead of easing her fear, obscurity made it grow.

Apparently, Yui had no such reservations. One moment she stood before the smoke, the next, she swept an arm, and the clouds blew away from her.

Keiko swore under her breath. Yui always maintained that perfect Japanese mask. Unlike what Keiko saw in other Japanese, though, she knew Yui's was just that – a mask. No, not a mask, a dam – and a weak one at that.

Across the floor, Yui crouched, fist rising to her chest. Light exploded from either side, shooting horizontally before solidifying into an angry lance. Blades of violent, pulsating yellow capped the ends like leering teeth.

"Yui!" Keiko shouted, her voice thin against the battle's thunder. "For God's sake, Yui, this is no time to be a hero!"

But either Yui didn't hear Keiko or she chose to ignore her, launching her shield-enveloped body into the air and landing near the edge of the cliffs. Keiko swore. Was she trying to get herself killed?

Five hundred feet from Yui, a great, clawed foot sliced through the smoke ahead and smashed onto the valley floor. A second gripped at the ledge and drove forward. Fiyorok's horns shredded the mist, its leering muzzle thrusting forward, burning spittle falling from its mouth like sparks. Yui looked so small, the dragon so huge. Keiko felt Yui's godlike power once in Tokyo and once in the White Spirit. But Fiyorok radiated the same, if not more. Keiko desperately wanted to believe this was a fair fight, but her senses said differently.

Undaunted, Yui attacked, leaping and catapulting from wall to boulder to ground, each summersault evading dragon fire, closing the distance. At fifty yards, she opened her palm to release multiple white-hot bursts of power. Slithering to the side, Fiyorok brought streams of fire just as Yui aimed a volley at its rippling shield. In an aggressive feint to the left, she hurled her lance to the right, intentionally throwing away from the line of tracers and through Fiyorok's shield.

Stunned, the dragon clamped its jaws together and twisted its head away. Flame-tipped lance met flame-colored armor in a symphony of sparks and blood. Fiyorok's head thrashed. Liquid fire sprayed from a wound below its horns, igniting whatever it touched. Yui grinned triumphantly and rushed forward.

Keiko could barely watch, but she couldn't look away either.

Fiyorok pivoted on its haunches. Momentum whipped its tail about its body like a flail, and the great mace-like end hammered Yui's shield with enough force to send her careening into the wall above the Keystone. The ground shook, and pulverized granite filled the air. Dust mixed with acrid smoke until it was nearly impossible to see.

Keiko took off at an awkward run.

Yui hit the ground a hundred yards away or so. She couldn't be far. Rubble littered what had been barren space, making it harder to locate Yui than she'd expected. The smoke didn't help either. At least it kept the dragon away. As far as she could tell, Fiyorok hadn't moved. Maybe it thought it killed Yui. Keiko thrust the thought aside, swallowed the lump in her throat, and quickened her pace. After what seemed like hours, movement caught her eye. She swerved toward it, her pulse easing when Yui pushed herself from the earth with her hands.

"Yui?" Keiko hissed, her voice quiet and low despite

the roaring fires around them. "Are you hurt? Can you move? We have to get out of here. I think I remember the way back. If you can get us into the air, I might be able to talk you through the tunnel."

The sound startled Yui. She dropped to her elbows and crawled the short distance to where Keiko sheltered behind a chunk of castoff wall. "It's too late for that." she whispered, shaking her head firmly.

"We have the advantage now," Keiko said. "We can hide in the smoke, just like Fiyorok hid behind the ice. It'll be our cover."

Yui's brows knitted. "Fiyorok *never* hides." Her voice was pensive. "It doesn't need to."

"What difference does that make?"

"Quiet! I need to think." Dirt covered Yui's face, and while she looked weary, the set of her jaw told Keiko she wouldn't back down. If Keiko couldn't talk Yui of out this madness, she'd have to find a way to help her. It's why she'd come.

She cleared her throat. "You know, when I was in high school, we had these lockers–"

"Not now!" Yui protested.

"Combination locks, not keys. If you weren't careful, someone could watch you open it from behind." She thrust her bottom lip forward, thinking. "Funny I'd remember that now, don't you think?"

Realization flashed across Yui's face. "It wants to know how to open the Gate." She sounded insulted. A stream of curses flew from her mouth as she glanced first at the Keystone and then over to Keiko. "We've reached a stalemate. We can't use the Keystone while Fiyorok is here, and it won't leave unless we do. We either have to distract it or lure it away."

"And just how are *we* supposed to do that?" Keiko

asked bitterly. "I can't do either one, and you're hurt. We're going to need help."

"My father won't leave Japan, and Aeryk and Seirin are too far away. Besides, I'm the only one who can get through Fiyorok's shield. Light and fire are tied together. The others don't stand a chance."

"You don't know that!"

Yui pushed herself unsteadily to her feet. Fiyorok prowled forward cautiously. "My father trusts me," she said, her voice flinty. "I can't let him down, not on my first assignment." She ignited her battle shield and bounded back into the air. "And I am *not* hurt. Stay here. I'll be back as soon as I can."

Keiko watched her go with a mixture of frustration and pride. Yui was courageous, but courage didn't always translate into victory. If she kept acting without thinking, she'd get herself killed.

Again, Yui slipped through Fiyorok's shield. She dropped onto its shoulders, lance primed and ready. Before she brought it down, though, the dragon pitched forward, and Keiko held her breath as Yui vaulted away. Fiyorok twisted after her, mouth agape. Fire followed Yui like the tracers in one of Masato's memories – World War II, a battle in the skies over London.

Ice-covered walls melted and cracked from Fiyorok's strikes. Huge boulders broke free and hurtled down, smashing into Fiyorok's shield, where they then turned into molten magma.

A large section of the near wall continued to fall from above, but instead of waiting for the avalanche to pass, Yui bounced from one boulder to the next until she was through. She hit the ground hard enough to gouge a large crater, but somehow managed to keep her footing. Her head came up, but this time, as she met the guardian's gaze, she stopped abruptly, her arms falling limply to her sides. The light in her eyes dimmed, and her body swayed rhythmically from side to side as if under a spell.

"Yui!" Keiko screamed. "What's wrong with you! You have to snap out of it!"

Helplessness washed over her. She felt sick, lightheaded. Takeshi warned her about this. He expected her to prevent Yui from rushing into a fight without thinking. She might as well stop a sunbeam. Where was the power she inherited? She needed it, but it wouldn't come. She'd have to do better if she wanted to become a guardian. Vissyus hadn't listened to Fiyorok, and look how that turned out.

Not knowing what else to do, she closed her eyes and concentrated. Focus her thoughts, Yui said. Push them out of her body. Back at the White Spirit, she'd sent them into Yui's head. She'd been angry then and had acted without thinking. Silently, she prayed she could do it again. One word, that's all she needed. She formed it in her mind and then, as if shouting, hurled it into the air. The faint scent of cherry blossoms filled her nose. It rode the wind, carrying her thoughts like a messenger.

"*Help!*" she cried, repeating the word over and over again.

29
RESCUE

Idiot! Yui seethed, staring helplessly into a sea of hypnotic fire. *Foolish*! *Naïve*! Three hours and a pair of mistakes, first in the village with the Sherpa, and now this potentially fatal one. Surgically, Fiyorok sliced through whatever defenses she managed to put in place ahead of the dragon's unstoppable thoughts. She hurled commands at her arms and legs while building barriers around her knowledge of the Keystones.

Frustrated tears ran stinging down her cheeks. *Father warned you.* She fumed. *Vissyus's guardians are different. Be smart, he said. Be careful.* He'd given her two simple tasks, and all she had to show for her efforts were two colossal failures. Sweat coated her body as Fiyorok ripped her defenses away, gloating over her for what felt like forever. The guardian was close to the deepest part of her consciousness, the place she'd move all of her secrets when its thoughts slowed and – amazingly – withdrew.

Yui's knees buckled, and she dropped onto them like a felled tree. A blur of golden red shifted in front of her and moved away. Blinking furiously, Yui dove for the ground and rolled to her feet behind the safety of a small hill. Her sight came back with agonizing slowness, and by the time she could make out more than blurred outlines, Fiyorok dug its claws into the earth and sprang away.

Someone else has seen you open the Boundary, Fiyorok leered. *Poor Yui. In Tokyo, I warned you about your ignorance. You should have listened.*

Yui's eyes widened as the full force of Fiyorok's words fell upon her. Her gaze shot over the ground, past the ravine, past the smoldering craters and tumbled boulders, flying to the series of rock outcroppings near the Keystone where she'd left Keiko. *Keiko!* she called, raising her shield and exploding from the ground. *Fiyorok knows where you are. Keep your head down and no matter what happens, don't move!*

Power flew from her conscious mind, capturing the light around Keiko and feeding her essence into the dull glow until she formed a makeshift shield around the girl. The defense wasn't perfect, not by any stretch of the imagination, and certainly not against Fiyorok, but it was the best she could do for now. She'd keep feeding the barrier as she flew and prayed it would hold.

Swallowing guilt, she accelerated, formed a sizzling javelin in her hands and hurled the weapon at the cliffs. Rocks tumbled into the ravine. Some blocked Fiyorok's path while others smashed into its shield and melted. Beyond, Yui glimpsed the top of her temporary shield, a yellow semicircle bobbing behind several overturned stones. The shield came up a foot or so more, and Keiko's head crested a large stone, the wind blowing through the shield and rippling her layered hair like waves of black wheat. Yui's gaze locked with Keiko's. She expected fear – accusation perhaps – anything but what she saw. Instead of terror, Keiko simply grinned and jabbed a finger at the sky.

As if in response, an uncomfortable tingling moved up and down Yui's arms. Again it came but more pronounced, stronger. Something tugged at the edge of Yui's awareness, a thought familiar and yet fleeting. The hair on her head stood out in all directions as if caught by the atmosphere, and at last she understood. She glanced into the energy strobing the chasm, into the charcoal-colored clouds with their sickening green hues and the blue-white motes flashing within.

Hope and chagrin swept through Yui – relief for the rescue, anger at its necessity. Skimming the far wall, she threaded her way through the fallen cliff face, determined not to draw Fiyorok's thoughts. She needn't have worried.

Fiyorok sensed the danger too. No longer charging, the dragon slowed its advance and moved warily – head tilted back, malevolent eyes scanning the top of the ravine as it growled menacingly and swished its tail from side to side. Overhead, wind and snow rushed in from above. Gales buffeted Yui's shield, and she had trouble controlling her flight. She nearly plowed into a large stone, before aiming for a bare spit of land to the right. Reaching the clearing, she skidded to a halt near Keiko's shelter and, hunching against the gusts, crawled the final few inches to where Keiko huddled against a large rock, hands over her head, the Keystone a good sprint behind her.

As exhausted as she was, Yui drew on a well of power deep within her spirit, cast a Delving into Keiko, and – satisfied the other girl hadn't been hurt – let out an explosive breath. "I told you not to move," she admonished. "You're lucky everything turned out all right in the end."

Keiko stared back incredulously. "All right? You call

this *all right*? Look at me, Yui! I'm singed and dirty, I've got bruises in places I didn't even know existed, and I just about had a heart attack. But yeah, other than that, I'm perfectly fine." She pushed herself to her feet and started dusting off her clothes when Yui grabbed her by her pack and hauled her back down. "What are you doing?" Keiko squawked.

Yui held up a silencing hand and nodded at the skies. A streak of silver-blue energy broke through the building clouds and slammed – jagged bolt after jagged bolt – into Fiyorok's fiery shield.

Keiko clamped her hands over her ears and hunkered down behind the shelter. Above, thunderbolts careened from wall to wall. Conductive ice channeled the electricity. It sizzled down the cliffs in weblike patterns. Smoking fissures appeared in the rock, the assaulted earth crackled, and blue light shimmered all around them.

"Aeryk Tai-Banshar has come," Yui said. "You summoned him, didn't you?" She tried to keep the edge from her tone. Keiko didn't believe in her either.

"I don't know," Keiko admitted. Head down, her voice came out muffled. "Maybe. I just sort of called for help with my thoughts."

Yui's breath exploded from her lungs, her earlier anger melting somewhat in the face of Keiko's announcement. "You've tapped into your power. We just don't know how much."

"And this is a good thing?" Keiko said without lifting her head. Lightning raked the far end of the canyon. Explosions shattered the morning calm.

"Better if you could form a shield and get to the Keystone by yourself." Yui inched up the rock. It held heat and burned her palms.

"So you can go back out there? Are you crazy?"

"He needs me," Yui said without looking back.

Keiko grabbed Yui's singed sleeve and spun her around. "That's not why we're here," she shouted, jabbing a finger at the Keystone. "*That* is. Come on, Yui. Use your head: Fiyorok's distracted. We won't get another shot at this."

Yui shrugged out of Keiko's grip but didn't argue. Resigned, she dropped to the ground with a regretful sigh and knelt beside Keiko. "Fiyorok already knows we're here," she said, saving as much face as she could. "We can use that Masking now." Quickly, she cast spiritual energy into Keiko's shield and watched the girl's small body fade away like an emptying shot glass. A tiny wavering in the air gave her away, but Fiyorok wouldn't notice unless it knew where to look. Satisfied, Yui shifted her attention to her own shield. "We move as soon as Aeryk appears. Keep your eyes open and be ready to follow."

"How am I supposed to follow if I can't see you?"

Yui ground her teeth. How many mistakes would she make before she entered the Boundary? Come to think of it, how many more would she make from here on out? She and Keiko were lucky to be alive. If Keiko hadn't called Aeryk – if Keiko hadn't stopped Yui and made her see reason, they might be in a whole world of trouble. Fighting to keep her composure, she linked her mind with Keiko's. *I've connected our thoughts*, she said. *You should sense where I am and where I'm going. Don't get distracted, though; you'll lose me if you do, not for long, but in the middle of a battle, long enough.*

A sniff sounded near her left shoulder. *I'll remember if you do.*

Yui smirked. Power or no power, Keiko looked after Yui as well as any guardian. Pushing the thought aside, she slipped from the shelter. She winced at the loud crunch of Keiko's feet and quickly hushed her. *We're trying to hide, Keiko. The Masking won't do any good if Fiyorok hears us.*

Sorry, Keiko whispered. Her footsteps grew quiet.

Yui let out a relieved sigh and loped across the valley. Vicious winds nearly threw her to the ground. She looked up. There, soaring within the thunderheads, was a single dark shape. It folded its great wings into its body and fell from the skies. The white down on its body had colored to match the charcoal gray-black of the clouds. A long sweeping tail tapered out behind it, equal to the neck in length and held rigidly extended. Electricity coursed through its darkening feathers like the heat lightning of summer. A pair of sharp lavender eyes surveyed the cavern floor in one great sweep. It fired lightning from its wings, twenty to thirty bolts at a time, each strike aimed at the cavern wall where Fiyorok knelt, not in fear but in readiness.

Ventyre, guardian of the winds, Yui said. *Its master will be close behind.*

Keiko stared at the guardian in wonder. *Unbelievable.* Her voice was breathy and full. *That's the most beautiful bird I've ever seen.*

And the most deadly. Come on. I need to pick up the pace. Stay focused and don't fall behind.

Keiko's wonder irritated her. She heard the defeat beneath the awe. Keiko compared herself to the other guardians and found herself lacking. She'd learn; she'd better.

They zigzagged through a minefield of lightning strikes, fire, and falling rock. Fiyorok churned boulders as it charged Aeryk's guardian. It closed rapidly – two hundred yards, one hundred, fifty, claws digging deeply into the earth, igniting whatever they touched. Fires burned throughout the gulf, a result of both the tremendous electrical discharges and the dragon's enormous power.

Yui grasped Keiko's Masked wrist and sprinted ahead. *Time's up, Keiko! We need to move!*

Across the ravine, shields warped and merged. Red and orange light blended with white-tinted purple and blue. Fiyorok lunged and clamped its jaws around Ventyre's neck, while the thunderbird slashed back with spearlike talons. Sparks flew from assaulted shields, though for all the attack's ferocity, the guardians beneath remained untouched. Ventyre broke free and pulled away as a shearing wind blasted in from the north. Fiyorok scampered back, its gaze fixed on the azure spark hurtling through the clouds above.

At first, Yui thought it was just another lightning attack, but as it dropped into the gorge, she saw the outline of a man within the cobalt globe. A loose shirt with three-quarter sleeves billowed like towering cumulus clouds over pants the color of midnight. His hair was dark and parted to frame a handsome face of ageless kindness that belied the hard, merciless look he threw at Fiyorok.

The same man I saw in my father's shop, Keiko mumbled. *He doesn't look any different.*

The etching was just ahead, and Yui marked its position in her head. If she lost sight of it while sprinting for the Gate, she'd have to relocate it quickly. The battle moved closer to her side of the valley – they were running out of time.

Yui steadied her breath and turned away from the guardians. She hurried forward. Her heart pounded in her chest, her feet pumping over rocks, blast craters, and burning ground. The wall loomed ahead of her, tall, gray, and forbidding. Gasping for breath, she half staggered, half stumbled toward it. Her palm came down upon the stone, and a shimmering door snapped open.

Hurry, she urged. *This way. Quickly!* Dropping their Masking, she pointed at an incoming wall of fire. "Fiyorok will know where we are now."

Keiko drew herself up and pushed past Yui. "Then I guess we'd better get moving," she said aloud.

Yui shook her head and followed Keiko into the Gate. She paused at the threshold and looked back.

"I thought you said you weren't planning on turning around." Keiko's head had reappeared through the Gate, looking strangely disembodied against the shimmering Boundary.

"No," Yui lied. "No, of course not." How had Keiko read her thoughts without her knowing? Keiko's power was growing, and her control as well. A shield would take a while, but it would come. Eventually.

"Good! Because you really need to get in here." Urgency filled Keiko's voice, and she disappeared back into the Boundary like a submerging seal.

Yui pivoted. Fiyorok had shaken off Aeryk's attacks and barreled toward her. The dragon was so big. It filled everything, blocked her view of the gorge and Aeryk. Her body tensed. Indecision ripped through her. She and the dragon had unfinished business.

"Yui!" Keiko shouted, breaking the spell. *"Come on!"*

Fire whipped across the ground toward her. Reluctantly, she turned her back to the firefight, determined to move forward – a simple action, but a difficult one. A hand materialized before her. She reached for it, and her resistance melted. Keiko waited for her inside the Boundary. She looked both confident and relieved to see Yui emerge from the wall.

Yui dropped her head to hide her burning cheeks. Until that moment, she believed she'd failed. Keiko obviously didn't see it that way. An ember stirred in Yui's heart. She reformed her shield, her hand still clasping Keiko's.

"Let's go, Keiko," she said, smiling. "We have a job to do."

"What about Mr Aeryk?"

Yui's smile widened. Sharing a burden, it seemed, lessened the load.

"We repay the debt." Her thoughts flew into the Boundary, where they touched both the White Spirit and Roarke's captured fortress. "I've done what I can. The rest is up to them."

She released Keiko's hand and threw their shield into the skies. An unfamiliar horizon greeted her, but she flew confidently toward it. Keiko's surprisingly strong presence steadied her, and for the first time since Masato left the White Spirit, she didn't feel so alone.

30
REUNION

Aeryk threaded his shield through fire and falling rock. Lightning struck from above and below, and, in the distance, the unmistakable signature of an opened Gate pulsed like a living beacon.

Ventyre! he called.

I see it. His guardian was only a few hundred yards behind Vissyus's charging dragon. Closer than Aeryk and shooting through the gorge in a blaze of amethyst light. *I'll hold Fiyorok as long as I can.* Ventyre pulled its wings close to its body and altered its course to intercept. *You'd better hurry, though. I'm picking up a huge surge close to the Keystone.*

Aeryk drew in a sharp breath and hurled his Searching at the Gate.

Half a mile away, behind a cluster of fallen boulders, the valley wall glowed. Red-and-yellow fire lit the gorge from within, smoke boiled from its roots, and an ominous hiss echoed through the narrows. The once-formidable escarpment became a curtain of liquefied rock that somehow remained standing. Inside a great presence seethed – an infinite power, a furnace of madness.

Vissyus.

Helplessly, Aeryk watched tongues of flame burst through and reach Fiyorok, striking and rippling across dragon scales like rekindled fire. Vibrant yellow streaked the outermost layers of the guardian's shield, while underneath, an angry orange surfaced to mix with red and shining white. Fiyorok vanished behind the incandescent colors until only its eyes remained visible – a pair of twin stars imbued with Vissyus's strength and spirit. They surveyed the battlefield in one sweeping motion, serious, and yet sparklingly amused.

Aeryk's eyes widened. *No!* he roared, wrenching his thoughts from the Gate and hurling them at Ventyre. Sweat coated his hands, guilt making it worse. *Fall back. You have to fall back!*

Ventyre didn't question, just did as he commanded, banking into a tight turn that seemed to take forever. As the thunderbird came about, a playfully thrown spark, a comet-sized afterthought, erupted from Fiyorok's shield. Ventyre saw the strike, but swerved too late. Fire overwhelmed lightning, and Aeryk held his breath as Ventyre slammed into the valley wall like a thrown doll.

Seirin taught him how to lessen their Bond, but in the confusion, he'd forgotten. Pain and disorientation exploded in his head. He lost control of his shield and quickly plummeted to the ground, the blazing sphere gouging a long trail through the earth. Standing groggily, he rubbed his eyes to clear his mind and found Fiyorok crouched behind a newly translucent shield. Watching him.

He staggered back. Through the smoke, from within the seared and glowing orb surrounding Fiyorok, a pair of burning eyes studied him. Fire pulsed inside them – flame within flame. Vissyus's eyes – unmistakable in the dragon's face.

"Aeryk?" Vissyus said through Fiyorok's mouth. "Is it really you?"

The question stunned Aeryk, not so much the words as the voice that spoke them. "I'm here, Vissyus," he said, his chest tight, his pulse racing.

"Is Teacher with you?" Fiyorok's eyes glittered at the mention of Seirin. "Where is she? She needs to see what I created for her."

"She's had a difficult day," Aeryk replied evasively. "I decided to let her rest."

Vissyus nodded. "Ah. Yes. I saw what she did to Lon-Shan. So much pain. You have to let me see her. I can help." His eyes bored into Aeryk, searching, eager. "I understood Lon-Shan better than either of you." Fiyorok frowned. "You weren't very nice to him, were you?" When Aeryk didn't answer, suspicion crept into Fiyorok's face. Steam belched noisily from its nostrils, an orange glow building behind its teeth. Fiyorok raked the valley with hellfire then paused abruptly. "Where are we? This isn't the ocean. This is the heart of the world." Vissyus swung the dragon's head back to Aeryk, realization darkening his tone. "You're here for the Rock Man, aren't you? *Aren't you*?" Spittle flew from Fiyorok's mouth, igniting small fires wherever it hit. "He turned the Teacher against me. Did you know that, Aeryk? No, of course you didn't. How could you? You weren't there when I brought Akuan to meet you."

Back down the canyon, Ventyre recovered from Vissyus's attack and took to the air. Aeryk sensed its approach and immediately ordered the great bird into the clouds. "I was delayed," he said, fighting to keep his face smooth. His gaze remained fixed on Fiyorok until he was sure Ventyre was safely hidden.

"Delayed!" Vissyus mocked. "I had something

momentous to show you. You asked for a miracle, and I delivered it: a child for Teacher... and for you. What could be more important than that? I gave you a life!" His voice dropped to a whisper, and a glimmer of his former self broke through. "Life," he breathed sadly. "Life for you, but death for me. After all I've done for you. I thought we were friends, Aeryk."

Fiyorok lifted its head. Tears ran over the dragon's scales, and though they boiled away as soon as they formed, the fine mist they left behind wreathed its head like a halo.

"We *are* friends. Let me help you." Aeryk moved forward a few hundred yards and extinguished his shield. Close enough not to threaten, far enough to protect himself if necessary.

Ventyre screeched a warning, but he pushed it aside. He and Vissyus had been close once. What if Takeshi was wrong? What if they could still save him? His oldest friend needed him. He couldn't just walk away.

Fiyorok thrust its head forward and growled. Its jaws gaped, but Aeryk held his ground. After a moment, it closed its mouth and looked away.

"You can't help me," Vissyus replied. "No one can."

"We shouldn't have asked you to risk yourself for us." Aeryk strode across the burning ground. "Give me a chance to make it right."

"I'd do it again." Fiyorok's defeated smile looked chillingly like its master's. Its chin drooped, and the clarity in Vissyus's eyes faded. "I'd do anything for you. For her."

Aeryk lurched forward. "No! You can't give up. I won't let you. I don't know what went wrong, but if we work together, maybe we can undo it."

"You'd like that, wouldn't you?" Vissyus snarled, all

traces of his old self vanishing like clouds before a dry wind. "Diminish me to become her hero."

Aeryk raised his hands, palms out in supplication. "It's not like that. You have to trust me."

"Trust you? I trusted you with Teacher, and you caused her nothing but pain. You'll pay for that, Aeryk. I promise you." The fiery globe surrounding Fiyorok contracted until the shield coated the guardian's scales like a second skin. Strands of fire twisted out of its aura – orange ropes, burning chains.

Aeryk scrambled back, painfully aware of his vulnerability. Pity opened him to attack, pity and hope and memories. Long ago, Seirin and Roarke tried to reason with the old Vissyus, and both had paid. Cursing his shortsightedness, Aeryk summoned his shield. He'd never been as fast as Vissyus; none of them had. This time was no different. Fiyorok's white-hot flames drilled through the air toward him before the shield appeared, their powers racing against each other, azure blue facing yellow-orange, shield against shield. One second. Another. One defense desperately forming, the opposing attack leaping across the valley floor.

Stone cracked and melted, and before Aeryk realized what happened, Ventyre was in front of him, its amethyst shield deflecting a second attack, its wings snapping open.

"Shield, lord!" it shouted, firing lightning from its charcoal-colored feathers.

Cursing his stupidity, Aeryk brought his shield to life and pushed into the air, at once embarrassed and relieved. "Thank you, Ventyre."

Ventyre grunted. "I need your help more than your thanks, lord." A few of its attacks connected with Fiyorok's shield only to fly off and strike bare patches of ground.

Aeryk muttered a curt apology and turned his attention to Fiyorok. A thought pulled devastating winds into the canyon. The southern gusts carried moisture, which the northern bursts froze. Snow and sleet pummeled Fiyorok's shield with enough force to drive it back.

The guardian dismissed Aeryk's advance, untroubled by either the ferocious storm or the tornados he launched from his splayed fingers. The whirlwinds drove Fiyorok into the far wall, but it quickly shook them off and charged again. Its shield flickered wildly. The pulses became more frequent, as did the lapses between them.

Puzzled, Aeryk was about to fashion a Delving, when Yui's voice erupted in his head.

Lord Aeryk, she said, briskly. *I wish I could greet you properly, but time is short.* Fresh tremors shook a spot of earth across the valley floor. *I've sealed the Gate, but I'm afraid Vissyus might still break through; even bound he is impossibly strong.* Despite her words, Aeryk sensed a renewed confidence. Something had changed Yui for the better. *My guardian and I have called for help. It should be here shortly.*

Guardian? When did you…?

Can you hold out? Yui asked, ignoring the question.

Aeryk glanced at the shaking earth and smiled. *We'll be fine.*

Good. Meet us inside when you can.

She cut the connection, and Aeryk turned to his guardian. *A change in plans. Can you coax Fiyorok to this spot?* He sent an image of quaking ground to Ventyre. *The rest will take care of itself.*

Ventyre snorted. *I think it's angry enough to chase me anywhere. Fiyorok will follow me into the ocean if I led it there.*

We go together, just to make sure. On my mark!

At Aeryk's signal, they rocketed past Fiyorok, Aeryk

aiming for a patch of ground less than two hundred feet in front of the Keystone, Ventyre covering his flight.

The violent quakes intensified as they neared the Gate. Deep cracks opened up beneath them, widening as they moved down the valley. The earth groaned, and a low rumble filled the air.

Aeryk's head whipped around. He spied a large dome pushing up from the pit. Thick jointed columns thrust in front of it. Silvery light surrounded them, each flexing and grasping hungrily at the air.

Well done, Yui, Aeryk whispered, grinning. Quickly, he shifted his thoughts to his guardian. *Double back, Ventyre. We'll pin Fiyorok down until Yui closes the Gate. After that, we withdraw.*

Ventyre squawked its understanding and came about in a sharp, rolling turn.

Ahead, a startled Fiyorok veered away. Ventyre swooped down to block its route, and it swerved again, this time into the path of a hulking stone giant.

Eyes the color of rust glared at the dragon from a chiseled face, brows drawn, full mouth frowning. Its jerkin was forged of cool black iron, as was the mace it brandished over its head. Lunging, the giant shot its arm forward and seized Fiyorok's shielded throat with its free hand.

Fiyorok thrashed wildly. It brought its head around, an injured expression flitting over its reptilian features. "Malog?" Vissyus asked, aggrieved. "Why, Malog?"

"My master seeks justice," Malog rumbled. Roarke's guardian had climbed out of the ripping earth while Ventyre kept Fiyorok distracted. It now stood between Fiyorok and the Gate. "You will pay for what you've done, Vissyus!"

"And what about my justice?" Vissyus snarled. "The

Rock Man led an attack against me, using my friends as soldiers. Many died because of him."

Anger sent powerful waves rippling through Fiyorok's shield. Vissyus pushed at them, throwing off the battle shield and reforming it into the glowing sphere. The force broke Malog's grip and thrust it away. Tottering backward, Malog lost its footing and collapsed like a fallen pillar.

"Did you think I'd forgotten, Malog? I remember what I did, how Botua tricked me into hurting her guardian." Fiyorok lifted a claw to the side of its shaking head.

The shockingly human gesture chilled Aeryk. He'd use the moment, though. He'd fight self-loathing and build a strike while his friend suffered.

At his command, Ventyre sent a curtain of lightning between the two guardians before aiming more bolts at Fiyorok. Electricity skittered over the dragon's fluctuating shield. A few perfectly timed forks connected with its hide, but they slid off like water over slick stones.

Fiyorok countered with liquid fire. Streams flew from its throat. It snapped its head back to hit Ventyre and then around to pummel the kneeling Malog.

Aeryk didn't know how much damage the giant's shield sustained, but he felt Ventyre's give. Instantly, he sent a macro-burst into the valley to help the struggling thunderbird. Trees flattened and rocks disintegrated. Near the Keystone, Fiyorok sank into the earth as if hammered. Its shield absorbed the worst of the blow, and it took a moment for it to crawl out and relocate Aeryk.

Aeryk readied another blast, but a new barrier slammed between his thoughts and the air. Vissyus had moved with lightning speed, seizing oxygen and hydrogen before Aeryk could command them. In seconds, Vissyus split the elemental gases at their most basic level and weaponized them. Aeryk raced to undo the damage before Vissyus ignited them, but as always, the Fire Lord was too fast.

Charges ran from atom to atom in a sizzling current that faltered as another power wrenched the Gateway from Vissyus's control. A figure stood against the shimmering Boundary, backlit and unmistakable in a suit of crimson armor.

"Takeshi!" Aeryk gasped. "No! Don't!"

Fiyorok's head whipped around. "Trickster!" Vissyus roared. "This time you won't get away!"

Bounding across the valley, Fiyorok raced for the Gate, and with one final surge, threw its body into the shimmering light. An eerie silence followed its disappearance, marred only by the soft crackling of fire and the occasional clack of falling rock.

31
AMBUSH

Takeshi withdrew from the gate and headed deeper into the Boundary. Fiyorok followed at a safe distance, neither closing nor falling behind. A minute earlier, Vissyus had thrown the guardian at him like a javelin. Why would he pull it back now? This was wrong. A trap, perhaps?

Vissyus couldn't take the Gate from a distance. He had to be close – close enough for Takeshi's Searching to detect. But Takeshi had blanketed the Boundary with a continuous Searching and found nothing.

Frown deepening, he sent his thoughts to his guardian. *I've lost Fiyorok. Can you see it? I need to know where it's gone.* An uncomfortable prickling grew between his shoulders, and he spun around, expecting to find the dragon bearing down on him.

It's disappeared, lord. Gaiyern sounded harried, fearful. *Vissyus too. I checked his section of the Boundary for Fiyorok, but it was empty. I'm sorry, my lord. It's the Weakening. He's found some way to move within the Boundary.*

Takeshi's pulse quickened. Empty. That meant Akuan was out too. Vissyus must have gone back for the ice dragon after he left Lon-Shan's Boundary. He hadn't expected that. The guardian should still be injured. How had Vissyus healed it so quickly?

We need to flush him out while we still have the advantage, Takeshi said grimly. Swerving, he opened a new pathway and accelerated toward it.

Gaiyern's response was immediate. *Fireball! Right Boundary, coming in fast!*

Starlike comets exploded out of a glittering wall ahead, and Takeshi rolled in a wide corkscrew to let them roar past. They missed by yards, intense heat buffeting him despite his shield.

He grimaced at the undeniable power behind them. The reality of Vissyus was far worse than a memory soothed over the eons. He'd grown complacent, arrogant even. If he wanted to survive, he needed to adjust his perceptions. Quickly. Looking over his shoulder, he opened a hole in the Boundary and dove. Light and shadow intermixed, shivering cold crisscrossed with boiling heat. Over and under he sailed until he broke through into the daylight of some alien world.

An overcast sky spread out before him, extending from one side of the Boundary to the other. The filmy clouds did little to blunt the sun's scorching rays, which had, over the centuries, turned the ground into a barren wasteland. He ignored the desolation, dipped below the lowering ceiling, and flew on as though the ruins didn't exist.

Fiyorok has changed its course, my lord, Gaiyern reported. *Has it broken off?*

No. It appears to be running parallel to you and picking up speed. I think it means to cut you off before you reach the next wall.

The temperature around him climbed unexpectedly, and he weakened his shield's outer layers to prevent accidental sparks. Not that it mattered. He couldn't have stopped the explosion anyway. As expected, the sharply rising heat ignited hydrogen and oxygen. A vortex pulled the burning gases into a pressure well, where they detonated with a low *whump*.

Takeshi banked away and sliced into the nearest Boundary wall. Below, a world of sand-crusted hills and lavender seas flashed by.

Where is he, Gaiyern? Why can't we find him? The Boundary gleamed in the distance. He picked up speed.

I don't know. Frustration filled Gaiyern's normally cool tone. *Heat and light are part of every Boundary world. He might use them to Mask his movements.*

We should still detect his spirit. His signature's different. Unique. Takeshi rubbed a hand across his chin. *Vissyus has put us on the defensive in our own territory. We need to regain the initiative.*

He crossed over the rugged landscape and came to a stunningly beautiful forest of rolling hills and evergreens. A big cat padded out of the underbrush to stare up at him, seventy-five feet long with fangs like spears. Takeshi's heart sank. Fa-Tan, a lesser guardian of animals. Its mistress, Tygrenne, must be here as well. A mistake. He had to leave... immediately. Turning, he made for the nearest Boundary wall, a ribbon of undulating light a thousand miles to his left.

The Boundary loomed in front of him. He relaxed. A few more miles and Tygrenne would be safe. He opened a portal, and fire roared out to meet him. Fiyorok burst through in a blaze of shield, smoke, and flame. Air whooshed toward the opening as if it was a chimney.

Takeshi slammed the path closed as the shockwave tossed him back into the temporary world. Too late. Fiyorok passed inside, igniting the air before the

Boundary resealed. Fire consumed everything, feeding on all levels of matter like some ravenous beast. Forests became kindling, seas boiled to increase the pressure. Fa-Tan's shield was far too weak to stand against the conflagration, and Takeshi watched in horror as the cat disintegrated into ashen fragments. He wished he had time to grieve; he wished for so many things.

Are you there, Gaiyern?

His guardian's voice drifted back to him, soft and sad. *I am so sorry, lord.*

We'll honor them when we've finished. Open a Gate over the Sea of Japan, and make sure you position it right behind me.

My lord?

Vissyus wants a way out. I'm going to give it to him.

But…

As soon as he arrives, invert the Boundary to trap him. If we're lucky, it'll take him a few moments to understand what we've done.

And then what? This section of the Boundary isn't as secure as his fortress. I'm not sure I can keep him from tearing it apart.

We can't go on like this, Takeshi snapped. *We have to lure him into the open.*

Fiyorok crested a distant mountain whose once-pronounced outline was now little more than a lump of melted earth.

We're running out of time. Do it. Now!

A huge circle appeared within the impregnable wall behind him. Beyond, lazy waves churned over a vibrant ocean. Japan's west coast filled the right half of the Gate, while, to the left, Korea and China framed a teardrop-shaped sea.

Fiyorok slowed its advance and moved as if to let something pass. Clouds mushroomed at its back while recurring explosions strobed within them. Gradually, the clouds rotated around some hidden eye, gaining momentum, shredding as they spun. A thermonucleic orb appeared at the storm's heart like a great, ringed sun, and there, hovering inside the inferno, Vissyus materialized from the flames.

"Trickster," he said triumphantly, his tone a breathy caress. "At last." A globe of blue ice floated over his right shoulder. Fiyorok moved back into place on the opposite side, its eyes glowing malevolently.

Takeshi inhaled to steady himself as they advanced. One mile, half. Just a little more.

Now, Gaiyern!

A sliver of the Boundary bucked and twisted and peeled away from the greater wall. Clouds shredded and then reformed as Gaiyern wrapped them around Vissyus and his dragons. Light flashed inside, muffled explosions filling the air. Takeshi circled it, taunting Vissyus with each pass.

I don't know how much longer I can hold him, Gaiyern protested. *He's set off a series of explosions along the inner ring. I'd forgotten how strong he is.*

Takeshi marked time in his head while Searching another section of the Boundary for Yui. *Just a little longer, my friend. Let his rage build. He won't hide this time. He'll come after me with everything he has.*

Fire and ice ripped through layer after layer, freezing and burning until brittle cracks formed around a tiny breach. Vissyus grinned and pointed a trembling finger at the Boundary. Smoke coiled about his wrist, flame orbiting his hand. Yellow light streaked away from his upraised arm to pound the fissures until Gaiyern's makeshift Boundary shattered.

Bits of burning debris flew at Takeshi, but he held

KEITH YATSUHASHI   301

firm as smoke poured into the chamber to hide him. Enshrouded, he slipped into another section of the Boundary, careful to leave traces of his passing for Vissyus to follow.

But Vissyus didn't take the bait. He lifted his chin proudly and raised his booming voice. "I can't do this anymore. I see where you've gone, and I know why you're running. I'd run too if I abandoned those closest to me."

He lowered his head and shook it as if to clear his thoughts. A flash of regret dimmed his eyes, but when he looked up again, accusation filled his face. "This game of yours is over. Finished! You can't keep me from Teacher any longer. She asked for my help, and I won't desert her. I will find her, Trickster, even if I have to obliterate every world within this Boundary until I do."

Vissyus waved a hand, and his shield pushed outward. A second layer formed around it, thermal energy building between the two. He looked at Takeshi, almost pleadingly, shook his head again, and let the increasing pressure trigger a massive explosion. Shockwaves pounded the Boundary's walls, though unlike the more temporary cage Gaiyern erected, these held firm.

Madness! Gaiyern cried. *You can't let him do this. We brought them here to protect the other Kami. What good is saving one world if we sacrifice so many others to do it?*

We'll save as many as we can, Takeshi said. *Reinforce the internal Boundaries! All of them!*

But some of the worlds are empty. We shouldn't dilute the Boundary to protect them.

If you only secure the sections holding Kami, you'll give their positions away. Let's not make it easy for him. And be sure to throw a Masking around Roarke's fortress… just in case. Quietly, Gaiyern. We don't want him to know what we're doing.

Shall I warn the others?

Takeshi shook his head. *No. See to the Boundary. I need to tell Seirin what's happened. We'll need her help for this.*

Vissyus may have left a Searching near Aeryk, Gaiyern warned, eliciting a frown.

I know. Unfortunately, we can't afford to wait. Add a second Masking to hide my message. Just to be sure.

He felt Gaiyern's energy seeping into his thoughts and instantly hurled them through the Weakening. Hurricane Point opened before him. Seirin was already asleep, and as much as he hated to tap her private thoughts, he knew his options were limited.

A gentle Delving would be enough to wake her. He slipped it into her mind, but once inside, once her raw emotions roared up to meet him, he reconsidered. She needed sleep to heal her wounds – the grief over Lon-Shan's treachery, the guilt over his death.

Instead of disturbing her, he insinuated himself into her dream. "Seirin," he whispered, calling to her subconscious spirit. "Can you hear me?"

"Takeshi?" she answered drowsily. "Where am I? What are you doing here?"

"I don't have time to explain."

Seirin bristled in her sleep. "You *never* have time. Not then, not now, not ever."

He let that pass. "I need to show you something. Will you allow it?"

She grunted her assent, and he relaxed. He fed images to her slowly, though she thrashed when he neared the end.

"I am very sorry, Seirin, but this is the only way. Now, one thing more. I need you to prepare the battlefield. Your power could save large sections of Tokyo. Will you do it?"

She nodded without speaking, as her thoughts drifted toward Japan.

"I apologize for the intrusion." Bowing, Takeshi withdrew his mind. "Sleep well."

As Hurricane Point faded away, he turned back to Gaiyern. "Have you secured the Boundary?"

"I did what I could, but I doubt the reinforcements will hold for long."

"It's enough." It had to be. He spun his shield and headed for a wall of pulsating energy. "Once I prepare the White Spirit, I'll take my position south of Tokyo. Be ready when I call you."

Outside the Boundary, exactly as Seirin promised, a heavy, soaking rain materialized over Tokyo in the middle of a perfect spring day.

32
RESOLVE

Keiko kept her eyes on the shimmering wall over her head as Yui flew deeper into the Boundary. A seemingly infinite plain spread out below, flat grasslands dotted here and there with delicate trees whose frond-like leaves rustled softly in the air. Keiko desperately wanted to take in the alien landscape, but she didn't dare, not with Fiyorok stalking them. Not knowing what happened to the dragon after they left the Himalayas made her anxious. The thing could be anywhere.

They flew on for several more minutes before landing near a spindly tree that looked like a shredded umbrella. Yui walked over, crossed her arms, and leaned against it.

Keiko stared at her, perplexed. "What are you doing? We can't just stand around. We have to find Mr Roarke before Fiyorok learns where we've gone."

A massive explosion rocked the Boundary, orange and yellow bursts flaring over its surface like fireworks. Yui's body tightened, but she remained where she was, her face pale yet determined.

"We need Aeryk's help," she said. "I asked him to meet us here as soon as he could."

Keiko started. Help? Yui didn't ask for help. Leaning forward, Keiko searched Yui's face. "What aren't you telling me?"

Yui swept her arm wide. "Roarke's fortress should dominate the landscape. It doesn't, which means he's hidden it. I've been trying to contact him since we entered the Boundary." She shook her head. "He refuses to answer."

The images Takeshi showed her from Earth's past filled Keiko's head: Seirin and Aeryk discussing a very young Yui, Takeshi disappearing with his family, a titanic battle on the edge of a lush basin. Keiko's eyes met Yui's.

"He doesn't know you," she said. "He hasn't seen you since you were a baby and can't verify your identity."

Yui nodded. "Fortunately, Aeryk can break that impasse. Roarke won't ignore him. He has too many questions. Where was Aeryk during the battle? Did he know his absence cost Botua her life?" She smiled at Keiko. "Calling for help not only saved us at the Gate, it may well have saved the world. Without Roarke, the Earth will burn."

Another boom echoed across the grass. It sounded different, less like an explosion and more like thunder.

Keiko turned and looked into the sky. A line of lightning-streaked storms emerged from the Boundary and rolled forward. "You have questions too, don't you?"

"No," Yui said, firmly. "Masato's dead I've accepted it. What does it matter if it happened a long time ago or within the past few weeks?"

"It matters to you," Keiko said. "What if... when this is over, I turn back time. I should be able to do that, right?"

Thunder sounded again, louder, closer. A howling wind followed, flattening the grass and blowing Yui's hair about her head. "Though I appreciate the offer, I don't think you'll be able to." She pulled a strand from her mouth. "Time unfolds as it's supposed to. You may divert it for a little while, but it will correct itself."

"But your father said–"

Yui lifted a silencing hand. "He said Masato influenced how a spirit moved through time. That's different than altering time itself."

Keiko frowned. She didn't understand the difference, and that bothered her. How much did she need to know before she could do anything? Using power without knowledge was dangerous. She might hurt someone, including herself. Not that she had much of a choice. Sooner or later, Yui would need her, and when that time came, she swore she'd be more help than she was in the Himalayas. Waiting for a response while Fiyorok held Yui – the uncertainty, the desperation – she didn't want to go through that again. She wouldn't.

Lightning flashed overhead, and her gaze drifted upward. Electricity arced from one cloud to the next, the wind carving them. Keiko admired the majestic guardian soaring between as much as she envied it. How long did it take to move with such confidence? As long as necessary, a part of her said.

Sighing, she watched Ventyre head for the horizon. Aeryk's azure shield emerged from the clouds a moment later, dropped quickly, and landed a few yards away. Aeryk strode toward them with the same self-assurance Keiko remembered from her father's shop, a smile creasing his handsome face, his shield unraveling in the wind like blue streamers.

"Yui." He nodded. "And Ms Yamanaka. It's been a long time."

Keiko's face flared. "I remember. And you can call me Keiko."

Beside her, Yui pushed herself from the tree and bowed. "Hello, Lord Aeryk. It is good to see you again. You must be happy to have Seirin back."

"More than you know, Yui." His voice was a rich baritone. "And thank you. I'm sorry it meant putting Takeshi in danger."

Yui shrugged. "He's safer in the Boundary than anywhere else." She said it casually, but her gaze flicked to the shimmering sky. Explosions continued to rock through it. They seemed louder without the storms.

"You're lucky Malog responded. I understand Roarke isn't as cooperative."

Yui crossed her arms. "He's completely silent."

"And you think I'll have more success."

"You're his friend," Yui said. "He trusts you."

Aeryk shifted uncomfortably. "He used to, but that was before our confrontation with Vissyus. Even Seirin thought I abandoned her." He sighed. "I'll do what I can. No promises, though." Arms lifting, he pulled his fingers closed, as if catching the wind.

A strong breeze cut across the plains. The gales snapped Keiko's robes and whipped her hair across her face to sting her cheeks. Deep booms accompanied the gusts as an infusion of warm air reignited the thunderheads. Lightning struck down from above, and a swarm of tornados touched down a mile or so away, tearing up grass, eating trees.

"I'm sorry, old friend," Aeryk said, sadly. "You left me no choice. We need your help, now more than ever."

A second rumbling joined the thunder. Loud and bottomless, it rose up from the ground like an anguished cry. In the distance, spindly cracks ripped through the landscape. The earth groaned and split, and a big, flat-topped mesa emerged from the ruin like an immense whale rising for air. Four cylindrical rock formations surrounded the structure, each connected to the one in the center by a single stone archway. If not for the quartet of small pillars and the mound's less natural symmetry, Keiko might have mistaken it for the great sandstone mountain in Australia's Outback. She'd always wanted to see that.

"Roarke's waiting for us just inside the foregate," Aeryk said, his face tight, anguished. "On the roof."

He ignited his shield and lifted from the ground without looking at either Yui or Keiko. Yui followed him into the air, glancing at the Boundary as she maneuvered in beside him. Her jaw tightened, and at first Keiko didn't understand why. Then it hit her: the explosions had stopped.

33
ROARKE

Yui kept pace with Aeryk as he led them toward Roarke's fortress. The Boundary's silence troubled her. She glanced at it time and again, worry gnawing at her. Her mind flashed back to her father's study. He stood in front of her, protecting her from Vissyus, not with his shield but with his body. Was this how he felt whenever she rushed into battle? He didn't hold her back because he doubted her. She saw that now. A spark stirred to life in her chest. She didn't need to prove herself to him. She was his daughter, and he loved her.

Keiko's voice drifted in from somewhere. "Yui? Are you all right? Why are we slowing down?"

"My father." Yui brought her shield about. "He needs me. If anything happens to him…"

Keiko shook her head, her earnest face firm. "You'd just give him one more thing to worry about. He can't fight and protect you at the same time."

Yui lifted her chin and stared into the Boundary, thinking, wondering. A loud shockwave rolled through it. She bit her lip as the sound blew past, indecision tearing through her. A part of her agreed with Keiko, while another part rebelled. Ultimately, the image of Vissyus's whip around her father's neck convinced her. Closing her eyes, she inhaled to steady herself. Keiko was right. She couldn't go back.

"Sorry." She turned away from the Boundary. "It won't happen again."

Keiko smiled sympathetically and patted Yui's arm. "I know."

Another blast shook the Boundary. Yui stiffened, but this time she didn't look back.

"Yui?" Aeryk called. His shield hovered over a wide prairie, Roarke's fortress dominating the lands behind. "Are you all right?"

"We are fine. Keiko and I needed a moment. We're ready now. You may go ahead."

Aeryk nodded his understanding and catapulted over the dusty ground. Powerful winds roared in behind him, flattening the grass below and carrying him forward at high speed. Yui flared her shield and followed, only to stop a mile from the large stone fortress.

"Aren't we going any closer?" Keiko asked, clearly unhappy. A pout curved her rosebud lips.

Yui shook her head. "We stay where we are until Aeryk says otherwise." Disappointment blanketed Keiko's delicate features. Yui should have expected it. The girl never liked to be left behind. "Since your power is waking, perhaps I can teach you how to do certain things. It will give us something to do while we wait." She smiled wryly. "A Searching shouldn't be too difficult."

"I don't–"

"Concentrate on what you want to see, and it will open up before you. Here, I will link our thoughts so you can feel it."

The world ahead rushed forward to meet them. Yui

felt Keiko's wonder as the vision stabilized. Two huge forms stood along the top of the escarpment. Aeryk's guardian, Ventyre, preened its wide, white-feathered wings under the sun, while an incredible stone giant to its left gazed unblinkingly at Aeryk's incoming shield.

"Amazing," Keiko breathed. "It's just like a telephoto lens."

"Do you think you can do it?"

Keiko nodded.

"Good. Let's try. Remember the feeling and slide your gaze between the guardians."

Yui surrendered her Searching to Keiko, who grasped the vision and moved it as Yui directed. Roarke appeared before them, tall, possibly taller than Aeryk – the immense guardians on either side made it difficult to tell. Yui hadn't seen him since she was little, though his big, rolling shoulders, thick arms, and huge hands had made an impression on her. She remembered thinking he was strong enough to move mountains.

He wore the same flowing robes of dusty orange from her memories over his rich, dark skin. A chain of dull iron circled his waist, knotted and tied simply just off his right hip. He fingered the links lightly as he waited for them to approach, eyes the color of desert sand measuring them.

"That's far enough, Aeryk," he called in a great rumbling voice. "I know why you're here." He slid a large black hammer from his belt, planted the head on the ground in front of him, and rested his hands atop the grip. "You're wasting your time. I'm not going back."

Aeryk inched forward, his azure shield painting the ground below. "The world needs us, Roarke. I know you don't want to leave it undefended."

"You don't know anything!" Roarke raised his hammer

and shook it at Aeryk. "You asked for my support before and look where that got me. As far as I'm concerned, Vissyus can have what's left of the world."

Yui had heard enough. She thrust her shield forward, half expecting Keiko to stop her. To her surprise, Keiko nodded encouragingly.

"My father thinks otherwise," Yui said in a ringing voice. "Botua understood Seirin's need better than anyone else but my mother. Am I wrong to think she asked you the same questions Seirin asked Aeryk?

Roarke staggered back. "Yui? Is that you?"

"Botua's flowers still bloom, Lord Roarke. As long as they live, a piece of her spirit remains. She's only gone if you let Vissyus burn them. Fight for her, Roarke; it's what she'd want you to do."

"You have no idea what Vissyus did to us the last time," Roarke protested. "You weren't there – either of you. We couldn't even slow him down."

"Takeshi did," Aeryk countered. "He brought the Boundary. I watched him do it."

Roarke frowned. "The Boundary." His gaze traveled out past his fortress.

Aeryk nodded. "He gave us a second chance. He knows what we have to do. I've worked with him since the last war. Trust me, Roarke. We can do this."

A glimmer of hope stirred in Roarke's dark eyes. "Who else?"

"Just the five of us: you, me, Seirin, Takeshi, and Yui. We'll keep the rest locked away until we're finished, both for their safety, and for ours. We can't afford any distractions. The more we bring to the battle, the more we have to defend. Only the strongest will participate, only those bound by pain and loss and suffering. We are the oldest, the originals. We were supposed to govern and guide all the other Kami. Join us, Roarke." Aeryk landed, snuffed out his shield, and extended his hand. "For Botua."

The light in Roarke's eyes grew. He drew himself up to his full height and took a deep breath. When he let it out again, it was as if he'd exhumed eons of despair. He smiled at Yui and reached out to clasp Aeryk's hand.

"Botua loved Vissyus like a brother. We all did. I know she'd hate what he's become. We have to release him."

Aeryk gripped Roarke's hand in his and shook it. Confidence flowed from his body like a summer wind, and yet his dazzling eyes dimmed. Yui sympathized. Despite his bravado, he hated what he had to do, they all did – everyone except for her. She'd only known Vissyus as a monster. Fervently, she hoped Aeryk's feelings wouldn't tear him apart when they needed him most.

Beside him, a look of controlled rage crossed Roarke's face. Yui didn't think Aeryk caught it because if he had, his smile might have faded.

Roarke had a score to settle.

34
ENIGMA

Seirin woke from a troubled dream. She sat up groggily, and glanced around her room. The horror of Lon-Shan's Boundary had faded to a dull ache in the back of her head. The discomfort remained but was manageable, which meant her increasing distress came from somewhere else. It felt different. Bigger. More tragic. She swung her legs over the edge of her bed and found a small globe of azure light hovering beside a delicate nightstand. Her body tightened. *Aeryk,* she thought, at once angry and anxious. *What have you done now?*

Tentatively, she slid her thoughts into the glowing ball and waited for it to pulse to life. "Yui's in danger," Aeryk's voice said. "I've gone to help her. I'll be back as soon as I can."

Incensed, Seirin drew moisture from the air, condensed the water into a tight ball, and fired the weapon at Aeryk's messenger. She watched in satisfaction as it smashed into the wall on the far side of the room and disintegrated.

Damn him! How could he leave her alone again? He knew she'd want to go, which was precisely why he didn't wake her. Now, she had no idea when he left or where he'd gone.

The message shunted something important to the back of her head. Cursing under her breath, she threw off her bedclothes and shrugged into a loose fitting sea-green tunic and matching pants. They were comfortable but had enough give for the rigors of battle. Once dressed, she shoved her feet into a pair of soft brown leather boots, cinched a belt of platinum seashells around her waist, and exploded from her room in a flurry of green, silver, and gold.

A simple thought opened the doors, and she swept through without closing them. Pink streaked the eastern sky, while below, the sea's rhythmic cadence called up to soothe her. The Observatory loomed ahead, its magnificent dome sparkling in the early morning. A rising sun drew her gaze, and as she landed inside the tower, her dream came roaring back.

She remembered everything – Takeshi's sudden appearance, his grave warning, his request and her answer, storms raging over Tokyo, Vissyus condemning the helpless.

"No," she whispered. "Vissyus. No. *Please*!"

Until then, he hadn't murdered anyone. He'd killed, certainly, but he hadn't understood the repercussions. He'd simply been... playing. Tears welled behind her eyes. Did he know what they planned to do to him? Was this his answer, some sort of justice?

Grief spilled from her body. The Atlantic became a boiling frenzy. Cyclones sprang from the ocean to join blackening clouds, tsunamis ripped the Pacific, and rain pounded forest and desert alike. At the poles, seawater carved ice shelves from glaciers.

Another wave took hold of her, but before she sent

more power into the oceans, a violent windstorm swept in from the east. She reached for it and wrapped it around her body as she entered the top of the tower, seeking comfort in Aeryk's sudden presence.

Seirin? Aeryk called. *Are you all right? What's happened?*

Frustration seethed through her like liquid fire. *It's Vissyus,* she answered, forcing the words from her tightening chest. *He's threatening to slaughter the Kami in the Boundary unless Takeshi releases him.*

The air about her chilled. *I'll be there as soon as I can. We just left the Himalayas. Roarke's with me, and Malog. Yui is here as well.*

The temperature moderated at the mention of Yui. *How is she? Your message said she was in danger.* Somehow, Seirin's earlier anger seemed inconsequential.

She's fine. If anything, the experience has left her both a little wiser and a little stronger. And Seirin… she has a guardian.

She has a what?

A guardian, Seirin. She hasn't Bound it to her, but it's a guardian nonetheless.

Aeryk's presence drifted away, leaving Seirin pacing about the Observatory. The news about Yui sent shivers through her. What type of guardian did she choose? And what would make it so difficult for Seirin to accept?

The more Seirin thought, the faster she paced. Aeryk said they'd just left the Himalayas, which meant they'd fly in from the east. Spinning around, she headed for the eastern windows and the Atlantic. There, she worked her thoughts past sodden African sands and mudstrewn mountains until she spotted five glowing shields north of the Bay of Bengal, three in front, two trailing.

The lead pair belonged to Aeryk and Roarke, which meant Yui controlled the one behind. Yellow gold rippled through rich purple-blue in a blending of elemental forces that took her breath away. Sunfire and spirit coexisting in a single shield? Awestruck, she chuckled to herself. What else could Yui do?

Her thoughts drifted to the guardian. Aeryk said Yui had one now, though, frustratingly, Seirin failed to see it. Ventyre's amethyst shield paced Malog's silver. Both served as a rear guard. Yui's should have been with them.

Seirin frowned, thinking. Where was it? Inside Yui's shield? But that didn't make any sense. Why would she need to keep it so close?

Intrigued, she probed deeper.

Yui was there, regally statuesque despite the soot of battle clinging to her clothes, skin, and hair. Seirin stared at her in amazement. How she'd grown. A half-abandoned hope rekindled. It *was* possible! She was right, and Yui was the proof! Her eyes shifted to the figure to Yui's left.

A young woman stood there, little more than a girl – small and slim with short dark hair, wide, innocent eyes, and a pixie face. She wore robes similar to Yui's, though instead of white striped with blue, hers were pure white silk.

Seirin's jaw dropped in disbelief. "Oh, surely not!" she said aloud. It couldn't be. It wasn't possible. Dubious, she Searched again, this time more thoroughly.

Looking for something? Aeryk's thoughts carried a triumphant edge.

You know perfectly well what I'm Searching for, having tricked me into it. She'd never hear the end of this.

Aeryk chuckled. *I knew you wouldn't believe me.*

He was right. One of the humans – what had happened to the world? She shook her head. *I don't know, Aeryk. Are you sure about this?*

I wasn't at first, but I am now. You'll understand better

when you meet her. Be patient, Seirin. We're making good time.
I should be there shortly.

The words sent a torrent of emotions through her.
She'd missed him, couldn't wait to see him. Confronting
Fiyorok like that without help... was this how he felt
when he arrived at the Boundary and found her gone?
She breathed a kiss into the clouds and commanded it
to his cheek.

Hurry home, Aeryk. I'll wait for you at the bridge.

She left the Observatory and descended toward the
pair of fluted spires at Hurricane Point's gated entry. Blue-
white lightning crackled from the tip of a tapered steel
spike, arced over a bridge of white stone, and connected
with its twin. She landed between them just as three
large spheres sliced through the distant cloud wall – sky
blue leading crystalline silver and yellow-haloed indigo.
The two guardians didn't appear. Their tower sat on the
opposite side of the fortress, though from what Seirin
learned from Kirak's Bond, they'd already arrived.

Aeryk landed first. His booted feet clicked loudly on
the stones in front of her and grew quiet. Roarke came
to rest next to him, as did Yui, though on his opposite
side. Their shields evaporated as quickly as his, but not
quickly enough for Seirin, who launched herself at the
Lord of Earth as soon as he landed.

"Roarke!" she shouted, throwing her arms around
him.

"It's been a long time, Seirin." Roarke's large hands
grasped her shoulders, and he pushed her back gently.
His sand-colored eyes darkened to a deep brown as he
regarded her.

"Too long." She touched his cheek. "Are you all right?"

He shook his head. "Time and solitude dull the pain,
but nothing can take it away." She opened her mouth

to speak, but he stopped her. "I already know what you're going to say, and maybe you're right. Botua wouldn't want me to live like this. She'd want me to be happy. Someday, I'll find peace, but right now, I want to remember what Vissyus did to her. It's the only way I can help you. I was close to Vissyus too."

Seirin's heart went out to him. She took his hands in hers and held his gaze.

"I'm sorry, Roarke… for everything."

Roarke lowered his head and nodded sadly. "Botua hoped for your success. She wanted the law changed as much as you did."

"I wish Takeshi explained the prohibition better in the beginning. I doubt I would have believed him, though." Ashamed, Seirin blushed and looked away. "He left when I needed him most. If only…"

Movement caught her eye, and her head came up in time to see Yui step out from behind Roarke. The small, elf-like girl followed, the index finger of her right hand twitching reflexively.

"Apologies, Lord Roarke, Lady Seirin," Yui said, bowing. "My father left so he and Gaiyern could build the Boundary. He debated long and hard whether or not to tell you, but in the end, he decided against it. Time was short, and he feared a delay would prove costly." She turned to face Roarke. "Unfortunately, he didn't finish as quickly as he hoped. He was greatly saddened by what happened to Botua."

Roarke placed a massive hand on top of Yui's head and smiled. "Little Yui," he rumbled. "You were very young, too young perhaps to see such horror." His sandy eyes hardened into agate stones. "You have lived your life in the shadow of war. I hope your father taught you the difference between duty and glory. One leads to honor, the other to ruin. Do not come to love war too much."

Yui's cheeks flushed. "He made sure I understood that, Lord Roarke."

"Roarke is right, Yui," Seirin agreed. "Glory is as elusive as mist. Those who chase it, never find it. For us, victory is no victory at all."

Regret lined Yui's face. "I wish my father had found another way. You shouldn't have had to suffer, any of you."

She was so like her father, yet so different. Takeshi rarely apologized, something Yui had done without thinking.

"It's all right, Yui. You don't have to defend him. Aeryk told me what he did for us. Because of him, we'll have a chance to right so many wrongs." Aeryk's eyes burned like a pair of sapphire stars. He seemed to know she aimed these words at him – a final act of forgiveness for what they'd put her through.

Yui smiled. "Karma."

"So it would seem," Seirin replied. She stepped back and motioned them toward the gates. "We still have much to discuss and very little time."

Aeryk's arm looped through hers. His touch brought goosebumps. "Have you prepared the Observatory?" he asked.

"I've seen to everything, including a bath and a change of clothes. I drew the water myself."

"Seirin, we can't afford the delay–"

"Nonsense. The stench of war clings to each of you, and Yui's clothes and skin are stained with dragon blood. A hot bath is exactly what you need to recenter yourselves." In truth, Seirin chafed at the delay too, but they needed the rest – all of them. Too many had died already; she wouldn't lose any more to fatigue.

A loud snort from behind Yui reminded Seirin of the peculiar guardian. "I hope it's more private than my last bath was," the girl muttered. She blinked then, as if wondering whether she'd spoken the words aloud, shrugged it off, and lapsed back into silence.

Seirin's gaze flicked from the guardian to Yui and back. What had Takeshi done now? How could he trust his daughter's safety to this child? Lightning flashed from the gate, the sound of thunder booming ominously through the fortress.

Yui must have noticed Seirin's disapproval. A frown creased her pretty face, her expression at once proud and defensive.

Seirin shook her head. Yui's loyalty was admirable, but it could easily get her killed.

35
AWAKENING

Keiko shuffled her feet impatiently and waited for Hurricane Point's big gates to swing back on their hinges. The courtyard beyond looked smaller than the one in the White Spirit, but not by much. At the opposite end, a wide, ornately sculpted palace with delicate, windswept eaves, pillared entrances, and a series of arcing ramps in place of staircases sat regally between the walls. The Observatory Tower launched skyward from the back, tall and proud, as if to punctuate Hurricane Point's majesty. It was a spectacular scene, one that had Keiko's head sweeping around in continuous circles as she tried to take in every detail.

"This place sure looks different up close," she commented to no one in particular.

"Perspective changes everything," Roarke said from her right.

Keiko started. The Earth Spirit had fallen in beside her without her knowledge – an impressive feat, considering his size.

"I remember a time when Aeryk filled Hurricane Point with music. Then, the palace stood on a great peninsula overlooking the sea. He must have ripped it from the earth after the last battle and brought it here to watch Seirin's Boundary."

Keiko couldn't tell if he was talking to her specifically or simply voicing a long withheld complaint.

"I'll never forget those sounds. Aeryk manipulated the air itself, changing tone and pitch, until the most beautiful music you'd ever heard swirled around you." Roarke's face darkened briefly, and then grew sad. "I understand he weaponized sound and armed the White Spirit with its power. Vissyus has much to answer for."

They walked the rest of the way in silence, Aeryk and Seirin leading them through the living quarters to their rooms. Yui, Keiko, and Roarke followed close behind. One by one, they disappeared behind richly carved doors, each given a reminder to use their time wisely and to be ready to meet as planned. Keiko's room was located at the end of a long corridor, its entrance abutting a winding ramp.

"One hour, Keiko," Aeryk said. He stepped back from the apartment with an affable wink. "Pay attention to the time. Seirin's baths are very relaxing. It's easy to lose track." He nodded to her. "Someone will come for you. Be ready."

A gentle puff of air opened the door for her, and she ambled into the spacious apartment with a wave and a promise. She closed the door and listened for the faint click of the latch as it caught. When she was sure she was alone, she turned to face the impossibly opulent room, tugged absently on one ear, and giggled. Being a part of this tickled her soul, the sense of belonging, the warmth of inclusion.

Keiko's room was three to four times larger than the spartan accommodations Takeshi provided. The windows opened to the night, and warm breezes played at a pair of sumptuously embroidered curtains – hand-woven – of pure white linen. In contrast, a pile rug covered the floor like rich, green grass. Mosaic tiles dotted the ceiling, blues and whites laid out in abstract patterns that reminded her of cloud-streaked skies. To her right, a few feet beyond the edge of the carpet, glossy white-marble squares disappeared into a pool of clear water. Wisps of steam rose from the surface, some clinging stubbornly, while others wafted lazily upward.

She dropped her small knapsack into a chair, removed her clothes, and slipped into the water, humming contentedly. The floor fell away gradually the farther she walked, though by the time the water reached her waist, the bottom leveled off. She lay back and let her body float within the pool. Incredibly, strength seeped back into her tired limbs; she didn't think she'd ever felt so relaxed. A wide, satisfied grin broke across her face. Aeryk had been right. Seirin's bath was amazing. If only she had more time.

She drifted between waking and sleeping, too relaxed to notice the tingling her wish had called from her body. Dimly, she felt her thoughts stretch out into space. A pair of giant metal arms appeared before her, one long, one short. She stared at them in astonishment, watched their rhythmic movement until her spirit opened.

Not knowing why, she placed her hands on each of the metal rods and held them. Vibrations beat against her palms, steady at first, but slowing. Before long, they ground to a halt and trembled. She imagined they waited for her to restart them. An odd feeling of satisfaction washed over her, and she felt her mind drift toward sleep.

Some time later, she couldn't say how long, a sharp

rap echoed inside her head. It came again. The third knock brought her out of a dreamlike sleep and back to consciousness. She groaned and waded to the edge of the pool.

"Coming!" She climbed out and dried herself.

Dressing quickly in the spare robe and pants she'd stowed in her pack, she headed for the door. When the rap sounded again, she realized it came from the balcony. She rolled her eyes. Only Yui would be crazy enough to fly up the side of the palace to meet her. Head shaking, she pulled on the satin cord and drew back the curtains, which parted to reveal a pair of beautifully wrought French doors with golden handles shaped like birds in flight.

Through the glass, unmistakable in the moonlight, stood Seirin, her hands clasped lightly in front of her, her dazzling smile open and friendly. She wore a fitted tunic of hunter green over a pair of matching pants, neither of which did anything to hide the ripe curves beneath. Intimidated, Keiko fumbled with the knobs, her sweaty palms making a sure grip difficult. She inhaled to calm herself and somehow managed to open the doors and invite Seirin inside.

"Thank you, Keiko, but some other time, I think." Though Seirin's voice was kind and light, she moved purposefully. "I see you've made good use of the bath I prepared." She eyed Keiko critically. "Can I assume everything was to your liking?"

Keiko blushed again. "The bath?" She shook her head as if to clear it. How could she have forgotten? "I'm so sorry, Ms Seirin, I should have thanked you right away. That bath was *incredible*. I haven't felt this good in..." She frowned, thinking. "I haven't ever felt this good. I don't know what you did to the water, but Yui was right, you really can bless it."

Seirin beamed, looking both flattered and intrigued. "She said that?"

Keiko squeaked a weak affirmation. Her cheeks flared. The woman's perfect beauty flustered her – that golden hair catching the moonlight, those sparkling eyes. No wonder Seirin always got her way. Refusing her, particularly for the men, must have been difficult.

"We were soaking in the hot springs. Yui said she prayed to you whenever she went there – said your blessing could make the water special."

"Well." Seirin laughed. "That's quite a compliment."

"She doesn't offer all that many," Keiko snorted. "Trust me."

Seirin laughed again. "Oh, I do. If she's anything like her father, I understand completely." Her emerald eyes drilled into Keiko. "Come to think of it, as a guardian, you must know her better than anyone but Takeshi."

Alarms sounded in Keiko's head. So *that's* what this was about. She should have seen it coming. "I'm not her guardian."

Seirin ignored the comment. "I haven't seen Yui since she was a baby. Perhaps you can tell me what she's like."

"She… young – maybe not in years, but emotionally. I'm not sure I can explain it any other way."

"I don't understand," Seirin frowned. "Responsibility accelerates personal growth, and Yui's been through more than most."

Keiko caught the hitch in Seirin's voice. The Lady of Water spoke from experience. "That's part of the problem, Ms Seirin."

Seirin tilted her head. "How so?" She took Keiko's arm and led her to the balcony.

"You all have your own expectations of her. Do you

have any idea what that's been like? Yui's always been on display, like an exhibit. Why do you suppose she leaps into things without thinking? She's trying to make an impression. She wants you to be proud of her, but she's also afraid she'll let you down."

"We really didn't have that much time with her." Seirin sighed. Though she hid it, Keiko heard the bitterness in her voice. "Takeshi took her away while she was still young, too young, I think for what you suggest."

Keiko shook her head. "That only made it worse. She knew the Weakening was coming, and she knew she'd see you again. She grew up knowing. Imagine what the anticipation's been like. I think it terrified her."

Seirin's thoughtful smile reminded Keiko of sunlight on the ocean. "You've been with us long enough to understand how much Yui means to us. We love her like she's our own child. She has to know that."

"I'm sure she does. But that only compounds the problem. You loved the child. Yui's a grown woman now. You need to start from scratch."

Seirin pirouetted, her platinum belt tinkling lightly. "Well then, I welcome your guidance." She studied Keiko for a moment. "You aren't like any guardian I've ever met – more brash and certainly more independent. Aeryk believes you've been good for Yui. I couldn't see how you'd serve her, but now that I've met you, I have to agree."

Keiko wasn't entirely sure what to make of the comment. "You have to treat Yui the way you treat everyone else." A part of her couldn't believe she was counseling a goddess, but another part – the part that yearned to become a guardian – spoke without hesitation. "Yui wasn't part of this to start with, at least not completely, but her birth set everything in motion."

For the first time since they'd met, Seirin appeared to be at a loss. Her beautiful face flushed furiously, and her eyes turned into wide pools of astonishment.

"Yui's hurting, Ms Seirin," Keiko continued, the words flowing easily now. "She has been for a very long time. Those expectations I mentioned? She's lived her whole life worrying about them."

"I need to remember to do something nice for Kirak," Seirin muttered. Her eyes burned in the night, a stunning green that defied Keiko's best efforts to describe. "Your fierce devotion will serve her well in the chaos to come. She's lucky to have you." Keiko beamed but said nothing. Seirin nodded and squared her shoulders. "Can you raise a shield?"

"No," Keiko admitted. "A brief Searching, but that's about it." The question stung. She wanted to do more than the few meager things she'd accomplished, especially with a battle looming on the horizon. Yui would need all the help she could get.

Seirin smiled gently. "It's all right, Keiko." Stepping closer, she brought her emerald shield to life. "I'm sure it will come to you."

Lost in thought, Keiko barely felt Seirin lift them from the ground and rocket up the side of the tower.

36
HONOR

Yui drifted in the middle of a wide, white-tiled pool with a clear head and healed wounds. The water wasn't as hot as she was used to, but it was more soothing. One touch cleansed her spirit along with her body, leaving her more refreshed, stronger, ready for the days ahead. Sighing, she let the water wash over her, and again her mood lifted. She wished she could stay. Just a little longer. The peace she enjoyed here wouldn't come again for a long time. Not once the fighting started. Regretfully, she kicked her way across the bath and was about to climb onto a carpet dyed to look like lush forests, when a voice sounded in her head.

Yui-chan, it called. *I wish to speak with you.*

Yui blinked and opened her mind. *Father? What's wrong? Has something happened?* Her father wouldn't intrude on her thoughts if it wasn't serious.

Vissyus, he said soberly. *He's destroying whole worlds within the Boundary.*

We know, Yui answered. *Seirin delivered your message. Are you ready for us?*

Not just yet, Takeshi said. The delay seemed to weigh

329

on him despite his words. *I want you to take command of the White Spirit. If we fail, pull it into the Boundary and draw the sanctuaries to you. Those inside will be this world's only survivors. You'll have to take care of them.*

Yui's bath turned icy. *You shouldn't think like that. We're ready. We can do this!*

I need you to prepare for the eventuality. We are responsible for the Earth's safety. I have to make sure I care for its people. Vissyus is so strong and so unbalanced. I've planned as well as I can, but events change quickly.

You will stop him.

Yes, Yui-chan, but we could easily perish in the attempt. The White Spirit must stand, whatever happens.

Yui didn't want to consider the possibility. Her father had always been the root of her strength. She'd railed against him, rebelled, and questioned him, but she always believed he'd survive. He was one step ahead of everyone – a blessing and a curse, at least for the daughter who thought to outmaneuver him.

A word of warning, Takeshi continued. *Another power moves toward you.*

Yui's head came up. She pulled back the obvious question to see how much her father offered.

Paitr Norwoska – Lon-Shan's first disciple – survived Seirin's attack and continues his lord's vengeance. The army Lon-Shan brought against Aeryk in the last battle is with him. The world rushes toward balance, Kami against Kami – disciple against disciple.

Yui's muscles tightened. The reality of their situation crashed upon her shoulders. She knew what her father implied and didn't want to face it. This wasn't a game; she'd learned that in the Nepali village and again at Kanchenjunga. *No!* she cried. *I don't care about balance! Keiko isn't a disciple, and she isn't a warrior. Turning her into one is wrong, Father. She deserves better!*

Well, well, well, Takeshi chuckled. *At last. This is what responsibility feels like, Yui. It's what separates great leaders from great warriors. Do what you can, but do what you must as well. I'm sure you've noticed that in her own way, Keiko is as proud as her father. Do not dishonor her.*

Closing her eyes, Yui drew in a shuddering breath and nodded. Despite the danger, her heart felt light. Her training, everything she'd been through mattered – both to her, and more importantly, to her father. He believed in her.

Thank you, she said. *The White Spirit will stand. You have my word.* She planted her feet on the bottom of the pool and bowed. Rising, she left the bath, dressed, and headed for the door. As she reached for the handle, the world lurched around her. The image of a great clock filled her thoughts, its gears moving backward before settling into a familiar rhythm.

Yui staggered. Was it possible? She glanced about her room and sighed. Keiko, she thought, shaking her head. It had to be Keiko. Turning, she strode from her room and made her way to Aeryk's Observatory, grim yet determined.

37
RUMBLINGS

Seirin raced up the side of the tower before slowing to a halt a few feet below the great dome. Keiko heard Aeryk's deep voice announce them, and Seirin's shield moved again. They reached a large, south-facing window and entered a spacious room with sparkling floors that reminded Keiko of diamonds.

Roarke stood on the opposite side, slightly behind and to Aeryk's right. He no longer had his hammer, but he still radiated power, not as much as Seirin or Aeryk, perhaps, but close. The pain in his eyes was there as well, though shrouded. The two men bowed their heads respectfully as Seirin entered, while Yui, as always, dipped from the waist.

Yui brightened when she saw Keiko and waved discreetly. Keiko returned the gesture, half laughing at how girlish Yui looked next to the others. Not that Keiko looked all that different. Apart from several inches in height they might have been sisters. Yui's similar garb made the comparison inevitable. Gone were the cumbersome robes and soft, serviceable boots she'd used for the Himalayas. Instead, she'd donned a matching tunic and pants – white, slashed with deep blue – close fitting for free range of motion. Her feet sported a pair of supple, bleached leather boots, ankle high and laced lightly for comfort. Even her hair, pulled into a ponytail and held away from her face with two white lacquered sticks, reflected a readiness to engage in brutal, unforgiving combat.

Keiko didn't like the reminder, especially with her own power still out of reach. She kept her comments to herself as she crossed the floor, trying her best to avoid notice. Not that she needed to worry. All eyes had shifted to Aeryk.

The Air Lord stepped forward and turned to face them. Like Yui, he'd changed into something more suitable for fighting. A white shirt hugged his athletic frame without hindering it. Loose pants of some dark gray material billowed about his legs like clouds, reminding Keiko of the pictures she'd seen of Persian princes or ancient sailors.

"I know you're expecting me to reassure you," he began. "I wish I could. The truth is, I really don't know what to say." He ran a hand through his hair and shook his head. "It wasn't supposed to be like this. Takeshi should be the one talking to you, not me. He understands the situation better than I do."

Yui stirred beside Keiko and started to move forward. Keiko seized her wrist. Aeryk hadn't finished, and she had the feeling his words would have a greater impact on Seirin and Roarke than anything Yui could say. Surreptitiously, she shook her head. Yui caught the gesture and returned to her spot, squeezing Keiko's hand in thanks.

"He hasn't lost what we've lost," Roarke grumbled. "I don't know whether that makes him more objective or more detached."

Aeryk grunted. "He's the Lord of Spirit, Roarke. He lost Vissyus and then a little more every time Vissyus killed or destroyed. Combined, our sacrifices pale next to his, and yet he's letting us right our wrongs. We've grown so self-absorbed. We don't even know the difference between want and need. I wasn't ready to fight for my dreams. I let Vissyus do that for me. We all did."

Seirin lowered her head, and to Keiko's surprise Roarke did too. Her eyes snapped toward Yui, who motioned for silence. Explanations could wait, she seemed to say. Don't interrupt, let them work it out for themselves. Somehow, Keiko knew she wouldn't ask again. Too much was coming for her to remember. Maybe she'd find out one day and maybe she wouldn't. She had her own memories to see to first. Either way, she guessed the answer wouldn't come for a very long time.

Roarke sighed. "All right, Aeryk. What do we have to do?"

"The guardians are the key. We will use the Bond against him."

Despite the law, Roarke accepted the idea without reservations. "Which one do we target? With all due respect to Kirak, Fiyorok's the strongest guardian I've ever seen."

Keiko did her best to hide her discomfort. Takeshi said the guardians were sacred. The Kami couldn't harm them – that was the law. Roarke didn't even question its violation. Keiko's stomach twisted. She looked at Yui, who shot her a warning glance before striding forward. The young spirit's thoughts touched her own, telling her not to interfere.

"The twin guardians are of equal strength," Yui replied. "Vissyus chained their souls to his spirit and infused them with his power. He can – and will – shift his attention to whichever guardian we threaten. In this respect, neither is weak. It is for other reasons that we target Fiyorok, Lord Roarke."

"Yui's right," Aeryk agreed. "We believe Vissyus uses Fiyorok as both a conduit and a receptacle for Akuan's Bonding." He looked over at Yui and motioned for her to continue.

"It's a curious anomaly." She moved forward so that all could see her. "It enables Vissyus to hold both Bonds without further damage to his psyche. As you know, a guardian takes the form its essence demands. Not so with Akuan, whose form Vissyus intentionally manipulated. We always wondered why he created a copy of Fiyorok. It seemed more work than was necessary. But as my father deepened his research, he came to the conclusion that, perhaps, Vissyus was more careful in his experiments than we thought – not that it helped him."

Yui folded her arms, her face unreadable except for the tiniest flicker of pride around a suppressed smile.

"It has taken my father thousands of generations to understand how the three are linked, but he finally uncovered the secret: Vissyus intertwined the powers of his distinctly different guardians with the use of a filter. Fiyorok became the buffer, the vessel apart from himself, and yet still linked directly to him. He knew how great a risk he was taking, and he would not chance direct contact with his spirit until he was sure it was safe."

Roarke's dark eyes narrowed thoughtfully. "Did it work?"

Yui shook her head. "We don't know. We have no way to verify it. The buffer, though, remains in place. He couldn't have altered it once he completed the Bonding." She paused to let her words sink in. "It still runs through Fiyorok."

"How long have you known about this?" Roarke
demanded.

"We only just learned the truth. Vissyus himself
provided the answer when my father showed Keiko
Akuan's creation."

A stunned silence filled the room. Seirin looked
stricken. Her face paled, and her emerald eyes glistened
with unshed tears. Beside her, Aeryk's body had gone
rigid. Only Roarke seemed unaffected.

He studied Keiko for a moment before returning his
attention to Yui. "You're sure about this?"

"We are sure, Lord Roarke. My father stands by the
assertion."

Roarke threw his enormous hands into the air and
moved about the Observatory like an earthquake. "What
a waste. What a horrible waste. Vissyus knew what could
happen, and he went ahead anyway." He exhaled loudly
and turned to face them. "So, we attack Fiyorok, then."

Keiko gnawed at her lip. Roarke was spoiling for a
fight. As much as Takeshi warned against Yui's rashness,
it paled next to the Earth Spirit's. Yui seemed to know
about Roarke. She even accepted his attitude. She and
Takeshi were planning something, but what? Balance,
harmony, that's what Takeshi wanted. What did that
mean for Roarke?

"Akuan is the obvious choice, Roarke," Aeryk said.
"Especially given Seirin's connection to it. Vissyus will
expect such a move." A grim smile split his lips, his eyes
twinkling like stars. "Which is precisely why we'll strike
there first."

"A feint?" Roarke grinned.

"A feint." Aeryk nodded. "If Yui's right, he'll leave
Fiyorok relatively unprotected."

Roarke folded his arms and shook his head in

admiration. "And who is to lead this mission? Will it be you, Aeryk, with Takeshi as bait?"

A shadow of pain flashed across Aeryk's face. He closed his eyes and looked away.

Keiko's heart went out to him. They'd used Takeshi already, and if Aeryk led the upcoming strike, only one option remained.

"That was what we originally intended," Seirin answered. Her right hand came up to stroke Aeryk's cheek as she walked past him. "But Vissyus meets Takeshi with violence. We need to hold him, not fight him."

"Then what...?" Roarke stopped. Realization shone in his sandy eyes. "No! Seirin, you can't. There's no telling what he'll do. He's unpredictable enough as it is."

Seirin crossed over to him. She looked pleadingly into his face, a hand flowing onto his wrist. "I've won this argument once already. Don't make me fight it again."

Roarke's breathing quickened, and he looked about to nod, when she planted her palms on his chest and pushed herself away. A look of pained outrage darkened his features. He rounded on Aeryk.

"This is madness. If anything happens to her, you won't be able to fight. Believe me, I know."

"It's her choice, Roarke." Aeryk's tone carried a hint of resignation.

"You're handing him a hostage."

"Not a hostage," Seirin answered. "At least not at first. Vissyus still wants something from me. It's the last thing he remembers, and it's very important to him."

"You are putting your faith in a madman. I understand why you're doing it, but I want you both to know that I don't like it." Again crossing his massive arms, Roarke looked first at Aeryk and then at Seirin. Neither moved.

He turned to Yui. "And Takeshi agrees with this?"

"He does, Lord Roarke. As do I." Yui's voice was proud – confident and commanding.

The declaration impressed Keiko. Roarke still treated Yui like a child, as did Seirin. Yui obviously meant to dispel the notion as quickly as possible. In Takeshi's absence, she represented the White Spirit. They needed to treat her as its emissary. Keiko tugged at an ear, convinced Takeshi expected as much.

"All right," Roarke huffed. "I know when I've lost. I'll drop my objections… for the moment." He tipped his head to Aeryk, who returned the gesture with a smile and a nod of his own before continuing.

This time, no one interrupted him, except to ask the occasional question. By the time he outlined their plan, night had come and gone. Another day had passed, and a gorgeous sunset dyed the surrounding clouds with vivid pinks and purples. A few stars speckled the sky, small and beautiful in the twilight.

Keiko gazed at them, marking the night's progress. Here, day ended, but in Japan, a new day was about to begin. The thought brought goosebumps to her skin despite the warm air. As she turned west, the Observatory's view lurched to the other side of the world. A deafening roar buffeted the great tower, loud beyond hearing, urgent beyond imagining. More sounds followed, these reminding her of a great, tolling bell, slow, somber, and funereal.

A long triangular shape appeared beyond the windows, tall and snow-capped and thrusting into the sky from a landscape of lakes and trees. The air to the southwest rippled and swelled, and when it calmed, a huge donjon – a castle nearly half as large as the volcano beside it – stood defiantly in the morning light.

"So," Yui said, walking up beside her. "The time has finally come."

Color exploded throughout the Observatory as the Kami brought their shields to life. Keiko moved next to Yui, who nodded and shielded them both. Aeryk rocketed past in a blur of dazzling blue, the green of Seirin's shield meeting his as they flew from the tower. Yui fell in behind Roarke and followed moments later. The guardians emerged from the fortress's lower towers, each peeling off to accompany its Kami through Hurricane Point's concealing storms.

Quickly, the North African coast flashed by, the Atlas Mountains appearing and disappearing like a surging wave. Huge thunderheads rose in the east to meet them as they crossed the Sea of Japan: towering, flat-topped shapes forty thousand feet high. Their torrential rains had stopped for the moment, but a drizzle lingered. Lightning flashed on, however, illuminating Japan's rugged west coast through the mist.

Seirin and Kirak banked toward Fuji's wide summit, while Yui raced northwest and angled for the White Spirit's central donjon. Behind, Keiko saw Roarke and his guardian whip past and drop into a hidden ravine along the volcano's rocky base. Behind him, Aeryk's azure shield shot into the lowering ceiling with Ventyre and disappeared. The shields winked out one by one until darkness returned, and an eerie calm settled over Japan.

38
FUJI

Takeshi surveyed the sweeping horseshoe-shaped bowl of Tokyo Bay with a Searching. Nothing moved over the ocean's surface, not boat, nor barge, nor buoy. The busy port cities of Yokohama and Kawasaki, Tokyo and Chiba, had ordered all ships to port, moored them, then waved off any inbound vessels to less dangerous waters. Along the shore, deserted derricks lined ghostly wharves, the empty warehouses beyond filling with dust and forsaken cargo. No dockhands worked the wharves this night, and no crewmen remained aboard ship.

Farther inland, the normally thriving cities around the bay stood equally still, their streets a darkened tangle of abandoned concrete and asphalt. Only gleaming towers and the litter of civilization gave testament to those who had once lived there – that and the mournful flashing of old, damaged neon signs or the occasional bleat of a forgotten radio.

Even so, Takeshi felt the anticipatory pall clinging to the air, almost as though some remnant of Tokyo's spirit lingered long after he'd shepherded its people into the Boundary.

The evacuation had taken less than two days – less than two days to turn one of the most densely populated areas on the planet into a ghost town. It was a monumental achievement – one born not of desperation or fear, but of a nation taught from infancy how to respond when called.

In Tokyo, where the threat was the greatest, his disciples had moved through the streets like lightning, searching house to house, building to building. Those who remained – foreigners mostly – offered the only resistance. Takeshi's forces systematically herded them to the nearest shelter along with the rest, their protests and demands all but ignored. The once-effervescent city became so desolate, so lifeless, that not even the sunbeams cresting the eastern horizon dispelled the fatalistic gloom hanging over it. This was where the sorrow began, here in what had once been the immense volcano home of Vissyus Sar Furcan, Lord of Fire.

Vissyus returned to his fortress after a brief assault on a number of worlds, some with Kami, some without, all now dust. That should have bothered him, but whenever he thought of the magnificent fires, he lost focus. Light and heat, twisting together in bright, burning beacons always set his soul ablaze. What was the world beside such purity? It cleansed and illuminated. All life contained a piece of it – all creation – a dormant spark, a hope in waiting.

He turned his attention to the Boundary. The Weakening called him back with the promise of freedom. More sparks lay beyond its wall, more souls needing release. He grinned at the thought, but, as he savored it, his mind shifted. A strong and powerful emotion overtook him. Was the Teacher out there? Was she waiting for him?

He had to find out.

Reforming his shield, he crafted flaming spears from the fires about him and studied the Boundary walls. A moment earlier he'd glimpsed a small change in a section ninety degrees above his castle's courtyard, a trace of smooth surface in the otherwise rippling fabric. He peered closer, adding power to his gaze. There. He saw it again, and this time, he was sure the calm came from an alignment of weakened layers. Clear blue sky peeked through the constantly moving Boundary, a peaceful swatch, an eye. A target.

Breath held, he launched his spears with a thought and waited through the eternal seconds. The barrage arced across the boiling sky, his calculations impeccable, his aim perfect. The first strike sent long, spindly cracks spiderwebbing from horizon to horizon. The second deepened the initial damage, and the third blew the whole ruined mass apart.

A thought ripped the once-eternal sky open; another sent his blazing shield through. Fiyorok pulled up to his left, Akuan to his right, and together they stared upon the world. Vissyus marveled at how much had changed. More water covered the surface, for one thing, and even if the liquid looked duller than he remembered, incredibly, most felt more flammable.

His gaze slid toward a small island chain in the southwest. That was new, but then so was the large, horseshoe-shaped bay beneath him. Once, his volcano rose from this spot, connecting Seirin's oceans to Aeryk's skies. He wondered where the great peak had gone, then remembered shattering the caldera and sinking the whole mountain into the sea.

He scowled disapprovingly. These were his lands,

and they looked so strikingly different than they should have, even after all this time. You'll just have to remake them, he said to himself. Change them back to how they used to be. Melt and remold them. Nodding, he flicked a finger, and huge solar flares broke from his shield, rocketed over the water, and climbed above the land like a rising star. Rock liquefied and water boiled, and Vissyus used the vapor to douse the earth the way a smith cooled a new blade.

Satisfied with his work, he spun his shield to the west and regarded the gleaming towers surrounding the unfamiliar bay. They were so many. How should he handle them? Precise strikes lengthened the fun and tested both skill and accuracy. A massive explosion, while lacking duration, was no less enjoyable, often more so. Which to choose... He shrugged and pushed his shield forward. A decision would come to him.

Fiyorok remained at his side. Smoke and fire flickered from its nostrils. Neck craning, it lifted its head to the skies and bellowed. He looked to his left, and Akuan took up the call, ice and fog rising to join Fiyorok's triumphal cry.

Water vaporized beneath his shield. The tall cranes along the wharves melted into twisted shards of glowing metal, fuel tanks in docked boats and abandoned vehicles ignited, and heavy machinery disappeared beneath inky clouds. The firestorm raced inland, but before the first orange tongues touched the city gates, his flames, so unstoppably perfect, sputtered and fizzled.

Glistening surfaces resisted him, the cloying dampness leaving nothing to burn. He blinked. *Could it be?* Mouth dry, he fired stakes of flaming energy across the ground. The more intense, blue-white flames caught this time, producing vast clouds of billowing smoke, thicker and blacker than a moonless midnight. None lasted more than a minute, though. Their intensity burned them out before they spread farther than a few thousand feet. The surviving fire met liquid power and quickly died.

His pulse quickened. *She was here*! Enraptured, he closed his eyes, let his body sway. She was here... the Teacher. She'd come to meet him. The burning city faded. Another fire seized his soul, one he couldn't control. His Searching exploded over the islands, toppling buildings, shredding storms, and igniting fires as he hurled his mind inland.

The loud tolling of hammers against iron bells followed him through the city. Shields erupted in the alarm's wake, opaque domes of spiritual energy cast to protect weak shelters from his fury. Vissyus smiled sadly and released firebombs into the protected sanctuaries.

Smoke and the stench of slaughter filled the air. Vissyus barely noticed the carnage; his mind was somewhere else, lost in an ancient dream that ended at a distant volcano's summit, a place so incredibly appropriate, so perfect, that he almost believed he was sleeping. Only he wasn't. Up he gazed, up the volcano's nearly perfect neck and past the snow-topped cone. There he found her, eight hundred feet above the crater, a vision to overwhelm his senses, a dream to devour. Tall, beautiful, and impossibly strong, Seirin floated unshielded in a clear blue sky. She held a hand over her head, palm tilted toward the heavens, a rainbow bursting from its center toward him, beckoning him to her.

"Teacher." The words were a whispered breath, his tone at once chaste and achingly perverse. "Is that really you?" He blinked, afraid his Searching had tricked him.

Seirin extinguished the light, lowered her hand, and smiled at him. "Vissyus." Her deep, musical voice made his name sound holy. "I was afraid you wouldn't come."

With a thought, he snuffed out his shield. The corona of reds streaked with yellow and tinted orange unraveled in the wind. Silently, he held up a hand and motioned his guardians to stop where they were. He advanced, looking at neither, seeing nothing but her.

"Teacher." He shook his head, his heart bursting. "You haven't forgotten me, after all this time."

"I'd never forget you," she said. "We've been through *so* much together."

Her words triggered a memory – the two of them dancing beneath a shimmering sky. Those were happy times. He frowned. Something wasn't right? If he'd been so happy, then why did the memory feel so... horrible?

39
CHAINS

Takeshi scrubbed a hand over his mouth and, sending his thoughts into the Boundary, drew enough power from his creation to form – panel by panel – a miniature version around Fuji. When he finished, a new barrier ringed the summit: invisible, imperceptible, and as strong as the Boundary, if infinitesimally smaller.

Do you think he felt that? Gaiyern's thoughts were troubled, uncomfortable even, but the guardian maintained its composure. *Seirin's taking a terrible risk.*

Takeshi grunted. "She knew the danger, and she volunteered anyway."

The distant storm clouds built again. Their leading edge streamed toward Fuji in a rush of thunder and lightning. Takeshi sent his thoughts toward the central eye.

All right, Aeryk, he called. *I've sealed them in as well as I can; the rest is up to you.*

We're ready, Takeshi, Aeryk said, driving the huge thunderheads forward. *I hope you're right about this.* Gusting winds assaulted the forests, vivid blue-white flashes strobing within the squalls. A single strike plunged like a dagger into the deepest of the five lakes ringing the volcano. Water spun around the lightning in a great, counter-clockwise swirl. Small whitecaps grew into pounding swells, turning the placid lake into a cauldron of turgid foam.

More scars would come, more devastation. Takeshi vowed to save Japan, but he'd sacrificed so much of it already. First Tokyo and now the ancient woodland around Mount Fuji. A weight settled over his heart. More disciples died in Vissyus's rampage than he expected: a weathered trainer, a blade master with a single eye, countless monks – some old enough to remember Masato. The youngest had pined after Yui until she brought him to the sparring grounds. He'd lasted maybe a second more before she pinned him to the mat with her thoughts. How would she react when she found out he'd died?

Takeshi opened his hand, blew into his palm, and set their spirit free. "I am sorry, my friends. I underestimated Vissyus's madness." Sadly, he turned his thoughts back to the Boundary, hoping Seirin wouldn't make the same mistake.

40
TEACHER

Seirin held her breath as Vissyus approached Fuji's summit, cut through a stray cloud, and drew up to her. She kept her back to the ruined city, unwilling to look. Unable to. Lon-Shan's words came back to her like an unwelcome guest, though they were as true now as when he'd first said them: *If you hadn't been so selfish, none of this would have happened. Vissyus would still be sane.*

Now, as she stared at her oldest friend, she couldn't deny the truth. Vissyus's boyishly handsome face was as open and inquisitive as ever, and his tawny hair whipped playfully in the breeze to complete the illusion of a lost cherub. Only his eyes were different. An odd light filled them, part uncontrolled madness and – alarmingly – part desire. Seirin's stomach fluttered. She hadn't expected him to look at her like that; they were friends, nothing more. He had to know that. He had to remember.

But what if Vissyus didn't see it that way? What if he never had? That uncomfortable idea made her see his approach in a new light, thinking how he darted for her like an adoring pet. An air of breathless anticipation surrounded him, increasing her anxiety.

"I did what you asked," he panted, shuddering to a stop a few feet from her. "Wait till you see. It's why you've come, isn't it? To meet our child?"

She tried not to shrink away. Child? What child? What was he talking about? Fighting to remain calm, she smiled at him.

"Akuan is magnificent – the things it can do." Vissyus gazed at the skies. "Your storms are very impressive; it takes a great deal of power to summon so much energy and even more to keep it caged at such a heightened intensity. Akuan wants to know how you do that. You'll teach it, won't you? It's eager to learn."

Seirin fought revulsion. "Of course," she swallowed. "I'd be happy to." It wasn't a lie, but it wasn't completely true either.

Vissyus relaxed. "Good. I've spent too much time with Akuan. I've neglected Fiyorok." A distant look crossed his face. "My guardian's fires are so strong; when we wield them together they are so… beautiful." Orange light flickered around him, dim, but enough for her to see. She needed to redirect his thoughts before he raised his shield; if he lost himself to the flames, he'd atomize the world.

"Have you shown Akuan how to draw moisture from our surroundings?" She leaned forward and placed a hand on his arm. Her touch sent a jolt through him. "That's the key. I taught you how to do it. Do you remember?"

Vissyus wasn't listening. He drifted to the edge of the crater and cast a thoughtful look into the space before him.

"You've sealed us in," he said, clearly puzzled. Somehow, he looked pensive, shy, and angry all at once. "Why would you do that? Do you expect someone to interrupt us?" He swooped in closer, his breath hot against the back of her neck. "Aeryk, perhaps?" A strong gust blew across the summit. She let it wrap around her, thinking of how often she'd dreamed of Aeryk coming to rescue her, had romanticized it. "I gave Aeryk something very special, but instead of treasuring it, he abandoned it when it needed him most. You deserved better."

The leading edge of the thunderheads rolled over Yamanashi Prefecture. Damaging gales surged out ahead, severe microbursts ripping through the Five Lakes. Updrafts lifted the wreckage into the air, only to blast debris at Vissyus's guardians. After nearly eight hundred years, the Divine Wind had returned to Japan with a destructive fury to match the one that reshaped the offshore islands.

Vissyus spun to face the incoming storm, but Seirin gently touched his wrist to stop him. "Forget Aeryk," she said, hating herself. "He abandoned me, remember? I'm not interested in anything he has to say." Seirin worked her lips into a pout and shook her head in mock disappointment. "I can't be with a man I don't trust."

Vissyus brightened and then frowned. "He's coming, anyway. Spurned lovers can be very dangerous." A pained, apologetic look crossed his handsome face. "I might have to deal with him."

He pressed his body into her back and pointed over her shoulder. "You see? He rushes to be with you." He tilted his head, turned his outstretched hand over, and spread his fingers. "Look how the storms dance upon my palm." The clouds appeared to hover in the middle of his opened hand, and then, in a flash, he curled his thumb around his forefingers to make a tight, quivering fist. He chuckled. "So powerful... So easily... crushed."

Seirin felt Vissyus's overwhelming strength through

the fabric between them. Fear overwhelmed her, anxiety groping her like an unwelcome lover. She had to fight the feeling. Aeryk depended on her. "Let your guardians handle him. He's not worth your effort." Winding her golden curls around a finger, she feigned a blithe smile, and pressed his arm down. To her relief, he didn't resist, though his strength made her feel as if she pushed a rusted lever.

"He won't leave without you. He'll think I'm holding you hostage." Vissyus pulled up a little and stared at her, his gaze moving over her, lingering in places, making her uncomfortable. She felt the anticipation in his body against her back, strong and tightly wound. "Maybe if you spoke to him."

Seirin crossed her arms and turned her back on the clouds, using the opportunity to move away. "We have nothing to say to each other."

"Then we'd better be ready. Ventyre is already here."

Seirin lifted her chin but didn't turn – her Searching would show her whatever she needed to see. She sent her thoughts past the mountain, through the Boundary, and beyond. The image of a large bird rocketed back to her. Snowy white wings colored to match the angry clouds, electric charges raging beneath dark, lightning-streaked feathers. Far ahead, the hint of a graceful neck blended into a noble, tufted head whose great, golden beak sliced through both cloud and smoke.

"Ventyre," she breathed. Her lips – hidden from Vissyus's sight as he repositioned himself several hundred feet behind her – broke into a smile.

The guardian's massive wings caught the air like huge billowing sails. Vapor plumed over the sleek body as the thunderbird dropped from the skies, gathering at the nape and blossoming into streaming trails behind an amethyst battle shield.

Battle ready, just another tool of war. Seirin grimaced, caught herself with a curse, and then returned her attention to the battlefield.

A rotating circlet of lightning exploded from each of Ventyre's folded wings. Sparks flew through the clouds, fifty-foot motes of pure electricity that bounced harmlessly from the dragons' shields before falling from the sky like tiny comets. A stray bolt careened out of control and crashed into Fuji's large crater. Seirin's world disappeared in a haze of smoke and dust. She felt Vissyus's Searching, felt his thoughts explode across the mountaintop. A second Cast of his power followed the first, and an area far to her right cleared. Warm air wafted out of the pit, ash and debris trapped within the climbing atmosphere. She gasped at his power, his control magnificent despite the madness.

"*Teacher*!" he cried, frantically. "Teacher! Don't go!"

Seirin's heart pounded. In desperation, Vissyus could flatten the entire volcano just to find her. Instead, he summoned a wall of solid flame – high, steep, and sheer – to stand between her and escape. It rocketed around the existing barrier's inner lining like a smokeless hedge of white-hot hellfire. A pair of two thousand-foot wide slits – eyes of searing red fire – moved wildly within the inferno.

She had to stop him before he did anything more, and that meant letting him see her. Quickly, she glided out of the fumes. Her shield was still down, and she made a conscious decision not to clear the area herself. Summoning that much power, given Vissyus's unbalanced psyche, was too much of a risk, too provocative, especially with Ventyre's recent arrival and the tightrope walk to come. "I am here, Vissyus," she said, calmly. "You don't have to worry. I won't leave you. This barrier is unnecessary."

"It will remain until I am sure of you," he hissed back. He hovered before the flaming wall, the massive eyes he'd conjured to amplify his Searching fading when he saw her. "Considering your feelings for Aeryk, I would be a fool to trust you completely." She tensed at that, and he chuckled at her discomfort. "You thought I forgot, didn't you?"

Seirin didn't answer. She hadn't seen this personality before, and she didn't like it – smart, proud, and overtly paranoid. Thunder boomed in the distance. Fierce, shearing winds cut across the summit. Chaos came at them from every direction. She gripped her leggings, searching Vissyus's face for an opening. The time had come to strike back at him. She knew what she had to do.

Drawing moisture from the air, she sent tiny beads into her hair to make it glisten in the light of his fires. Her lips were wet with the promise of kisses, her clothes just damp enough to cling seductively to her body. She peered up at him through heavy lids. "You are as brilliant and as strong as ever." Her voice was low and husky. "The others are far too set in their ways to listen to anything I have to say. You're the only one who understands. They turned their backs on me. Even Aeryk tried to talk me out of this." She pushed her lower lip forward, pouting. A hand came up to her heart. She pressed it against her breast, tightening fabric, showing skin. "You're the only one I can count on. I need you, Vissyus. Show me what you've learned. Please. I've waited so long."

He smiled, and a dagger of ice pierced her soul – for the briefest of moments, he looked frighteningly sane.

41
DRUMS

Yui knelt on the tatami mats of her father's study, cradling Masato's staff in her hands. She'd come back to the room shortly after Vissyus reappeared, watching as long as she could before emotion overcame her. Tears still spilled from her eyes. Tokyo was as much her home as this castle. The city was part of her, and now it burned. Forming a Searching, she let her power transport her into the downtown area.

Shinjuku's proud skyscrapers were a pile of ash, Tokyo Tower little more than twisted metal. Ginza Station had disappeared beneath a toppled building. The intersection where she'd lost Keiko was a tangle of melted wire, soot, and shattered neon tubes. The acrid scent of charred wood and chemical fires blended with the coppery tang of blood. Their monks did their best, but she never expected them to save everyone. Her father tried to hide *that* from her too, and now she understood why.

She felt the monks' souls – lifetimes and memories forever lost to the world. A battle wasn't some game; she understood that now. The ruined city was proof enough for her. So much destruction with so little effort. What would happen when Vissyus unleashed his full power?

Shivering, she hugged Masato's staff and lowered her head. Where was his strength when she needed it?

Keiko raced back to her rooms, grabbed her camera from her pack, and bolted to the top of the White Spirit's tall central donjon. Sweat covered her skin, as much from the tension in her body as from the heat of Vissyus's sunfire shield. A glance to the south provided a perfect view of Fuji's blazing summit. Quickly, she lifted the camera to her eye and waited for something – anything. A tingling in her hands, a rush of energy.

Neither came. Frustrated, she slumped against the tower's stone walls. After the Himalayas, she'd been so sure. Back then, she sent her thoughts from her body – called to Aeryk, cast a Searching – but the two most important things, a shield and her command of time, eluded her. Instead, she came away with her stomach tumbling and her hands shaking. She wasn't any worse off than she had been, but she wasn't any better either. And she had to be better. Takeshi and Yui were counting on her.

But for what? That was the question. Yui said they were to stay behind and secure the castle. Not that Keiko minded. What Vissyus did to Tokyo – so fast and so effortlessly – felt like a warmup to something far worse. Explosions still rocked southern Yokohama and Chiba like aftershocks from an earthquake that ended long ago. Keiko shook her head, recalling the excitement she felt when she first saw those great cities from the plane. Her stewardess said she grew up in Hokkaido but now lived in Yokohama. A nice woman. Keiko hoped she was working a flight somewhere far away.

She thought about the concierge at her hotel (a fastidious man who bowed so often she wondered how he maintained his happy paunch), about the family she'd seen in a small park, her fellow tourists. What happened to them? Were they still alive? She wanted to help them, knowing she couldn't. Tears formed in her eyes, but she scrubbed them away with the back of her hand.

Her place was with Yui. She promised her father – she promised herself. Resigned, she turned her back on the burning city. The stairs were a yard or two away. She moved toward them, only to stop after a few steps. Something felt wrong – like a presence in an empty house. She prowled around the donjon until she came to a window overlooking Aokigahara. The shutters were half closed, but she pushed them open and peered through.

Her gaze found the western wall, noted nothing of interest, and moved on. Deeper into the forest she probed – past the hill she'd flown over with Yui after fleeing Tokyo, over the steep ravine at the base. Thought merged with sight, and a Searching came to her. Blood roared in her ears, but the triumphant cry building in her chest died before meeting her lips.

There, fifteen miles away, her Searching found a shadowy mass racing through the trees. Dark and menacing, it moved through the forest like oil over water. The nape of Keiko's neck tickled, her skin prickling despite the heat. Horrified, she backed away from the window and rushed for the stairs.

Yui, she thought as flight after flight rolled by. She had to warn Yui. The darkness was deadly, her instincts said so. Yui had to see to their defenses before the threat, whatever it was, reached them. How much time did they have? And how much did she waste descending from the top of the tower. Once again, she cursed her inability to form a shield, or better yet, to hold time until she reached Yui. Distracted, she didn't see the large doors to

Takeshi's study until she was on top of them. Grasping the simple handles, she threw open the shojis without knocking, and stormed into the room.

Yui sat cross-legged on the mats in a short white robe expertly fastened around her waist with an elegantly embroidered obi of blue and yellow silks. A long, red-hafted spear balanced across her knees. Her back was to the door, and while she neither moved nor spoke, she held herself like an all-seeing cat, ready to pounce on anyone or anything foolish enough to sneak up from behind.

"What is it, Keiko?" she asked without turning. Her tone was soft and melodious despite its tautness. She faced the now familiar platform – perfectly placed in the middle of the room and draped with the silken banner. The proud, circular crest – a radiant sun rising over the shoulder of Mount Fuji – practically glowed in the gentle light of the lamps.

"I felt something," Keiko began. "I mean, I saw something... out in the woods. A black shadow under the trees, big, and coming this way."

Yui was silent for a moment. If Keiko hadn't seen her back expand and contract with each deep breath, she would have thought she'd turned to stone.

"I felt it as well." Yui uncoiled her legs and rose. As she turned, an aura of golden-haloed indigo sprang to life around her. She held the tall, elegantly carved rod upright and stepped lightly to one side. The staff lifted from the floor and flew back to the alcove that once held Takeshi's armor.

Gone now, Keiko thought. Gone with Mr Takeshi to war. Her eyes shifted to Yui. "You know what's out there, don't you?"

Yui brushed past her and strode to the open shoji. "Paitr Norwoska, Lon-Shan's first disciple. He's here for revenge."

Keiko shouldered her camera and fell in beside Yui. The young spirit's thoughts surged through and past her, obliterating everything else in her head. A window to her soul opened to Yui's call, shining burgundy light filtered through, tantalizingly close, yet still blocked. Dazed, she followed Yui back upstairs and into a wide corridor. The hallway was a blur of white, crimson, and gold that ended at an open shoji and a large observation deck. Dark clouds streamed across the sky beyond then broke to reveal a brilliant sun. More formed and rolled in behind the first, the sky alternating between clear and stormy as the Kami's powers roared around Mount Fuji.

Blinking under a patch of bright sun, Keiko stepped onto the balcony and stared in wonder at the fortress's main training grounds. Row upon row of armored men filled the vast space. Their stances, though perfectly still, seethed with caged violence. Each wore a suit of traditional samurai armor, complete with helmets adorned with family crest or sigil. They'd strapped beautifully crafted swords to their backs, the graceful hilts positioned behind and above shoulders for easy access. Some held long spears in gauntleted hands in addition to the blades, while others hefted staves pulsing with living energy.

Physical weaponry? That didn't make any sense, given what they were up against. And their armor, though sparklingly new, still seemed antiquated and wildly out of place. Why did they need it? Any of it?

"Because they are samurai," Yui said, her voice drawing a squeak from Keiko, who only just realized she'd spoken aloud. "Their fathers were samurai, and their fathers' fathers. The swords and spears they carry are forged from their thoughts and given form by their spirit. They fight with weapons familiar to them and their history. Close combat or not, they will be deadly, I assure you."

"But where did they come from?" Keiko asked. These were the first soldiers she'd seen about the castle.

"Our monks look different once armed." The yellow flecks in Yui's eyes glowed like embers within the smoky browns of her irises. She looked different, content.

Keiko walked to the protective railing and planted her hands on its smooth surface. Fuji stood tall in the distance. Yui joined her. A glimmer of light reflected off the armored men. It saddened Keiko.

"If the others fail, the fate of the world rests with us," Yui said soberly. "This castle must survive for that possibility. I am here to make sure that happens." She nodded solemnly and sent her thoughts to a far corner of the fortress.

Keiko followed Yui's mind over the open ground, past rows of samurai, and up the towering rear wall, where another contingent stood guard. Each man held a huge baton above his head, poised and ready. At Yui's command, the batons came down in one fierce motion. They struck the great *taiko* drums lining the ramparts, and a loud, rolling boom shook the donjon. Again the wooden sticks lifted, and again they fell, hammering on and on, filling the air with their pounding.

Yui met Keiko's questioning look with a knowing smile. "The power of sound. Wielded correctly, it can be as painful as a physical blow. See what it does to our enemy." She pointed to a spot beyond the wall.

The black cloud was less than ten miles away. Though it still raced toward them at high speed, the sound waves were having an effect. Cracks appeared in what was once a solid carapace, and as they widened, Keiko glimpsed a large black ball deep within. Gasping, she clutched her throat and shivered.

Yui followed her gaze into the wood. "You feel him, don't you? This close his presence is unmistakable. He brings an army with him, an army much like himself, distorted shells and fragments of a once-noble Kami." She lifted her chin and called her shield to life, her eyes bright.

"What are you doing?" Keiko's heart pounded. She rushed forward. "You can't go out there alone!"

"I'm sorry, Keiko. You're not ready for this. I'll be back as soon as I can. Wait for me in my father's study." Leaping from the balcony, she hovered over her forces, her thoughts ordering them to battle.

Keiko gripped the railing and thrust her body forward. "Don't you remember what happened the last time! You need me. Yui! Wait!"

Strong gusts snatched her words away, the drums drowned them, and even if Yui could hear her, Keiko knew she wouldn't come back. She'd made up her mind.

This was bad. But what could she do? Yui was right; she wasn't ready. The Yamanakas' vaunted power lay untapped inside her. A whisper was all she felt. Not enough to protect Yui in battle. Not enough to protect herself. Her mind raced. What would bring her power to life? What hadn't she tried?

The answer came quickly. Despite everything she'd been through, she hadn't faced a direct threat, not by herself. Maybe if she had to fight for her life. Without Yui's help – without her father's.

Pulse racing, she climbed onto the balcony's stone railing and closed her eyes. This was a bad idea. It was crazy. It was her only hope. She drew in a deep breath to steady herself. And jumped.

42
LIGHTNING

Aeryk ran through a narrow ravine at the base of the volcano. The walls on either side felt like they were closing in on him as he sprang from rock to rock, his eyes glued to the northern sky. A pillar of red and yellow fire lanced upward from a spot several miles away. Fuji was there, and Seirin. He needed to know what happened – if she was all right. A Searching would show him, but he didn't dare cast one, not with Vissyus out there. The Fire Lord would expect him to do something that foolish and was probably looking for it.

Desperately, he swerved toward the nearest cliff and climbed. Knots formed in his stomach, tightening as he scaled inch after torturous inch. His chest heaved, both from exertion and tension. The earth was still slick from the rains and morning mist; how cruel the power he loved so much now conspired against him. He lost his footing halfway up and again near the top. Despair overwhelmed him as his body pitched back. How many delays would he suffer, how much time had he lost? Seirin: he prayed nothing had happened to her. He fell and was about to ignite his shield, when a hand –

transparent and filled with what looked like swirling galaxies – shot down, seized his wrist, and hauled him out.

"My master thought you'd try something like this." Gaiyern's featureless face stared back at him, its body – now roughly his size – carefully positioned between him and the volcano.

"You shouldn't be here, guardian." Aeryk stepped to one side, but Gaiyern moved to block his path.

"Nor should you. You're *supposed* to be in the thunderheads – where Vissyus expects you. Seirin went to a great deal of trouble to hide your descent, don't throw that advantage away now, my lord. It's too soon."

"Out of my way, guardian! *Now!*"

"Forgive me, lord," the guardian replied. "Lord Takeshi forbids it."

"Takeshi can't forbid *me!*" Cyclones swirled around Aeryk's wrists. He brought them up and aimed at Gaiyern's chest.

Perhaps he can make you listen to reason then. Takeshi's calm voice bloomed in Aeryk's head. He chuckled ironically. *I see history repeats itself. At least this time I arrived before you did something foolish.*

Aeryk lowered his head. Takeshi was right. Seirin volunteered for this. He remembered her hand on his cheek, her liquid eyes. Love as deep as the oceans had filled them. She did this for him, to help him. If he went after her now... He inhaled. *I'm sorry, Takeshi. When I saw that...* He pointed at Fuji's shielded caldera.

I know, Takeshi agreed. *I worry too. It's the price we pay to love.*

Aeryk ran a hand through his hair. *I don't know if I can do this.*

You can, if you believe in her. The world demands harmony.

Good and evil, sanity and madness, even the need to right past wrongs. Seirin confronts herself as much as she does Vissyus. She has to do it, Aeryk; she won't find peace unless she does.

How can killing a friend bring peace?

Letting Vissyus live would bring a far greater guilt, I promise you. Be strong, Lord of Air, Takeshi said, his voice fading. *For Seirin and for Vissyus. A part of him begs for release. Better to come at the hand of a friend.*

"Friend," Aeryk spat. "What kind of friend have I been to him?"

"The kind who shows mercy in justice," Gaiyern said as its body dissipated.

Aeryk watched it go before gazing at the volcano. *Justice*, he thought. *When was fratricide ever just?* The guardian must know something he didn't because this didn't feel like justice. It felt like murder.

Ventyre burst from the thick clouds over Mount Fuji. Akuan's shield floated a few thousand yards below, Fiyorok about the same, though farther to the right. Sparks from Ventyre's earlier attack still crackled on the dragons' shielding like dying stars, while behind them, Vissyus ringed the volcano's summit with a wall of fire. It was a heartbreaking sight. Vissyus, Fiyorok – they'd been friends once.

Ventyre's body – a body built to soar – felt suddenly leaden. *Why did you do it, Vissyus? What was worth the risk?* Shaking its head sadly, Ventyre cupped its wings and dove from the skies. Instantly, Searchings surged in, one from the south, another from the north.

Too late.

Ventyre fell between the twin guardians before they could fire. Wings snapped open to rake Akuan with lightning. Cold battered the left side of Ventyre's shield, heat pounded the right. Akuan hissed as it passed and then, forming its battle shield, charged after. Farther back, Fiyorok followed, fire matching ice speed for speed.

Lake Sai lay five miles northwest, close enough, and yet, with the dragons in pursuit, seemingly a world away. Ventyre's feathers bristled. This was madness. It shouldn't have agreed.

A quick glance behind showed the dragons gaining. At least Ventyre hadn't lost them. Satisfied, the guardian opened its mind to Lord Aeryk. *I have them, my lord! Things did not turn out exactly as we planned, but I do have them... both of them.*

Akuan roared out of the clouds, spraying the air with sleet. Fiyorok appeared moments later, burning battle shield searing away the gloom.

Good. How far is the lake?

I'm still a few miles out, but closing rapidly. I should be there within minutes. Forested treetops tickled Ventyre's belly. Its passage snapped some branches, burned others.

No chances, Aeryk warned. *We can't back you up until you reach Lake Sai. Do you think you can stay alive until then?*

White water appeared through a gap in the trees, only to disappear behind a range of short, blunted foothills.

Ventyre squawked back at him. *We had our hands full with Fiyorok in Nepal. Imagine how much fun I'm having with the two of them. I hope you like roast poultry. The lake doesn't provide too much cover.* At least Seirin taught them how to lessen their Bond. If the dragons hurt it, its master wouldn't suffer.

Try not to think about it.

Easy for you to say.

Ventyre rotated around a burst of icefire. The attack clipped its feet as it hurtled past and slammed into a far shore with a loud boom. Abandoned boats, violently wrenched from their moorings, lay tossed about like driftwood. The nearest froze instantly and then shattered from the concussion. Submerged roads turned to ice, and the few remaining buildings toppled.

Ventyre hoped Takeshi had cleared the area. Without shields, nothing could survive. Fortunately, the Spirit Lord prepared for everything. The people might not feel so lucky when they emerged from their sanctuaries and saw what Vissyus had done, though. Men created monuments so history wouldn't forget them. It's how they measured success. Likely, the loss of their cities would hurt as much as an actual wound.

Akuan fired again. Ventyre's instincts overcame reason as the great bird beat its wings and climbed to avoid the strike. A mistake. Fiyorok had anticipated the move and hurled a stream of fireballs into the air above. Ventyre flew right into them. Its shield handled the first volley and even the second. The next barrage burned through layers too thin and damaged to stop. Scorched feathers left a trail of smoke behind, and the blasted chunks of flesh brought blinding pain. Remaining airborne became a struggle.

Ventyre limped past foothills and ruined hotels. The lake opened ahead, and with one final surge, Aeryk's guardian heaved itself clear, scissored over, and worked its massive wings against the wind. At the far shore, the dragons closed. Immediately, Ventyre seized the warm surface air and fed the drafts into a rotating updraft. A massive cyclone sprang from the lake, Kirak's blue shield sizzling to life within. Anger filled those wise eyes – made them deepen.

Ventyre saw the challenge in those bottomless pools, an ancient grudge rekindled, a gauntlet thrown down. It smiled grimly. Thus far, their plan was a resounding success.

43
ANGUISH

"*Kirak*?" Vissyus roared. He stabbed a finger at the lake and rushed forward. "Your guardian attacks me!"

"What did you think would happen?" Seirin let a hint of anger creep into her voice. "You've come to me with a superior guardian. Akuan's a direct threat, the first of its kind. Kirak's reacting the only way it knows how. My guardian doesn't understand or care what Akuan means to us. I wouldn't, if I were in its place."

Vissyus pulled back, his dubious expression holding a moment before brightening. "Perhaps it's time to let the serpent go. You have options."

"That won't help Akuan." Seirin pointed past the volcano's slopes. "Kirak is desperate. Unless you reinforce Akuan's abilities, our new guardian could lose." Somehow, she maintained a neutral expression despite her racing heart. "Fiyorok is the more powerful of the two, and the better at defending itself. I advise draining a portion of your will from the elder guardian and redirecting it into Akuan."

A deadly light flickered behind Vissyus's eyes. He frowned suspiciously. "How would you know about that? I haven't told anyone." He bent forward and searched her face.

Seirin fought to remain calm. She had to distract him, had to find a lie he would believe. "Akuan's a water spirit." Her voice was impossibly serene. "A part of its mind calls me."

Vissyus considered that for a moment. "Of course." He smiled shyly. "Something else we share." He presented a hand – presumably to lead her back to Akuan – when a howling gale roared out of the northwest. Curious, he dropped his arm and turned away from her. "Aeryk?" He flew up to the Boundary. "You're too late. She's with me now! Of her own free will. If you turn back, I'll forget this. Turn back, Aeryk. I don't want to hurt you!"

The wind howled in reply. Seirin fixed her eyes on the lakes, determined not to give Aeryk's location away. She'd helped him hide, had brought the fog and drizzle that covered his flight from the storms. They'd fooled Vissyus – a small victory considering the struggle to come, but an important one. However this fight ended, it would begin on their terms.

In the distance, Fiyorok rocketed into the heavens, tearing clouds, shredding them. The largest, a huge, black thunderhead, splintered into a thousand tiny pieces. The smell of ionized ozone filled the air, strong and pungent and hot enough to sear the lungs if inhaled.

Akuan blew through one of the smaller squalls. The darkened clouds were so thick and so black that it must have been impossible to see more than a few feet in any direction. Seirin hid a triumphant smile. Akuan's Searchings would be useless inside, bouncing off crystalline water and pelleted ice, both infused with layered Maskings.

Defeated, the guardian dropped below the storms.

Rain and lightning skittered harmlessly off its shield. To its right, a long, cigar-shaped funnel cloud broke away from a disintegrating squall. High winds pulled air and moisture into it before slinging both away with even greater force. Vissyus stared at it thoughtfully. He ordered Akuan to a halt and fired a Searching into the eye.

Seirin's heart pounded in her chest. A spark at the base of the volcano called out to her, but she refused to turn her head. She heard it sizzling through the air, felt it coming closer. Vissyus wheeled about, and only then did she look its way. Far below, a streak of glowing azure whipped around Fuji's rugged base in a wide, sweeping arc – hard and fast and accelerating.

Aeryk.

She closed her eyes, but found she couldn't keep them shut. These moments with him – his battle, his life – were precious to her. She needed to see what happened, had to know whether he lived or died. Every memory they ever shared filled her mind: images of love, loss, and hope. As they ended, she watched him lift his hands. Air swirled around them, building in strength and power. He aimed his fists at Akuan and launched severe, tornado-like drills into the guardian's shield. The first hammered Akuan hard enough to send it into a sickening freefall. The second kept it from regaining control. Stunned, the dragon dropped from the skies like a frozen meteor.

Aeryk pressed. Layer by layer, he chipped away at the blue shield – first with whirling vortexes, then with knifing microbursts. He was close to piercing one weakened section, when Akuan put its head down and fired a blast of ice at the ground below. Quickly, a single, immense column – one thousand feet tall or more – climbed into the sky, a living, growing pillar that raced upward to provide sanctuary.

Higher it raced, splitting the skies like a spike. At two thousand feet, when the tip was a few yards below Akuan's tail, the guardian stopped feeding the ice, threw out its talons, and grabbed on. The claws carved deep fissures into the slippery surface, but they eventually slowed Akuan's fall. Glittering sapphire armor coiled around the ice to stop momentum, as the guardian regrouped, its frigid belly against frozen water, its mane whipping in the wind like a tattered flag. Muscles bunched and bulged, and when they looked near to bursting, Akuan sprang back into the air with a powerful thrust of its legs, jaws agape, icefire streaking across the skies.

Helplessly, Seirin looked on as Aeryk deflected the shot with a fierce gale and hit Akuan again. She wanted to be with him, beside him, sharing the danger. Was this how he felt all those years ago? Knowing she fought for her life. Alone. Without him. Fuji had become a trap, a cage, another Boundary. Then, she had no say, but now, here, she chose for herself. Keeping Vissyus from fighting, that was her part. She could do it. She had to. For Aeryk.

Chin lifting, she let her thoughts leech onto the battlefield, probing, testing, searching Akuan's power. Aeryk's winds had broken through Akuan's weakened defenses and sliced across its neck. Though muted, Seirin felt pain. The injuries, while not serious, reminded her of an earlier failure. A glimmer of hope raced through her. These were independent thoughts, untied to Vissyus. Her pulse quickened. Some small sliver of Akuan's spirit remained. If she could just reach it…

"Akuan!" Vissyus shook a trembling fist into the air. "What's happened to you, Aeryk? Attacking a guardian. There's no excuse!" His rage-filled thoughts surged into the clouds to link with Fiyorok.

Seirin bit down on her tongue to hide her excitement. Patience. She needed patience. Already, Vissyus redirected his will to Akuan in a ferocious attempt to save it.

The ice dragon's shield came back to life in a flash of cold light. It shrugged off its injuries, spun around, and prepared to charge. Leering rabidly, it raised a dense curtain of fog and, drawing upon the frozen moisture, swiftly crafted hundreds of deadly projectiles out of the ice, discarding any shards deemed too small or too fragile in favor of larger, power-infused chunks. These it saved, cast into missiles, and hurled at the blue globe streaking toward it, rounding in for the kill, coming in fast.

Akuan recovered faster than Aeryk expected, and he immediately abandoned stealth in favor of a quick, devastating hit. Fiyorok's shield had lost some of its brilliance, which meant Vissyus shifted his power from fire to ice. He called to his guardian.

I see it. Ventyre banked sharply and doubled back. Lightning streaked its feathers. Strong downdrafts leveled trees as it flew over them. Along the shore, damaged buildings collapsed. Ventyre had used the brief lull to heal most of its wounds and now soared upward.

Fiyorok's still too far away, Aeryk said. *If we abandon Akuan now, Vissyus will know what we're planning. A hard strike should lure Fiyorok out of the storms.*

If Vissyus shifted his power from Fiyorok…

Akuan will be dangerously strong, Aeryk finished. *It's what we want, Ventyre. We can't defeat Fiyorok otherwise.*

Ventyre grunted its agreement. *So long as Akuan doesn't defeat us first.*

Closing its mind, Ventyre raced toward Akuan's

thickening fog. A fresh volley of lightning exploded from its wings. Most of the bolts cut harmlessly through the mist, but a few hit home. The multiple strikes – those that missed and those that didn't – illuminated the clouds enough to reveal the dragon's darkened form within.

Aeryk circled around to the left, his guardian's words echoing ominously in head.

Vissyus's mind drifted, passing through a pair of barriers and into the open air. The world around him blurred as he floated, his spirit light, almost insubstantial.

"Akuan is running out of time, Vissyus," the Teacher warned. Her voice was soft and distant, as if coming from far away. "Aeryk's already discovered a way through its shield. It needs more of your power. Vissyus? Vissyus... do you hear me?"

Her words guided him, gave him both purpose and direction. Instinct sent him racing over mountains and rivers – something was out here, something precious. He needed to protect it, no matter the cost. His thoughts reached for a small spark in the distance, diving into a wall of gray fog, drilling through layers of mist.

Physical sensations returned to him: the beat of an enormous heart, the smell of moisture, its touch against his armored skin. He swung his head – the movement strangely languid – and faced a barrage of lightning, bolt after bolt, filling the mist like an electrified net. A faint voice in the back of his mind railed against him – a spirit tethered to him, Bound to him. He smothered the complaint with a thought and drew the charged fog toward him, manipulating and trapping as much of the moisture as he could.

The work brought a rush he'd nearly forgotten. Others discovered this before him – first Teacher and then Yui

– but he would perfect it. The Teacher tried to hide the knowledge from him, but her water remembered, speaking to him through the Bond they shared with their child, the one he now protected.

She would like that. He knew how important it was to her, and yet... The thrill of discovery had taken hold of him. His was a lifetime of achievement, a legacy no other Kami could match. The others were too timid, too constrained by worry, too overly cautious. The Teacher, Yui – their accomplishments impressed him, but they barely realized their works' true potential. He would have to show them.

His target approached from the southwest – a perfect ball of bright azure light. A part of his mind recognized the orb and instantly argued against what he was about to do. He ignored the warning and drew lightning-infused fog into his green shield, lacing vapor with dormant fire. Adrenaline boiled his blood. Mouth agape, he sent bands of frigid water through lips that looked like elongated, sapphire covered jaws.

He frowned at that, but only for a moment. Liquid met lightning, one becoming a conduit for the other. If the incoming sphere maintained speed and trajectory, his weaponized streams would reach it in seconds.

He leaned forward in anticipation. The Teacher's voice echoed in the far reaches of his mind, pleading with him to stop. But it was too late. Jets of lightning-infused water had already reached the shining orb. They broke around the shield like crashing waves, embedded lightning meeting elemental air, power against power, each recognizing the other through a Guardian Bond.

Impatiently, Vissyus counted the hits. How many would it take? Why hadn't the shield let them through? Frustrated, he readied the few remaining bolts when the shield abruptly absorbed the energy into its core. Once inside, his dormant fires burst to life. Burning red overwhelmed shining blue, turning it black. The shield buckled. Flaming cracks tore across its surface, splintering it. Breaking it apart.

Vissyus's heart soared. A triumphant cry flew from his lips. The Teacher would be pleased. He saved their child. He couldn't wait to tell her. Before heading back, he glanced at his work one last time and stopped, stiffening.

A limp body had emerged from the wreckage. Momentum carried the figure through the air in an arc whose fall seemed to take forever. Time slowed. Vissyus studied the man: the white shirt, the dark hair, the face – a face he knew. Aeryk's face. His friend. A hole opened in Vissyus's stomach, and he cursed his clearing mind. If only he didn't know, if only he hadn't seen. Teacher would hate him for this. And he'd been so close to winning her heart too.

Anguished, he lost control of his thoughts. Shock paralyzed him, sent him tumbling back to the volcano. As he fell, a new idea took root in his mind. A piece of his soul whispered to him, tempted him. The Teacher was his now – nothing stood in his way. In time she'd forgive him.

If only he could forgive himself.

Vissyus stirred. His body shuddered, and he shook his head as if to clear it. Guilt twisted his boyish face, and his eyes were feverish. "What have I done?" he whispered, staring down at his hands. The light of his fires cast red shadows over his palms.

Seirin barely noticed. She stood rigidly behind him, unable to look away. The same attack. Akuan used the same strategy she'd thrown at Lon-Shan. How did it know? Then, in a moment of clarity, it came to her. She had set the tone, and Akuan – a water spirit – drew its instincts from her experiences.

Anger exploded within her. "Monster! He was your friend. The best friend you ever had!" Hot tears streamed down her cheeks, and for the first time in eons, she confronted him, not as an enemy but as a friend who had done the unthinkable.

"Monster, am I?" Vissyus's voice was low, hollow, and sad. "He came here to kill me, Seirin, not to renew acquaintances, but to wipe me from a world that used to belong to all of us. If I didn't defend myself, my guardians and I would be dead."

The sudden use of her name jolted her. Her heart ached at the sound of it. She heard a hitch in his voice, a flash of remorse – a remembrance, perhaps, of the close bond the three of them once enjoyed. For a moment, neither of them moved, unable or unwilling to say anything further. Pity welled up in her heart. She reached for him, tentatively lifting a hand and placing it onto his shoulder.

He shrugged her off and floated over to the flaming wall, never once raising his head to meet her gaze. His wide shoulders slumped, and his muscular body withdrew into itself.

"I've played your little game," he said in a voice thick with emotion. "I've danced your little dance. I knew your bond with Aeryk was too strong for you to betray him, but I had to see for myself. You'd never love me the way you love him."

"Vissyus, I–"

"There's nothing more I can learn from you, Teacher." Raising his chin, he drew a deep breath. "It is time to end this."

44
COMMAND

The fall was worse than Keiko imagined. Gravity and momentum pulled her body in opposite directions. Her insides went up, while the rest of her went down. She panted and screamed and prayed it would stop. It didn't, though, which was both a good thing and a bad one. The great taiko drums pummeled her body and, coupled with the roaring of both wind and blood in her ears, made it hard to concentrate. If she couldn't summon her power, she was as good as dead. Yui didn't see her jump and was halfway across the courtyard by now.

Keiko's panicked mind caught a flash of indigo light streaking toward the outer walls. She closed her eyes, determined not to look. Yui wasn't the answer, and seeing her shield tempted Keiko with something she couldn't have – a crutch, a way out. She had to ignore it, knowing she had a few seconds at most before she hit the ground. Doubt filled her, and adrenaline made it grow. This was a mistake. A stupid, tragic mistake.

She tensed, but instead of the impact she expected, Yui's thoughts sounded in her head.

Disciples! The Lady of Light and Spirit calls you! Fight for

*the honor of your fathers! Fight for your home and for your
world! Together we will break the darkness! It ends here! Today!*

The words awakened something inside Keiko. Her
eyes flew open, and the window to her soul shattered.
Power rushed in, suffusing her body and exploding
outward. A nimbus of burgundy light flashed around
her. She hardened the glow with a thought and before
she realized what happened, she guided her newly
formed shield into the air.

"I did it!" She laughed aloud and stared at the shield
in stunned disbelief. "I finally did it!" The ground was
frighteningly close, but she barely saw it. Her heart was
too light, her mind too far away. Tears rolled down her
cheeks. She wiped them away and headed off to find
Yui.

Below, the rows of armored samurai moved out in
long, snaking lines. They broke apart at the edge of the
training grounds, scattered throughout the fortress's
perimeter, and climbed. A short, wide-shouldered man
spotted her and barked a command. As one, his line
stopped, turned, and drew their weapons. The soldiers
Keiko recently questioned now looked deadly. Energy
sizzled around blade, lance, and bolt, sure hands holding
them steady.

Keiko uttered a stream of curses. She'd been careless.
The White Spirit was a tripwire. Something unusual
could easily set it off. Something like an unfamiliar shield
behind its defenses. Already, a second row of samurai
noticed her. An armored figure stepped from the line.
Keiko's breath caught. She recognized Brother Seki's
square face and stocky body.

The monk peered up at her, searching, questioning.
"Yamanaka?" he said, uncertain. Their eyes met, and
his expression changed from suspicion to wonder.

"Yamanaka-sama!" Unsheathing his sword, he stabbed it into the air. "*Yamanaka-sama*!" The samurai around him rippled like fields of windblown wheat. They gazed at her, and a hush fell over them. Again, Brother Seki raised his sword. "*Yamanaka-sama*!" More brandished their weapons, more pointed and shouted.

Overwhelmed, Keiko covered her mouth with a hand. Not long ago, her world had collapsed. She had nothing: no family, no home, no future. And while the future was still a question, the present had settled. She'd found a home at the White Spirit. Lifting her chin, she caught a tracer of indigo light approaching from the northern wall. Keiko lowered her hand and smiled. She'd found a family too.

Yui stopped a few yards away, and the men below fell silent. "Congratulations, Yamanaka-san." She inclined her head, her expression proud but troubled. "I only wish I had more time to train you."

Her gaze drifted past walls gleaming in the filtered morning light. Sunbeams broke through the storms rolling over Yamanashi Prefecture. To the east, Seirin, Aeryk, and Roarke tried to hold the world together. Fires touched the heavens, rain beating down upon them. Ventyre wheeled over a vast crater. Fiyorok's fiery shield dropped from Fuji's summit, Akuan climbing from its base.

"Don't worry about me," Keiko said. "I'll be fine. Just do what you have to do." She nodded to Aokigahara. The darkness was closer and accelerating. It seemed to speak to her. Her heart fluttered, but she fought it.

Yui looked from Keiko to the wood, flecks of golden light streaking those stunning eyes. She nodded in understanding. Whirling, she made for the gates. "Samurai!" she cried. "To your posts! The enemy is five miles from the northern wall and closing. I want archers in place along the parapets and ready to fire. The lancers will hold one half mile back, enough to form rank and charge. All swordsmen are to stay hidden unless I say otherwise! This is your day. Become my hammer and my sword. Come, my samurai. I order you to destroy our enemy!"

Her words rang out across the fortress, from the walls to the grounds and into every tower and holding area. They raced down the ramparts with the wind, rising even above the sound of the drums. Their power stirred Keiko to life. Inhaling deeply, she stared into the Sea of Trees, determined to face her fears. Trees bent and snapped as the darkness swallowed wide swathes of the forest. She shook her head sadly. So much power wasted on hatred. What could ruin a soul like that? Anger burned inside her chest, and with a start, she realized the cause was irrelevant. Her heart told her it was beyond redemption.

Yui's shield was well below her, a slash of purple light before the castle's white stone. Time had moved on, while Keiko remained behind. She berated herself and sent her shield into a dizzying drop. The walls to her left and right blurred, the tower behind turning into a solid white streak. Her stomach climbed into her throat, her blood raced. It was a wild, exhilarating ride, and somewhere along the way, she realized she enjoyed every second of it. The chills running through her added a sense of freedom she didn't want to end. She laughed again. No wonder Yui flew like this.

She spotted Yui's dual-colored shield less than fifty feet below and growing larger by the second. If she didn't slow down soon, she'd plow right into it. Unfortunately, the actual braking proved more difficult than she anticipated. Time seemed to simultaneously race and plod. Whenever she looked at Yui, however, the indigo shield had zipped closer. She swallowed, cursing and praying all at once. Whether through a miracle or something she did, her shield stopped a few feet from where Yui hovered over the archers – above the walls and in the exact center of their line.

This close, the black mass wafted from the ground in clinging spirals that looked like the fingers of a spectral hand.

"I see you're learning how to master your shield." Yui glanced at Keiko and nodded. "Good. You will need it now."

Lifting her arm over her head, she held it motionless for what seemed like an eternity, a beautiful statue on the edge of a toxic sea. Second after second ticked by until finally, just as the mist peaked, she brought it down in a single slicing motion.

"*Launch!*" she cried.

Her free arm came up in front of her face. Beams of blazing yellow light lanced from either side of her clenched fist. They curled back and around at the tips like the horns of some massive ox. A shimmering arrow formed at the bow's center, a sharp, triangular head that shot from bow to strand in a two yard-long shaft. Yui drew back in one smooth movement and let the arrow fly. Hundreds followed, though none outpaced it. Alone, it pierced the darkness. The archers' volley hit seconds later, brilliant flashes strobing within the black covering like fireworks.

Keiko peered into the darkness, and her stomach tightened. Shapes massed near the front of the failing obsidian mist, thousands of them. Light drove them there, working them into a frenzy. They fled the dying veil, creatures ten to twelve feet tall with hornlike ears and eyes as dark as bottomless wells. Their leathery wings beat rhythmically against the air as they took to the skies.

A few noticed the samurai along the parapets and fell on them in a blur of talon and fang. Wave upon disorganized wave followed, forming and breaking and searching for prey. The massive taiko drums pushed some back, but after a while they grew immune to the shockwaves.

Keiko grimaced. The power of sound – music as a weapon. Her thoughts wandered back to her apartment and the piano she treasured slightly less than her camera.

"Keiko!" Yui called, snapping her back to the present. "Stay alert! This is a battle, not an outing. I need to move. Pay attention and you might stay alive." She swept an arm around her back and motioned Keiko behind her. "*Hurry!* We have to go."

She led Keiko away from the walls and drove for the eastern stanchions. The samurai lining the narrow walkway split evenly at her command. As planned, they abandoned their entrenched positions, rounded the corner turrets, and reformed along the eastern and western ramparts. The one to the north – the one directly in the enemy's path – she left unmanned.

"What are they doing?" Keiko shouted. "There's no one left to keep them out."

"I don't *want* to keep them out," Yui answered. "We can't let them reach Fuji. Their leader will either defend his forces or die – I plan to give him no other choice. Once I have him here, I'll keep him pinned down until the others have dealt with Vissyus." Her eyes glittered under the sun. "Unless I finish him first."

Keiko opened her mouth but saw Yui no longer paid attention.

"Again," Yui shouted, pulling back on her longbow to unleash another volley as she flew.

Bursts of white, gold, and yellow blew across the sky, lighting one after another, drawing closer together as Yui's forces herded and slaughtered as many creatures as possible. A small group in front wheeled around, if for no other reason than to feast upon the remains of the fallen. The sight turned Keiko's stomach. The amazement she'd felt at the dazzling arrows faded when the creatures turned on each other. Enemy or not, the dead deserved better than this.

Yui left the distracted hordes for her closest archers and pushed the main host between the castle walls. Occasionally, a few broke off – one or more detecting the vibrant shields, so near, and so inviting. Raising the great bow to her eye, she aimed and struck again. Over and over, she reloaded, targeted, and fired with incredible precision and speed.

The main force struggled toward Fuji, but the archers' constant barrage eventually turned it. Keiko felt a surging pride. Those men, people like her, fought the nightmare without fear. She watched them gather the beasts as Yui ordered and push them over the unprotected wall like a cresting wave. A man with a sickle on his helm raised a fist in triumph, one of many Keiko had picked out of the crowd, thinking he looked too young to be here. He brought his fist to his face and loosed an arrow just as a creature punched its claws through his chest. The nearest men brought the thing down, but not without losses.

Keiko tried to put them out of her head, but their faces stayed with her. Maybe winning would ease the pain. She had to believe their sacrifice meant something. Beside her, Yui looked on. Apart from her stiffening shoulders, she seemed unaffected, peering into the writhing mass as if searching.

"What?" Keiko asked. "What are you–?"

Yui shushed her with a finger and gazed into the darkness.

"A shield," she whispered. Instantly, her bow lengthened and straightened into a long, sharp-bladed spear.

Keiko followed her eyes, glimpsing the big, spherical inversion of light hidden behind the monsters.

"Pull back to the tower," Yui commanded, throwing the words over her shoulder as she advanced. "No questions. Go! *Move!*"

Yui put Keiko out of her mind and plunged headfirst the hundred or so feet to the northern gate. Once there, she drew her shield close to her body and hurled herself into the unsuspecting rearguard, firing tracers of light from her shield in long sustained bursts. Clouds of blood, darker and richer than human blood, spattered against her, but the sizzling light around her body boiled it into wisps of noxious steam before it touched her skin.

She accelerated through the grisly debris – here the charred stump of a clawed hand careening off her shield, there a severed head tumbling to earth – until finally, she saw the black sphere through the carnage. Its zigzagging flight avoided most of the incoming fire, but it also slowed its progress.

Yui let go of her spear and charged. A surge of power built within her hands, bright and deadly and growing as she flew. Thrusting her palms forward, she directed the energy through the gap and hurled a white-hot pillar toward her enemy. Streaks of white and purple spun below the surface in an angry corkscrew of light and spirit that chased down the fleeing sphere, hitting it hard enough to send it flying out of control.

A wiry man appeared within the unraveling shield – Paitr Norwoska, her father called him, Lon-Shan's first disciple, a survivor of Seirin's attack. He was dressed all in black – shirt, pants, belt, and boots – with a mop of black hair framing a sharp, angular face split by a long aquiline nose. Fury glinted in his cold, blue eyes, the only spots of color on the man other than the white, pasty skin of his hands, neck, and face.

Yui scowled back at him. Paitr Norwoska would die today.

45
NECESSITY

Kirak pushed the huge cyclone toward Lake Sai's southern shore. Water swamped the wide peninsula, while overhead the spout's great foaming muzzle came about like the barrel of an enormous gun. Akuan was out there, a streak of cool blue slashing in front of the volcano like a sword. Already, Vissyus's new guardian pelted Ventyre's shield with endless attacks. Kirak admired the thunderbird's determination. Icy daggers thrown by the thousands slammed into the amethyst barrier, and still the bird refused to move.

How is he, Ventyre? Kirak asked.

Aeryk lay below the guardian in an unconscious heap.

He hasn't regained consciousness. Forked lightning surged from Ventyre's wings, striking Akuan's shielded scales, doing no damage. *I've had neither the time nor the opportunity to evaluate his injuries.* A note of frustrated acceptance deadened Ventyre's tone. It would do what it could for as long as it could, but once Vissyus decided to strike, the end would come.

Kirak shook its head in disbelief – Lord Aeryk down, Lady Seirin imprisoned, Japan in ruins. Vissyus had beaten them so easily. They might as well have been flies. Kirak needed to do something. The surrounding lakes wouldn't provide enough ammunition to damage either dragon, but they might provide an adequate, if short-lived, defense. Images of liquid spikes flashed through Kirak's mind, two hundred feet long and ten feet in diameter. Nodding, Seirin's guardian crafted the thought into weapons and filled the lakes with them. When they were ready, Kirak let them fly. Rainbow-filled showers welcomed the missiles into the air, a phalanx of lances that raced over the tortured ground like horizontal rain.

Time crawled. Battles always seemed to unfold this way – incredibly fast and painfully slow. Kirak's weapons crossed the skies one heartbeat at a time, one moment closing on Akuan, the next shooting past as the ice dragon banked away.

Kirak muttered an oath. They needed something larger. But what? The giant waterspout? Yes. That would do – it had to. A new thought pressurized the great watery tornado spinning around Kirak's body. Blue water collided with blue energy, white foam against white ice. Together, they shot from the spout like cannon fire. Akuan slowed beneath the tremendous pressure, crawling forward a few more feet before the weaponized liquid pushed it back.

Ventyre! Kirak called with its thoughts. *Can you heal him?*

I don't have enough time. Akuan will be back, and Fiyorok is still out there. We need to move him. The White Spirit's close. Ventyre gestured northwest with its tufted head. *We'll take him there and hope Lady Yui can help.*

She's just a child, Ventyre. She can't possibly help.

You don't know her. She's smart, and she's strong. Lord Takeshi groomed her for this. He trusts her, and so do I.

Enough to risk your lord's life? Kirak was unmoved. *If he dies, our hopes die with him.*

Lord Roarke then. He's closer, and he has Malog with him.

Kirak shook its huge head. *Lord Roarke stays where he is. Too many threats will draw Vissyus away from the volcano. Besides, we need him for what's to come.* Kirak gazed up at that caldera, and its heart sank.

A dark, almost pitch-black cloud rose over Fuji's rear shoulder. Twin spots of fire burned inside the haze like a pair of embers at the heart of a riotous inferno. Horns of glittering red-gold cut through the haze, thin vapor trails streaming from their tips like speared pennants. A torrid Searching raked across the sky ahead, as dry as the desert and ten times as hot. Power rammed into Kirak's thoughts and snuffed them out as if they were tea candles.

Too late, Ventyre! Do what you can to hold Akuan while I see to Fiyorok.

Ventyre hissed at the mushrooming cloud. *What chance do we have against them? Akuan brought Lord Aeryk down without any help.*

We don't have a choice. My mistress will know what to do. She won't let anything happen to your lord. We'll just have to hold them until she finds an opening.

Ventyre muttered something that sounded like "*suicide*" but nodded. Its eyes locked with the incoming ice dragon. *I'll do what I can, but you saw what the traitor did to my lord.* Despite its words, electricity rippled through its feathers. *Go on. And be quick about it.*

A minute, Kirak promised. *Maybe less. What can you give me for weaponry?*

Ventyre's lavender eyes glittered behind its shield. Images of electrically charged water appeared in Kirak's thoughts.

Kirak nodded. *Agreed. Hold your fire until I'm in position. You'll know the time.*

Seirin's guardian waited for Ventyre's grunted reply before surging out of the lake with the waterspout in tow. As planned, Ventyre fired a short burst of ball lightning at a precise spot five hundred feet ahead. Kirak angled toward the strike, snaring the sphere with the cyclone's outer rim. Electricity flickered throughout, growing in intensity, blazing and burning until finally, when it looked as if they were about to explode, Kirak hurled the water at Fiyorok.

Heartbroken, Vissyus raised his massive shield and headed out. This world – everything he dreamed it could be – was as much a prison for him now as the Boundary had been. He had to cleanse his memory and start over. He'd take the Teacher with him, of course. He could forgive her anything, even this.

As if summoned, she rocketed up to him. Golden hair streamed behind her, her eyes the leaden gray-green of an ocean in turmoil. "Don't. It's wrong. Somewhere deep inside, you have to know." An arm pressed into her stomach as if to hold back emptiness. "Vissyus. *Please!*"

The words clung to the air between them, faint and anguished and yet passionate enough to make him pause. Her emotions triggered something in his soul. Hadn't she asked for a favor? One he granted? Maybe showing her would make everything all right.

A loud concussion shook the mountaintop. He felt the force through the dual shielding fencing him in. The blast jarred him a little, but otherwise did nothing to break the tension. Less than a thousand feet below, Fiyorok cast off its black shroud and, red-golden scales shining against the darkness, raced to join the fight.

Dropping his shield, Vissyus turned away from the battle and moved toward her. She loomed before him. He'd pledged himself to her ages ago, had promised happiness. But as he looked at her now, he saw only deep pain. Tentatively, he touched a finger to her cheek. Water dotted the tip, a small dome of clarity within a raging world. The liquid shuddered briefly before vaporizing and when he looked at her, his heart seemed to stop.

"I…" he began.

To his surprise, she planted her hands on his chest and thrust him away. "How could you?" Her ragged voice reminded him of shredding clouds. "He loved you. We both loved you."

Behind her, Fiyorok fell from heaven like a streak of living fire: powerful, strong, and unstoppable. Its massive, horn-crowned head parted the clouds, glittering scales burning them off.

He should call his guardian back, but he couldn't think.

"You… *love* me?"

A warm rush flooded his body. He blinked at her, afraid to believe. She stared back, eyes widening in shock. A light sparkled in their opaline depths. It wasn't there a minute ago – at least he didn't think so. And then, everything about her changed – a shift in her posture, a slow softening of her features. The anger she showed him melted into longing, her body moving close to his, her breath tickling his cheek.

A part of his mind screamed at him, warned him to be careful. Another piece roared back to smother his doubts. He'd dreamed of this moment forever; now was not the time to question, no matter how odd the change in her seemed.

"I love Aeryk too," she said, interrupting his thoughts. "We have a history."

He heard the distant rumble of thunder, saw tongues of long, reddish-orange flame lick the sky. A torrential downpour swept in to douse them, only to freeze into deadly spears that spun about and shot back to the ground.

"But you can give me something he can't, or won't." Her tone was hard and frigid. He believed her. "He wasn't even willing to try."

Vissyus's pulse quickened. He lifted his hands to his chest, touching where hers had been. "I tried. Just as you asked."

"I know you did. I never doubted you."

A long-buried memory tried to resurface, a phantom of the man he might have been. He turned his back to her. "I gave up my dreams to do it," a part of his spirit said. "I barely remember them now."

Her hand was on his back, her touch sending shivers through him. "What if you could reclaim them? Show me what you've done. I need to see it."

Vissyus beamed at her. "Akuan wants to know you too. Did you see how well it played with Kirak?"

She nodded but didn't speak. Tension flitted through her, concern over her guardian's feelings, perhaps.

"Don't worry, Teacher. Kirak will be fine. You don't have to replace it if you don't want to."

Seirin's head came up, and she studied his face, her eyes bright. "We'll worry about Kirak later." She looped her arm through his. "I think I've waited long enough to see what you've created for me."

She leaned into him and followed his eyes past the confines of the mountain, down its sleek, rocky neck, and into the ragged hills beyond. Her breath was hot against his cheek. He felt her muscles tensing in anticipation.

"Show me," she said at last. Her breath tickled him, made him swoon. "Show me what I mean to you."

Seirin closed her eyes and lowered her head. She threw her thoughts into the battle below and reached for her guardian. Regretfully, she severed the lifelong Bond between them, paused to embrace Kirak, and then released it from her service.

Forgive me, she said sadly. *There's no other way*.

"No!" Kirak bellowed. "Mistress, you must not! It is forbidden... it is too dangerous!"

46
DELIRIUM

Seirin left her physical body and followed Vissyus's thoughts from the volcano. A mile west, Akuan circled Ventyre like a shark, peppering the thunderbird with power-laced ice. To the east, Kirak grappled with Fiyorok in a ball of steam and fire. The vision of her guardian facing the world's strongest guardian darkened Seirin's heart. She hoped Kirak understood what she'd done and why. At least the Unbinding hadn't slowed the great serpent, not that she'd expected it to. Learning how to thin the Bond had also opened this possibility to her. If a Kami could call and Bind a guardian, it stood to reason one could also dismiss it. Lon-Shan had already done so. If he could, then so could she.

Just a little farther. Vissyus intruded into her thoughts.

Startled, she slammed a wall between her conscious mind and his. How long had he been there? Had he heard? Did he know? Fortunately, he seemed too preoccupied with Akuan to notice. She needed to be more careful.

The dragon loomed before her. This close, its ferocious beauty took her breath away – ice-blue shield over shining sapphire scales, a sea-foam mane billowing out behind as it flew. Something about Akuan's wild, untamed appearance seemed more akin to Vissyus than Fiyorok ever had. The thought brought a lump to her throat. He'd poured his soul into the dragon, and he'd done it for her. Desperately, she wanted this to be over. No more ghosts, no more reminders. Dutifully, she trailed Vissyus's mind through Akuan's frigid shield and into its soul despite her misgivings. Vile, filthy, and nearly without conscience, the once-noble guardian had become a twisted maze of emptiness. Only a determined effort, combined with her love for Aeryk, kept her from recoiling.

Akuan, she called, her words stronger and more commanding than she felt. *Come to me, Akuan. I am your rightful lady. Let me save you.*

Vaguely, she felt Vissyus slide up beside her. She refused to look at him, couldn't face the betrayal she'd see in his eyes. Akuan was supposed to belong to them both, and she was taking it from him. She felt unclean.

Why? he asked.

She tried to ignore him, but couldn't. How could one word hurt so much?

Akuan needs me. She turned to face him. *It's in pain. Can't you see that?*

No! Vissyus cried. *I won't let you take it. Akuan is MINE!*

Back over the mountain, back in their physical form, Vissyus built circlets of fire around his wrists; a third ringed his head like a halo. Seirin tensed for the blow only to watch him let his power go. Despite her betrayal, he couldn't hurt her. She considered using that against him, no matter how much it turned her stomach.

Instead, she turned her thoughts to Akuan and intensified her hold over the guardian. Vissyus's mind weighed upon her. She thought she felt him... watching her. She shuddered, afraid he'd stop her before she finished. But then, just as she fought to maintain her composure, a faint, featherlight spirit reached out from the darkness.

Mistress, it called weakly. *Help me. Please.*

Akuan? Elated, Seirin's consciousness rushed to embrace Akuan's fallen soul – to heal it and draw it from the shadows. But as she hurried forward, she rammed into a wall of hidden triggers. Heat and fire surrounded her conscious mind, as real and as painful as a candle against her skin.

Beaten back too many times, subjugated and punished time and again, Akuan's essence fled in terror. Desperately, she reached for the fleeing spirit, pounding through the traps Vissyus left to protect his Binding, determined to not let the guardian escape.

I made it for us, Vissyus cried. *Akuan is our child, the best of us both.* He swayed slightly as he spoke, and hope flooded through her. Takeshi was right about the Binding!

Takeshi.

Memories of a dream erupted from a corner of her mind. He knew this moment would come. He tried to tell her. She smiled as pieces of an ancient puzzle came together. She understood exactly what she had to do.

Thoughts formed in the shielded part of her head; power filled them. When she was ready, she sent them racing into the skies. They leapt from one water molecule to next. Each jump erased the one before, and by the time she finished, a line of clouds rolled in from the bay and thickened over Tokyo.

Light showers – so typical for late spring – wheeled in from the sea. They reached the Kotoku-in Temple in Kamakura, where a forty-foot statue of Amida Buddha sat contentedly at the top of a steep rise. Lush, tree-filled woodlands surrounded the stone square about it, while here and there, the sweeping tops of temple roofs peeked out of the underbrush.

None stood taller than the statue, however, and when the weak storm front approached from the east, its gentle rains drummed against the figure's wide shoulders like a bell struck with a thousand softened hammers. Water rolled down the arms to pool in its neatly folded hands. A faint, greenish glow surrounded the upturned palms, pulsing once before bleaching to a pure white light.

Takeshi opened his hidden Gateway in Kamakura and, Masking in place, slipped back into the world. Unseen, he flew to the Tsurugaoka Hachimangu Shrine, where he drew upon a secret well of spiritual power. Turning, he cascaded over a series of stone stairs like some ghostly waterfall where he reached the broad plaza below. There, he paused to survey the area.

A pair of snarling, doglike dragons perched atop two cylindrical posts on either side – ancient and weathered protectors of the shrine above. Torii gates were visible over the top of a squat temple, the tall red structures dwindling into the distance. He leaped over the building and hurtled through the gates like a phantom, hugging the ground as he traveled. Nothing moved in his wake, no blade of grass bent or swayed, and no tree rustled. He caught Seirin's essence and followed it through the sky and into Akuan's consciousness, careful to shield his thoughts from Vissyus.

Inside, he opened his mind to the guardian spirit. *Hello, Akuan*. His thoughts were both calm and soothing. *It's been a very long time*.

Akuan's broken spirit recoiled. *Lord Takeshi! Please*

forgive me. I've done things. Terrible things.

Takeshi wove serenity into his thoughts. *And now you will set them right. This wasn't your fault. Vissyus summoned you, and by law you had to obey.*

Vissyus. Regret filled Akuan's spirit. *He wanted to do so much.*

Yes. But that was a long time ago. Takeshi's will hardened. *You know why I'm here, Akuan. You know what I require of you.*

The dragon froze. *No. I can't. I'm sorry.*

Your mistress has already freed you, guardian. She's here, looking for you. Go to her, help her. She needs you. Now more than ever.

Free? Akuan spoke the word as if testing it.

Takeshi felt hope grow in its soul. *Free but vulnerable. Vissyus can still retake you. Don't give him that chance. Seirin is your only hope.*

Determination flared in Akuan's heart. Purpose suffused it, faith making it grow. Takeshi withdrew his thoughts and veered away. From a distance, he watched Akuan's baleful steel-green eyes reawakened to the pure arctic blue of its spiritual light. It nodded once to him before hurling itself at the volcano.

Mistress, Akuan called, frantically circling Fuji's summit, its body trembling. *I am here, Akuan, Spirit of Water. You summoned me. Command me, lady. What would you have me do?*

Seirin's voice sounded in its head like church bells, loud, clear, and urgent. *Fiyorok. You have to stop Vissyus's guardian before it's too late.*

Akuan lifted its head proudly. *Yes, my lady.* The guardian ignored the sunfire heat surging up beside her. Arching its back, it rolled away from the mountain and dropped from the heights like a stone.

Mist and fog lifted, and the once-humid air became as dry as a desert wind. New blasts rocked the distant countryside, huge, glowing orbs of crackling light that sent flame-infused lightning into the heavens. Shockwaves shattered stone and leveled hills, while, at its center, Akuan sensed a dying spark courageously clinging to life.

Vissyus roared up to Seirin and stabbed a shaking finger at the fleeing dragon. "How could you? You've ruined everything!" He fell away without another word. Smoke swirled about him, and he wrapped the thick black bands around his body to hide himself. He couldn't let her see him like this. She'd think less of him – maybe even pity him.

His hands flew to his spinning head. What was happening to him? Control. He had to regain control. Remorse swamped desire and then burned it to ash. A spark of conscience scolded him for torturing and murdering millions upon millions of people. He bowed before it like a penitent child, only to have a bestial fury seize his thoughts.

He pointed again, this time to the west. "Fiyorok has broken Ventyre. You're too late." He stared back at her through his gritty, ebon clouds. She'd spurned him, after everything he'd done for her. And now, Aeryk would pay.

"As long as he lives, it's not too late." Seirin's hands were balled into fists at her side, her expression harder than he'd ever seen it. She shook her head vehemently. "You would have understood that once. You know what it's like to give everything you have for someone you love."

He stared back at her in astonished silence, then hung his head and nodded. His thoughts turned to his guardian. He should stop it. She'd want that. But her actions – he couldn't believe what she'd done. She took what they were supposed to share and let it go.

Far below, out over the ruined ground, Fiyorok slammed its body into Ventyre.

Vissyus smiled as the thunderbird's shield collapsed. He always wondered if those beautiful feathers would burn, and now he knew. Fiyorok's scales ignited a line of fire from Ventyre's beating shoulders to the end of its long tail. The Teacher screamed at him.

He barely heard her.

The struggle below mesmerized him – smoke and flame, guardian against guardian.

Ventyre rolled its body in a wild attempt to dislodge Fiyorok. The bird would have to do better than that. Fiyorok had buried its shielded claws in deeply. Aeryk's guardian would never wrench them free.

In desperation, Ventyre did something Vissyus never expected, deliberately wounding itself with four perfectly synchronized electrical discharges. Brilliant puffs of blue-white light blew large chunks of flesh from its back, each detonating beneath Fiyorok's claws. With nothing to grasp, Fiyorok flew from the thunderbird in a hail of scorched feathers and showering sparks.

Pain filled Vissyus's head. First Akuan and now Fiyorok. His time in the Boundary had dulled his senses, softened him. He looked at Teacher. Her face had paled. Her body trembled. She knew what was coming. The guardians' fight had taken Ventyre away from the unconscious Aeryk, leaving him alone and undefended at the bottom of the pit.

He frowned. She'd blame him for this, at least at first.

In the end, she'd understand. This was the only way they could be together – free from memory, free from everything, including the world.

Silently, he backed away and entered the clouds. Smoke obscured his sight. He smiled. If he couldn't see her, she couldn't see him. Without his presence to remind her, she'd forget his involvement. He'd reappear when this was over and reclaim her. A perfect future stretched before them. Once she understood that, she'd apologize for causing him grief. The clouds around him thickened. A blast of heat reached up from below, calling him. He turned his thoughts toward the source and shook his head to clear his troubled mind.

He'd been in the middle of the sweetest dream – something about a time yet to come. The fires burned it away. They were *so* beautiful. If he could just... touch them.

47
FULFILLMENT

Paitr's shield tumbled away from Yui like a dying meteor. Translucent stripes slashed its once-opaque surface, and momentum rather than controlled acceleration sent him hurtling toward the central donjon. Yui was less concerned about the damage the impact would inflict on the tower than she was about the man inside. Paitr was dying. The power Lon-Shan gave him sputtered like a spent candle. She felt it, and she knew it made him dangerous. Unpredictable.

She slowed, waiting for his shield to slam into the castle before advancing. Black marks seared the tower facing, the center of which remained clear. There, spreadeagled and upside down, Paitr's body hit the wall. He remained in place for a moment before sliding onto the thin balcony below like a crushed insect.

Spinning on all fours, he hurled a pair of dark spheres at the ironbound doors blocking the castle entrance. Wood splintered, iron melted, and sooty rubble vanished into what looked like a shrinking hole of nothingness. With the entrance clear, he sprang forward and disappeared.

Yui cursed her hesitation. She raced to the broken

doors only to stop well back of them. Paitr could be close – just inside, readying an ambush. Carefully, she studied the wounded tower with a Searching, then, satisfied, pressed ahead.

"I hope you're not thinking of going in there by yourself," a voice called.

Startled, Yui whirled around. A burgundy shield bobbed erratically in front of her. Keiko stood inside, hands on her hips, her expression daring Yui to comment.

"What are you doing here?" Yui fought shock and irritation. "I thought I told you to pull back."

Keiko's brow climbed. "I'm sorry. Was I supposed to go a *different* tower?"

"Stop twisting my words. You deliberately followed me." Exasperated, Yui jabbed a finger at the smoldering gash in the donjon. "You have no idea how dangerous that man is."

Keiko maneuvered her shield over. It slipped to one side then bounced to the other like a ball on smooth pavement. She spun around to face Yui, over-rotated, and readjusted. "And *you* haven't learned your lesson. You can't do everything by yourself. You need my help and the sooner you admit it the sooner we can get started."

"And if I refuse?"

"It's either the tower or the battlefield." Keiko pointed at the bloodstained courtyard, where bodies of both samurai and shadow monster littered the grounds. "Your choice."

Yui glared at her for several seconds, uncertain. She didn't think Keiko would actually do it, but she couldn't be sure. "All right, Keiko. You can come. But I'm warning you–"

"I know. I know. He's dangerous. I got that part."

Yui ignored the comment. "He's cast a Masking to conceal himself. We need to stay alert."

Keiko's eyes traveled up the donjon, measuring it. "This castle is huge. It could take weeks to search the whole thing. Do you even know where to start?"

Yui nodded. "The foundations. The only light down there is what you bring with you. That's where he will be."

"If it's such an obvious place, wouldn't he avoid it and set up somewhere else?"

Yui shook her head. "Doubtful. Our knowledge of these buildings gives us an advantage. He'll need the darkness to even the odds. I'm afraid he'll be strongest there too."

"I hope you didn't think he'd make it easy for you."

Yui smiled in spite of herself. "We'll need to draw him out. This is an ambush. He won't show himself until he's ready to attack. We can help that along if we keep our weapons down. Do you understand? No Maskings, no shields, and no weapons of any kind. He has to *believe* we're vulnerable."

"Better and better. I suppose a flashlight's out of the question."

"You don't have to come." Yui sniffed, stepping over the broken doorframe and extinguishing her shield.

As expected, Keiko fell in behind her.

The tower was darker than it should have been, and it took a moment for Yui's eyes to adjust. After perhaps ten paces, she pulled up short and gestured for Keiko to stop. The walls ahead were streaked with blood. Unnaturally red and pungent, the liquid oozed onto the floors and ran the length of the long corridor to the stairwell, where it then cascaded through a wide opening and splashed grotesquely into the darkness.

"Careless." Yui stared at crimson trail in disgust.

"What do you mean?" Keiko had covered her nose, and her light voice hummed oddly through her pinched nostrils.

"The blood's too thick. It can't be his. More likely his soldiers'."

"So we're both playing games." Keiko's disapproval was obvious. "He wants us to think he's wounded."

Yui nodded and headed for the stairs. "Be ready for anything."

The light faded as they made their way into the castle. Keiko shuffled her feet, carefully probing the steps before she committed her weight. Falling would be disastrous, as much for the noise as for the threat of injury. Thankfully, a soft glow appeared a few feet in front her.

Yui stood a flight below, her right hand wrapped around a thin pole perhaps a yard long. A small, lighted sphere hovered an inch or so above the tip. Yui nodded and pointed at the floor.

"The blood no longer leads us," she said.

Sure enough, the thick liquid fanned out in all directions.

"What do we do now?" Keiko's feet came down on stone, and she moved to Yui's side.

The space beyond stretched in all directions. She couldn't tell how far it went, not with shadows cutting the light to a few feet. The area was at least as large as the tower above, probably larger. She hoped it didn't cover the grounds as well. That had to be – what? – several square miles. At least. They could search for days and not find anything. Biting her lip, she twirled her hand, gesturing for Yui to answer.

"He obviously wants us to take the main corridor. I

think we should indulge him."

Keiko rolled her eyes. "You *do* know he's trying to kill us, right?"

Yui didn't reply; she just kept staring into the darkness. She looked eager, bouncing on her toes, her body taut, ready.

Keiko sighed heavily. Warrior Yui was back, which wasn't necessarily a bad thing, not with Paitr hiding in the darkness like a cobra. Biding his time. Waiting to strike.

Paitr watched the two women from the shadow of a cross corridor. The beautiful, young spirit clad in shining blue and white was the one who attacked him. He frowned at the curious object in her hand, wondering how it pierced the dark nets he'd woven throughout the underground. He sensed light in her, and that made her dangerous.

Disgusted, he crouched low and waited for her to move down the hall with her tiny companion before lifting from the ground and rounding the corner.

Keiko fought to keep up with Yui's longer stride but soon found herself falling behind. Her legs felt like lead, and her thoughts were a jumbled mess of horrific images – of men falling and dying. Or being eaten alive. She'd never seen anything like it. It haunted her, left her hurt and empty and shaking. Roarke was right: wars weren't glorious, not even wars between gods. She pushed the thought aside and increased her pace. Lingering fatigue slowed her, but she made good progress.

Fortunately, Yui had stopped and now stood in the middle of two intersecting corridors, the torch held high, her gaze sweeping the surrounding passages. She looked angry, furious even. Her eyes found Keiko's, and she

touched a hand to the back of her head where her long
ponytail stood, streaming in a newly forming breeze.

Alarmed, Keiko whirled about. Yui told her to pay
attention, but she'd been too busy thinking about the
battle. She swore at herself and concentrated on the
strengthening draft coming in from her left, a strong and
insistent movement in the air. How had she missed it?
Something approached – just like Fiyorok in the subway.

She turned, the motion quick and sharp and yet
seemingly eternal. Paitr Norwoska's black shield
barreled down on her, the threat jarring her instincts,
reawakening her power. Limitless energy built within
her – arms and legs, head and chest. It exploded outward
to form not one shield but two.

The first became a blazing nimbus around her body.
The second expanded like blown glass. Keiko stared at
both in disbelief. What had she done? The world outside
stopped as if frozen, Yui couldn't reach her, and, worst of
all, she somehow managed to capture Paitr's black shield
within her own.

She watched him advance, cautious now, like a
lion that underestimated its prey. This close, his shield
appeared less solid and filmier, its translucent texture the
same as smoke. Keiko peered inside and found a man
with a long, pointed nose and pinched features glaring
back at her. His sneer looked permanent, his lips thinned
by years of cruelty.

Keiko's stomach roiled. Seeing a man, a person, a
living being, instead of a faceless ball made it harder for
her to attack. She had never hurt another soul, and she
wasn't about to start now. Maybe if she talked to him,
maybe if she knew why he did such horrible things. It
was better than fighting – anything was better than that.

She drew herself up and struck what she hoped was a

confident pose. "What do you want?"

Paitr's shield stopped. "What do I want?" His voice was thin and nasally. She addressed him in English, and to her surprise, he responded in kind. "I want vengeance. I was supposed to live forever. Lord Lon-Shan promised me!"

Keiko raised her hands plaintively, palms outward. "Maybe I can help you. You have to let me try. Look! Out there." She flicked her head at Yui. The Kami's shield remained frozen in the air, everything surrounding it as motionless as a photograph. "Time. That's my power. It's what I do. You can't have much left." She slid her foot forward. "If you just lower your shield."

She wasn't entirely sure she could help him, and even less sure she wanted to. Saying it bought her time, though, which was all she wanted. Or needed.

Paitr's eyes hardened. "You'd like that, wouldn't you, guardian?"

"I'm *not* a guardian." Keeping her tone level proved difficult. A touch of bitterness seeped in, not enough for him to notice, not enough to make him believe her.

"Do you think I'm stupid? I'm dead as soon as this shield comes down."

Was he right? Would she kill him? Could she? Her stomach tightened. The guilt would torment her. She didn't think she'd get over it. Ever. She hesitated, and her concentration slipped.

Paitr sensed her weakness. A triumphant smile broke across his face. He swept an arm in a wide arc, and the shadows around him swirled. Another movement straightened them into long, quivering spears.

Somehow, Keiko held her ground. After Vissyus, Paitr was nothing. "This is your last chance." Her voice was tight but steady.

"Lord Lon-Shan was my last chance!" Paitr cried, launching his attack. "He's dead now, and so are you – all of you!"

Keiko lifted her chin defiantly. She didn't look away, not when the first explosion slammed into her shield, not when the rest pushed her back. Dust and smoke filled the corridor, thick and choking and deep enough to hide Paitr. Not that it would do him any good. Yui taught her how to form and manipulate Searchings, and she was fairly sure she could make one on her own. At least she hoped so. Warily, she pushed her thoughts into the smoke.

Paitr was still there. She saw him move to the right and hug the wall. His Searching scoured the area. It was more focused than hers, more precise, which was probably why he hadn't found her yet. A flash of jealousy jolted her. She managed a Searching, but barely. Hers was clumsy and overwrought compared to his. Even now, it expanded well beyond her intended range, swamping the corridor, slamming into Paitr, stripping him bare.

Everything he was, everything he did, opened to her. His whole life rolled through her head. What she saw sickened her. Hundreds of townspeople went into his dungeons, only to come out as tortured corpses. No one was immune: not friend, not family, not even Lon-Shan, who he planned to challenge once his immortality was assured. Killing Paitr would do the world a favor, but deep down, Keiko knew she couldn't do it. She didn't have it in her.

Fortunately, Yui did.

Keiko just had to hold him, find a way to lower her shield, and get Yui to kill him. She scowled. Why did everything have to be so difficult? She'd overwhelmed his Searching, and that showed him how much stronger she was.

That was careless, she thought. *Careless and provocative.* Already, she felt him panic, felt him turn and run. He wouldn't get far, not with her second shield in place. By the time he discovered he couldn't move, it'd be too late. He'd have to turn back, and if he did, Keiko was sure he'd attack.

She had to be ready; she needed to stop him. But how? Absently, she scratched an irritated spot on her neck. Her camera strap snaked over her shoulder, digging into her skin, chafing it. Keiko's eyes flew open. The camera! She couldn't believe she'd forgotten it. It was there, it had always been there. Just like her power. Just like her father.

Her hands embraced the cool metal case. How many times had she used the little metal box? How many pictures taken? How many moments captured?

Confidence slowed her breathing. She could do this – after a lifetime of practice it came to her instinctively. Lifting the camera, she sent her thoughts into the lens. This time she wouldn't overreach. Not here. Not now. Her finger hovered over the shutter button, and as Paitr neared her outer shielding, she pressed down.

Burgundy light seized the fleeing shield. A thought sent it a few minutes into the future. Paitr clawed at the air after it, unable to do anything but watch it shoot away.

"I tried to warn you." Keiko shook her head sadly and lined up another shot.

Paitr's plans were in ruins – his lord was dead, his army defeated. Even his shield had betrayed him. He'd never felt so exposed. So naked. Like the women he brought to his dungeons. Had they known a fear like this? He tried not to think about them, but their faces filled his head. He saw them, heard their mocking laughter in his ears. Covering them wouldn't help, and neither would running. He did run, though. Another darkened corner, a cell, or abandoned room, that's all he needed to regroup. Now that he knew what to expect, he could better prepare. But first, he had to escape. He had to go before that cursed guardian alerted her mistress.

She was a guardian, no matter what she said. Her power proved it.

His last hiding place loomed ahead. He estimated he had less than a minute to reach the intersection before they caught him. The seconds ticked on, but, to his dismay, he found the corridor no closer than when he'd turned toward it. A strange droning filled his ears, slow and deep, though with a cadence that might have been speech had it not been so slurred and distorted. Again, he heard it – though this time its pitch was different: lighter, crisper, and more commanding.

Reflex urged him to turn his head. He tried, but found he could not do so. It was almost as if a giant vise held his body in its grip, as if something had paralyzed him. He ordered his eyes to the right... nothing. Over and over he tried, hands and feet, arms and legs. Still nothing. Not even the sweat clinging to his forehead, stuck and motionless on his face, had so much as moved, not by a fraction of an inch.

He screamed, but no sound came out. His mouth was frozen, his tongue stilled. His mind shrieked the curses he couldn't utter. What had she done to him?

As if in answer, a slight pressure – no more than a pinprick – irritated a spot between his shoulders. It was almost infinitesimal, an annoyance. But it built slowly over time, grinding and digging into his flesh, breaching skin. Searing pain flooded through his body. He couldn't believe something could move so slowly or inflict so much pain for such a long time. That he endured it only added to his misery. He wished it would end, but was unwilling to die.

By the time the spear ran him completely through, his mind was too far gone to understand what had happened. The void called out to the last remaining spark of life within him. He felt his soul lift, felt time resume, and then, after one flickering moment, he felt his life go out.

Paitr's body slid from Yui's lance and hit the ground like a piece of bad meat. The darkness swirling about him lifted, but it couldn't erase the cruel curve of his lips or the horrific images burned into Keiko's psyche. She wouldn't forget them, and she wouldn't feel guilty for her part in his death. Not after what she'd seen. The world was a better place without Paitr Norwoska.

Squaring her shoulders, she joined Yui in the corridor and nodded her approval.

"Thank you Yamanaka-san," Yui said. "This fight was shorter than I expected. Thanks to you." She lowered her weapon.

"Shorter for you, maybe, but not for him. I held him for a *very* long time."

Yui's eyes widened. "Really?" Her voice was breathy and low. "I should have known. You did well. *Guardian*."

"Guardian," Keiko murmured, testing the word. She smiled. "I think I like the sound of that."

48
SANCTUARY

Takeshi skimmed over a war-ravaged landscape. Pits smoldered to his left and right, some shallow, some shockingly deep. Seirin's rains had reduced the fire's effects, but they also transformed the sprayed earth into rivers of mud. Hills lay toppled, pounded, or blasted.

The sight troubled him. He expected Roarke to minimize the damage, but the Earth was quiet, too quiet. He sighed. Another wrinkle to correct, another scale to balance. He'd deal with Roarke's grief when the time was right. He couldn't afford the distraction now. Aeryk needed him. Desperately.

Moving faster, he threaded his way through a maze of boulders, downed trees, and thrown earth. Aeryk was close, but circumstance made it feel much farther. The space between Takeshi's shoulders prickled. Despite the Masking, he felt vulnerable, exposed. Seirin kept Vissyus and Akuan busy; Ventyre did the same for Fiyorok. But for how long?

A Searching showed Aeryk's unconscious body lying at the bottom of a deep crater. Fiyorok darted toward it, while a wounded Ventyre did its best to harass the dragon. A low rumble shook the ground. The earth cracked and tilted, and, as Takeshi approached, Aeryk tumbled down a growing hillside toward him. Fiyorok roared in the distance, but the sound grew strangely muffled. Dull booms rolled beneath the Earth's surface, and he immediately threw a Searching at them.

A huge mound covered Aeryk's crater like piecrust. Severe tremors rattled beneath, growing louder, more insistent. Ignoring them, Takeshi sprinted for the base of the hill where Aeryk lay in an unconscious heap. He landed at the bottom of a steep incline, grasped Aeryk under an arm, and quickly secured both shield and Masking.

Roarke's voice bloomed in his head as he sprinted away. *My apologies, Takeshi. I would have acted sooner but… I was distracted. I'm sorry. That hill isn't as strong as it should be. It won't hold Fiyorok for long.*

Takeshi's lips compressed into a thin line. Yui was right about him. *I am very sorry about Botua. But you need to control yourself. Vengeance has no place here.*

A cold silence stretched between them. *I'll do my part.* Roarke's voice was flat. *Small though it may be.*

You're the only one who can do this, Roarke. Without you, the Earth dies. Self-pity might make that seem small to you, but it isn't to the billions we protect. You know how losing something precious feels. Don't let anyone else feel it too.

I won't, Roarke said bluntly. *That much at least, I can promise you.*

Takeshi started to say more, but Roarke had already cut the connection. He considered turning around, then quickly discounted the idea. If either Fiyorok or Vissyus spotted him… Instinct told him to trust Seirin, even if he couldn't trust Roarke. Not that he had any choice. Grinding his teeth, he hurled his shield north.

He'd built a sanctuary deep in the Shosenkyo Gorge some ninety-five miles south of Nagano. There, a small, Masked portion of the Boundary protected the southernmost section of the chasm. Vissyus wouldn't find them inside; the shields he built there were too strong.

Reaching the Chichibu Mountains took less than ten minutes, the longest ten minutes of Takeshi's life. Each rustle, each crack of the Earth's crust, brought a backward glance. If Fiyorok escaped and caught them… He let out a relieved sigh the moment he spotted a deep cleft in the mountains ahead. Dropping into it, he came down next to the Arakawa River at the bottom. He eased Aeryk onto a wide rock and cast spirit into his body to heal him.

Aeryk stirred, and he intensified his casting until Aeryk's eyes fluttered open.

"Welcome back," Takeshi said. "I am happy to see you awake."

Aeryk grunted. He lifted a hand to massage his temples. "Where are we?" His gaze drifted up the breathtaking ravine. Tall limestone cliffs protected them on either side, the unmistakable sound of a large waterfall rumbling in the distance.

"North of Kofu City, about eighty miles from Tokyo." Takeshi's crimson armor clinked as he shifted a hand to the simply carved hilt at his waist. The other draped over one knee. "We will be safe here for the moment – unless Vissyus decides to come looking for us. I doubt he'd search near *Tengu-iwa*, though." He pointed at the looming boulder beside them. "Demon Rock is another Boundary seal. It would feel too much like a trap to him. You should have enough time to heal."

"Time is one thing we don't have." Aeryk stood unsteadily. The towering cliffs were no more than a few hundred feet apart, but Vissyus's pillar of fire remained visible between them.

Aeryk tensed at the sight, anguish contorting his face. He threw a pained look at the distant volcano. "I have to go."

"I understand," Takeshi said. He expected it. "But first, I need to tell you something."

A wall went up around Aeryk's emotions.

Takeshi's thoughts shifted to Yui and the White Spirit. He understood Aeryk's pain, shared it even. "It's not what you think," he said, quickly. "Seirin's done something remarkable! Even I didn't expect it."

"What?" Aeryk demanded. "What are you saying?" Despite Takeshi's assurances, his face remained grim.

"She released Kirak's Bond and then wrestled Akuan away from Vissyus."

"She did *what*?" Aeryk's worried expression melted into a look of fierce pride. "I don't believe it."

"It's true all the same. She's given you another weapon to use against Fiyorok."

Aeryk frowned, uncertain. "Can we trust it?"

"I've seen Akuan's spirit. It's wholly committed to her."

"And Vissyus? Did the Unbinding affect him?"

"He is disoriented. Just not enough – he can and will raise a shield if threatened. We need to do more. Fortunately, Akuan will help us."

Aeryk's frown deepened. "I don't see–"

"Akuan and Fiyorok's shields know each other. One allows the essence of the other through without question. Surely someone as clever as you will know how to use that to his advantage. History teaches many things. Sometimes, the most beneficial lessons are the ones that wound us most."

A smile crept across Aeryk's face. Trust might come slowly – it might not come at all – but if using the ice dragon meant saving Seirin, Takeshi knew Aeryk would do it. He was counting on it.

"Ventyre is too badly injured to join me." Aeryk's voice took on a commanding tone – crisp, confident, and assertive. "That leaves the two Water Kami. Kirak is free to do as it wishes. Will Akuan bow to Seirin's former guardian?"

"It will do whatever it can to save her," Takeshi assured him.

Aeryk nodded. He strode to the middle of the gorge and turned. "Have Roarke standing by."

Takeshi wondered if he realized he'd just ordered the Lord of Spirit as he would a lieutenant.

"As long as Vissyus controls the volcano, he can restore some of his power. We need to prevent that." He glanced at Takeshi. "I'm afraid your presence would only enrage him. I'm sorry, but you'll have to stay behind. Our success depends on keeping Vissyus passive. If he fights, we die."

"I'm sure you are right, Aeryk." Takeshi lowered his head to hide a satisfied grin.

Aeryk and Seirin had suffered for a very long time. They needed to set things right, alone and without interference. That was the only way they'd forgive themselves for what they'd done.

Takeshi moved aside, and Aeryk brought his shield to life. Azure light filled the gorge, brighter and more vibrant than Takeshi had seen before. Aeryk's faith had returned along with his strength. He was at peace.

"Look after Ventyre for me." Aeryk pushed from the ground and adjusted his shield for battle. "It will probably try to follow."

Takeshi nodded. "I know how to handle a guardian spirit. I've had a good deal of practice."

"That won't help you with Ventyre." Spinning away, Aeryk rocketed into the sky and disappeared behind the gorge's eastern lip.

Takeshi snorted. He could manage any spirit. His thoughts shifted to Mount Fuji. Any spirit but Vissyus. He hoped Seirin fared better than he had. If not…

Suppressing a shiver, he opened a hole in the Boundary and slipped into it with a heavy heart.

49
ATONEMENT

Aeryk roared over the rugged hills and tree-lined slopes of Yamanashi Prefecture like a devastating typhoon. Two of the five lakes, Motsosku and Shojiko, flashed by on either side, while to the south the White Spirit's shining towers soared above Aokigahara like small mountains. Several miles east, Mount Fuji's smooth neck climbed into a curtain of blazing fire. A pair of huge shapes hurtled away from the volcano, closing on the spot where he'd recently fallen.

He stared at the area, unable to recall what happened, amazed by the perfectly circular mound that covered the blast crater. Explosions hammered the dome from beneath, and a large section in its center looked as if it had started to melt. His Searching took him below ground and into a cavern sealed and protected with spiritual energy.

Fiyorok raged inside, pounding the roof with fire, overwhelming Roarke's power, breaking it.

Aeryk swore under his breath. Once free, Fiyorok would turn on the incoming guardians. If Vissyus's dragon killed either Kirak or Akuan, the odds of victory turned against them. He had to call them off before it was too late. Already, Kirak neared the withering dome, Akuan's cool shield visible several hundred yards back. Aeryk's thoughts screamed toward both, surging through the tortured sky with the force of a hurricane. His mind shredded smoke and blasted through storms, and just when he thought Kirak readied a strike, the great serpent changed course and sped toward him.

"Lord Aeryk!" Kirak called. "I'm happy to see you alive." It slowed to a stop a hundred feet from him.

"I could say the same to you, considering." Aeryk's eyes shifted to Akuan. Seirin's new guardian wisely kept its distance. "I suppose this means Seirin's forgiven you. You'll have a harder time with me. Let me be clear, Akuan. I don't know if I can trust you, but I *do* need you. Earlier today, you breached my shield. Can you do it again?" He didn't know what the Unbinding had done to Akuan's memory. He didn't know too many things.

"Lord Vissyus conducted the attack," Akuan replied, not even trying to defend itself. "His mind drifted in and out of my body. I saw what he did; I can replicate it."

Aeryk's eyes widened. Vissyus. How was that possible? He pushed the thought aside. "Good. When I tell you, I want you to use it on Fiyorok. Do you understand?"

"Yes, lord, though I can't see what good it will do. I used your storms against you. With Fiyorok..." Akuan shrugged. "None of us can wield fire."

"We won't have to," Aeryk said. "Fiyorok's shield knows you. Send your thoughts through. I'll handle the rest." He studied the skies. "The air's too thick here. We'll need to go above the storms where it's cleaner." The sound of sliding rock rolled over them like an avalanche. "I'm afraid I'll need you to cover us, Kirak."

Kirak nodded grimly. "I expected as much. A

coordinated assault gives us the best chance. The affinity between the twins will do the rest."

"Agreed," Akuan said. "But I need to be close, within a few yards. Any farther and Fiyorok's shield will not be fooled."

Kirak paused, its cerulean eyes stormy. "And that is the only way? You are certain?"

A fiery rope exploded out of the shaking hill, bathing Akuan's face with flickering orange light. The guardian lowered its massive horned head and nodded.

"Unfortunately so." Aeryk thought it sounded more apologetic than fearful. "I'll use what I've learned from Fiyorok's battle with Lady Yui. My attack on you, Lord Aeryk, will serve as a foundation. I know how to pierce its shield. Fiyorok will fall."

"You're putting Seirin's life in danger," Aeryk interrupted. Doubt gnawed at him. He studied the dragon, Searching for deception. "We have to find another way."

"This is the *only* way," Akuan's eyes were bright in the firelight. "Payment, I'm afraid, for an evil life."

"She'll never let you go. Don't you understand what will happen to her?"

"Of course I do. I've known all along. Why do you think I left the Bonding unfinished?"

"You what?" Aeryk swore and glanced at the volcano. An unfinished Bond meant she didn't have complete control. Aeryk's unease increased. This was madness.

"A broken heart is easier to mend than a broken body," Akuan said. "This is my choice, Lord Tai-Banshar. I've committed unspeakable crimes; I need to pay for them."

Aeryk ground his teeth. How much was he willing to risk? Akuan sounded sincere, but he'd seen the dragon as an enemy for a very long time. Feelings like that didn't turn quickly. He closed his eyes, but couldn't concentrate. Faith often meant deciding against reason. Another flaming spear exploded out of the Earth. Rock melted, and sand turned to glass. Aeryk's Searching haunted him. He saw Fiyorok's horned head rise from the ruined ground like a demon.

"All right, Akuan." He couldn't believe he was saying this. It felt wrong. "Head for the anchoring storm. I'll come in from the west while Kirak buys us the time we need."

"We're not going together?"

Aeryk shook his head. "Splitting up adds uncertainty – not much, perhaps, but it's the best we can do." He moved aside and motioned Akuan past. "Go! And don't stop until you've cleared the thunderhead."

As if in a dream, he watched Akuan fall away from him. Sunlight broke through the clouds, and the guardian's sapphire scales sparkled magnificently as it flew from one pillared ray to the next. Far below, Fiyorok climbed out of the pit and took to the sky – searching as it flew.

Akuan noted Fiyorok's approach and headed for the storms in a blur of blue and green. Steam burst from its nostrils to cover its flight, the huge, pluming clouds building between them, cutting visibility, blocking it from Fiyorok's sight.

Against any other guardian, the strategy might have been effective, but Fiyorok was too experienced with Akuan. Immediately, the older dragon vaporized the fog with a massive burst of fire. Clouds boiled, and the mist lifted. Exposed, Akuan sprayed another layer of fog into the air, only to have Fiyorok blast it away.

Kirak wheeled in from the southeast, but even with its assistance, Akuan wouldn't shake Fiyorok without his help. Aeryk tested the atmosphere, Searching, probing. Akuan's clouds gave him an idea, a risky one, but one that was passive, nonthreatening. Heart pounding, he sent his thoughts into the skies. The air aloft plummeted, fed upon the warmer surface atmosphere, and refueled Seirin's storms. Hurricane-force winds swept in from the northwest, accompanied by macrobursts and massive dust clouds.

Debris, caught and carried within the gales, confounded Fiyorok's Searching enough to prevent the guardian from locating the three incoming Kami. The red dragon's expression became a portrait of frustration, its response wildly reckless. The slightest movement prompted atomic fire – here incinerated boulders, there liquefied steel and cindered wood.

Aeryk smiled as smoke and refuse added to the airborne clutter. He wondered if Fiyorok understood the enormity of its mistake. Lost in a cloud of its own making, unable to see or read its Searchings, Fiyorok flew on blindly. From above Kirak dove and began a new battle to buy some time. Climbing away, Aeryk headed for the cool shield waiting for him above the storms.

"Are you ready, Akuan?" He focused on the dragon's eyes to avoid looking at its face – a face he'd always hated.

"Yes, lord, but be quick. I don't care to face Fiyorok unshielded."

Aeryk's eyebrow climbed, but he stayed silent. If Akuan could breach Fiyorok's shield, then the reverse was also true. Didn't Akuan realize that? Head shaking, Aeryk threw his thoughts into the air's moisture. The memory of his first success brought a sharp pang: his waterspout, Seirin's pride-filled hug, her light, flowery scent.

"Try not to move. I have to alter the air around you to build a weapon. If you don't hold still, you won't capture it. Do you understand?"

Akuan nodded, and Aeryk continued to work, feverishly separating air into hydrogen and oxygen and then adding methane and other explosive gases. When done, he positioned the mixture in front of Akuan's shield.

"Let go of your shield," he ordered.

The icy globe vanished, and he moved the weaponized gases into place. Sweat beaded his forehead, exhaustion working into every muscle and bone.

"All right," he grunted. "You can reform the shield."

Sapphire scales shone vividly against the lighter blue of the sky until a new barrier, a nimbus of glowing energy – emerald touched with cobalt – blazed to life around them.

"Wait as long as you can to fill your lungs. When you attack, the air will do the rest."

"As you command, Lord Aeryk." Akuan bowed.

Aeryk wanted more time to test the weapon, but with Fiyorok rippling through the clouds like living heat, he knew they'd exhausted what little they had.

I mark Fiyorok at roughly six thousand feet and climbing, Kirak reported from the overcast skies. The bright fireballs flying from Vissyus's guardian gave its position away as well as any Searching.

Aeryk's eyes locked with Akuan. "I won't forget this. I'll make sure Seirin knows what you did for her. She'll be very proud of you."

"I can't let you destroy a guardian," Akuan said, turning away. "You've suffered enough and neither you nor my mistress should live with any more pain."

Akuan's sapphire scales disappeared into the turbulent

storm just as Fiyorok vaporized its covering clouds. The two welcomed each other with orange-sheathed flame and razor-sharp ice, arctic blue met yellow fire, the mist around them evaporating.

Heat struck Akuan's shield and skittered away, drawing a relieved exhalation from Aeryk. Charged air surrounded Akuan, air imbued with his power. Fiyorok might be able to strike through Akuan's shield, but as long as he controlled the air inside, he could protect the guardian. For a little while.

The dragons passed each other in midair, and for a moment, it looked to Aeryk as if a single dragon moved in front of a mirror, flying and pivoting before breaking away to leave its reflection behind. The two came apart, looped around, and accelerated back together as if caught up in some deadly dance.

A quick Searching showed thousands of frozen lances spewing from Akuan's gaping mouth and racing toward Fiyorok's shield faster than wind-driven snow. Harder than diamonds, the projectiles broke through the other guardian's fiery shield. Ice appeared on red scales, hundreds of shards covering Fiyorok's hide, each driving through the golden armor, each seeping into muscle, tissue, and blood. Melting, they joined the other liquids in Fiyorok's body, and, once inside, heat and pressure ignited the whole. Heartbeats pushed the explosion on, each pulse blowing a piece of Fiyorok apart from the inside.

Somehow, the great dragon still had enough control to whip its head around and face Akuan. Fiyorok's eyes bulged grotesquely. "At least I have the pleasure of taking you with me," it snarled. Spittle dripped from its mouth in bright, blazing sparks.

Akuan said nothing, just hovered in place as Fiyorok's

head came apart. Burning flesh splattered its shield, blood painting the inside red as a growing fireball overtook the rest of the viscera.

Horrified, Aeryk watched waves of elemental energy hurtle across the skies. Akuan stood against them, neither moving nor trying to run. At last, Akuan's shield shattered. Light flared and overcame the proud body. For a moment, Akuan's shadow floated proudly within the fires. The guardian tipped its head first at Aeryk and then at Fuji and Seirin. A final blast of power roared from the wreckage and flew to the mountain, where it then blended with the air's moisture before fading to nothingness.

The image seared itself into Aeryk's mind. He bowed his head and swallowed bitterness. He'd sent Akuan to slaughter a guardian he'd known and loved for a very long time – before the madness changed Fiyorok forever.

With Fiyorok down, he turned his attention to Vissyus. He tried to think, but grief muddied his head. Once, they'd been inseparable; friends, comrades, and brothers. The task that always seemed so noble now tore his soul apart. Murderer – that's what he'd become. A coldblooded killer.

He lifted his eyes to the mountain. He and Seirin wanted to share their dreams with Vissyus, but now they had to live with their nightmares. Seirin was right: this was their fault… all of it. They should have been more careful and less self-absorbed. Images of Vissyus passed before his eyes, of his boundless energy and infectious happiness. He hated himself for what he was about to do, but he'd hate himself even more if he allowed Vissyus to destroy the world. With a regretful sigh, he sent his shield into a dizzying climb.

He slowed to a stop near the top of the Boundary and

stared into its shimmering, flame-encircled prison. He wished the Boundary would hold as it always had, but as he stared into the light, he felt the layers open for his thoughts. Reluctantly, he sent them in. Air thinned and dissipated at higher altitudes until, finally, none remained above twenty thousand feet. He'd created a vacuum, a perfect void, within which no fire would burn.

Aeryk lowered his head and began his lonely vigil.

50
PEACE

The loss of Akuan opened a hole in Seirin's heart. Her chest tightened, and she couldn't breathe. The guardian was gone, another death at her feet, another life sacrificed. She turned to the volcano, tracing the flows of steam, ash, and soot wafting up from below. Vissyus was down there, somewhere within the chaos. He was the last, the most significant. The hardest.

A Searching showed him plummeting through the skies. His hands were on his head, and his body thrashed from side to side as he fell in a wild, rotating descent. Losing his guardians stunned Vissyus just as they hoped it would. But for how long? His strength made guessing impossible. Then there was the madness. Who knew how that affected the Unbinding? Seirin needed to finish this before he recovered.

His smashing into the caldera might further disorient him, but she couldn't chance it. Rock and dust – thrown high into the air from the impact – churned angrily over Japan in great, mushrooming clouds, and when the skies parted several hundred yards to the east, Seirin's blood froze.

There, moving through the wreckage, repairing the damaged ground to create a smooth path, Roarke stalked toward Vissyus, hammer held high.

Roarke! Seirin hissed. *No! Stop. Please.*

But Roarke didn't answer, and he didn't stop. Cursing, Seirin measured the distance to the ground and accelerated. She tried to land quietly, but the attempt proved pointless. As soon as Roarke saw her he pulled himself up and bellowed. "Out of my way, Seirin!" he roared. His fingers tensed around his great hammer.

You don't want to do this. Seirin said into his head, desperately trying to keep Vissyus from hearing them. *If Vissyus fights, we're as good as dead.*

"He murdered Botua!" Grief darkened Roarke's sandy eyes, and for an instant he looked as insane as Vissyus. He took a step forward, brandishing his hammer. "If you don't move I swear I'll–"

A small, subdued voice, carried through the air on fiery currents, cut Roarke off. "Is it true, Seirin?" Vissyus asked. "Is Roarke right? Did I kill Botua?"

Seirin spun, ready to defend herself, expecting to die. "Don't think about it." She flashed a dazzling smile despite her leaden soul. Again, he'd used her name, calling her Seirin instead of Teacher. She'd seen a hint of his old self earlier, and now it was back. Maybe his madness wasn't permanent. Maybe losing both guardians somehow reset his psyche. Hope fluttered inside her. They didn't have to do this. They'd find a way to save him. "Come over here, Vissyus." Slowly, she lowered herself to the steaming ground. "Sit with me so we can talk."

"Did I do it?" he asked again, this time more forcefully. She noted his trembling hands, the force with which he hurled the question. "It felt like a nightmare, but I can see it in your face. So many dead, so much burned. I…"

He shook his head miserably. "I just wanted to make you happy."

The words sickened Seirin. Emotion laced them, shame and defeat and most of all love. He'd done this for her – all of it. She couldn't let him die. She had to save him, even if she died in his place.

Roarke stirred beside her but didn't attack. Apparently, Vissyus's return to sanity had as great an impact on him as it had on her.

"Vissyus," Roarke repeated.

A look of intense pain crossed Vissyus's face. His eyes flicked to Roarke. "I'm so sorry." When he returned his attention to Seirin, she watched his spirit fade. "I've done bad things." He sounded like a lost child. His knees buckled, and he fell like a broken statue. "The Rock Man is right. I must be punished." An ominous glow sprang to life around his fingertips. The ground shook, and thin, spidery cracks appeared beneath their feet like shattering glass. The sharp exhalation of gas preceded a heated blast of gas and steam as the sealed caldera melted.

"*NO!*" Seirin wailed, fighting to raise her shield. "*Vissyus! NO!*"

Magma fountained into the sky toward her. She struggled against the firestorm, watching Vissyus's unshielded body slip beneath the lava. A silver globe burst through the molten earth and inched toward her.

"What have I done?" Roarke said, his head down, his face anguished.

A hundred miles northeast, Mount Hakone erupted. Mount Bandai followed, and then Mount Azuma. Quakes rocked the islands as more peaks exploded.

Roarke's face paled. "What's he doing?" His voice was barely audible over the groaning Earth.

You heard him, Seirin said into his head. *He's punishing himself, and he's taking the world with him.*

"Seirin," Roarke gasped. "I–"

"I understand," Seirin said, cutting him off. "I would have done the same." She maneuvered her shield until it was even with his. "Takeshi must have known this would happen. That's why he brought you here. You're the only one who can stop him. You did it before, remember? I saw you stop the eruptions when Vissyus first Bonded Akuan."

A light bloomed behind Roarke's eyes, and his pain eased.

"Go!" Seirin urged. "Avenge Botua by saving the world."

Roarke nodded. "Thank you, Seirin. Tell Vissyus... Tell him – Botua and I...we forgive him." Then, hefting his diamond-encrusted hammer, he lowered himself into the chaos.

Seirin held her breath as the eruption subsided. Flame and lava drained back into the earth, the smoke dissipated, and Mount Fuji's perfect cone reappeared. Roarke had done his work as she'd expected, but Fuji's reformation had taken her by surprise. A lump formed in her throat. She lowered her head sadly and peered down.

"Where are you, Vissyus?" she whispered, startled by the duality of the thought.

Far below, the lava bed churned. A series of perfect rings spread out in rising waves to slam at the cone's inner lining. Molten earth heaved over the rim and down the volcano's neck. At the summit, a column of viscous fire shot hundreds of feet into the air. Vissyus's unshielded body exploded out of the liquid earth like some surreal phoenix.

Seirin watched him climb, and quickly raced to be

with him. She drew close, half expecting him to attack. He didn't, and together they streaked toward infinity like twin comets, one green and one gold.

He caught Seirin's eye, and something in his gaze said he knew what was happening. "Don't be sad, Seirin," Vissyus said. "It's better this way." This was the end – the end of so many things. Soon, he'd be gone; she'd never see him again, never hear his voice. Never have the chance to apologize for asking him to give so much. Releasing her shield despite the danger, she formed a sheer barrier of elemental water to protect her skin from his fires and leaned in to kiss him on the cheek. Astonished, he touched a hand to his face. Love bloomed behind his eyes, and for a moment, they sharpened. "Vissyus?" she asked. He was there, the spirit she once knew. She felt him. Desperately, she grabbed at his fading essence, fought to wrap it within her mind. Tears stung her eyes, and her heart felt leaden in her chest. Heavy. Like an anchor secured to the Earth. "No!" she cried, wanting to keep pace with him.

"I've loved you for a very long time, but you belong with Aeryk. I've always known that."

Stars appeared in the sky overhead, Japan dwindling to a series of volcanic rocks below. The Pacific raced eastward toward the arcing horizon, while the sun moved inexorably forward.

Seirin wished she could stop it. "You have to fight it." Her golden hair, once whipping in the thick air, had stilled along with the roaring wind. "You can. I know you can. You have the strength."

Vissyus shook his head. "I need that strength to keep from fighting." His face contorted as if some internal struggle went on inside him. "You have to go. I'm not sure I can do this if you stay." A wry smile curled his lips despite the pain. "I found myself again." He gasped. "The loss of my guardians helps. My other personalities – they're disoriented. You'll be able to do what you need to do. No guilt, Seirin. You aren't taking my life. I'm giving it."

Seirin bowed her head. At last she understood. Ultimate sacrifice – this was what it meant to love. Aeryk had done it, and so had Takeshi. The others had given so much for her, time and again, without asking for anything in return. And she'd taken. She'd taken and offered nothing. But not anymore.

"You have to leave." Vissyus panted. *"Please!"*

The air was so thin; Seirin had trouble pulling it in. She couldn't stay, but didn't want to leave. Ignoring her breath, she reached for him, took his hands in hers. She drew him to her, pressed her lips to his. This was her gift to him, a realized dream to sustain him. Aeryk would understand, though she didn't know if she would ever tell him. She'd sacrifice this for him, the lie she'd live with to the end of time.

Her lips moved to Vissyus's ear. "You taught me what it means to love."

She kissed him again, harder this time. It took her to the edge of fidelity, but she didn't turn back. This was for Aeryk, her way of saving him. "I'll never forget how much you loved me."

"Go." He pulled away. "I want this to be my final memory."

Seirin brushed a stray hair from his face and nodded. Resigned, she let him slip from her arms. The distance between them opened at a crawl. She savored it, knowing she'd never see him again. He smiled at her. Then, closing his eyes, he rocketed into the black clouds above.

• • •

Aeryk watched Vissyus break through the clouds and hurtle toward the stars. "This is wrong." He knew what would happen once he finished draining the air from the Boundary, and he hated himself for doing it.

Takeshi appeared beside him out of a shimmering haze. "The alternative would be worse. You didn't see him inside the Boundary. He destroyed whole worlds. The same would have happened here. A harsh truth, but an indisputable one."

"And Seirin prevented it," Aeryk said sadly.

Takeshi nodded. "Yes, my friend. For a little while."

They fell silent as Vissyus climbed into the upper atmosphere. Aeryk felt air passing through Vissyus's lips, in and then out, growing weaker, slowing, stopping. Momentum carried him perhaps a thousand feet higher. Aeryk thought he'd fly on forever, but before his lifeless body escaped the Earth's pull, gravity caught him and drew him back.

Aeryk shook his head. "I'll never forget this. Vissyus was my friend, and I failed him."

"Don't blame yourself, Aeryk. We're all responsible – for the beginning and the end. If I hadn't kept to myself so much, if I'd been more sympathetic, then maybe..." Takeshi took a deep breath and gazed at the heavy, gray clouds above the mountain. "You'll have to be strong. Seirin will need you – now more than ever." He gestured at the spark of emerald light slashing through the smoke. "We fought Vissyus from a distance. Imagine what it was like for her."

Seirin dropped her shield and approached Vissyus's body. She reached for it and drew him against her.

Aeryk nodded. "I never understood the last part of your plan. It didn't seem necessary."

Seirin landed on Fuji's western summit, positioned,

Aeryk saw, so she could look past the rim of the volcano and into the setting sun. Her arms held Vissyus tightly, as if she'd never let him go.

A sad smile crossed Takeshi's lips. "And now?"

"I can't believe Lon-Shan was right, but he was smarter than any of us. We can't stay here, we're too much of a danger." The admission lifted some of the weight from Aeryk's shoulders. "We have to split up and find worlds where we can–"

"Build a family." Takeshi folded his arms into his robes.

Aeryk's breath caught in his throat. "What about the law?"

"Vissyus showed why it was necessary, but he also showed us what is safe and what isn't." A wistful smile crossed Takeshi's face. "Remember the buffer? Vissyus knew the truth, but he ignored it."

"Because he loved Seirin so much."

Takeshi nodded. "His instincts were right, as were Seirin's. She believed having a child with you was safe. She believed it with all her heart. I'm sorry, Aeryk. I should have seen it. Teras, Seirin, Botua – in this, they were wiser than I." He gazed at Seirin. "Go to her. Be with her, mourn our loss."

Nodding solemnly, Aeryk left Takeshi alone with his thoughts and dove through the skies. Fuji lay beneath him, its fires silent – at peace. Seirin was on her knees at the summit's edge. Tears streaked her radiant face, and she cradled Vissyus's head against her breast as if she'd just rocked him to sleep.

"It's finished, Aeryk," Seirin whispered, somehow sensing his approach. "He was like a child... at the end." She sighed bitterly and hugged Vissyus tighter. "I know I wanted one of my own, but not like this – never like this." Aeryk knelt beside her and cupped her chin. She needed his touch more than his words. Wrapping his arms around her, he drew her close and held her without speaking. "What will happen to him?" she asked after a pause. "We can't just leave him here."

"Roarke promised to entomb his body within his former palace. A fragment of it remains intact beneath Tokyo Bay, embedded in rock too hard for mankind to break. It is a fitting spot for him, the most fitting, perhaps, of any."

Still weeping, she looked into his face. "I am so sorry, Aeryk."

Aeryk pressed a finger to her lips. "It's over now." He drew her closer and lifted his eyes to the horizon. The world spread out before him, the world they'd threatened and then saved. The world they had to leave now. He sighed and kissed Seirin on the top of her head, oddly serene despite his loss.

51
YUI

In the days that followed, life in Japan returned to normal. Hidden shrines throughout the country threw open their doors, and those who had come seeking shelter slowly made their way back to their devastated homes. As a people, they had been at the heart of something momentous, something profound. And while few remembered more than pounding rains and shaking earth, collectively they felt as though the world had been cleansed, their lives spared. Those closest to the battle bowed reverently at the beautiful volcano in the distance. No trace of the violent eruption marred its surface, a miracle many believed, and further proof of its mystic power.

The lands around the mountain had not been so fortunate.

Wherever the people looked, they saw signs of a cataclysmic struggle. Most of the buildings within the Five Lakes region lay in ruins, stone, steel, and concrete pulverized as easily as wood and paper. None of the roads were fit for travel, and those that weren't covered with debris had either been melted or washed away.

Huge craters pitted the landscape, and more often than not, charred stumps and piles of cooling ash surrounded them. The massive fortress that appeared at the edges of Aokigahara had vanished as well, though strangely, the ground where it had stood was the only area to have escaped the carnage.

Stranger still, sightings of gigantic creatures flooded local authorities in Japan and beyond. Several airliners radioed their towers as they flew into Asia, each claiming to have spotted a huge white bird winging its way over the Philippine Sea. On the waves below, a number of cargo ships steaming through the same area frantically called to port with identical descriptions of a serpentine creature racing just beneath the surface; one hundred fifty to two hundred feet long, with vivid turquoise stripes running the length of its aquamarine body.

In Nepal, the pilot of a small sightseeing plane told his home base that he'd seen a massive stone giant standing on the top of Mount Kanchenjunga's highest peak. Incredibly, a large dark-skinned man sat contentedly in one opened hand, a diamond-and-gold encrusted hammer balanced on his knees. Banking through a flurry of low-level clouds, the pilot brought the plane's nose about for another look only to find that the giant had all but disappeared, two enormous footprints in the glacial snows marking where it had been.

A short time later, in the middle of the Pacific, the USS *Ronald Reagan* led a small, tactical group of warships through a series of training maneuvers. Less than three days out of Pearl Harbor, it steamed easily across the open seas on a heading that would take it into a deserted stretch of ocean. In the distance, where there should have been nothing but the slow, graceful arc of the horizon, a huge atoll rose out of the waves before it.

Puzzled, the captain ordered a slow halt and lifted his binoculars to his eyes for a better look. Abruptly, he pulled back in shock, blinked, and looked again, certain his mind had tricked him. But then, as soon as he'd adjusted the lenses, he saw them again: a tall man wearing a flowing white shirt over dark pants and a pair of stout, leather boots. His hair was a deep brown, cut short and framing a handsome face. Beside him, strolling along happily with her hand in his was the most achingly beautiful woman he had ever seen. Golden hair cascaded over a filmy dress the color of tropical seas. The garment shimmered as she moved like the sun glinting off the waves below.

The two had reached the edge of the limestone rock when the captain saw her turn her head toward the man, and – after throwing him a dazzling smile – raise a hand over her head, her face radiant. As if in response, the seas boiled. Gales swirled around them, appearing from nowhere to join a climbing wall of water, the two pushing the whole into the heavens. The storm lasted for only a minute, hanging suspended over the Pacific before collapsing, the water rushing back down to meet the ocean like a monsoon. The atoll gone as though it had never existed.

Takeshi Akiko sauntered over a simple wooden bridge, his face lifted to the sky. "Ah," he said wistfully. "They have gone." He slowed to a stop near the end of the Uji Bridge and the entrance to Japan's most sacred shrine: Ise City's *Naiku*, legendary home of Amaterasu Omikami, the Sun Goddess.

Yui was only a few steps behind him, her long, black hair pulled away from her face and held in place with a clip resembling a white crane in flight. She had forsaken her robes in favor of a more comfortable tunic of fine white silk, worn over a pair of black pants that whisked rhythmically as she walked. Pausing, she bowed her head only to have Keiko stumble into her.

"Honestly, Yui," Keiko grumbled. "You can't just stop in the middle of the bridge. Not with someone right behind you."

Yui's eyebrow twitched as she glared down at Keiko. "I stopped to pay my respects to my friends. Perhaps if you'd been watching where you were going instead of gawking, you might have noticed."

Keiko sniffed and tossed her head. "I was just taking in the sights. I *am* on vacation, remember?" She wagged a finger under Yui's nose in an attempt to gain the moral authority she knew she lacked. "Lucky for you you're not going back to your old job. I mean, really, how can you call yourself a guide when you don't even spare a minute to tell me anything about this incredible place?"

Yui's eyes widened. She looked as if she was about to respond when her father interrupted.

"Yui warned me you were inquisitive." Takeshi's eyes twinkled. "I hope her replacement will not disappoint you. He is... untrained."

"I'm sure you'll do just fine." Keiko gave his arm an affectionate – if inappropriate – pat. "If we ever get there, that is. I've been dreaming about this ever since you suggested it, and if you don't mind, I'd like to be on my way as soon as possible." Moving to one side, she bowed and swept an arm down the bridge. "After you."

"Careful, Father," Yui chortled, falling in behind Takeshi as he smiled and led them down the bridge. "The guardian sometimes forgets which of us is the Kami, a flaw I trust you can smooth over... given time." She sighed sadly. "I still don't understand why you won't leave her with me. She Awakened because of my summons. She belongs with me."

The hitch in Yui's voice made Keiko pause. She didn't want to leave Yui either – they'd been through so much together. "We've been over this, Yui. You saw what I did in the White Spirit. I have to learn how to use this power before I hurt someone."

"I thought you wanted to stay."

"I do," Keiko said. "More than anything. When my father died, I thought I'd lost everything. Coming here, meeting you – all of you – you're my family, the family I didn't know I had."

"But you're giving it up." Yui sounded injured. "After fighting so hard to find it."

Yui's words tugged at Keiko's heart. "I have to. I don't think I could live with myself if I did something bad by accident. We've all seen what happens when we do what we want instead of what we should. Vissyus died because of it, others too. Thousands of them. It has to mean something, Yui, and it won't if we forget why it happened."

Yui stared at her for a moment, then lowered her head and nodded. She'd lost this argument once already, and she knew she'd lose it again. An uncomfortable silence settled over them, broken now and again by birdsong and the slow gurgle of the Isuzu River.

Eventually, they passed under the unpainted torii gate marking the end of the bridge and continued down a long, stone path cut into a forest of ancient cedars. Checkered sunlight spilled onto the ground at their feet, filtered and muted by the tree's thick green leaves. The temperature dropped under the wood, making their journey more comfortable. For a long time, none of them spoke, either content to drink in the shrine's majesty or reflecting on the past, both recent and distant.

After a while, the path gave way to a steep flight of wide gray steps. The climb was long, though not particularly arduous, and Keiko soon found herself walking through a series of gated enclosures leading to the Inner Shrine.

A pair of bronze hinged doors swung inward as they approached a formidable wooden building. Once inside, Takeshi brought them to the end of a short room, where an empty dais sat upon an elevated platform. A ball of white light formed before him, growing and opening until another world appeared on the other side.

Beyond it, a beautiful woman shimmered into focus. She was clad in flowing silver and white, her hair pulled away from her face and held back with three simple red-lacquered sticks. Kind, yellow-tinted eyes shone out of an oval-shaped face so like Yui's that Keiko had to turn to make sure the younger Akiko still stood beside her.

"Hello, Teras," Takeshi said, his eyes as bright as hers. "I would like you to meet someone very special." Stepping aside, he eased Keiko forward. "This is Keiko Yamanaka."

The woman's bow was fluid and willowy. "You have my eternal gratitude, Yamanaka-san." Her voice was light – like Yui's – and filled with comforting warmth. "I am Teras, Lady of Light, known to you as Amaterasu, the Sun Goddess."

Keiko returned the greeting with a perfect bow of her own: slow, graceful, and proud. "A difficult charge, my lady. But I managed."

The lady's eyes widened. "Is that so?" She laughed, the sound coming out like the ringing of clean, clear chimes. "The lack of a mother's touch, I fear, has roughened her a little around the edges."

"Nothing a good man can't fix." Keiko shot Yui a meaningful look.

"True," Takeshi chuckled. "So true. Now, if you don't mind, I would like to have a few private words with Yui before I go. Please say your goodbyes and join Teras in the Boundary. She promised to look after you until I can join you."

Bristling with excitement, Keiko scampered over to Yui and threw her arms around her. "You are the best friend I've ever had, you know that, right?" The words rushed out of her mouth, her eyes teared. "And because I wouldn't trust this to anyone else…" She removed her pack and rummaged through it. A second later, she lifted her beloved camera, its metallic casing resting atop her open palms. "I don't need it anymore, and, thanks to you, I've learned how to make memories of my own."

Overwhelmed, Yui extended her hands and took the camera. "Thank you, guardian." She bowed. "I shall cherish it. It will have a place of honor in the White Spirit."

Keiko nodded back and climbed onto the platform. Pivoting, she took one last look at her world and inhaled. Adventure waited for her on the other side of that Gateway, infinite worlds and infinite beauty. She couldn't wait.

"I will hold you to your promise, old man." She jabbed a finger at Takeshi. "That was the deal. You show me everything, and I let you train me."

"So it was, Yamanaka-san." Takeshi chuckled. "I always keep my promises. You should know that by now." He gestured at the Gate. "Go on ahead. I'll be with you shortly."

Keiko bobbed her head in reply and raised her shield. It was easy for her now, as easy as running. A contented sigh escaped her lips as she squared her shoulders and walked into the Gate's shining light.

•••

Once they were alone, Takeshi walked over to Yui and embraced her. "I could not be more proud of you, Yui-chan. You have grown into a remarkable woman, one with heart and courage and wit and wisdom to match. That's why I decided to leave this world to you."

Yui blushed at the compliment, and while she wanted to lower her eyes, she did not, preferring to bask in her father's love a little longer. "I will do my best. Vissyus and Lon-Shan left deep scars."

Takeshi shook his head sadly. "A fine example we turned out to be. Still, if anyone can show them the way, it is you, the youngest of our kind, born into this world and a part of it. I have every confidence in you, daughter."

"Thank you, Father." Yui hugged him back. "I will come through the Boundary from time to time to report to you, and to ask for guidance when I need it. Your faith honors me, but I wish you would let Keiko stay behind. I'll need a guardian to help shape the future."

Eyes twinkling, Takeshi put his hands on her shoulders and squeezed. "Summon one then. A new one, one that can work with you. You may be surprised by what responds." He patted Yui's shoulder one last time before following Keiko into the Boundary.

It was some time after that parting before Yui returned to her new chambers in the White Spirit. She'd spent her days traveling from one shrine to the next, reblessing them and meeting with her father's disciples to brief them on what had happened. To them, she assigned the arduous task of rebuilding Japan.

One week later, when the emperor entered his throne room to welcome the American president and his promise of emergency aid, he found Yui seated upon the

Chrysanthemum Throne. Her eyes locked with his, and he fell to his knees. He swore his life to her before his brow even touched the tatami mats. She flashed a kind smile, blessed him, and then flew into the skies without looking back.

For the better part of that week, she crisscrossed the globe, inspecting the Gateways before closing them. When she left the portal into Seirin's world, she flew from the Caribbean, and headed directly to Hurricane Point. Seirin may have moved her palace to the Pacific before taking it from the world, but Aeryk had kept his here.

She found it exactly where he said it would be, floating over the southern Atlantic within its massive cloud walls. Aeryk offered it to her as an outpost in the west, a base from which she could watch events in the Americas and in Europe and take action if necessary. She had accepted, bowing lower than custom allowed.

Exhausted, she returned to the White Spirit the following day, and finally, after a visit to the hot springs and a well-deserved rest, she made her way into the main hall. Gone were her simple blue-and-white tunic and pants, replaced with an elaborately embroidered kimono, indigo slashed with yellow sunfire and belted with a golden obi. Soft white slippers covered her feet, and as she folded them beneath her body and lowered herself onto the raised dais, she closed her eyes and opened her mind to the void. Her thoughts raced through infinity in search of a kindred soul, one that would respond to her unique blending of spirit and light.

For a moment, she was afraid none would come, that Vissyus had frightened the lesser Kami too much to chance serving one such as she, one who could command two elemental forces. But then, just as she was about to recast her summons, the mats below began to shimmer. Cursing under her breath, she started to stand, her mind already selecting a more suitable spot for the guardian to craft a new form for itself, one large enough to accommodate even Ventyre's great body and wingspan.

By the time she'd lifted herself to her knees, however, the guardian before her took shape. "I am here, mistress," it said, its tone strong and resonant, its voice unbelievably familiar. Her eyes flew open. A man knelt before her – head bowed and face half hidden in robes of periwinkle blue.

"So have I been summoned, so have I come," he intoned. "I, Masato Yamanaka, guardian of Heaven, submit myself to you, to protect and serve you until the end of the world."

Yui staggered to her feet and took one tentative step from the dais. "How?" Her chest tightened. She was afraid. As much as she ached for this, she worried it might not be real.

"I left a part of myself within my daughter. When Lord Takeshi found what I had done, he ordered me to continue guiding her. As a reward, he released me from my oaths, except the one I made to him. He said he would use that when the time came."

Yui moved from the platform to stand in front him, her eyes never leaving his face. As she crouched down, her hand came up to stroke his cheek. Her thoughts raced to the back of the room. They lifted his staff and brought it out of the alcove in a blaze of amber light. Tears, joyous and disbelieving, streaked her face. When she could no longer stand it, she broke with tradition, threw her arms around his neck, and wept tears of joy.

Lost in emotion, neither noticed the glassy eye of a twenty year-old camera at the back of the chambers, its strap looped around the neck of Takeshi's crimson armor. A faint, muffled click rose from the shutter, too quiet for them to hear and useless for the camera's lack of film. It captured the scene nonetheless, the images hurtling across time and space, reaching into and across the Boundary where a self-congratulatory sniff and a wide, teary eyed smile awaited them.

ACKNOWLEDGMENTS

I would like to thank a whole host of people for making *Kojiki* a reality. I'll start with the team at Angry Robot: to Marc Gascoigne for believing, to Phil Jourdan for making this happen, and to Mike Underwood for first noticing *Kojiki* on Twitter and bringing my manuscript to his colleagues. Massive thanks to Thomas Walker for a truly magnificent cover. A very special thank you to my fantastic agent, Laura Zats of Red Sofa Literary Agency. Laura, you're a joy to work with, and I consider myself very lucky to have you representing me. To my incomparable independent editor, Lorin Oberweger of Free-Expressions.com. Lorin, what can I say? You've been my mentor for so long, much longer than you needed to be. You taught me to walk then run then fly. *Kojiki* wouldn't exist if not for you. Finally, for my family: Kathleen, you're my inspiration for everything; Caitlin, you're too much like me – you know how to make your dreams soar; Jeffrey, your dedication and quest for perfection has taught me so much; and Justin, when you find something you love, you put your heart and soul into it – always practicing, always trying to better yourself. Your example showed me how to keep going with *Kojiki*, no matter what.

So, dear reader, you might wonder where this journey began? Well, when I was little I spent so much time in our local bookstore. You might think this is perfectly normal for a would-be author, but the truth is, I really wasn't much of a reader. Ironic, right? If I didn't like to read, then why would I keep going back to the bookstore? The answer might surprise you. Back then, before the internet, books were the only place to relive my favorite movies. No streaming, no VCRs, no way to see what you wanted to see at the click of a mouse. This was it. I moved on from the film and music section to travel and art. In both places, I saw pictures of incredible places – real or imagined – that I wanted to visit.

Fast-forward a few years. Brandon Sanderson once told me that everyone has a gateway book, that one story that makes you a reader. For him, it was Robert Jordan's masterful *The Wheel of Time* series. For me it was JRR Tolkien's *The Lord of the Rings*. A friend recommended it to me, and once I started reading I never looked back. After *The Lord of the Rings*, I read as much epic fantasy as I could get my hands on. I started with Terry Brooks's *Shannara* series before moving on to David Eddings's *The Belgariad*. Of course, I came across some books that didn't fit my tastes. Just when I wondered if I'd ever read another *Lord of the Rings*, I found *The Wheel of Time*. Robert Jordan's epic had everything I loved about fantasy: beautiful prose, an action-packed story, incredible settings, and characters you cared about. These books made a huge impact on me. I've always been a daydreamer, and I had so many crazy thoughts in my head. Reading *The Wheel of Time* made me believe I could write a book of my own. Not long after that, I began.

Anime played such a huge part in crafting the story. You'll find homages to my all-time favorites: *Space Battleship Yamato*, *Giant Robo*, and Hiyao Miyazaki's gorgeous *Nausicaa*, *Laputa: Castle in the Sky* and *Spirited Away*. The most important piece, Vissyus's fall, came from somewhere else entirely. Here, I thought *Billy Budd* and *The Phantom of the Opera* – Andrew Lloyd Webber's award-winning musical – resonated best with Vissyus's tragic story. The Lord of Fire is the book's only character whose actions are pure and selfless. Only Vissyus helps his closest friends realize their dreams. Everyone else, aside from Keiko, wants something for himself or herself. So I ask the question, dear reader, who is *Kojiki*'s real hero? I'll let you decide for yourself.

KY

JOIN US

angryrobotbooks.com

twitter.com/angryrobotbooks